was born on March 3 1797 at the Old Palace Yard, West
Seventh daughter, one of fourteen children, of William Eden, the
First Lord Auckland—an influential politician and diplomat,
a successful writer and friend of Pitt—she moved in select and
exclusive Whig circles at their peak in those days of the Reform
Bill. Considered one of the most delightful women of the age, she
was a prominent political hostess and a close friend of Melbourne.
Indeed society gossiped of their marriage after the death of
Caroline Lamb, and Caroline Norton considered her sufficiently
a rival to dub her "the virgin Eden". Chief in her affections though
was her family—her sisters Fanny and Eleanor, Lady Buckinghamshire and, most particularly, her elder brother George, the
second Lord Auckland. When Melbourne appointed George
Governor-General of India in 1835, Emily accompanied him and
spent the next seven years there. She wrote two books on her
experiences in India, *Portraits of the People and Princes of India*
(1844) and *Up the Country* (1866). Her *Letters from India* were
published posthumously in 1872.

Emily Eden's second novel *The Semi-Detached House* was published, anonymously, in 1859. Its enthusiastic reception encouraged her to publish *The Semi-Attached Couple*—written thirty
years earlier, but first published in 1860. She wrote for pin
money, and to amuse herself and her friends. In both aims she
was successful; praise was showered on her by the great of the
day, and though this is their first paperback edition, *The Semi-
Attached Couple* and *The Semi-Detached House* have constantly
reprinted since they first delighted readers one hundred and
twenty years ago.

After her return from India Emily Eden continued to act as
hostess for her brother until his death in 1849. For the remaining
twenty years of her life she lived at Eden Lodge, Kensington
Gore, finally retiring to Richmond where she died in 1869.

THE
SEMI-ATTACHED COUPLE

BY THE
HON. EMILY EDEN

WITH AN INTRODUCTION BY
VALERIE GROSVENOR MYER

Virago
London

Published by VIRAGO Limited 1979
5 Wardour Street, London W1V 3HE

Introduction Copyright © 1979
by Valerie Grosvenor Myer

ISBN 0 86068 116 5

Printed in Great Britain
at The Anchor Press Ltd, Tiptree, Essex

INTRODUCTION

The Hon. Emily Eden (1797–1869) was an aristocratic spinster, shrewd, well-read and observant, and above all witty. She was an invalid who had enough energy to leave behind her the two novels in this volume, *Portraits of the Princes and People of India* (1844), *Up the Country* (letters and journals written in India) and reasonably accomplished sketches and watercolours. She was in India from 1836 to 1842, travelling with her brother, Lord Auckland, who was governor-general. She was a Whig hostess, who held "morning receptions" because dinners would have been too much for her. But "morning" in those days went on all day till evening dinner; a "morning fete" in *The Semi-Detached House* begins at three o'clock. Emily's letters are full of lively political commentary and gossip, yet the world of politics, so important in her daily life, is only lightly touched on in the novels. In her journal for June 14 1838, she wrote: "I am interested in Indian politics just now, but could not make them interesting on paper." She made documentary use of her Indian experience, but restricted her fiction to the world of London society, though her life extended far outside. It was richer, more varied and interesting than that of most women at any time.

Her eye was sharp; her books are comedies of manners and her dialogue is racy and amusing. Unlike greater, but less aristocratic novelists, she knew how the upper classes in the nineteenth century talked among themselves, and we believe her. Both novels are rich mines for the social historian. *Nouveaux-riches* characters pepper their talk with French phrases; the more secure laugh at them for it. The amiable, jolly (and perfectly *comme il faut*) Lord Chester in *The Semi-Detached House* speaks of a friend's "old woman" and his "kids".

The Semi-Detached House was published anonymously in 1859, appearing only as "edited by Lady Teresa Lewis". Lady Teresa was an old friend who successfully negotiated "£300 and very early publication" as requested. Its success encouraged Emily to acknowledge it and bring out her bottom-drawer novel, *The Semi-Attached Couple*, written thirty years earlier. In her preface, she says she decided against revising it: the only thing to do was to offer it as a "record of vanished manners".

The Semi-Attached Couple is about the early adjustments of marriage. A character in it becomes prime minister, but it is not a political novel. An interesting sidelight is thrown when Eliza Douglas, aged eighteen, writes home to ask which side she is expected to be on in the forthcoming election campaign. The quarrels of young Lord and Lady Teviot take place in settings of enormous luxury, and their problems may seem remote and trivial to us. But Emily Eden observed the isolation and grief that the "splendid" marriage must have brought to so many of her contemporaries. Girls married off from the schoolroom to men they hardly knew, required to adapt to new roles, suffered various forms of shock. The misunderstandings between Lady Helen and her husband arise convincingly from the socio-economic context.

Helen comes from a large, loving family, youngest of three sisters. It does not occur to her that her husband, a spoilt only son, is jealous of these relatives and of her attachment to her home. He sees these loyalties of hers as a threat. Helen is only eighteen, their "courtship", a distant and formal affair, lasted for only six weeks. She goes into marriage in a depressed and doubtful state, unsure of her husband's love. She is afraid of his domineering temper and sarcastic tongue. She is affectionate and outgoing, while he is reserved and inhibited. She waits for permission to show warmth towards him; he suffers in silence, burning with resentment because she does not offer it. As his world is that of the aristocratic male—hunting, shooting, fishing—while hers is that of entertaining, with boudoir gossip about jewels and trousseaux, their minds hardly meet. Their expectations of marriage are different because of the differences in their formative experiences. Emily Eden is as aware as any post-Freudian of the importance of nurture. The dilemma of such marriages must have been real enough, but Emily was unable to find a true fictional solution. Lord Teviot falls seriously ill while travelling abroad and Helen flies to his side to nurse him. The convention that sickness ennobles both the sufferer and the nurse was to run tiresomely through Victorian fiction. As a means of reconciling Helen and her husband, it is a transparent plot-manipulation; in real life, such couples doubtless went their separate ways.

Dickens and George Eliot were later to show the disastrous consequences for the married relationship of the Victorian oppression which fashioned infantile women. There is nothing of this in Emily Eden; like Jane Austen's heroines, Emily's are restricted socially, but seem to notice it less than Jane's do, perhaps because they are grander and richer. Although Helen is unrestrained in her intimacy with her sisters, in her relationship with her husband she operates largely under the social code of discretion in which she has been strictly schooled by her mama. As Lady Eskdale is an idealised character, Emily Eden does not, I think, criticise the conventional upbringing Helen receives; but she does recognise and depict the problems caused by the separation of men's lives and women's in her society.

There are frequent affectionate references to Jane Austen, and her influence on both books is marked. Emily Eden's satire is sharp and convincing, though less savage than Jane Austen's; like Jane Austen's, Emily Eden's observation and pointed wit make us give sudden snorts of laughter. *The Semi-Attached Couple* refers explicitly to *Pride and Prejudice* and could be described as basically the same story with the equivalent of the Darcy family as the main characters. The story of the Douglases (who have a daughter, Eliza, who marries Helen's brother, a grand match) is a framing device to open and close the plot.

Mrs. Douglas is a splendid bitch, drawn with truth and accuracy. Her theme-song is how her friends have aged since she saw them last. Mrs. Douglas had never had the slightest pretension to good looks; in fact, though it is wrong to say anything so ill-natured, she was excessively plain, always had been so, and had a soreness on the subject of beauty, that looked perhaps as like envy as any other quality. As she had no hope of raising herself to the rank of beauty, her only chance was bringing others down to her level; people may go on talking for ever of the jealousies of pretty women; but for real, genuine, hard-working envy, there is nothing like an ugly woman with a taste for admiration. Her mortified vanity curdles into malevolence; and she calumniates where she cannot rival.

Emily Eden's quality is shown by the unexpected adjective "hard-working", normally a term of approbation; its application to envy is piquant, for we realise that Mrs. Douglas brings to her spiteful, self-absorbed malice all her vital energies, which might profitably have been used for more worthwhile things. Her husband's response (he has married her for her money, not her looks) is to "let her have a reasonable share of her own way, and spend a reasonable portion of her own money; he abstained from all vivid admiration of beauty within her hearing."

The Semi-Detached House, written later but published first, is a better book, more original, better plotted. A few days after *The Semi-Detached House* appeared, Emily wrote to a friend, "*Semi* has had more success than I require, and considerably more than I expected." The same year, 1859, she wrote to Lady Teresa about a letter she had received:

He says the grandest things of *Semi*, which he had read on Saturday evening, and says that a bystander would have thought him quite mad; he was screaming with laughter by himself, and that he is ashamed to add that all next day it *would* come back to him. "It really haunts me." He was longing for Monday to read it aloud to Lady L, and he says that he must, at all events, be a good judge of a confinement.

Young Lady Chester's husband is called abroad on a diplomatic mission, so she rents a semi-detached house in the London suburbs, where her baby is born. There are echoes of *Persuasion*; the bluff seafaring Captain Hopkinson remarks of the dubious Baron that he is unlikely to set the Thames on fire, a comment made in *Persuasion* by Admiral Croft about Sir Walter Elliott. But Sir Walter represents a dying rural squirearchy, while the Baron represents a new threat, the deplorable world of mushroom financial empires. Business is now king; landowners no longer live on rents, timber and other produce; they indulge in speculation. There are financial crashes. There is a thread of malicious anti-semitism in this part of the plot. There is some fun at the expense of those members of Parliament, "radical in politics and unpolished in manner, who had manfully voted for the removal of Jewish disabilities. Whether they knew what the disabilities were, or what would be the effect of their removal, is doubtful; but they somehow had an idea that they were voting against gentlemen and bishops, and church and state, and they felt proud of themselves." Emily expects her readers to respond by sharing the prejudices of her time and her class.

Emily Eden, in her position, could hardly be expected to take a radical line herself. She takes the standard aristocratic view that polished manners and intelligent conversation are desirable when they can be found, but, failing the cultivated arts, goodness of heart is the next best thing and is to be cherished. "It is really refreshing to hear conversation about facts, not about people," says Lady Chester. There are several literary allusions, and leading characters know Shakespeare, Wordsworth and Byron well enough to quote extensively. But there is sympathy for the uncultured but goodhearted Mrs. Hopkinson, who, faced with the prospect of meeting a cabinet minister, gets all flustered because she "cannot read *The Times* and should not know a reform bill from a budget".

"Tact, which is only another name for consideration of the feelings of others, is compatible with unpolished manner," writes Emily in the authorial voice. Mrs. Hopkinson's confusions delight us, but her unaffected goodness earns respect.

INTRODUCTION

Mrs. Hopkinson is bewildered by the literary conversation of the clever, unhappy, detached Rachel (a modern character), niece to the odious Baroness. Rachel, in danger of being asked to make an inventory for a removal, responds,

> Ye household cares, vex not my mind
> With your inglorious strife,
> Nor seek in sordid chains to bind
> My free aesthetic life,

a poem she tells us she made up herself on the spur of the moment.

Mrs. Hopkinson is puzzled by the word "aesthetic", which was newly fashionable at the time and had not acquired the associations it now holds of affectation, pose, perversity and idleness. It was used with approval by cultivated people when they were talking about the arts. Rachel wonders how it would be possible to manage without it. Rachel is alienated by her intelligence and the only use she can find for her analytical powers is to account for her own unhappiness. She recognises it is her loveless childhood that has made her "what I am – cold, distrustful, unloved and unloving."

She marries the gloomy widower Willis, who makes a great parade of being inconsolable for a wife he did not truly love. There is an element of macabre farce about the present he chooses for his little boy: the gift is a model tomb, with a skeleton on a spring which jumps out when the lid is opened.

But Willis is the necessary touch of shadow in a sunny picture. The gloomy puritanism of the nineteenth century does not weigh very heavily on these characters, who are in general cheerful, though it is sketched in on the periphery of their lives. Of one minor character it is said, "Some people think him rather too evangelical . . . he does a great deal of good in a quiet way. . . ." Evangelicalism had advanced enough for it to be clear that the correspondent who so enjoyed the book could not have read it aloud to Lady L on a Sunday, but had to wait till Monday for this indulgence.

Valerie Grosvenor Myer, 1979

PREFACE

This story was partly written nearly thirty years ago,[1] before railroads were established, and travelling carriages-and-four superseded; before postage-stamps had extinguished the privilege of franking, and before the Reform Bill had limited the duration of the polling at borough elections to a single day. In re-writing it I might easily have introduced these and other modern innovations; but as I believe the manners of England to be as much changed as her customs, there would have been discrepancies between my scenes and characters: the background would not have harmonized with the figures.

When I wrote it, I thought it a tolerably faithful representation of modern society; but some young friends who are still living in the world, from which I have long retired, and who have read it with the indulgence of happy youth, condescendingly assure me that it is amusing, inasmuch as it is a curious picture of old-fashioned society. Therefore, in giving it to the world, I trust that to my own contemporaries it may have the charm of reminding them of their youth, and that to the young it may have the recommendation of being a strange Chronicle of the Olden Time.

E. E.

---

[1] The book was first published, it must be remembered, in 1860.

THE SEMI-ATTACHED COUPLE

CHAPTER I

"WELL, I have paid that visit to the Eskdales, Mr. Douglas," said Mrs. Douglas in a tone of triumphant sourness.

"You don't say so, my dear! I hope you left my card?"

"Not I, Mr. Douglas. How could I? They let me in, which was too unkind. I saw the whole family, father and mother, brother and sisters—the future bride and bridegroom. Such a tribe! and servants without end. How I detest walking up that great flight of steps at Eskdale Castle, with that regiment of footmen drawn up on each side of it; one looking more impertinent than the other!"

"There must be a frightful accumulation of impertinence before you reach the landing-place, my dear; for it is a long staircase."

"Don't talk nonsense, Mr. Douglas," said his wife, sharply. "I shan't go again in a hurry. That whole house is hateful to me: Lady Eskdale with her dawdling, languid manner, and her large shawl, and conceited cap; and that Lord Beaufort, with his black eyebrows and shining teeth. Lady Eskdale looked as old as the hills, with all that lace hanging about her face. She has grown excessively old, Mr. Douglas. I never saw anybody so altered."

"Did you think so, Anne? I thought her looking very handsome yesterday, when I met her in her pony carriage."

" Ah; that pony carriage; that is so like her nonsense. Pony carriages are the fashion, and she has taken to drive. I should not be the least surprised any day to hear that she had broken her neck. Why cannot she go out in her britzska, and be driven by her coachman? and as for looking handsome, it is not very likely that she should at her age. Lady Eskdale is as old as I am, Mr. Douglas."

" You don't say so," was again on the point of escaping Mr. Douglas's lips, and after a pause he bethought himself of the lovers as a safer topic than Lady Eskdale's beauty; he had tried that too often in his life. " Did you see Helen, my dear? "

" Oh! to be sure. She was sent for. ' Dear Love,' as Lady Eskdale drawled out, ' she is so happy; and you must see Teviot, he is such a darling; if he were my own son, I could not love him more.' So in they came, the dear love and the darling. You know how I hate those London sort of men, with their mustachios and chains and offensive waistcoats, and Lord Teviot is one of the worst specimens I ever saw of the kind——"

" And Helen? " again said Mr. Douglas.

" Oh, Helen! " said Mrs. Douglas, and then paused. She was in imminent peril of being forced to praise, but escaped with great adroitness. " Well, if Helen were not one of that family, I should not dislike her She is civil enough, and promised to show the girls her trousseau; but she is altered too. I think her looking dreadfully old, Mr. Douglas."

" Old at eighteen, Anne! what wrinkled wretches we must be! Has Helen grown gray? "

" No; but you know what I mean: she looks so set-up, so fashioned. In short, it does not signify, but she is altered."

Mr. Douglas had his suspicions that Helen must have been looking beautiful, since even his wife could not detect, or at least specify, the faults that were to be found in her appearance. He had seldom seen her so much at fault for a criticism. Mrs. Douglas had never had the slightest pretensions to good looks; in fact, though it is wrong to say anything so ill-natured, she was excessively plain, always had been so, and had a soreness on the subject of beauty, that looked perhaps as like envy as any other quality.

As she had no hope of raising herself to the rank of a beauty, her only chance was bringing others down to her own level. " How old she is looking! "—" How she is altered! " were the expressions that invariably concluded Mrs. Douglas's comments on her acquaintances; and the prolonged absence of a friend was almost a pleasure to her, as it gave her the opportunity of saying after a first meeting, " How changed Mrs. So-and so is! I should hardly have known her; but then, to be sure, I have not seen her for a year—or two years," etc.

People may go on talking for ever of the jealousies of pretty women; but for real genuine, hard-working envy there is nothing like an ugly woman with a taste for admiration. Her mortified vanity curdles into malevolence; and she calumniates where she cannot rival.

Mrs. Douglas had been an heiress, which perhaps accounted for Mr. Douglas having married her; but though no one could suppose that he married for love, he had been to her what is called a good husband. He let her have a reasonable share of her own way, and spend a reasonable portion of her own money; he abstained from all vivid admiration of beauty within her hearing; he had a great reliance on her judgment, and a high opinion of her talents; and though he was too good-hearted to hear without pain her sarcasms on almost all her acquaintance, he seldom irritated her by contradiction, but kept his own opinion with a quiet regret that his wife was so hard to please.

The Eskdales and Douglases had been near neighbours

for many years, and had always been on sociable and sometimes intimate terms. Mrs. Douglas could almost have become attached to her neighbour, had it not been for the prolonged youthfulness of Lady Eskdale's appearance, and the uninterrupted and increasing prosperity of her family. The provocation grew too great for endurance. The ladies had become mothers at the same time, and the comparison of their babies, monthly nurses, and embroidered caps had been the commencement of their intimacy; then came the engagement of nursery governesses, and discussions on the comparative merits of Swiss *bonnes*, highly accomplished French governesses, poor clergyman's daughters, or respectable young, ignorant women. Then the respective right shoulders of Sophia Beaufort and Sarah Douglas took a fit of growing, without due regard to the stationary dispositions of the left.

There are two years in every woman's life in which the undue size of her right shoulder is the bane of her own life, and of everybody about her. Mrs. Douglas called constantly at Eskdale Castle to satisfy herself that Sophia was growing absolutely deformed; and Lady Eskdale owned she should fret dreadfully about her poor darling if she did not think Mrs. Douglas so much more to be pitied on her dear Sarah's account.

The girls grew up perfectly straight, of course.

This period of reclining boards and dumb-bells was the most flourishing age of the Eskdale and Douglas friendship. After that it gradually declined. There was a slight revival when the two ladies entered into a confederacy against an exorbitant drawing-master; but he was shortly reduced to terms; and when he had consented to walk fifteen miles, and give a lesson of two hours for fifteen shillings, instead of a guinea, all farther community of interests on the subject of accomplishments ceased. The Eskdales soon after received an accession of fortune, and passed a great part of each year in another county, and also in London. The Ladies Beaufort grew up, came out, were admired, and became what Mrs. Douglas called " disgustingly fine."

The Douglas family remained in the country, mixed more with their second grade of neighbours, in default of their great friends; and the Misses Douglas were, Lady Eskdale said, "the dearest, most amiable girls in the world"; she only wished they " dressed better, and that Lord Eskdale did not think them vulgar; but unfortunately their voices annoyed him, so that she could not ask them to dinner so often as she could like for dear Mrs. Douglas's sake."

Still a certain degree of intercourse was kept up. An occasional letter passed, and at last a dreadful blow fell on the unsuspecting Mrs. Douglas—an announcement from Lady Eskdale of the marriage of her eldest daughter. It began in the terms usually employed on such occasions,— " I cannot bear that my dear Mrs. Douglas should hear from anyone but myself, that my darling Sophia's fate is decided; and that in giving my precious child to Sir William Waldegrave, I feel no doubts," etc., etc. The remainder is easily imagined: high principles, good looks, long attachment—six weeks—worldly prosperity, mother's fears, these were the catchwords of the sentences. Mrs. Douglas wrote her congratulations, and kept her astonishment and comments for home consumption. Twelve months passed, and another letter arrived, but Mrs. Douglas was prepared for the worst this time, at least, she said she was; and that it would not surprise her at all if Amelia were going to be married. Again Lady Eskdale could not bear that Mrs. Douglas should hear from anybody but herself, that dearest Amelia was to marry Mr. Trevor; another delightful young man with still higher principles, more good looks, a still longer attachment—

two months, at least—and the mother's fears, and the trousseau, and all the rest of it, followed in due order. The letter wound up with a gay assertion that little Eskdale Waldegrave was such a splendid child, that she forgave him for making her a grandmother at eight-and-thirty.

Mrs. Douglas read the communication in a tone expressive of extreme ill usage. Neither from herself nor from anyone else could Lady Eskdale hear that either of the Misses Douglas were about to be married. They had not even a disappointment to boast of, not a report about them to contradict, and Mrs. Douglas's chance of being a grandmother at all seemed hardly worth having. She began to rail against early marriages—hoped Mr. Trevor would help Amelia to play with her doll, and guessed that Sir William Waldegrave had repented long ago that he had not taken time to find out Sophia's temper before he married her.

There was only Helen left—Helen, so beautiful, so gentle, so light-hearted—the pride of her parents, the petted friend of her sisters, the idol of her brother, and loving as warmly as she was beloved. Yes, I knew Helen from her childhood, and had thought that such a gentle, gay creature could never be touched by the cares and griefs that fall on the common herd. " It was very much to the credit of my benevolence, though not of my judgment," as Sneer says. Why was she to escape? I do not wish to be cynical; but if a stone is thrown into our garden, is it not sure to knock off the head of our most valuable tulip? If a cup of coffee is to be spilled, does it not make a point of falling on our richest brocade gown? If we do lose our reticule, does not the misfortune occur on the only day on which we had left our purse in it? All these are well-known facts, and, by parity of reason, was it to be expected that anyone, so formed as Helen was to enjoy as well as to impart happiness, should escape the trials that ought to have fallen on the peevish and the disappointed—on me, for instance, or such as me?

Helen came out the year after her sister Amelia's marriage. "Lady Eskdale is so lucky—in fact, so clever—in marrying off her daughters, that it would not the least surprise me if she actually caught Lord Teviot for Lady Helen," was the spiteful prophecy of many who were trembling at the idea of its fulfilment. Their hopes and their fears were both confirmed. Lord Teviot, the great *parti* of the year, with five country houses—being four more than he could live in; with 120,000*l.* a year—being 30,000*l.* less than he could spend; with diamonds that had been collected by the ten last generations of Teviots, and a yacht that had been built by himself, with the rank of a marquess, and the good looks of the poorest of younger brothers—what could he want but a wife? Many people (himself among the rest) thought he was better without one; but he changed his mind the first time he saw Helen, and then it signified little whether other people changed theirs. He danced with her, evening after evening. He gave balls at Teviot House, breakfasts at Rose Bank, whitebait dinners on board the *Sylph*, and finally paid a morning visit at Lord Eskdale's at an unprecedentedly early hour. Mrs. Fitzroy Jones, who lived next door, and passed her life in an active supervision of all Eskdale proceedings, declared that his cabriolet waited two hours in the square, so she was sure he had proposed. Lady Bruce Gordon, who lived at the corner, asserted that she saw Lady Helen go out in the open carriage with her mother later in the afternoon, and that she looked as if she had cried her eyes quite out of her head (this was figurative); so she had no doubt that Lord Teviot had jilted her. But Mr. Elliot was looked upon as the highest authority, as he happened to be passing Lord Eskdale's door at half-past seven, and saw Lord Teviot go in, though he had ascertained that there was no other company expected. What did that mean?

The next day the marriage was declared. For the three following weeks Lord Eskdale's porter had a hard place of it. He said himself that it required two pair of hands to take in the notes and letters of congratulation, to say nothing of the interesting-looking parcels, wrapped in silver paper, that were sent by attached friends, and the boxes and baskets which arrived from distinguished milliners and jewellers.

At the end of the fourth week, Mrs. Fitzroy Jones and all the little Joneses, Lady B. Gordon and all the little Gordons, Mrs. Elliot and all the little Elliots, were drawn up at their respective windows, watching the packing of the huge waggons which were stationed at the Eskdale door, and reasoning themselves into a painful conviction of the melancholy fact that they were to be defrauded of a view of the wedding. Perhaps not, though. It may take place to-morrow. But, No! The next day brought the travelling carriages to the door. Mrs. Jones saw the family depart, then " turned with sickening soul within her gate," and said, " I must say I think it very ill-natured not to have the wedding in town." Mrs. Douglas thought so too—or rather she thought it very ill-natured to have the wedding in her neighbourhood, not only forcing on her the sight of so much prosperity, but, by an unfortunate train of events, actually obliging her to form part of the show. Eliza Douglas was asked to be one of Lady Helen's brides-maids.

CHAPTER II

However, we have not come to the wedding-day yet. There was the usual difficulty about settlements which attends all marriages, whether there be any property to settle or not, and the delay gave the neighbourhood the full enjoyment of watching the Teviots in the interesting character of lovers; and nothing excites so much curiosity, or affords such a fine mark for criticism, as the conduct of any two individuals who are placed in that critical position. Mrs. Douglas, as we know, had given herself the advantage of a regular morning visit and a formal introduction to Lord Teviot, thereby acquiring a lawful right to make all her remarks by authority; and this visit was followed by an invitation from the Eskdales to dinner—the invitation including the two Misses Douglas as well as their father and mother. So the Douglases took very high ground on the great Teviot question.

The other neighbours had various degrees of good fortune. Mrs. Thompson, the curate's wife, had a very fair share of luck, considering, as she said, that she was sure to be looking the other way when anything worth seeing was going on. But she had just called in at South Lodge with a tract, when she saw several ladies and gentlemen riding up the avenue, and she understood the happy pair were of the party; so that though she could not distinguish who was who, yet she had a right to say she had seen " the marquess." She really thought those large parties must prevent young people from making acquaintance: they ought to be left more to themselves. Mrs. Birkett, the apothecary's wife, had had greater good fortune: she had crossed in her walk an open part of the pleasure-ground, and she had seen Lady Helen sketching, and a tall, dark-looking young gentleman standing by her. "A most noble-looking young man is the marquess—he reminds me of what Mr. Birkett's cousin Sir Simon was when he was young. I own I was a little surprised—I won't say shocked—to see his lordship and her ladyship without a chaperon; but in high life I fancy there is a great deal more ease than we should think right. But I can't say I approve of young engaged people being left so much to themselves. However, I am glad I have seen them; and I was much nearer to them than Mrs. Thompson was."

However fortunate these two ladies had been, Sunday was the day that was looked to for the general gratification of public curiosity, and the church had not been so well attended for months as it was on that particular day. It was obvious to the whole neighbourhood that the Eskdales wished to avoid observation by coming early to church, for they arrived before the end of the first lesson—a most unusual degree of punctuality; but this sign of timidity did not prevent the whole congregation from fixing their eyes intently on the tall young man who followed Lord Eskdale into church, and who took a seat opposite to Lady Helen in the pew. Never was the congregation so alert in standing up at the proper opportunities. Old Mr. Marlow, a martyr to rheumatic gout, and Mrs. Greenland, who had, for two years, made her stiff knee an excuse for sitting down during the whole of the service, were both on their legs before the psalm was given out. The clerk, who had a passion for his own singing, saw his advantages, and gave out five verses of a hymn, with repetition of the two last lines of each verse. Seven verses and a half! but nobody thought it a note too long. Moreover, Lady Helen dropped her prayer-book, and the tall young man picked it up for her. Such an incident! Mrs. Thompson, as usual, missed it, because she was unluckily tying her little girl's bonnet-strings. There was a rush into the churchyard the moment the sermon was over, to which nobody had attended, except those who were watching for " Lastly." And when Lady Helen came out, leaning on her father's arm, and Lady Eskdale followed, attended by the tall young man, and when they all bowed and curtsied, and got into the open carriage, the father and mother sitting forwards and the young people opposite to them, and when Lord Eskdale took off his black hat and bowed on one side, and the young man took off his gray hat and bowed on the other, nothing could exceed the gratification of the assembly. Lord Teviot was exactly what they expected, so very distinguished and so good-looking. Some thought him too attentive to his prayers for a man in love, and some thought him too attentive to Lady Helen for a man in church; but eventually the two factions joined, and thought him simply very attentive. They all saw that Lady Helen was very fond of him, and nobody could be surprised at that. It was a most satisfactory Sunday; and as most of them were addicted to the im- moral practice of Sunday letter-writing, the observations of the morning were reduced to writing in the evening, and sent off to various parts of England on Monday morning. But hardly had the post gone out, when an alarming report arose that the real, genuine Lord Teviot had gone up to town on Saturday, and that the " observed of all observers " was an architect come down to complete the statue gallery. It was too true: the reaction was frightful, and, as usual in all cases of reaction, the odium fell on the wrong man. The architect, who was in fact an awkward, ungainly concern, remained in possession of distinguished looks, and with the glory of being very attentive to Lady Helen; and it was generally asserted that

Lord Teviot kept out of the way—as he was quite aware of being ill-looking; that he was not attached in the smallest degree to Lady Helen, or he would not have gone to London; and that he was very unprincipled, not to say an atheist, or he would have gone to church.

CHAPTER III

THE day of the wedding drew near. The whole Eskdale family, with the exception of the Waldegraves, were assembled for the ceremony. Lady Amelia Trevor and Helen had always been friends as well as sisters. There was a difference of little more than a year in their ages, and on every point of amusement or interest—in their childish griefs, or their youthful pleasures—their trust and confidence in each other had been unbounded. Amelia's marriage had made no difference in their relations to each other, for Helen liked Mr. Trevor, and he admired her with all Amelia's enthusiasm, and loved her with all Amelia's fondness.

Amelia was in ecstasies on her arrival at Eskdale. She thought Lord Teviot charming. Helen had never looked so beautiful. Everybody ought to marry—a married life was so happy; and then it was so lucky that she and Mr. Trevor had brought a set of emeralds for Helen, for the Waldegraves had sent a set of pearls, and she had once thought of pearls herself. Lord Teviot was quite as desperately in love as she had expected—just what he ought to be; in short, she worked herself up into such a state of prosperous cheerfulness, that when she went into Helen's room, three days before the appointed wedding, she was as childishly gay as when she had run into it five years before, with tidings of a whole holiday, or a child's ball, and now, to her utter discomfiture, she found Helen in tears.

"Helen, my darling, what is the matter? what is it,

31

love? Are you tired with your long ride? I said you
would be."

"No, Amy, I am not tired; we did not ride far," said
Helen, trying to stifle her tears. "Have you and Alfred
been out?"

"Yes—no. Oh! I do not know; never mind where we
went, but tell me what is the matter. Do, dear Nell.
Don't you remember how in former days I always used to
tease you out of all your secrets? and you must not cry
without telling me why."

"I do not know that I can tell you, dear; perhaps I do
not know myself. I dare say I am tired, I often feel so
now; and then I have so much to think of"; and she
leant her head on her hand with a look of painful weariness.

"Yes, so you have, but they are happy thoughts too,
Helen, in most respects. Oh, dear me! how well I
remember the week before my marriage, going to my own
room and sitting down comfortably in my arm-chair, just
as you are now, and thinking I would be thoroughly
unhappy about leaving dear papa and mamma, and you
and Beaufort, and I meant to cry about it, and to make a
complete victim of myself. And at the end of half an hour
I found I had been thinking of nothing but dear Alfred,
and wondering whether there ever had been in the world
any creature so happy as I was——"

"And yet you were leaving home!"

"Yes, but not for ever," said Amelia, laughing; "only
for three weeks. I knew I should come back, and bring
dear Alfred with me; and so will you, and bring dear
Teviot. Now, Helen, do not look so deplorable; nobody
can possibly pity you, I assure you."

"No, I suppose not," said Helen, in a low tone.

"Alfred and I have settled to remain here till you come
back from your great castle in the north," said Amelia,
determined to talk away Helen's low spirits. "So you

need not fret about mamma's loneliness; and besides, I never saw her so pleased with anything as she is with your marriage. I had a horrible fit of jealousy yesterday, thinking poor Alfred was neglected—I may say, quite cut out; but mamma has taken a little more notice of him to-day. Oh, dear! what fun it will be when we visit you in your own house! I hear it is an actual palace. Alfred went there once for some shooting when he was a boy; and then I have never told you that I like Lord Teviot so much."

Helen raised her head, but her lips quivered, and she leaned back again without speaking.

" I was so very anxious to see him, and to make acquaintance with him; because, you know, if I had not liked him, life would not have been worth having. You would have found it out, and would have thrown me off at once as your friend."

" Never, never!" said Helen; " I am sure I never should."

" Oh yes, you would, dear; and you ought. You will soon see how naturally one acquires a distaste for any ill-judging individual who presumes not to like one's husband. You would give us all up in a moment for Lord Teviot's sake, if we——"

" Oh, no, no!" exclaimed Helen, clasping her hands; " I shall cling to you all more than ever, and none of you must give me up. Amelia, promise to be kind to me, to love me more than ever when I am married; indeed, indeed, I shall want your love "; and she threw her arms round Amelia's neck, and sobbed violently.

" Why now, darling, how silly this is! how can I love you more than I do? You are nervous and tired, and just see what a state you have put us into: only look at me, with my eyes as red as ferrets', and you know how I hate to cry. Now we must not have any more of this nonsense.

c

There, you lie down on this sofa, and I will sit at this window, and pretend to read, while I cool my eyes. I won't speak another word; and if you fall asleep, so much the better, you will wake up quite in spirits again."

Helen threw her handkerchief over her eyes, and, leaning back on the sofa, seemed inclined to follow her sister's advice. Her sobs ceased; and Amelia sat quietly at the window, in the fond hope that her directions were all obeyed and that Helen was asleep.

In half an hour she saw Lord Teviot walking on the terrace below; he stopped under the window, and looked up at her.

" Is Helen there? " he said.

Amelia leaned forward, and, putting her finger to her lips, made signs to him to be silent.

" What is the matter? Is Helen not well, Lady Amelia? " he said, in a tone of vexation.

" Oh! bless the man," murmured Amelia, " why can't he hold his tongue? he will wake her. She's asleep—asleep, I tell you," putting her head quite out of the window, and speaking in a loud whisper.

" Who is it that you are talking to? " said Helen.

" There now, Lord Teviot, you have woke her. I told you how it would be, only nobody ever can be quiet. She was tired with that hot ride you took her."

" Well, ask her, Lady Amelia, if she will not come and sit in the shade a little while, she will find it much pleasanter than it was when we were riding."

" No; she says she is sorry, but she must keep quiet till dinner-time."

" Did you tell her it would be pleasanter? "

" Yes; but she don't seem to believe it."

" Ask her if I may come and visit her in her sitting-room."

" No; she says you are very good, but she does not wish

you to take that trouble. There, Helen, he is gone; but why would not you let him come here? I wish you had seen him, and then you could not have said no. I cannot imagine how you could have been so unkind to such a *héros de roman* looking man. Whether he is more like Lord Byron, or the superbe Orosmane, or Sir Philip Sydney, or Alcibiades, I cannot decide, never having seen any of them; but he certainly is the most distinguished-looking individual I ever saw. Oh! but, Helen," she said as she passed the dressing-table, "who gave you this splendid brooch?"

"Lord Teviot; he gave it to me this morning."

"Well, I never saw such lovely rubies—no, never. And you would not even come to the window to look at the man who gave you such a brooch, and who is so extremely well worth looking at, as I tell you he is. What an unfeeling little wretch! Well, good-bye, darling, you are better now, so I will leave you."

"No, don't leave me; I am better now, as you say, and I should like to have a little talk. What was it, Amelia, that you were saying about mamma—that she is pleased with my marriage?"

"Oh! delighted with it; she said that she was the happiest mother in the world, and that she was sure it had made dear papa ten years younger."

"And yet, if they had been told only six weeks ago that I was to leave them——"

"Ah! but, my dear, if it is your happiness."

"Yes, *if:* what a frightful word that *if* is, Amelia!" said Helen, turning to the table so that her sister could not see her face. "Did it ever occur to you before your marriage, that if your engagement were broken off——"

"Oh no, dear, I never thought of such an impossibility. I should have died of it; besides, Alfred was naturally too much charmed with the precious treasure he had gained to think of throwing it away—he is much too sensible for that."

"Oh! I did not think of *his* changing his mind; but if *you* had found out that you did not love him as much as he expected—that he had some great fault, a bad temper, for instance, would you have broken off your engagement? Would you, Amelia?"

"No, decidedly not; I should have married him, bad temper and all, and have turned it into a good one; I could never have given him up. Fancy me going through life without Alfred. How can you put such shocking ideas into my head? Only think of the sin of breaking one's promise, and of the poor man's mortification, and of what papa and mamma would have said; and of the explanations and the disgrace of the whole business. I should have gone mad. I should have shut myself up in a nunnery, if I could have found one. I never could have shown my face again. My dear, what could have put such a notion into your head?"

"Oh, nothing," said Helen; "'it is talking for mere talking sake,' as our governess used to say."

"Helen," said Amelia, after a pause, "you have frightened me; but I see now how it is. I suspect that you and Lord Teviot have had some little quarrel to-day; indeed, I am sure of it. You were fretting about it when I came in, and he was evidently very anxious to make it up when he came under the window. Dearest Nell, a slight unmeaning quarrel may be an amusing little incident, but it should not last half an hour, and it should not happen more than once. Be kind to him, dear, when you come down to dinner. You have had your fit of dignity, and the pleasure of putting yourself rather in the wrong; and now make it up, and let it be peace and happiness for the rest of your life." She ran out of the room, thinking she had said enough, only adding as she placed the brooch in Helen's hands, " There, you ungracious little thing. Look and repent."

" Ay, repent indeed," said Helen, throwing it from her; " and unless I were as cold and as hard as those stones, how can I but repent? She will not understand me; she will not help me; and how can she unless I had courage to tell her all? Oh! but the disgrace would, as she says, be too great; and then papa and mamma, and the day fixed, and so near. Oh! what shall I do!"

The dressing-bell rang, so it was clear that the first thing to be done was to dress for dinner; and happy for us is it that these ordinary domestic habits of life watch over its imaginative distresses with the sagacity and decision of sheep dogs, and bark and worry them till they fall into the proper path of the flock.

CHAPTER IV

THIS was the grand day of the Douglas dinner. They arrived. Mr. Douglas prepared to dine and to talk, and to be thankful if the cookery and conversation were good; Mrs. Douglas, perfectly ready and able to detect what might be amiss, and to say what would be disagreeable; and the girls, charmed with the new gowns that had been manufactured in honour of the occasion, and full of mysterious curiosity about Lord Teviot, and of real affectionate interest in Lady Helen.

Lord and Lady Eskdale and most of the guests were assembled. Amelia, for a wonder, was ready in good time; she was anxious to see her sister and Lord Teviot meet, and had taken her station near the door on purpose. Helen appeared soon after the arrival of the Douglas family, and received the friendly greeting of Mr. Douglas, and the meaning pressure of his daughters' hands, with the kindest cordiality. She looked flushed and excited when first she entered, but after a glance round the room her agitation subsided, and it was evidently a relief to her to see that Lord Teviot was not there. Dinner was announced, and he had not appeared.

"Are we to wait for him, Helen?" said Lord Eskdale, with a smile.

"Oh no, papa. Mr. Douglas, you must take pity on me. Do you remember the first day I dined down, how you protected me in to dinner?"

The whole party marshalled themselves, and went on to the dining-room.

"How disappointing!" whispered Sarah to Eliza; "I wanted to see them together."

Helen always sat on one side of her father, whatever guests there might be; and Amelia observed with pain the earnestness with which she tried to induce Mr. Douglas to take the chair next to her on the other side; but he laughed and left her, telling her he preferred going of his own accord to being sent away. Lord Teviot came in just as the soup and fish were taken away. He took his accustomed place, but without looking at Helen, and not till the second course came did any conversation pass between them, and then it seemed to be short and constrained; but she talked to her father in apparently good spirits. Sarah and Eliza looked at each other, and wondered whether that would be the right manner to adopt under similar circumstances. The ladies rose to retire. Helen had dropped her bracelet. Lord Teviot stooped for it, but with an air of such unwillingness that Helen said, "Pray do not give yourself so much trouble, I will send for it presently."

"As you please," he answered coldly, and stepped back to let her pass.

"Stay, Nell," said Trevor, "I will find it; Amelia has brought me into excellent training. I am quite in the habit of groping about under the table for all the things she drops. I am much more pliable than Teviot."

"That you are," said Helen; "thank you, dear Alfred"; and without another look at Lord Teviot she passed on.

Amelia did not at all like the aspect of affairs, but consoled herself with the hope that it was a mere lovers' quarrel, and would end in a burst of sentiment; and in the meantime she was glad to divert Mrs. Douglas's attention by showing her Helen's trousseau. It was indeed "showing her eyes to grieve her heart"; but if her saturnine dispositions could exhaust themselves on the senseless gowns and the poor dumb trinkets, it would be better than allowing her to make remarks on more sensitive victims. Sarah and Eliza were in good-natured rapture with the whole show—from the Brussels lace wedding-gown to the very last dozen of embroidered pocket-handkerchiefs, and they were quite sorry when a summons to coffee took them back to the drawing-room.

" Thirty morning gowns! " whispered Sarah, as they went down stairs. " The idea of a new gown every day for a month. Now I call that real happiness."

" Not such real, lasting happiness," answered Eliza, half laughing, " as eighteen bracelets, and then those heaps of gloves and handkerchiefs. A quarter of them, Sarah, would free our miserable allowances from embarrassments for life."

" It must be very pleasant to be so rich——"

" And to be going to be married," said Eliza; and this sage conclusion brought them to the drawing-room door.

Helen would perhaps have given them a different opinion. She began to doubt much whether it were happiness, or anything like it, to be going to be married. She had accepted Lord Teviot on an acquaintance of very few weeks, and that carried on solely in a ball-room or at a breakfast. She knew that her sisters had married in the same way, and were very happy. No one, not even her mother, had seemed to doubt for a moment that Lord Teviot's proposal was to be accepted. And except some slight misgivings as to whether she liked him as much as Amelia had liked Mr. Trevor, she herself had had no distrust as to her future prospects till she came into the country. Then she found every day some fresh cause to doubt whether she were as happy, engaged to Lord Teviot, as she was before she had ever seen him. He was always quarrelling with her—at least, so she thought; but the real truth was, that he was desperately in love, and she was not; that he was a man of strong feelings and exacting habits, and with considerable knowledge of the world; and that she was timid and gentle, unused to any violence of manner or language, and unequal to cope with it. He alarmed her, first by the eagerness with which he poured out his affection, and then by the bitterness of his reproaches because, as he averred, it was not returned.

She tried to satisfy him; but when he had frightened away her playfulness, he had deprived her of her greatest charm, and she herself felt that her manner became daily colder and more repulsive. His prediction that she would be happier anywhere than with him seemed likely, by repetition, to insure its own fulfilment. Even their reconciliations—for what is the use of a quarrel but to bring on a reconciliation?—were unsatisfactory. *She* wished that he loved her less, or would say less about it; and *he* thought that the gentle willingness with which she met his excuses was only a fresh proof that his love or his anger were equally matters of indifference to her. No French actor with a broken voice, quivering hands, a stride, and a shrug, could have given half the emphasis to the sentiment, *J'aimerais mieux être haï qu'aimé faiblement*, than Lord Teviot did to the upbraidings with which he diversified the monotony of love-making. This very morning he had persuaded himself that Helen would have preferred riding with her brother. She found the sun hot, and proposed to return. This was a fresh offence, and he declared that it was only a desire to avoid him that made her wish to shorten their ride. Then he worked himself up by a repetition of his wrongs to a degree of violence that would have surprised himself at another moment. At first she laughed at his accusations, then she was shocked at his bitterness, and at last, gay and giddy as she was, her spirits gave way; and when he helped her to dismount from her horse, he saw that her cheeks were pale, and that big tears were rolling over them. To his entreaties that she would

stay only five minutes more with him, she shook her head
and said faintly, " No, I am too tired now, I can bear no
more "; and as she left him the thought rushed into her
mind, " Perhaps he is right. I do not love him as I ought;
it is not yet too late."

It was in this mood that Amelia found her. One word
of encouragement would have given her spirit to break off
her marriage; but Amelia, who had been in love with Mr.
Trevor from the first hour of their acquaintance down to the
present speaking, could not realize her sister's feelings, and
gave the only advice that she would herself have taken in
Helen's position. Helen went down to dinner irresolute.
Nothing in Lord Teviot's manner tended to reconcile her
to him; and she thought that in the course of the evening
she would bravely seek him to dissolve their engagement.
But perhaps he saw something in her ease of manner that
alarmed him: dinner, that useful counsellor, had smoothed
his ruffled temper; perhaps the instinct that always leads
a man to foresee when an impending explanation is not
likely to end in his favour prompted him to divine that
he should have the worse of this. And the result was, that
when he came into the drawing-room, and saw Helen conversing gaily with Mrs. Douglas, he drew quietly towards her,
and sat down, looking very penitent, on a wretched, hard,
cane chair with a straight back, immediately behind her.
Gradually he edged himself into the conversation, took an
opportunity of throwing Helen's work on the floor, partly
that he might stoop for it with all Trevor's pliability, and
partly that in the course of that process he might contrive to touch with his lips Helen's hand, unperceived even
by the sharp-eyed Mrs. Douglas; and that *amende* being
made, he took his accustomed place on the sofa by her side,
and was so gentle and so pleasant that her resentment faded
gradually away, and all her magnanimous resolutions were
forgotten. Her misgivings as to the degree of affection

she felt for him remained; but she supposed Amelia was right: it would be shocking to break her promise. And, in short, she was too young to act for herself, and too much devoted to her parents to ask them to do for her what she knew would give them pain; and so the evening ended peacefully.

CHAPTER V

THE Douglases rolled home in their family coach.

"Pray, may I ask, Mr. Douglas, if you thought that a pleasant dinner?" said his wife in an insidious tone.

"Yes, my dear, I did indeed; good cookery, pleasant company, and very pretty women—I ask nothing more. Ought not I to have liked it?"

"Oh dear, yes! I am glad you did; easily pleased, that's all I can say. Perhaps, too, you thought your beauty, Lady Eskdale, looked well in that floppety cap?"

"I have not the good fortune to know what a floppety cap is, my dear; but I thought she looked very handsome, even by the side of those two pretty daughters of hers."

"Well, it is to me the strangest delusion of yours, that about the beauty of the Eskdales. Perhaps, too, in the extremity of your benevolence, you think Lord Teviot is very much in love with Helen?"

"Is not he? I took it for granted that he was, because, in the first place, most men who saw her would be; and in the next, because I presume he would not marry her if he were not."

"What his reasons may be for marrying her I do not know; but I never saw a more unpromising-looking business than that. He seems to me to be about the most ill-tempered, disagreeable, odious young man I ever saw; and he does not care two straws for Helen. Girls, I am sure you must have observed it: he never spoke to her at dinner, and I am convinced she is very unhappy."

"Oh, mamma, do you think so?" said Eliza. "I

think Helen, when she is married, will be just like Lady
Amelia; and I am sure *she* is happy enough."

" She carries it off very well," said Mrs. Douglas; " but
in my humble opinion Mr. Trevor is rather a poor creature,
and Amelia is sharp enough to find it out. After all the
fuss that has been made about Lady Eskdale's luck in the
marriage of her daughters, I see nothing in it. The
Waldegraves are never here, to begin with."

" Oh, because he was obliged to go to Paris about that
money of his uncle's."

" Ah! so they say; I never believe those stories of people
going rambling about in search of their uncle's money. I
suspect he is very unsteady, and Sophia's temper must be
a trying one, I am sure; and probably they do not wish
the Eskdales to see how unhappy they are. So much for
one daughter. Then Amelia is married to a man who looks,
I think, though nobody will agree with me, like a fool, and
moreover his father is alive, and may live for ages, or marry
again, and have heaps of children; so in a worldly point
of view that is a deplorable marriage."

" My dear, how you do run on imagining grievances!
The Trevors are very well off."

" How can you know, Mr. Douglas? Nobody who has
a father alive ever is well off; and besides, they are very
extravagant; you will see that they will get into difficulties;
and then Helen, we were told that hers was to be a model
marriage—the greatest piece of luck that ever was known.
Now I am not easily taken in, but I really did expect to
see a tolerable chance of happiness for that poor girl;
and there she is going to be the wife of that horrid savage."

" Oh, mamma! he does not look like a savage."

" No, my dear, savages would not be so affected; but I
was alluding to his temper, which is evidently a savage
temper. I am sorry for it, for Helen is rather a favourite
of mine, and I see she will lead a wretched life; and

taking all these circumstances together, I cannot wonder that with all this care and anxiety on her mind Lady Eskdale looks as old and haggard as she does."

" Well, Anne, you have settled that family thoroughly," said Mr. Douglas; " nobody can accuse you of too much benevolence in your opinions."

" No, my dear, I don't set up for that sort of character, because I happen to see things as they really are, and I am never taken in by the cant of prosperity, and that sort of pretension. So really, without offence, I must be allowed to observe that I do not envy Lady Eskdale her sons-in-law; and that I hope we shall not be asked to dine there any more this year, that is all."

And on this conclusion the family rested till they arrived at home.

CHAPTER VI

" I WISH mamma did not hate dining at Eskdale Castle,"
said Eliza to her sister when they went to their own room;
" and I wish they would ask us a little oftener; I think it is
very good fun going there."

" Do you? " said Sarah, in an absent tone.

" Yes, I like their large rooms, and the armchairs, and
the sofas, and the sort of smell of wealth that there is about
the house. And the dinner itself is so good. How lucky
it is that mamma does not hear me! It is the sort of thing
she would hate me to say; but the soup was perfectly
delicious, so unlike our dull Scotch broth; only I wish it
had not been spilt on my new gown, and on the front
breadth too; just look, Sarah. What a pity! and it was
all the fault of the servant. Those great tall footmen
frighten me out of my senses, and I wish they would not go
on offering one all the dishes, it is so tiresome; I go on
saying ' No, no, no,' all dinner-time. Lord Beaufort said
I ate nothing."

" Ah, by the by, miss," said Sarah, rousing up, " how
came you to contrive to sit by Lord Beaufort? You are
always taking the best places, and as I am the eldest, I
ought to have my choice sometimes."

" Yes, but as I am the youngest, other people have their
choice," said Eliza, laughing. " However, you need not
mind it this time, Sarah. Lord Beaufort was obliged to
take the only place that was vacant, because he did not
come in, you know, till dinner was half over, and so that

47

was the reason why he sat by me. He spoke to me three times, and asked me to have some wine. Did you observe his waistcoat, Sarah? 'such a love!' as Lady Eskdale would say."

"How you do run on, Eliza! I wish you would let me have the looking-glass for one minute, if you have looked at yourself enough."

"Law, my dear, you may have it for a week if you like. I was only taking a last fond look at this dear gown, before I take it off. I shan't have an opportunity, probably, of wearing it again for the next six months; not that I shall actually have any great pleasure in it again, because of those grease spots. I wish that servant had not done it. So awkward and provoking! However, I hope we shall dine there again some day or another."

"And I hope we never shall as long as we live," said Sarah, emphatically. She had taken one look at herself in the glass, and then threw herself into a chair with an air of deep despondency.

"Never dine there again as long as we live!" repeated Eliza. "Why, Sarah, what is the matter? You can't be well. What can have happened?"

"Something dreadful," said Sarah, in a deep tone.

"Why, what can it be? You have not greased your gown too?" said Eliza, starting up as if she had made a great discovery.

"No."

"What then? Have you lost anything? forgotten your fan? dropped your bracelet?"

"Oh, no; worse than all that; it is something dreadful that has been said of us."

"Good gracious! what? What can they find to say of us?"

"Something quite shocking!" and Sarah actually coloured at the mere thought of repeating it.

"Well, tell it, at all events; I should like to know the worst."

"It was just when you were sitting by the pianoforte, and I was behind the sofa, and Mr. Trevor came up to Lady Eskdale and said, looking at the flowers and the silver comb in your hair, 'Don't you think those silver épergnes full of flowers would look better on a dining-table than walking about a drawing-room? I know nothing of dress, but is not that a little in the May-day line—rather chimney-sweeperish?'"

"No, did he really say that?" and Eliza looked aghast. "What a horrid man!"

"Yes, but that is not the worst. Lady Eskdale said, 'Don't laugh at those poor girls, Alfred; they are dear good creatures, though they are vulgarly dressed.' There, Eliza, now is not that dreadful, and so hard too, when we took such pains about our dress, and thought it was so nice?" and Sarah's voice quivered with vexation.

"Oh, never mind, dear; don't fret about it, you did look very nice. I'm sure I thought so; and if we wore too many flowers to-day, next time we will wear none; and as for that Mr. Trevor, I dare say he knows nothing about dress."

"But I wish we were not like chimney-sweepers."

"I say, Sarah, it would be rather good fun to go to Eskdale Castle with our faces blackened, and we, covered with flowers and tinsel, dancing round Mr. Trevor, rattling our shovels."

"Don't talk nonsense, Eliza. I never thought we were vulgar."

"Nor I; but we cannot help it if we are. I think we are two very nice girls, and Helen does not despise us. Oh, Sarah, how beautiful she is, and how I should like to be going to be married to Lord Teviot! that is, I should not like it at all except I were Helen. I should be afraid of him as I am."

D

"Ah, she looked very pretty," said Sarah. "She had no flowers in her hair," and with a deep sigh, Sarah unpinned a gigantic bunch of camellias, "and her hair was braided quite smooth"; and Sarah gave a desperate tug at a highly frizzed set of bows which she had built up on the top of her head with some pride.

Eliza burst out laughing; Sarah's distress seemed to her to be out of all proportion to the calamity, and she was too merry and too light-hearted herself to be discomposed by such a trifle. "I hope they will ask us again," she murmured as she sank to sleep.

"What shall we wear if they do?" Sarah responded.

"Black jackets, tin foil, and calico roses, with shovels for fans," said Eliza, in a sleepy voice; and in another moment their troubles were forgotten.

CHAPTER VII

ELIZA's wishes were more than fulfilled, for the following day she received a very kind note from Helen, asking her to be one of her bridesmaids, and this was accompanied by a very pretty dress, with Lady Eskdale's " kind love," and a note to invite Mrs. Douglas also to the wedding, and Mr. Douglas and Sarah to the breakfast that was to follow it.

Mrs. Douglas could hardly do less than make a very great grievance of what was intended as a kindness. She hated a wedding: it was just the sort of thing that the world chose to make a fuss about, but which she thought the most uninteresting ceremony on earth. She did not see why she was to dress herself out in satin and blonde just to go and hear two young people make foolish promises that they never could keep. What could be more absurd than to assemble a crowd to witness a man and woman promising to love each other for the rest of their lives, when we know what human creatures are,—men so thoroughly selfish and unprincipled, women so vain and frivolous? This wholesale way of dealing with her fellow-creatures was one of Mrs. Douglas's favourite methods of treating them. " I should like to go in my garden bonnet and coloured muslin gown, just to show how I despise their love of fashion," she said, as she sealed the note to her milliner, which was to order the well-chosen dress and bonnet on which she had determined for the occasion; for the energy with which she declaimed against dress did not at all interfere with her inclination to spend a great deal of money on it.

So to the wedding she went, and this is her description of it.

"My dear Sister,

"You will expect to have some account of the Esk-dale wedding, so I may as well write to-night, though I am completely knocked up. You know what a wretched sleeper I am, and of course I could not close my eyes till five, from feeling that I was to be called an hour earlier than usual; and then, what with breakfasting in a hurry, and dressing, and fancying we were too late, I was quite ill by the time we arrived at the Castle. Eliza was to be one of the bridesmaids, and Lady Eskdale gave her her dress. I must own I thought it a shabby present; but as Eliza was pleased, of course I did not say so. When we arrived at the Castle, there was poor Lady Eskdale looking ninety at least, though Mr. Douglas will not see how old she is grown, and the tears rolling down her cheeks, while she kept saying, 'We are to have no crying, that is all settled, and no melancholy leave-takings on account of poor dear Helen; we are none of us to shed a tear.' I am the worst person in the world, you know, to enter into these *prettinesses*. I could only say, 'There was no use in crying,' or some platitude of that sort, for sentiment bores me. Lady Amelia stayed with Helen till almost the last moment, and then came and made the sort of fuss with her mother which all that family make with each other. Amelia's beauty is one of those delusions I have never given into. Large eyes and dark eyebrows, and a great display of hair—I presume it is all her own—and a way of playing her features about as if she were more intelligent than other people. It may be natural, but it looks like affectation. We all went in solemn procession to the chapel, through rows of servants. What the expense of that establishment must be I cannot imagine, nor how the

Eskdales have gone on so long without coming to a stop. As soon as we were arranged in our places, Lord Eskdale and Helen came in at one door, and Lord Teviot and Lord Beaufort at another; and they all went straight to the altar, with a great tangle of bridesmaids behind them. I thought it all a most theatrical arrangement. Why could they not come like John and Jane Smith to be married, like other people, at the village church? Helen was so covered with Brussels lace that I cannot say how she looked; some of the company, of course, declared she looked beautiful. I saw nothing but a veil—a mere lace veil; and besides, I have always set my face against the absurd idea that all brides look pretty. She shook very much, and though I am the last person, from my friendship for the Eskdales, to hint at the real state of the case, I have a sad foreboding that Helen marries with the prospect of being one of the most unhappy women in England. And I do not wonder at it. Lord Teviot is one of the worst specimens of the class dandy I ever saw; and I am much mistaken if his temper will not be a sad trial to poor Helen. However, don't quote me. You never saw such a frightful effect as the coloured glass had on Lady Eskdale's looks; and I think Lord Eskdale's hair has grown suddenly gray. It may have been the reflection of the blue glass; but it gave me the impression of gray hair: and I suppose all his worries must tell upon him at last. The chapel was all dressed out with flowers; and I could hardly attend to the ceremony, because I was expecting every moment to feel faint with the smell of the lilies and heliotrope; and then I thought I should catch my death of cold by standing on the marble pavement. To be sure, the manners of the present day are very different from what even I can remember. I saw Lord Beaufort shuffling a cushion about with his feet, and thought that he was of course going to give it to me to stand on, when down he went on his knees,

and began saying his prayers, without the least consideration for my chances of cramp. After the ceremony there
was a long scene of congratulation, and we all embraced
each other, without sparing age or sex. I had a narrow
escape of a ' salute ' from Robinson, the old tutor, and
Lizzy was frightened out of her wits by a kiss from Lord
Eskdale. There was a great breakfast immediately after
the wedding, to which most of the neighbourhood were
invited. Helen went to change her dress, and Lord Teviot
stalked about amongst the company for a little while,
looking bored and sullen. I always pity the bridegroom
on these occasions. The bride is supported by her father,
and attended by her bridesmaids, and everybody is or
pretends to be in a fright, lest she should faint or cry; and
she has all the protection of a veil in case she should be too
shy, or not shy enough; and there is a general sympathy
in her feelings. The poor man has to walk himself up
alone to the altar, where he stands, looking uncommonly
foolish, without even the protection of his hat. There is
the mother sobbing at him for carrying off her child; the
sisters scowling at him because he did not choose one of
them; the clergyman frowning at him for not producing
the ring at the right moment, or for neglecting the responses
in their proper places; the brothers laugh at him; the
bride turns from him; and the only person who pays him
the slightest attention is the clerk, who tells him when he is
to kneel, and when to stand, and which is his right hand,
and which his left, and helps him to the discovery of his
waistcoat pocket, in which the ring may or may not be.
Lord Teviot is not a man to look foolish, but he decidedly
looked cross.

" Two carriages-and-four were waiting at the door, and
an immense crowd was assembled round them. We all
went and stood on the marble terrace above, and in half
an hour Lord Eskdale led Helen out from the cloister door,

and handed her into the carriage. Lord Teviot stepped in, and they drove off, followed by the other carriage, in which all the dressing-boxes and the jewel-cases and the valet and the maid had been packed up for some time. You know that Lady Teviot's maid is that pert Nancy who originally waited in my school-room, and of course I am rather amazed at her presumption, calling herself Mrs. Tomkinson, and travelling in a carriage-and-four. Lady Eskdale came back to the company, still crying, and still declaring it was the gayest wedding she had ever seen, and that she was so glad there had been no tears. I was dead tired when I got home, and am very glad that the Eskdales have married all their daughters, and that we have no more weddings to do. Adieu, my dear sister. Is it true that your son has sold out of the 15th? If I were you, I would advise him to live less at clubs, and not to keep so many horses.

" Yours ever,
" A. Douglas."

CHAPTER VIII

AND now, whatever might have been Helen's fears or hopes, her fate was sealed. She had turned to that page of life over which she had lingered with distressful doubt; and now it must be read, though on herself partly must she depend for the interpretation of the characters it bore. St. Mary's Abbey, at which her honeymoon was to be passed, was the most magnificent of all Lord Teviot's residences. It almost calls for a formal description; but how can anyone be expected to write what no one ever reads when it is written? That pert Nancy, now by the grace of presumption styling herself Mrs. Tomkinson, addressed a letter to Mrs. Hervey, the housekeeper at Eskdale Castle, in which she gave her views of St. Mary's Abbey, and in her sketchy way she succeeds so well in the descriptive art, that it is impossible to join in the total contempt with which Mrs. Douglas looked down upon her from the marble terrace.

"DEAR MRS. HERVEY,

"I hope this will find you in good health and sperrits—not forgetting all other friends at the old house. Me and my lady are quite well, and have no reason to complain that we have changed our abode for the worst. We were very nervous that day what we left you, me, in particular, that had been sitting in the Bruche, baked to a jelly, and watching all those jewel-boxes while my lady was bidding good-bye, and with that great mob of people staring at me. But Mr. Phillips was very attentive, and helped me to bow to them as we driv off. He

56

seems a superior young man, quite a London-bred servant, and quite confidential with my lord, which was the reason why he was left at St. Mary's during my lord's courtship, because he knew all the plans about the furniture. We went at such a pace that I was quite giddy, but found great comfort in the sandwiches, and gingerbread, and chicken and buns you put into the carriage, which was a kind thought, for otherwise we should have gone the whole fifty miles without refreshment. When we had arrived all but a mile, my lord's tenants met us, and took the horses off from my lord and lady, and dragged them their own selves; and they came to drag us, but Mr. Phillips explained that we was only own man and lady's maid, and that our horses were to be let alone. So they hurraed and threw flowers, and it was very agitating. When we arrived, my lord made a speech, and my lady made a curtesy, and I got the imperials and boxes in as soon as I could. I was terrified lest any of our new troosso should be stole. Dear Mrs. Hervey, St. Mary's is a most beautiful place, and the great mirrors in the ball-room are alone worth coming to see, and I have not power to describe the scenery. There is a lake quite full of water, like the lakes abroad, and endless woods filled with the finest trees, that seem to run for miles and miles, and gardens that beat our gardens at the castle all to nothing. The furniture would please you in particular, chiefly silk and damask, but some rooms with velvet; and my lady's suite of rooms is what I can't describe—straw-coloured satin embroidered with real flowers—and such cabinets and china, and on the dressing-table a service of gold plate with my lady's name on it. Mrs. Nelson won't like to see it, she was so set up about her lady's. In every respect I feel satisfied with the accommodations for me and my lady, except that I was obleeged to ask for another wardrobe, and to tell Mrs. Stevens that I was accustomed to a larger looking-glass in my own room.

Mrs. Stevens and me seem inclined to be very friendly; she is the very moral of a housekeeper in a romance, quite an old lady. We are a princely establishment, and sit down twelve in the Steward's room, with wine, and a man and boy to wait. Mrs. Stevens and me joke each other about our beaux, for there are ten gentlemen, and only us two ladies, and Mr. Phillips has, of course, the precedence. I hope to pick up a little French between the cook and the confectioner. I wish you would ask Mrs. Warren whether, when Lady Amelia married, she did not get all her lady-ship's shawls with the rest of the things. My lady kept her suit of Brussels, and I had nothing to say again that, for I believe Brussels lace is what every lady have a right to keep; but she also kept two shawls, which I believe are my perquisites, as my lady wore them before my lord proposed. I want to know if you and Mrs. Warren and Mrs. Nelson think that their being real Ingee makes a difference. My mind misgives me, it does. It is not for the lucre of gold I speak, nor that I would grudge my lady the shawls, nor the gown off my back if she wanted it, but I hate to see poor servants defrauded, and if the shawls is my due, I shall take the liberty of mentioning it. I had not time to tell you of the pride of that Mrs. Douglas, who met me on the wedding-day, and said ' Fine times for you, Nancy; your head will be turned.' I was mad with myself afterwards for having made her a curtesy, and said, ' Yes, indeed, ma'am,' when I might as well have said something sharp. If Lady Eskdale asks if you have heard from me, will you, please, make my duty, and say that my lady is quite well, and has had no cold or headache. Mrs. Stevens thinks her the beautifullest lady she ever saw, and compliments me high on my manner of hair-dressing.

    " I remain, dear Mrs. Hervey,
          " Your kind friend,
             " Ann Tomkinson,"

CHAPTER IX

IT is not worth while to give any of Helen's letters to her family. Some years ago it was the fashion of all newly-married people to write word to their friends that they were the happiest of human creatures. Heaven alone knows if it were true, but so they always said. Now this romantic state of bliss has been laughed at in society, and sneered at in novels, till nobody dares say a word about it. It may be wiser, but it is not quite satisfactory. The domestic novels of the day have described with such accuracy, and with so much satire, all the little fidgety amiabilities of life, that a wife who is inclined to praise her husband checks herself, for fear she should be reckoned like Mrs. Major Waddell. An active mother has a suspicion that she is laughed at as a Mrs. Fairbairn, and the kindly affections of the heart are now so carefully wrapped up and concealed, that it seems just possible that they may die altogether of suffocation.

Helen did not commit herself by any asseverations of extraordinary happiness, and made no mention of any fresh trait of perfection that every day must have revealed in Lord Teviot's character; but there was St. Mary's to describe, and the neighbourhood to explain, and all the various congratulatory letters she received were duly quoted, and her own regularly ended with " Teviot's love to all "; and Lady Eskdale was satisfied. Amelia read her sister's letters with greater distrust. She thought they were written in a constrained, guarded tone, and she remembered the week that preceded the wedding with pain and doubt. She hoped in another fortnight to see and judge for herself; but Mr. Trevor and she were summoned into Sussex by the sudden death of his father; and ten days after Helen's marriage Lord and Lady Eskdale sat down, for the first time during the last ten years, to a *tête-à-tête* dinner. Poor dear people, it fairly puzzled them. They were more attached to each other than many husbands and wives are after twenty-four years of married life; and they had been in the daily habit of taking a comfortable half-hour's talk in Lord Eskdale's library, uninterrupted by any of their children. But they had never contemplated the possibility of dining and passing the whole evening together, without a child to come in to dessert, or a daughter to look at and listen to. Then who was to make breakfast the next morning, and to answer notes, and to receive visitors? Lady Eskdale was quite posed. She actually ordered a riding-habit, and declared she would begin riding again with Lord Eskdale, who hated going out alone, and had always been accompanied by one of his children. Then she thought she could rub up music enough to play to him after dinner; but when the evening came she was fast asleep on the sofa, half dead with the fatigue of her morning ride, and she almost cried when a note was brought to her that required an answer—partly because, as she said and thought, she missed Helen so much, and partly because she was too indolent to sit up to write.

" I don't think I can ever exist in this way, Lord Eskdale," she said. " What is to be done? here is this note to be answered."

" Give it to me, Jane; I will be your secretary."

" Thank you, that is very good of you. It is a great relief for this once; but how am I to get on when you are out? To be sure, that poor dear Lord Walden might as well have put off dying just for a month, and then the

Trevors could have stayed here. I am utterly lost without Amelia. There never was anything so unlucky. I wish Beaufort would marry. A daughter-in-law would be better than nothing; or if the Waldegraves would come back to England, Sophia might come here. It is really very hard to have no daughter at all, after all my trouble "; and Lady Eskdale's voice faltered.

"The schoolmistress, my lady," said the groom of the chambers, "is waiting for directions about the children's stuff books."

"There again, now! What am I to do? I have mislaid the patterns. Very well, tell her I will send to her. Now, Lord Eskdale, you know you cannot settle about the school-children's frocks; that was poor Helen's business. Dear child! I do trust she is happy, but it is sad work marrying off one's daughters; it makes me very low at times. Lord Eskdale, do you think if I were to ask Mrs. Douglas to let me have Eliza here, that it would bore me very much?"

"You must be the best judge of that, my dear Jane; at all events, take care to ask the right daughter, not the one with the voice."

"No, no; I mean Eliza, who was Helen's bridesmaid. You know you thought her very pretty that day. She plays very well on the pianoforte, and I could take care that she should be always well dressed; and she would write my notes, and see the school-mistress, and help to entertain the company. She is a good-humoured, amiable girl, and I have always felt that I could be fond of her; and it would be such a thing for her, for the Douglases see so few people. I wish I could guess whether I should like this plan or not. I can ask her for a fortnight only at first, and if it does not do, then there would be an end of it."

"As you please, my love; it concerns you more than me."

"Yes, but I wish you would say what you think best;

I am so little in the habit of making up my own mind. Helen always knew what I should like. I must say we have been unlucky in our daughters all marrying rich people. If any one of them had married a younger son without a shilling, they must have lived with us; but my girls had no time allowed them to look about them and choose for themselves; and so they have all married men with country-houses of their own, and I have lost them all."

And, roused by this overpowering calamity of wealthy sons-in-law, Lady Eskdale sat up to write her note to Mrs. Douglas.

CHAPTER X

"Mamma," said Eliza Douglas, as they were sitting working in the evening, "did you know that the Trevors had left Eskdale Castle?"

"No, my love; how should I know anything about the Trevors? Lady Amelia never deigned to call here but once, and then at an hour when she knew I should be out."

"Yes, another time with Mr. Trevor, mamma. If you remember——"

"Well, Mr. Trevor wanted to see your father, and she was obliged to come with him; I do not call that a visit."

"And then on Sunday, mamma, after church?"

"My love, what is the use of contradicting me? If Lady Amelia did call then, she ought to be ashamed, with all her pretence of goodness, to pay visits at all on Sunday. And all these little trifling facts make no difference, in my opinion, that all these young women are much too fine to pay any attention to their mother's old friend. Who told you they were gone?"

"Mrs. Birkett told Sarah, and Betsy said, when she was dressing me, that she had seen Lady Eskdale's maid, who had mentioned it."

"Well, now, I should like to know what business Betsy had to be talking to Mrs. Nelson. It will not at all do for our servants to get a habit of gossiping at Eskdale Castle; not that I shall be at all sorry if it obliges me to speak out and to make a thorough reform in our household: I am always glad of an opportunity to tell servants what a thoroughly bad race I think they are."

" That must be encouraging to them," said Mr. Douglas,
" and produce a great increase of attachment to yourself."

" Oh! my dear, that is one of the subjects you do not
understand, and so you may as well not talk about it.   If
you would let me send away that old Thomas of yours, the
house would go on much better.   Mrs. Birkett, and Mrs.
Dashwood, and everybody says I manage servants better
than anybody; and I know I do, by never letting them
have their own way on any one point; and as for attachment, you might as well expect it from this table."

" I should think so, under the circumstances," said Mr.
Douglas; " but whatever you do, do not interfere with
Thomas."

A silence followed while Mrs. Douglas was thinking
what a clever manager she was, and how well she contrived
to make her servants hate her; and then her thoughts
recurred to the Eskdales.

" So Amelia is gone; I suppose to some gay party at a
country-house.   I must say, that after all the fuss that has
been made about those girls, it is not much to their credit
that they leave their parents quite to themselves in their
old age, while they are flying about in search of amusement.
I will answer for it Amelia went off because she thought it
dull."

" Are you speaking of the Trevors? " said Mr. Douglas,
who was reading the paper.   " I see his father is dead,
and they have been sent for into Sussex.   Trevor is now
Lord Walden."

" Oh! " said Mrs. Douglas; and there was another long
silence.

" Well," she began again, " I do pity Lord Eskdale:
I do not see what he is to do, after being accustomed to
the society of his daughters, and used to having one of them
always with him.   Those die-away, languid airs of Lady
Eskdale's must be rather trying.   To be sure, she is not so

young as she was, whatever you may say, Mr. Douglas;
but she might exert herself to be a little more of a companion to him. She has none of my ideas that a wife is
bound to exert herself for her husband's good."

" I met them riding together to-day," said Mr. Douglas.

" Riding, my dear! "

" Yes, riding, Anne."

" You must be dreaming, Mr. Douglas. Lady Eskdale
on a horse! "

" No, my love, on a mare; the gray mare Helen used
to ride."

" Impossible! How was she dressed, Mr. Douglas? "

" In a habit, my dear, and hat, with a veil. I can
swear to the hat, for it became her particularly."

" Well," said Mrs. Douglas, with a scornful laugh, " I
think this is by far the most amusing thing I ever heard.
Lady Eskdale doing the youthful, galloping about the
country flirting with her husband; I suppose she will
begin dancing next. Lord Eskdale and she are probably
at this moment practising the Gavotte de Vestris up and
down the saloon. I don't know when I have been so
diverted; but to a person of plain commonsense like
myself, the tricks and ways of these London ladies are
amazingly entertaining."

" However, you must allow, Anne, that this is not a die-
away, languid air; and as you take such a kind interest in
Lord Eskdale's fate, you will be happy to hear that he said he
was quite delighted to have his wife riding with him again."

" Oh, my dear love! unless you mean to make me quite
ill, you must not offer me the mawkish idea of Lord
Eskdale making pretty speeches to his wife; I really
cannot stand that. And pray, are this promising young
couple likely to remain long in their solitary paradise?
or are they going to St. Mary's? or is there any company
coming to the castle? "

E

" I think they are expecting a large party at home. Lord Eskdale was beginning to say something about it, and then she gave him a look, and he stopped short."

"What! I suppose we are not to know, for fear we should expect to be asked. Why, it is just the very thing I would go miles out of the way to avoid, and the last society into which I should like to take my girls."

" Oh, mamma! " said Eliza, " I wish you would not say that; and I wish they would ask us constantly to their house. It is very odd, that though I feel afraid of everybody all the time, there is nothing I like so much as dining there. And I am sure, mamma, it would be very good for my manner, which you say is so unformed at home. Before I have crossed the hall at Eskdale Castle I feel quite refined," she said, laughing.

Mrs. Douglas laughed too, for though she rarely lost any opportunity of speaking malevolently of her neighbours' children, she was very much disposed to admire her own. And her own misanthropy found a pleasant relief in Eliza's enjoyable views of life.

CHAPTER XI

LADY ESKDALE's note of invitation arrived, worded in the most engaging manner. She begged Mrs. Douglas to consider her forlorn situation, and to lend dear, gay Lizzy to her for a few days—the few days not to be construed literally, but to extend to a fortnight if Eliza could bear to leave home for so long. She feared it would be very dull at first, but hoped that some friends who were expected would amuse that *très amusable petite personne*. If Mrs. Douglas consented to this plan, the carriage would come for Eliza and her maid the next day.

Mrs. Douglas was excessively surprised. It was unlucky that she had just said so much against the manners and customs of Eskdale Castle—protests made, too, in vain, for she had no hesitation in allowing Eliza to accept the invitation. The friends who were expected might include a second Lord Teviot. That horrid, rude Lord Beaufort might be at home, and she could magnanimously forgive his nefarious conduct at Helen's wedding, if there were any chance of her officiating at his own in the capacity of his mother-in-law. Visions of grandeur rose before her eyes; and when Mr. Douglas, in the consultation held between them on the subject, asked if she had not said that the society at Eskdale Castle was not what she would like for her daughters, she boldly took Falstaff's line of defence when accused by Justice Shallow of having broken into his park and stolen his deer. "I have, Mr. Justice, I have—and so I hope that's answered."

"Yes, my dear, I said so, but what of that? It is rather

hard to be tried in the morning for every little careless word spoken over-night; nothing provokes me so much as to be accused of inconsistency, when it does so happen that I am remarkably consistent. However, I am decidedly in favour of Lizzy's going, so it does not much matter what I said. We may as well tell her."

Eliza was in raptures. "A whole fortnight of visiting! and only think, mamma, of Lady Eskdale saying she would send for my maid. Why, I have none."

"You must take Betsy, I suppose, and my maid must dress Sarah. It will turn Betsy's head, and make her rather perter than she is; but it cannot be helped."

"What fun it will be! only what shall I do about going into the room alone? and I hope I shall not be sent out to ride with Lord Eskdale, for I do not know how to talk to him. And then about dress, mamma, what gowns am I to take? and then poor Sarah, left all alone, how unhappy she will be! Oh, no! she won't though, because of Mr. Wentworth's coming here; and besides, I shall write to her every day."

This hint of Mr. Wentworth was well thrown in. Sarah was just beginning to wonder whether she ought not to be affronted because Lady Eskdale had not invited *her* ; but the handsome manner with which Mr. Wentworth was made over to her—he being the only semblance of a lover that had ever appeared at the house—quite appeased her, and her affection for her sister was always strong enough to conquer any little feelings of jealousy awakened by Eliza's superior popularity.

"Yes, you must certainly write every day," she said when they were alone, "and describe all your little difficulties. I think you will be very fond of Lady Eskdale."

"Yes, I am sure of it; she is ' such a dear,' as she would say herself. But Lord Eskdale, Sarah, is very alarming, is not he?"

" Rather so; but perhaps he will not take much notice of you. If I were you, Lizzy, I would read the newspaper more than you do; and then you can talk to him about trials, and murders, and politics, and accidents: I observe that those are the kind of topics he likes."

" Oh, goodness, Sarah! think of me talking politics to Lord Eskdale; a nice mess I should make of that. No, I had better not think about it. I must take some pretty work with me, something that will not annoy Lady Eskdale in the drawing-room; and then music is always a resource. And my daily letter to you; and, Sarah, mind you send me every particular of Mr. Wentworth's visit, and what he says, and looks, and thinks. Oh dear! if you should write me word he had proposed, what a state I should be in ! "

" Oh, nonsense ! " said Sarah, " there is no chance of that "; but the idea led her into a dream of happiness; and when Eliza and her Betsy, her embroidery and her best gowns were all carried off the following morning in Lady Eskdale's carriage, Sarah saw her depart without one twinge of envy, for Mr. Wentworth had sent word he should arrive in time for dinner.

CHAPTER XII

THE Teviots had reached the end of the second week of their honeymoon undisturbed, except by the visits of two or three neighbours. It was almost time that there should be some change, at least Mrs. Tomkinson wished to goodness there might soon be what she called " a little staying company " in the house, if it were only that my lady might wear some of her bettermost gowns; and she also thought my lady seemed rather moped somehow. Mr. Phillips gave it as his humble opinion that " our folks had had enough of their own company for one while." It has never been definitely stated what period of time " one while " comprises, nor whether there is a plural to the substantive, and " two whiles " represent a certain number of days or weeks. However that may be, Phillips and Tomkinson had judged with their usual discrimination. That same day Lord Teviot went into Helen's boudoir with some letters in his hand.

" Helen, here is some company for you. Lady Portmore has offered herself for Friday."

" That is rather a short notice, is it not? "

" Yes—no; I do not think that signifies. We should be glad of her visit, either on a short notice or a long one. *I* shall be delighted to see her, and she must know she is welcome at St. Mary's—always has been, and always will be."

" Are you expecting any other friends? " said Helen, putting aside the question of the Portmore welcome.

" Yes, two or three men. Lady Portmore says she is

sure we shall have been too much occupied with each other "—and he smiled rather scornfully—" to think of arranging a pleasant party, and that we shall be obliged to her for inviting a few people we all know."

" I am not sure that I am obliged to her just now," said Helen, hurrying on through her sentence. " My letters had given me the idea of a totally different plan. The Trevors have been obliged to go to Walden, and papa and mamma are left quite alone; and I thought we might surprise them with a visit now, instead of next month, when you promised to go to them. How I should like it! but, if we cannot put off Lady Portmore——"

" We neither can nor will," said Lord Teviot. " I am sorry you are already tired of your own home; but, such as it is, I am afraid I must trouble you to stay in it. And though *my* friends are not, of course, to be compared to yours, I cannot begin by affronting them all."

Helen made no answer, and after a moment's pause took up her work. Lord Teviot walked to the window, and began playing with the tame bullfinch that stood in it. The silence that ensued was long and awful, but was broken by him as he said, in a constrained voice, " Have you had no other letter but that from your mother? "

" None of any consequence."

" Did not Beaufort write? I thought I saw his hand."

" There is his letter; there are all my letters, if you like to see them," said Helen—a faint suspicion dawning on her mind that Lord Teviot was jealous of her family. He seemed to waver, but she placed them on the table, and, moving her work-frame nearer to the window, left the field open to him. He took up the letters with a slight sensation of shame. Lady Eskdale's was as usual affectionate and amiable; and though she expressed strongly her wish to see her daughter, she said she knew it was not likely Lord Teviot could leave his home again so soon;

and she mentioned her invitation to Eliza Douglas, which she hoped would satisfy Helen's doubts of her comfort. "It is a sad change, my darling, but as it is for your happiness I cannot complain, and your letters are the greatest possible comfort to me. Do tell your idle husband to write to me." Lord Beaufort wrote from London, where he had seen the Portmores, and he said he should have joined their party to St. Mary's, but that he was seized with a fit of filial duty, and meant to run down to Eskdale Castle, to console his respected and deserted papa and mamma. "They fancy, poor deluded creatures, that they miss you dreadfully, and that no one can fill up your vacant place. Strange illusion! which my august presence will instantly dispel. After I have raised their spirits to their proper pitch, it is just possible that I may raise my own, by coming to see my little Nell; so tell Teviot to expect me, and to turn his attention towards partridges and pheasants." There was a third letter in a hand-writing Lord Teviot did not know. "Am I to read this, Helen?"

"If you like. It is from my friend Mary Forrester, of whom you may have heard me speak."

"Yes; I have seen her at the Portmores: a very handsome girl. Where is she now?"

"At Richmond, with her aunt."

She, like the other two, seemed full of deep interest in Helen, and it was with a strange mixture of pride in the affection she inspired, and jealousy of those who expressed it so warmly, that he perused these letters. He saw how tenderly Helen had always been treated; how dear she was to her family. He himself loved Lady Eskdale almost as a mother. Lord Beaufort was one of the young men of his own standing, whom he liked best; but when he looked upon them as his rivals in the heart of his wife, he could not bring himself to speak kindly of them, at least not to her. He hardly knew how to begin the conversation again.

Helen seemed to have no curiosity about his guests; but he recollected a paragraph in Beaufort's letter that might help him.

" Did you observe that Beaufort says your cousin Ernest is coming here? "

" Yes, I supposed he was—at least, that he was asked; he is sure to be included in the Portmore list."

" That is a hit at Lady Portmore, I suppose," said Lord Teviot, again on the point of taking fire; but he checked himself. " It will be a great pleasure to you to see Ernest, I should think? "

" Yes," said Helen, faintly; " he is rather amusing."

" More than that, he is clever, and can be very pleasant when he chooses. I am going to answer Lady Portmore! Have you any message? She asks if she can bring anything from town for you? "

" Nothing whatever, thank you."

" Have you any letters for the post-bag? "

" I shall have one for papa."

" To your father? " said Lord Teviot; and suddenly the thought occurred to him that she was going to write to complain of her situation. She was silent. " Might I ask, without being considered impertinent, what is this sudden fancy for writing to Lord Eskdale, and when the idea entered your head? "

Helen stooped down, and, taking a letter from the work-basket that stood by her side, broke the seal. She pushed away her work-frame, and passing quickly by the table at which Lord Teviot sat—

" I must go and breathe the fresh air," she said, and her voice sounded low and dispirited. " There is my letter to my father; will you seal it and send it? If you like to write in this room, you will find pens and paper there, and you will not be disturbed, for I am going out." She went without waiting for an answer.

"So! I drive her out of her own room, if I come into it," thought Lord Teviot. "She thinks I am jealous, or curious, or she would not have shown me all these letters. She cannot say one kind word; she does not even look kindly at me, and she evidently thinks of nothing but her own family. I suppose she compares me with all these doting relations, and thinks me cold and hateful; and yet which of them can dote on her as I do if she would let me? She would actually have gone back to them without me, I believe. No, I remember she said *we* ; but still she called Eskdale Castle her home. My house is clearly not her home; and she has not asked one of her friends to come and stay here. Does she think I should not like it, or is she afraid that they will see she is not happy? Not happy! Helen, my own Helen, whom I could have loved, whom I do love, as I never loved any human being. There are moments when I think she hates me. Now here is this letter to her father. How quick and angry she was about that! I did not ask to see it. I did not know she had written to him till she said so herself. I have a great mind to write to Lady Eskdale, and to ask her to come here. She and Lord Eskdale, and Beaufort, and that Miss Douglas, and the whole clan, and that will show Helen I am not jealous of them, and it is the best chance I have of pleasing her. I dare say, that because *I* ask them, she will not be glad to see them. Who's knocking there? Come in. Come in, I say. Good heavens, how I hate to be made to roar out ' Come in ' ten times over ! ''

"It's only me, my lord," said Mrs. Tomkinson. "If you please, my lord, her ladyship has left her bonnet here."

"Very well, Mrs. Tomkins, look for it."

"Her ladyship will be ready in a moment, my lord," said Mrs. Tomkinson, who could not resist the chance of a little talk. She had an ambitious idea that she was diving into my lord's character.

" Very well; shut the door."

" Umph!" thought Mrs. Tomkinson, as she obeyed; " how very uncivil; and calling me Tomkins, too! I hate to be called out of my name. Now I should like to know what he's doing of with all those letters. I wonder whether my lady chooses for him to be ransacking her papers, and whether that's the right thing with married people. Here's your ladyship's bonnet. I could not lay my hand on it rightly, because of my lord's sitting so just at the writing-table."

" Is my lord writing?"

" His lordship seemed to be busy with some papers as was on the table," said Mrs. Tomkinson, guardedly, and with a look of curiosity to see if the hint told. The pause that ensued left her still in doubt. " Shall I step back and tell my lord your ladyship is ready?"

" No," said Helen, absently.

" I can easily go back on pretence to see for your lady-ship's gloves"; and Tomkinson began to think the case was assuming great interest.

" No, no," said Lady Teviot, thoroughly roused; " don't disturb Lord Teviot; he was so good as to offer to finish and seal my letters; don't run in and out to disturb him."

" Law, my lady, how good his lordship is! It quite pleased me to see him sitting so comfortable and at home in your ladyship's beautiful boudoir. I wish Lord and Lady Eskdale were here to see how happy your ladyship is. There! there's my lady gone; I declare I think she looks very bad; not a hatom of colour compared to what she had. I ain't quite sure yet but what I think my lord a brute; at least, I shall make a point of thinking so if he plagues my lady. And calling me Tomkins, too—such an idea!"

CHAPTER XIII

LORD TEVIOT wrote all his invitations; then he thought of showing them to Helen before he sent them; and then again, he felt some difficulty in renewing the conversation. The waywardness of his temper had so often displayed itself, that between him and Helen many of the commonest topics of conversation were attended with awkwardness; and he had discovered that she not only abstained from contradicting him on any point that had once inflamed his temper, but that she never even alluded to the disputed point again. Even this caution offended him. A bright thought now occurred to him; he would ask Lady Portmore to bring Miss Forrester with her. He knew they were acquainted with each other, and the arrival of Helen's favourite friend would reconcile her to the Portmore visitation, and to the consequent delay of her return to Eskdale Castle. And then if her family came, he did not see anything of which she could complain; he had done all he could to please her; she ought to make allowance for his manner, for he owned that it was at times rather taunting; but she ought to be above such trifles. It was a pity Lord Teviot had never read Hannah More. Her prose would have been of great use to him; but even her poetry would have taught him that

> " Since trifles make the sum of human things,
> And half our misery from trifles springs—
> Oh ! let the ungentle spirit learn from thence
> A small unkindness is a great offence."

And, consequently, a series of small unkindnesses is very offensive indeed, and it would not have been surprising if Helen were offended. But she was not; she was depressed, half frightened, and half unhappy. Lord Teviot's expressions of affection were almost as alarming as his anger; he was so energetic in all his professions, so violent, as it seemed to her who had been accustomed to the gentle love of her mother and the playful tenderness of her brother and sisters, that she did not know how to answer his vehement protestations and eager upbraidings. And then his sudden starts of temper puzzled her. In short, she did not understand him; and amidst all the grandeur that surrounded her, and the magnificent gifts which Lord Teviot heaped on her, she felt troubled. She longed to be at home again, and at her ease; but she was too gentle to be resentful.

When Lord Teviot had despatched his letters, he found her in her garden; not one of the old-fashioned gardens, full of roses and honeysuckles, and sweet peas, suggestive of the country, and redolent of sweetness—but in a first rate gardener's garden, every plant forming part of a group, and not to be picked or touched on any account; all of them forced into bloom at the wrong time of the year; and each bearing a name that it was difficult to pronounce, and impossible to remember. Helen was standing apparently absorbed in admiration of a *Lancifolium Speciosum*, which she had been assured by her gardener was "a better variety" of the *Lancifolium Punctatum;* but in reality she was thinking first of her mother, wondering when she should see her again; and next what she could find to say to Lord Teviot at dinner. She hoped he would not look for her before that; but just as she had devised an inoffensive remark, which might be hazarded before the servants, she saw him standing beside her, and the conversation had to begin forthwith. The flowers were a safe topic, *Lilium Punctatum* played its part; that led to admiration of the place. Then Lord

Teviot, who, as well as Mrs. Tomkinson, perceived that "My lady had not a hatom of colour," offered her his arm, and, finding no signs of resentment, thought that it would be a greater support if he put it round her waist; and once established in that confidential and highly conjugal attitude, he felt he could explain away more easily the misunderstanding of the morning. And when he saw the delight with which Helen heard of the arrangements he had made, and the ecstasy with which she looked forward to the arrival of her family, his heart smote him for the pain he had inflicted on her. His kindness gave her courage and spirits.

"And so you have written yourself to Mary Forrester; how pleased she will be! Oh! I hope she will come. And you have really asked Eliza Douglas, your own particular guest? Mrs. Douglas will be enchanted, and of course say something bitter about it; but still she will think that ' that Lord Teviot has some good qualities; at least, she tries to think so for poor Helen's sake; and, at all events, he is very civil to us.' "

"Poor Helen," repeated Lord Teviot, as he pressed her fondly to his heart; "and may I ask why you are poor Helen with Mrs. Douglas? "

"Oh! because everybody who is not a Douglas is poor something or somebody. She has for years pitied poor mamma, who has never known what grief is; and I heard of her saying that the high spirits of poor Lord Beaufort would end by wearing out himself and everybody belonging to him."

"And would she pity you now? "

"Not at this moment," said Helen, gaily and carelessly.

"And even a moment of happiness is to be prized," he answered, coldly; "happiness seldom lasts much longer. However, let us hope you may overtake it again on Thursday. I suppose you will have your family here then."

" Did you name Thursday ? "

" I said the sooner the better—that you would be very uneasy till they came, and that I should hardly be able to persuade you to stay at St. Mary's much longer without them."

" It was only because mamma was alone that I wished to go to her now," said Helen, timidly, for she felt a change of tone in the conversation, " and I thought she would be unhappy."

" Oh! it requires no excuse; nothing can be more natural. It is only a matter of surprise to me, Helen, how you ever prevailed on yourself to leave her. I ought to be flattered that I had influence enough to persuade you to take such a step, though it is rather a check to my vanity to find I cannot prevent your regretting it."

" Dear Teviot, I have never expressed any regret, I am sure."

" No, you are much too guarded, too careful of giving offence, I mean; and besides, let us hope that even moments of happiness, since you can have no more——"

" Has that offended you? Oh, Teviot, how you *will* misunderstand me! "

" I am very unfortunate, certainly; my want of comprehension is most distressing. Perhaps if our feelings were more the same, my obtuseness would not be so great; but, as it is, I am not sufficiently cool and guarded to judge calmly. I hoped I had at last found a way to please you; however, it is of no consequence. I have intruded on your ladyship's horticultural pursuits, I fear," he said, with a bad imitation of playfulness; " you must have wished me away repeatedly, and as I have hardly time for a gallop before dinner, I have the honour to take my leave."

" I thought you meant to ride in the evening, but I can be ready in a moment."

" It is just possible that I may be able to ride twice in

one day, and that for once I may choose to ride alone. I have been long enough in your way now, and so good-bye."

"Now, what can I have said that has annoyed him again?" thought Helen; "but so it always is; he never understands me. I wonder why he married me; and yet at first how different he was from what he is now! When we danced together in London, how pleasant he was—so gay, and so ready to talk and laugh and to be amused! but then I was different too, and more amusing, I should think, for I feel so grave and dull now; and whenever I try to be in spirits, I say something that vexes him. Well, papa and mamma will be here soon, that is one comfort, and dear Beaufort. Nothing ever puts him out of sorts; but I must not think of that."

Helen wandered home, absorbed in ruminations over her new position: and she was so absent that Mrs. Tomkinson's distrust of my lord was confirmed; and it seemed almost time to hint her very low opinion of him to Mr. Phillips.

The evening passed away better than Helen had expected. Lord Teviot's gallop had put him into better humour; and Helen's spirits rose when she was dressed for dinner. I have often observed that the petty vexations and worries of the early part of the day are taken off and folded neatly up with the morning gown; and a fresh fit of spirits and good-humour put on with the evening adornments. It is a change for the better, personally and mentally.

CHAPTER XIV

Thursday came with its promise of guests. There was no answer from the Portmores; so, besides the interesting uncertainty of their arrival, it remained to be seen whether Mary Forrester would accompany them. Lady Eskdale had written one line of joyful acceptance, apologizing for bringing Eliza Douglas; but adding, that she was a dear good girl, and the idea of paying Helen a visit pleased her so much, that Lady Eskdale could not resist bringing her, if Mrs. Douglas gave the consent for which Eliza had written to ask.

As I consider the Douglas papers valuable, not only for their own merits, but as proofs of the exact truth of this history, I shall make use of some of Eliza's letters.

" Dearest Mother,

" I do not know what you will say to it, but Lady Eskdale desires me to ask if you have any objection to my going to St. Mary's with her and Lord Eskdale to-morrow? I hope you will let me go. Lord Teviot asked me himself, for Lady Eskdale told me so; and besides, my name was in his letter, which was lying open on the breakfast table, so I could not help seeing it. I am very happy here, though rather sleepy in the evening, because they sit up so late. There never was anything like Lady Eskdale's kindness. She has given me two beautiful gowns and a bracelet,—two pomps and one vanity,—and she takes such care of me, that I am quite ashamed of never feeling ill; she is always asking how I

F   81

am. I write in such haste, that I have not time for more than several very important questions which I want you to answer. What am I to give the housemaids here? and do you object to my reading novels, if Lady Eskdale says there is no harm in them? They look very tempting, particularly one called *Pride and Prejudice*. And when we go to St. Mary's, that is, if you let me go, ought not I to sit backwards in the carriage, though Lord Eskdale is so civil, he will be sure to say not? I play to him every evening; he is so fond of music, I am glad I can play. Every evening he says, ' Now, Miss Douglas, are we to have a little harmony? ' May I sing to him? My love to papa, and I wish he would advance me my next quarter's allowance; and pray tell Sarah my work is turning out beautiful, and that gowns are still worn without any trimming. I wish she would hear Susan Dawson her catechism while I am away, else she will be sure to forget that long answer to ' What is thy duty to thy neighbour? ' And it has been such a trouble to teach it to her. It nearly wore your poor little Eliza quite out. Lord Beaufort came last night, and is also going to St. Mary's.

> " Ever, dearest mother,
>> " Your dutiful and affectionate,
>>> " ELIZA DOUGLAS.

" Please mention what papa's politics are. They talk a great deal about government and opposition, and I do not know which I am for."

Mrs. Douglas's answer was propitious; and she was so gratified by the prospect of her daughter's amusement, that she assured Mrs. Birkett, much to that worthy person's surprise, that Lady Eskdale was one of the most warm-hearted, amiable people she knew; not that she joined in the common cant about warm hearts and kind dispositions, because she happened to know what men and women really were; but still there were exceptions, and from long intimacy with the Eskdales, she was able to say, etc., etc.   In short, she evinced a spirit of benevolence that took poor Mrs. Birkett quite by surprise, and spoiled her visit.   She had come armed with some little anti-Eskdale anecdotes, and with a small supply of malevolence, which would, she had expected, make her visit unusually acceptable, and she was left without a word to say for herself.

CHAPTER XV

ELIZA wrote to her sister immediately after her arrival at St. Mary's:—

" I begin my letter after I have come up to bed, dearest Sarah, for there is so much to say, that unless I write at night, I never shall have time to say it all. This is such a beautiful place; but you hate descriptions, and so do I. We arrived an hour before dinner, and met Lord and Lady Teviot at the first lodge, when Lady Eskdale got out, and walked home with them. I wish you could have seen how pretty and happy Helen looked. Lord Eskdale and Lord Beaufort arrived just after we did, and we had not been half an hour in the house before a number of other people came. A Colonel Beaufort, a horrid man, like that Mr. Brown we used to call Ape Brown—though Colonel Beaufort is very good-looking—but he is so grand and conceited. Then, there are two Mr. Sterlings and a Sir Charles de Vere, and one or two others, and at last there came Lord and Lady Portmore, and with them a Miss Forrester, a great friend of Helen's. Don't you remember how Mrs. Duncombe used to talk of her, and say how clever she was, and that she was going to be married to somebody, I forget who, who liked somebody else? I do not like Lady Portmore at all. She came in just as if she were mistress of the house, and as if it were her place to receive the guests; and she called everybody by their names, and without their titles. ' Oh! Teviot, why did not you ask Melmoth to meet me? So, Beaufort, you are

here, that is right. Ernest' (meaning Colonel Beaufort),
' you should have sent to my house before you set off;
I wanted you to bespeak horses for me on the road. Well,
now we must go and dress, it is almost time for dinner.
I have my old room, I suppose, Teviot; so, dear Helen,
you need not come with me, I am quite at home, so stay
where you are. Who is that with your mother?' ' Miss
Douglas,' Helen said. ' Oh, Miss Douglas, rather pretty,
is not she?' Now you know, Sarah, that I am not vain,
nor perhaps even rather pretty, but I longed to say ' Yes,
quite beautiful,' just to quell Lady Portmore, who walked
off, saying, ' Well, good people, will you all go and dress,
I hate waiting for dinner.' I should have liked to put it
off for half an hour, for the pleasure of thwarting her,
though I was rather hungry myself. I have such a pretty
room, with a dressing-room, and such looking-glasses and
sofa and arm-chairs, mamma would be shocked. Lady
Eskdale was so good as to send for me before she went down-
stairs, and Lord Beaufort took me in to dinner, so I was
less frightened than might have been expected. He is so
good-natured, I am not at all afraid of him. I wore my
blue gown. This is such a magnificent house. How I
should like to be married to a very rich man, with a very
fine place!

" Your affectionate sister,

" E. Douglas."

Helen was quite happy at dinner, with her father on one
side of her, and Mary Forrester sitting next to him, and
her mother nearly opposite to her. She had been all day
preparing for the arrival of her family, surveying their
rooms again and again, and adorning them with flowers.
The books that she thought would amuse them were
placed on their tables. The claret cup which Lord
Eskdale drank after dinner had been ordered and tasted

by herself; even the bill of fare, which was usually submitted only to Lord Teviot, was looked over by her, lest
the boiled chicken for Lady Eskdale, and the *potage* which
Beaufort liked so much, should have been omitted. And
now they were all there, the guests and their *comestibles*, and
she felt at home again. She had more questions to ask
her father about Eskdale Castle than he could possibly
answer during one dinner, for she was obliged to do the
honours to the rest of the company; but that was no
trouble to her. Her eye was bright, and her cheek flushed
with happiness. She was willing to laugh at every joke,
and to break through every silence, for there was a pleasant
consciousness about her, not only that the good things of
life were collected very handsomely and becomingly
around her, but that those she loved best were with her to
share them.

" Upon my word, Lady Teviot," said her father with a
gratified smile, as the ladies rose to withdraw, " you seem
to me to be a very finished specimen of the lady of the
house; that little head will be turned, and my little Helen
will be spoiled."

She kissed his hand as she moved on, but the gloomy
look with which Lord Teviot regarded her as she passed
him at the door might have satisfied Lord Eskdale that
there was still a chance that his daughter would not be
utterly spoiled by unqualified indulgence.

CHAPTER XVI

IT was a beautiful August evening—a real summer's evening—and the ladies, instead of betaking themselves to the drawing-room, strolled out on the lawn. Helen, passing her arm through her mother's, contrived to draw her away, and turned into the shrubbery, having whispered to Miss Forrester to take charge of the others; and Lady Portmore, who hated walking, sat down on one of those wretched gridirons commonly called garden chairs, and desired Mary to take another. Eliza thought she should be in the way, and was quietly withdrawing, but Lady Portmore, who had seen Lord Beaufort talking and laughing with her, and had heard Lady Eskdale call her "Dear Liz," thought it would be the right thing to make much of her.

"My dear Miss Douglas, you must not leave us; I foresee that you and I shall be great friends. Pray sit down with Mary and me. Mary is one of my dearest friends; and you must not be afraid of her, though she is the cleverest creature in the world."

"There is one of the prettiest creatures in the world," said Mary, waving away the compliment to herself, and pointing to Lady Teviot's receding figure; "and there Miss Douglas will agree with me, I see."

"And I, I am sure," said Lady Portmore; "in fact, you could not speak to anyone who is such an authority on the subject of Helen's beauty as I am, for I was the very first person who discovered it. The night she came out at H. House, just as she entered the room, so that nobody else could have seen her, I said to the Duke, ' There is the prettiest girl that has appeared this year '; and I remember turning round and instantly saying to Count Czernischeffski, the man with the scar, you know—Princess Saldovitch's hero—*Voilà, M. le Comte, une jolie débutante;* and after that, all the world, English and foreign, raved about her beauty. I really set that fashion."

" I suppose," said Mary, " that when she appears next year as Lady Teviot—that is, if she does appear——"

" How do you mean, my love? What is to prevent her appearing? "

" Nothing but her own good will and pleasure," said Mary, laughing: " it is a foolish expression; but I meant to say that I hope Helen will not adopt the reigning fashion of young married women, and lead a life of balls and parties. I think she will be a stay-at-home wife."

" I don't understand," said Lady Portmore, fussily; " if she stays at home, what becomes of her position, and her rank, and Teviot House? And you forget her diamonds. But that is the way with you clever people; you so often overlook *the* important point which we silly ones remember. If she shuts herself up, what is the use of her having married Teviot? "

" But she liked him, did she not? " said Eliza, who looked aghast at Lady Portmore's reasoning—or rather calculation—for reasoning was not Lady Portmore's strong point. " I think if I were married to anybody I liked, I should prefer staying at home with him to going to a ball."

" You dear little romantic thing; now that is so like me! I foresaw we should suit each other exactly. There is nothing equal to the comfort of a long evening at home for the husband and wife; but then, you know, other people must be considered—the people who invite one to their houses—and one must go, for fear of not being asked again; and that is the rock on which my domestic happiness splits."

There was a pause while Lady Portmore mused sadly upon this shipwreck of her domestic felicity; and then the conversation began again with the Teviots.

" Did Helen's marriage take you by surprise, Mary ? "

" I could not be surprised at any amount of admiration that Helen might excite; but I was in the country at the time, and I had heard very little of Lord Teviot. It was a short romance, you know ? "

" My dear Mary, there is nobody who knows so much about it as I do. Miss Douglas will think me very vain, but as she does not know me, I must just let her a little into the secret of my character. She will say I am frank, too frank perhaps; but the fact is, as all the world knows, that before his marriage Teviot almost lived at my house. It was his home, literally his home. He is the most warm-hearted creature on earth, and chose to take a great fancy to me. Why, I am sure I can't guess; but he was on that footing at my house that my own brother might have been. It was the sort of thing that the world might have talked of; and I never know how I escaped all sorts of ill-natured remarks. In fact, but this is between ourselves, I *did* say to Lord Portmore, ' If you think Teviot had better not come so much to our house, only tell me so, and I will contrive that he shall not dine here so constantly—and yet there shall be no scene, no *esclandre*.' I thought this right; don't you agree with me ? "

" And what did Lord Portmore say ? " said Eliza, who was listening in breathless delight to what she thought a very odd and slightly improper story.

" Oh! it was a most gratifying answer to me. He said he had not the smallest objection to Teviot's dining with us as often as he liked, and that he saw no opening for any scene, and no necessity for any explanation ; in short, he evidently placed the greatest confidence in me. This was in June, and there were constant fêtes at Teviot House and the Villa; and I was rather annoyed by the notion that the world would say they were given for me. And one day, I remember it as well as possible, it was at a breakfast at the Villa, I said to my friend Mrs. Hanbury, ' I charge you, Cecilia, if you hear any ill-natured comments made on my being at all these fêtes, that you will give me warning in time. I can tell Teviot they had better be given up.' And she said in her odd way, ' Why, my dear, what do you mean? Don't you know that he is desperately in love with Helen Beaufort? I believe he has proposed; if not, for mercy's sake say nothing to him, or you may do mischief.' I do mischief! I! who am the last person in the world to think of such a thing. I went to Teviot directly, and said, ' My dear Teviot, tell me the truth. The world says you are in love with Helen. Are you quite sure of your own feelings? Will she suit you? ' and so on, exactly what his own sister might have said to him. And I am as much convinced as if it were told me by an angel from heaven that I made that marriage, for he proposed the next day, the very next day. I suspect he had been a little piqued by my easy way of talking of it, for when he came to tell me it was settled, I never saw a creature in such a state of agitation. It was a very hot day, and he asked directly for a glass of iced water, which shows how nervous he was. I took my line at once, and wished him joy, and said that I would call on Helen, and that I was much flattered that he had put me in his confidence the day before; and then he grew calmer. But he laughed and talked a great deal, and was certainly very much excited, and hurried away again, so unlike him. After that I saw him but little; indeed, I kept out of his way, as I guessed the Eskdales would wish to keep him to themselves; but as soon as he was married, I was so anxious for his sake and Helen's that there should be no awkwardness, no coolness between us, that I offered to come here—actually offered myself—and you saw how well the meeting went off."

" Perfectly," said Mary; " nothing could be more commonplace—more easy, I mean."

Lady Portmore did not look as if she quite liked the answer, and was on the point of turning to Eliza to extract a more flattering opinion, when the gentlemen appeared, and her thoughts took a new direction.

Lord Teviot looked round as he came out on the lawn, and seemed to miss someone, though he asked no questions; but Lord Beaufort said immediately, " Where's Helen? Miss Douglas, have you a mind to come and look for her? I saw her and my mother go up that walk."

" I should like to go," said Eliza, " but——"

" Oh dear! yes, we want a chaperon, I forgot," said Lord Beaufort; " perhaps my respected father will have the kindness to act ruffian to us babes in the wood."

" Not I," said Lord Eskdale; " I can't stir a step without my coffee; but there are your mother and sister in sight, at the end of that avenue, so you may go in all propriety and join them."

" Will you come, Miss Forrester? " said Eliza.

" Now, Miss Douglas," said Lord Beaufort, " let us be off, or they will be here, and our excessive attention in going to look for them will not be appreciated. Don't ask that Miss Forrester to come," he added, as they walked away, " I can't abide her."

" Oh! why not, Lord Beaufort? I like her looks so much."

" Her looks then are deceitful above all things. I am not going to add that she is desperately wicked; but she affects to be desperately good, which is nearly as bad."

" I dare say it is not affectation. Why should she not be really good? Now, Lord Beaufort, what right have you to judge of either real or affected goodness?" she added, laughing.

"That right, Miss Douglas, which lookers-on assume of knowing most of the game; and as for Miss Forrester's game, I admire neither it nor the way in which she has played it. Neither do I admire her, and let me advise you not to be taken in by her, as Helen is."

"I am afraid your advice will be thrown away. I feel frightfully tempted to like her. I like everybody, except Lady Portmore, by the by. I am very willing to dislike her, if that will satisfy you."

"Ah! poor Lady Portmore, all women hate her. I wonder why? but we have not time to discuss her now. Well, Helen, my beauty, we are come to conduct you and our well-beloved mother to coffee. Have you finished your confidential communication? and can you listen to a few original remarks in the Repton line, which Miss Douglas and I are prepared to make on St. Mary's?"

"Is it not pretty, Eliza?"

"More than pretty—beautiful. Oh! Helen, how happy you must be here!"

"So I have been telling mamma," answered Helen, with a faint smile; "and she has been making me jealous of you. You are creeping into my place. She says you take such care of her."

"I should be very ungrateful if I did not," said Eliza, gliding round to Lady Eskdale's side, and pressing her hand.

"No sentiment, dear Liz," said Lady Eskdale, "for we must all put on our company faces and company manners now."

They joined the rest of the circle, and found Lady Portmore proving to Lord Eskdale that she had brought about most of the political changes of the past year: and that she knew beforehand all that were likely to take place in the ensuing one.

CHAPTER XVII

"WHAT will you all like to do to-day?" said Helen one morning after breakfast, "drive? or ride? or stay at home? or go to Langley ruins? Lady Portmore, what is your good will and pleasure?"

"I hardly know," she said, with an air of mystery. "Let me have a little talk with you in your dressing-room; a real comfortable chat, before I decide."

"Good heavens, how inhuman!" said Ernest Beaufort, who was lolling on a sofa, supported by countless cushions, and reading the paper; "you are not going to make that guiltless Helen endure the agony of a regular talk at this early hour of this broiling day. Besides, what is there to talk about?"

"A thousand things. I have not seen Helen for ages; and we have so much to hear and to say."

"And are you, Lady Portmore," he said, giving the cushion that supported his back a languid push, "are you still going on with all that old humbug of being glad to see people, and of having something to say to them? Has not everything been said forty times over? and is not any one individual quite as good as another?"

"Now that is so like you, Ernest. How odd your theories are; and yet how true! I said myself the other day, that one never hears anything new till it is old; and Cracroft the poet, who was sitting with me, laughed very much at the originality of the idea. You and I think so exactly alike, Ernest."

"Perhaps then, Lady Portmore, you are thinking of

picking up the supplement of the *Times*, which I have had the misfortune to drop. In the similarity of our dispositions we are probably of opinion that it ought to be picked up by one of us."

" Now that is too bad. Oh, Miss Douglas," she said, as Eliza stooped for it, " you are spoiling that wretch! "

" Miss Douglas, the wretch thanks you; your attentions to me in my old age do you infinite credit. When I was as young as you, a period which my enfeebled memory can scarcely recall, I doubt whether I was equally mindful of the infirmities of the old."

" And what may be your age? " said Lady Portmore.

" It is a painful subject. You have probably observed this morning that I am unusually grave and meditative. To-day is one of those eternal birthdays of mine which are always coming round, and with shame I avow that for six-and-twenty years I have now existed in this very tiresome world, bored and boring. Now don't all begin to wish me many happy birthdays. I am tired of good wishes. If you like to make me any presents, you may; but I am tired of things too—so do not give yourselves any trouble. I am twenty-six, and can't help myself."

" Oh! we must leave him, Helen, he is really too odd. Come and show me your boudoir."

" Directly," said Helen. " Teviot, as you and Beaufort are going to the stables, will you order the open carriage for mamma? and the pony phaeton will be wanted. Shall I ride with you? " she said, timidly.

" Your attention, my dear, is most gratifying, but as you know that the Smiths, Beaufort, and I agreed to have our first shot at the partridges to-day, your obliging offer is made in all safety."

" I am glad you will be so well employed," answered Helen, speaking as unconcernedly as she could, for she saw Mary looking inquiringly at her. " Then I will make my own arrangements, as I am discarded by you. Mary, you have brought your habit, of course, and there is a charming horse which Teviot provided for me; but papa has given me my old favourite, so we will ride after luncheon. Now for Lady Portmore. Shall I get off under an hour of confidences? "

Mary shook her head, and the party dispersed in various directions.

CHAPTER XVIII

THE library at St. Mary's was of a high, old-fashioned form, and within it was a small flight of steps which led to a light gallery built round three sides of the room, giving thus an easy access to the higher shelves of books. The room itself was full of odd, deep recesses, and was altogether a dangerous style of apartment, for the occupants of the gallery were not necessarily visible to the occupants of the room, so that if any two conversable guests were inclined to discuss the character of a third, there was a very reasonable probability that their conversation might be overheard by the party most concerned. Mary Forrester had entered this gallery from a door above, and was standing in one of the recesses, with a book under her arm, which she meant to take to her room, and another in her hand, which she read as she stood. And while she was thus occupied, Lord Beaufort and his cousin came into the room below. "We can get out through that window," said Lord Beaufort.

"Oh! then I need not announce myself," thought Mary.

"Why, so we can; but won't it be a great deal of trouble? I wish, Beaufort, you would tell me why you hate her, before you drag me any further."

Again Miss Forrester was on the point of saying, "I am here," when a name that had the power to arrest her at any moment drove her back.

"Why, on that poor Reginald Stuart's account: she led that man on to attach himself to her in the days of his prosperity, and threw him over the moment his little money peccadillos came to light."

"That's bad," said Ernest; "but I dare say they were dead tired of each other. It is so difficult to go on liking the same person for ever and ever; and besides, as Reginald was ruined, they could not have lived on air."

"No, but she had had a large fortune left her, and jilted him just when she might have helped him; and that is what people call a saint. And there is that unfortunate Stuart getting into no end of scrapes, for he has become reckless, and will be thoroughly dished."

Mary could stay no longer. As quietly as she could, she glided to the gallery door, and, certain that she could not be recognised, allowed herself the natural solace of letting it fall with a slight tendency to a bang, and rushed along the passage to her own room. The sound of the closing door made the two gentlemen start. "Who's there?" said Lord Beaufort in a very guilty voice. "Is there anybody just come into that gallery?" he added, as the silence continued.

"Nobody just come in, but somebody just gone out," said Ernest, drily. "If it were Miss Forrester, you are about as much dished as Stuart. My chief merit happily is that I am a good listener"; and he sauntered on to the anteroom.

Lord Beaufort rushed up the steps, still with a vague hope of finding a deaf librarian, or a dusting housemaid; but no, there was nothing but a handkerchief, and on one of its corners an intricate arrangement of forget-me-nots and roses represented to an acute decipherer the word "Mary." Lord Beaufort laid it down again as if it were made of glass, walked down the steps as if he were treading on ice, and, following Ernest, whispered to him, "We never must open our lips again in that confounded room."

Mary, on her part, was promising to herself never again

G

to fetch a book from that same unlucky apartment. She would never enter that gallery again. She would never speak to Lord Beaufort as long as she lived; or perhaps she had better annoy him by talking to and at him constantly, though she was not quite sure whether she would not leave St. Mary's at once. But she would tell Helen to explain to him all the Stuart history, and then crush him by the most lofty contempt—not that she cared what he said or thought, in fact she rather enjoyed his malice; and then she burst into a violent fit of crying, and found she had dropped her handkerchief. There is nothing like a good handsome flood of tears when these atrocious attacks on our good name or good looks are detected. The whirl of resentful thoughts, the angry resolves, the crimson cheeks, the burning eyes, the swelling heart, and the twitching fingers—all these moral and physical symptoms of injured innocence are instantly alleviated by a hearty cry. Mary felt better directly, and then she began to look at her mortification rationally, and not passionately. She still thought Lord Beaufort very unjust, because she had really behaved so uncommonly well; she had taken such pains to do what was right in that business; but she began to see how her conduct might have been so represented as to take a selfish colouring; and then the recollection of Lord Beaufort's hatred of her as a saint made her smile as she thought of the fit of temper to which she had just given way. "Oh! that I were one," she said, "in the genuine sense of the word!" and, in pursuing that train of thought, the momentary mortification she had suffered sank to its proper dimensions. Better feelings resumed their sway, and though she ended by thinking it a great pity that Helen should have such a detestable brother, and should live in a house that contained such an absurd room as a library with a gallery, yet she thought there was no necessity for leaving St. Mary's; that Lord Beaufort might have some good qualities, though she could not guess what they were; and that Ernest, who was at first involved in his cousin's disgrace, was not to be treated as a criminal at all. By degrees she began to see that it was for her good that her vanity had met with such a check; her natural good temper and her acquired humility helped each other, and when she joined the rest of the party at luncheon she was almost as cheerful and as benevolent as she was when she left them after breakfast.

Helen's morning had not been passed much more prosperously. Lady Portmore had talked unceasingly for an hour and a half; and though from the vague diffusiveness of her words, and the hopeless entanglement of her ideas, it was difficult to ascertain the precise purport of her remarks, Helen felt that the general result was irritating, though she hardly knew why. She had not the remotest idea what Lady Portmore meant to convey when she said—

" Dearest Helen, you will be candid with me. You will understand me when I implore you to tell me frankly if you think my visit likely to do harm. Helen, you know my heart; you may trust me—say, am I welcome? "

" Dear Lady Portmore, why should you doubt it? Of course I am delighted to see you, and so is Teviot; and as you have asked your own party, I hope you will be amused."

" Helen, you are a noble creature; I see you understand me."

Helen felt thoroughly puzzled, but tried hard for a look of intelligence, so that she might escape a long explanation.

" We shall be friends—we are friends; and as a proof of confidence, before I say anything further on the subject which is at this moment uppermost in both our hearts," (" I wonder what it is," thought Helen), " I will ask your advice on a point that more immediately concerns myself. It is a difficult case to explain, Helen; cannot you guess what I mean? "

" No, indeed, I cannot imagine the point on which I should be capable of advising you."

" Oh, what a relief! I was afraid you were condemning me all this time; that you thought it so strange I had let him come."

" Let who come, where? " said Helen. " Pray remember the seclusion in which we have been living; and have pity on my ignorance."

" Oh, yes! I forgot, you lost all the end of last season; but you must have heard—in fact, you must have seen yesterday, how it was—Ernest! Helen, do you think that I was wrong in asking him to come here? "

" Certainly not; we always expected him this week. He had promised to come when——"

" Yes, yes; but, my love, you must know (this is of course in the strictest confidence); but you must see that Ernest is desperately smitten with me. It is almost ludicrous; for he is not the sort of person from whom I should look for sentiment; but he has been too absurd. I had really been completely blind to the whole thing, till one day at my house, your brother said to me, with one of his meaning looks, ' If I want to find Ernest, Lady Portmore, I always come here.' I caught his eye; I felt myself colour to my finger-ends; and I instantly guessed what the world was saying, and what was the warning Beaufort intended to convey. I shall always feel obliged to him for the candour and courage with which he put me on my guard. How *he* came to be so very clear sighted it is not for me to guess. I was rather puzzled what to do, for, Helen, you and I have, I know, the same high ideas of a wife's duty— and I really hate scenes; but it is so difficult to make that strange creature, Ernest, understand hints. He made the most absurd excuses for calling: the streets were so hot, or he wanted luncheon, or dinner; and if I looked grave, he affected to be bored, or to fall asleep. At last I thought of coming here; and I said honestly to him, ' Now, Ernest, I positively forbid your following me to St. Mary's'. And what do you think was his answer? ' My dear lady, there is nothing I should dislike so much as following you; the roads are so dusty, I should be smothered; so I will go before you.' "

" How like Ernest! " said Helen. " However, that does not sound very sentimental."

" But, my dear, if you had seen his look—I know Ernest's looks so well. You do not understand your cousin, Helen; but I must teach you to know each other thoroughly. You will like him."

" Like Ernest! why, my dear Lady Portmore, I have known him and liked him all my life. He was brought up at Eskdale Castle. I think I told you so when I introduced him to you in London."

" Ah, true! but he is so reserved; and yet there is a good deal under that dry manner that I am sure you will like," said Lady Portmore, who invariably claimed a right to be the first and only friend of all her acquaintances. " It would have been foolish, don't you think it would, if I had put off our visit when I found that Ernest had contrived to include himself in the party? I think apparent unconsciousness is the most dignified line to take, don't you? You see, Helen, what confidence I have in your judgment."

" You are very good; I am sure you will do what is right."

" No speeches, my love. Thank you for your attention and advice; you have put me quite at my ease; and you must not think ill of poor Ernest from what I have told you; he is an excellent creature, you may take my word for it. And now, my dear, talk to me about yourself: are you quite happy, Helen? "

" What a question! dear Lady Portmore," said Helen, affecting to laugh; " you must really find out the answer for yourself."

" My love, do not misunderstand me; I see," she added, looking round with rather a vexed air, " that you have all the luxuries of life in profusion; but I am sure that you are like me, and do not care for those kind of things, and that Teviot's feelings——"

" I beg your pardon, I care very much for the luxuries of life," said Helen, determined to pursue that safe subject. " It is a real pleasure to me to look round and see the absolute perfection of my room; and besides, most of my pretty things are gifts, and I love them for the sake of the givers. Do look at this beautiful gold dressing service, which Teviot gave me on our wedding-day."

" Ah, very handsome, beautiful! Lord Portmore wanted to give me just the same set; at least I told him of one I had seen, and he would have given it to me, only he thought it would be useless; but to return to Lord Teviot."

" But just look first at my sapphires; I have heard you admire sapphires."

" Yes, so I do in the abstract; the blue is beautiful, and Lord Portmore would have given me a set if I had wished for them; but don't you think—not that I wish to put you out of conceit of your stones—but don't you think they are less becoming than rubies? "

" Do you think so? " said Helen, raising the tray on which they were placed. " I suppose papa agrees with you, for he gave me these; but Teviot and I like the others best."

" You agree in that then. Ah! similarity of tastes, even in trifles, is a blessing; but now, my love, shut that box, and let us talk rationally. I know Teviot so well that I am sure I can give you some useful hints."

" Do you think this miniature on my watch is like him? "

" Yes, very like; I have seen it before," said Lady Portmore, impatiently. " Of course I know all about it; I recommended Holmes to Teviot. But it is of himself, and not of his picture, that I wish to speak; for though you seem to fly from the subject, let me tell you, Lady Teviot——"

" Nothing of my husband, Lady Portmore," said Helen, firmly. " Mamma told me that married people were never, under any circumstances, to make each other the subjects of discussion or comment; so tell me nothing of Lord Teviot."

Lady Portmore was completely defeated, and it seemed to her quite marvellous that such a child as Helen should presume to withstand and baffle her. But even she could not renew a conversation so pointedly interrupted, and after settling her plans for the afternoon, and advising Helen to have her sapphires reset with more diamonds, she left the room, saying as she passed—

" Now, my love, you are not angry with me. I quite agree with you that we wives should say nothing and hear nothing about our husbands. I should fire up just as you did if anyone spoke to me about Portmore; but I know Teviot so well, and am so aware of all the little shades of his character on which everything depends——"

" Yes, yes; but I mean to see nothing but lights—no shades; and so good-bye, luncheon will be ready at two."

" Ah! you are very discreet, but I respect you for it "; and she walked off rather mortified, while Helen soothed herself by repairing to her mother's room for the rest of the morning; but she first threw her windows wide open, having a vague idea that nothing short of a thorough draught could drive Lady Portmore's conversation thoroughly out of the room.

CHAPTER XIX

THE gentlemen all dropped in to luncheon, beginning by wondering how people could eat at that time of day, and ending by seating themselves and enjoying a good hot dinner. Beaufort came in last, with a very guilty countenance; but Miss Forrester was talking to Sir Charles Smith, and showed no sign of mortification or pique. He began to dislike her more than ever. The walk with the game-keepers was apparently given up, as Lady Portmore was imparting to Ernest in an apologetic tone that Teviot insisted on driving her in the phaeton.

" And what vehicle is ordered for me, and who is to drive me? " said Ernest, languidly. " Helen, will you take a little more care of the rest of your guests? "

" You may ride with all of us—Mary, papa, and Beau-fort, and me. Sir Charles goes with mamma and Eliza in the britzska, and we are all to meet at the most beautiful ruins you ever saw."

" So be it," he said, " I shall be a beautiful ruin myself by the time I have ridden an hour in this sultry weather; but I am resigned "; and the party set off.

" I shall be dreadfully frightened if we get mixed up with that crowd of people and horses," said Lady Portmore, as she took her place in Lord Teviot's phaeton. " Cannot we take some other road? "

" Certainly, if you are afraid, but my horses are very quiet; and if you wish for a pretty drive——"

" But all the drives are very pretty. Let us go down that road, and I will give you my advice as to any improvements that may strike me. Nesfield says I have a good eye for the picturesque; but above all, I want a quiet talk with you, and we should be interrupted if we went with the others. Is that Helen's new horse she is riding?"

"No; Miss Forrester is on Selim."

"Well, I wonder Helen did not prefer your gift. I am sure that from sentiment I should never allow any human being but myself to ride a horse that had been given to me by the person I loved best in the world."

"That is an interesting and romantic idea; but as I shall probably have the honour of furnishing Lady Teviot's stud to the end of our days, it is not very likely that she will refuse to lend a horse to her friends when they come."

"Oh dear, no, that would be selfish; and you know how I hate selfishness. I often say there is nobody thinks so little of self as I do. Still I wonder Helen did not ride Selim."

Lord Teviot was silent.

"Are you well, Teviot?" said Lady Portmore with an air of great interest.

"Quite well, thank you."

"My dear Teviot, do you know I am not quite easy about you. You certainly are not in your usual spirits. Do tell me, is there anything the matter?"

"What can be the matter, Lady Portmore? Pray do not put fancies of illness into my head, and allow for a little additional steadiness in a respectable married man."

"Yes, that is all very well, my dear friend, but I know you too well to be satisfied with that sort of joke. Come, Teviot, shall I put you at your ease at once? that pretty little wife of yours is not the least in love with you, and your vanity—men are so vain—is a little hurt. Is not this the truth?"

"If so, it is another proof that *toute vérité n'est pas bonne à dire*," said Lord Teviot, hastily, for he was stung to the quick by the remark. Why is it that fools always have the instinct to hunt out the unpleasant secrets of life, and the hardiness to mention them?

"But I am speaking entirely for your good, and you must not be angry with me. You know what a warm friendship I have for you, and the interest I take in your happiness; and I really look upon Helen as a sister of my own. So I want to make out why it is that you are not so happy together as I wish to see you. Perhaps you expect too much from Helen. She is a child, you know, and a petted child; and she has been idolized at home, so it is natural that she should love her own family. I see you think she is too much devoted to them, and perhaps a little afraid of you." Lord Teviot gave the reins a jerk, in the fond hope of giving Lady Portmore a fright; but she went on. "Perhaps that is the case now, but you must give her time. Her little head was turned by your rank and position in the world, and she married without that attachment that a girl older and more experienced would have felt. But trust me, Teviot, she will fall in love with you some of these days. It is impossible it should be otherwise; and then you will forget that now her father and mother and all that Eskdale clan are more to her than you are."

This was the pith of Lady Portmore's harangue. Lord Teviot hated to hear what she was saying; he hated her for saying it, and himself for listening; but yet, because she fed the delusion under which he laboured, because she talked to him of himself, and because she was handsome and foolish, he allowed her to go on putting "rancours in the vessel of his peace," confirming all the painful suspicions against which he had struggled, and extracting from him avowals that he wished unmade the moment they were uttered. Lady Portmore prevented Lord Teviot from meeting his wife and guests at the ruins. She put into words thoughts most repulsive to his better feeling. She told him all that he had rather not have heard; and he came home dispirited and annoyed, but convinced that Lady Portmore was an excellent friend, and that it was most kind of her to persuade him that his wife did not care a straw about him.

CHAPTER XX

" Law! Mrs. Nelson and Mrs. Hunt," said Mrs. Tomkinson, when this riding party set off, " do make haste to look at our folks—here, put your heads out, but don't let them be seen for all the world."

" Well, what a many! " said Mrs. Hunt, who was the original Betsy of the Douglas young ladies, but called Hunt on her travels. Her manners were not quite equal to her position. " Well, what a sight of company, to be sure; and what a show of horses! "

" Mrs. Hunt," said Mrs. Nelson, who was prim, and considered rather pompous in her own set, " I must trouble you not to squeedge my sleeve."

" There's another window," said Mrs. Tomkinson; " you go there, Mrs. Hunt; you can see quite as well. She's shocking uncouth, Mrs. Nelson," she added, as Betsy bustled off to a distant window.

" She squeedges, certainly, and pushes about too much; but she has had no time to learn manners. Rome was not built in a day. There's your lady getting on her horse, Mrs. Tomkinson."

" Yes, and your young lord a-helping of her; and there's the old lord helping Miss Forrester; and there's them Smiths! "

" Who are they, Mrs. Tomkinson? "

" The heavens above only know, Mrs. Nelson; there is such a tribe of Smiths in this world. I see Miss Douglas goes with your young lady in the bruche. Between ourselves, Mrs. Nelson, what's the meaning of this fancy for the Douglases?"

"I have not been consulted, Mrs. Tomkinson; but my lady's as full of fancies as an egg's full of meat. I can't rightly account for it, except, to be sure, that it is lonesome for her now all the young ladies is gone. However, the girl's pretty, and civil enough."

"Well, and if there ain't my lord and Lady Portmore driving off by theirselves! I do declare, if I was my lady I would not stand that. Do you know, Mrs. Nelson, now that there Betsy don't hear us—do you know, I can't tell what to think with any certainty of my lord. He don't stand high in my good books by any means."

"I am sorry to hear you say so," said Mrs. Nelson, in her primmest manner, "for of course a person's servants is the best judges; but I am sure my lady has no idea that anything is amiss."

"Oh, and my lady makes no complaints; but still, you know, if one has eyes one must see what's under one's nose; and my lady has not half the fine sperrits she had."

"She feels strange, poor young thing, I dare say, at first."

"Yes; but ma'am, I'm sure it's more than that. My lord has one of the most naggingest tempers it's possible to see; and it's my belief he frets and worrets her ladyship till she wishes herself back at her old home again. And as for that Lady Portmore, if all's true as I hear, she's not one as I should choose to see driving about in a curricle with my husband."

"What do they say of her?" said Mrs. Nelson; "those Portmores have never come much in my way."

"Oh, I heard enough of her when I lived chambermaid with the Stuarts: they say she has no more respect for Lord Portmore than she has for the hearth-broom; and that all she is at from morning to night is to catch up admirers; and she don't care for other people's husbands

being other people's husbands, but likes all the better to
make them follow her. And that is just the sort of lady
who says poor servants ain't to have any followers at all,
not even to keep company. I have no patience with her;
and if I was my lady, I should look after her pretty sharp
with my lord."

"These are early days for subspicions, Mrs. Tomkinson,"
answered Mrs. Nelson, dogmatically; "and I hope your
lady will never have cause for any."

"I hope so, too, ma'am; but I don't quite like my lord";
and so they parted.

One of the odd channels scooped out by Lady Portmore's
restless vanity was a persuasion that she was the world's
universal confidante; and she would enter into long arguments to prove that she must necessarily have foreknown any
piece of intelligence or gossip that was imparted to her.
Like all very vain people, she was contradictory; and
this, added to her pretensions to universal knowledge,
rendered her conversation a glorious mass of inconsistencies.

"I have heaps of news," she said one morning when she
came down to breakfast. "I dote upon letters, particularly
from clever people, though it is a sad thing for me, having
the reputation of a good letter-writer to keep up. You know
there is no vanity in saying so, for my letters *are* very
original."

"Particularly so," said Ernest, "for they always seem to
me to consist of rows of rather crooked lines, without either
vowels or consonants."

Lady Portmore gave him a look which meant to imply to
the company at large that Ernest was committing a little
indiscretion by letting out that she corresponded with him.
She put on an air of pretty confusion, and said, "Pray
what do you know about my letters?" and then went on :

"But now for my news. One of my great favourites is
going to be married—Charles Wyndham."

" Yes, here is an account of the wedding in the paper," said Lady Teviot.

" What, already!   Well, I have shown my discretion.   I take you all to witness I never said he was going to be married? "

" Did you know it? " said Ernest.

" Of course I did, because the Wyndhams are my second cousins—at least, we are connected somehow; but now I have another piece of news about Reginald Stuart."

Lord Beaufort could not resist a look at Mary.   She seemed quite calm.

" I am so vexed about Stuart, as you may well guess. He is such a dear creature, and he has actually gone off to Scotland with that dancing girl, Pauline Le Gay.   I am sorry for him, and still more for myself.   It will put me into such an awkward position as to visiting her.   He is actually married by this time."

" I doubt it," said Lord Teviot, quietly.

" I wish I could," said Lady Portmore, with a deep sigh ; " but there is no use keeping his secret any longer."

" Not the least, unless you mean to let him have the pleasure of telling it himself.   He will be here to-day."

" Stuart here!   Then he is coming at last.   I thought he would—I made such a point of it ; but he will marry that horrid girl at last, you will see."

" There is one strong reason against it."

" You would not think so if you were in his confidence," said Lady Portmore, most mysteriously.

" To a certain degree I am," said Lord Teviot, " for he tells me here ' That fool Reid has actually carried the Paulina off to Scotland, and took the precaution to change his name for fear of pursuit, though who was to run after them except her dancing-master remains a mystery.   However, he has cleared me of the odium of being supposed to *courtiser la belle Pauline.* Now, Lady Portmore, are you satisfied?"

"Yes, but not at all surprised. I remember Reid applauded her so in that stupid ballet, 'Rose d'Amour,' that I said he must be in love with her. Mary, you were with me that night; you must remember it."

"Was I?" said Mary, with an air of doubt; "I do not recollect——"

"Oh, but I did indeed; I always foresee these things. I am so glad I persuaded Reginald Stuart to come here, out of the way of that girl. Mary, my love," she said, lowering her voice, and affecting great interest of manner, "have you a headache? you look pale this morning."

"Oh no, pray don't have the headache, Mary," said Helen, indignant at this instance of Lady Portmore's want of tact. "I beg that both my young ladies," she added, smiling at Eliza, "will look their very best, for there will be a large party to amuse, to say nothing of Colonel Stuart."

"*I* can promise to take some of that trouble off your hands, *young* ladies," said Lady Portmore, in a tone of pique. "Colonel Stuart comes on my invitation." It was an unlucky morning for her. She had been vexed by the total failure of her letters and her news; and when her vanity was in a state of mortification, she became more than usually untact. She complimented Helen on her dress, and asked if it were Teviot's taste—"but I am sure it is, for he used to complain of your style of dress as too simple before he knew you well, so I must congratulate you on the improvements he has made: you are *tirée à quatre épingles* this morning." This pleasant speech made three people uncomfortable. Helen did not like to hear that Lord Teviot had ever found fault with her,—Lady Eskdale was hurt that it was supposed she had dressed her daughter ill,— and Lord Teviot did not choose it to be supposed that he had made Lady Portmore his confidante, and that on the very important point of his wife's dress. Then she tried a little sportive condescension, in the shape of a joke to Eliza on Lord Beaufort's attentions; and that made Eliza colour till the tears came into her eyes, as, in the primitiveness and innocence of her home education, she looked upon love and lovers as sacred mysteries never to be profaned by a jest; and, moreover, expected that Eskdale Castle would fall down at the mere idea of Lord Beaufort's condescending to admire her. Lady Portmore finished by what she thought a noble touch of magnanimity. Taking Mary's hand, and saying in an audible whisper, " You must forgive me, my love, if I distressed you by what I said of Colonel Stuart. You know how thoughtless I am; but we won't allude to that history any more. Pray say you forgive me." What a woman! and what a fine quality, what an absolute virtue Tact is. Lady Portmore never had a grain of it—a misfortune that fell more heavily on her friends than on herself.

CHAPTER XXI

COLONEL STUART arrived; but another change took place in the society at St. Mary's. Lord and Lady Eskdale were sent for by Lady Sophia Waldegrave, who had had a sudden attack of illness; and Sir W. Waldegrave requested her mother to come and assist in nursing her. There was a consultation and a demur, and a fuss about Eliza's destination. Lady Eskdale thought Mrs. Douglas would not like her daughter to be taken so far from home as the Waldegraves', so she was left to Helen's care till Mr. and Mrs. Douglas should come and fetch her. Eliza's letters to her sister give an accurate account of St. Mary's at this time.

"MY DEAREST SARAH,

"I would give anything for a good hour's talk with you. You have not told me half enough about Mr. Wentworth, and that walk to the Mill, and your fit of dignity about the music book. It is so interesting, and quite as amusing as one of Miss Austen's novels; and this is all true, and your happiness is concerned in it; so you may guess how I pore over your letters. If he does not propose soon, I shall think he is behaving very ill, and shall hate him; but I know he will. We go on very happily here; at least, I hope dear Helen is happy; but I do not feel quite sure. Lord Teviot is very pleasant, I dare say, and very clever, but he is sometimes rather cross, and he seems to tease Helen. I always wish when he does that I were a lady of great consequence, and could speak out and tell him what I think. Talking of great ladies, that Lady Portmore is worse than ever. I am sure Helen cannot like her. She takes up so much of Lord Teviot's attention; and yet she is not satisfied with that. Last night when Colonel Beaufort came and sat down by me, she actually called to him to come to her; and though of course I did not care whether he went or not, it was very uncivil of her. He is very amusing. I was quite wrong when I said he put me in mind of Ape Brown, and he is always trying to persuade me that I shall be bored, and that life is nothing but a trouble; and you know, I never was bored in my life, and I think life very good fun. There is a Colonel Stuart here, who was once engaged to Miss Forrester, they say; but it cannot be true, or she would not seem so unconcerned as she does; and he does not take so much notice of her as he does of Helen. He is a great friend of Lord Beaufort's; and Lady Portmore says he is a great friend of hers, but so she says of everybody. She says the same of Colonel Beaufort, and yet one day after she had left the room he said, ' Bless that fair lady! she talks greater nonsense than ever. She has been talking rural economy for the benefit of the country neighbours. I would give £100 to hear her explain the poor-laws to Harriet Martineau; she is capable of it. She becomes a greater treat every day.' Now that does not seem as if he liked her; does it? If mamma comes to fetch me home, I wish you would send my other white bonnet. I suppose there is no chance of mamma's letting me stay here till Lady Eskdale comes back. I shall be very glad to be at home again; but it is so seldom we pay any visits, I should like to stay here a little longer. When I said that Colonel Beaufort was amusing, I did not mean that he made jokes, and laughed a great deal; but he says odd things in a dry, grave way, that make other people laugh, without seeming to take any trouble about it himself. I am afraid mamma will think him affected; not that it would signify, only I do not think he is.

" Yours affectionately,

" ELIZA DOUGLAS."

Colonel Stuart's history, which Miss Douglas could not explain, was simply that he had been as much attached to Mary Forrester as it was in his nature to be, and his peculiar talents for pleasing had not been exerted less successfully with her than they had in many other instances of which she knew nothing. He disguised his faults for a time, and when Mary discovered that he was extravagant, that he played, and that he was totally without religious principle, she found that the determination to give him up, which followed her discoveries, was accompanied by bitter feelings of regret. But Lord Beaufort was wrong in his assertion that she jilted Colonel Stuart on her accession to wealth. Their engagement was at an end some weeks before the unexpected death of a distant relation gave Miss Forrester her fortune. This circumstance added to the mortification which Colonel Stuart felt; and if he had not actually said that her sudden prosperity had induced her to change her mind, he had allowed it to be said by his friends. He was a popular man with men, and there were many of his partisans who made it their business on this occasion to talk of Miss Forrester as cold-hearted and capricious; and who, when they meant to go the extremist lengths of vituperation, accused her of being actually a saint. But this awful assertion was of course made in a low tone of horror, and mentioned only in strict confidence. Colonel Stuart for some time kept up an appearance of attachment and regret. Perhaps he thought it impossible that any woman whom he had condescended to love could give him up and forget him. But when the consistency of Miss Forrester's conduct convinced him that she was in earnest, he returned to his former courses, played higher, betted more, and flirted more determinedly with married women; and whether his love of Mary were really or not forgotten in the bottom of his heart, he met her in society with apparent indifference, and in general seemed to forget that they had ever been on more intimate terms. He did not know that she was at St. Mary's when he accepted Lord Teviot's invitation; but her presence, when he found her in the drawing-room, appeared to give him neither pain nor pleasure.

Lady Portmore talked to him in the evening for two hours and a half, in a low, confidential tone, making him thoroughly uncomfortable by assurances, that she was his constant friend with Mary Forrester.

" Now, my dear Stuart, I am not paying you a compliment when I assure you I feel quite justified in persuading Mary that she ought to relent at last. She will be a model wife; and I know you have too much good taste not to give up play, and any other little pursuits, when you marry."

" My dear Lady Portmore, for propriety's sake don't talk of my other little pursuits in that meaning tone; and for my sake, do not propose in my name to Miss Forrester. She might accept me."

" Well, and you know you are dying to marry her. Now you must have no disguise with me, Stuart; we know each other too well for that. You are a little mortified—yes, you know you are—at Mary's perverseness. Come, own it at once, and then trust to me for taking up your cause warmly."

" Good heavens, Lady Portmore, what a strange way you have of proving your friendship! I will trouble you not to assume that I wish to pay court to your *rich* friend, or, if I did, that I am not able to make my own cause good. But I see how it is. You wish to get Miss Forrester out of the way. She has evidently been tampering with some of your victims. Has Ernest wavered in his allegiance? "

Colonel Stuart had often found that there was no way of checking Lady Portmore's remarks but by a bold impertinence addressed to herself. She had not wit enough to answer it, nor discretion enough to seem *not* to understand it. So it threw her into long verbose explanations, during which she lost sight of her original topic.   And now she had, in her character of the most virtuous woman in the world, to repel with becoming scorn the imputation that Ernest should admire her at all, and, in her character of the most attractive woman in the world, to explain how it was that he should admire her so much.   It took her nearly twenty minutes to conduct this argument with herself to a satisfactory conclusion, during which time Colonel Stuart took a survey of the rest of the society, and at last broke in with the abrupt question, " And how about our host and hostess?   Are they very tiresomely in love still?   or have they begun to be good company again ? "

" Teviot is a great friend of mine," said Lady Portmore, with a look of great discretion.   " So there is no use in trying to extract from me any opinion about him, poor fellow ! "

"What!   Is it come to poor-fellowing him already? That's awkward.   Come, out with it ; you know you are longing to tell me all about it—is he bored ? or jealous ? or what is it ?   If he is not desperately in love with that little jewel of a wife, I am surprised at his taste, that's all ; but those wealthy dogs never are satisfied, and I don't wonder at it.   Wealth is not allowed its rights in this strait-laced country.   It is monstrous hard that a man who is rich enough to pension off his old wife when she grows tiresome, and marry a new one, should be obliged to go plodding on in the old routine, with the same woman sitting everlastingly opposite to him at his own table.   But Teviot can't be bored already.   Is he?   I am half in love with his wife myself."

" I will not have any remarks of that shocking kind made, and above all to me ; and, what is more, Stuart, I must insist upon it that you talk no nonsense to my little friend Helen.   She does not know you so well as I do, and it might put ridiculous ideas into her head—and then Teviot's temper—— But that I say nothing about, only let me tell you Mary Forrester will not take very well any marked attentions of yours to Helen."

" Won't she? Suppose we try," said Colonel Stuart, and, rising, he joined Lady Teviot, and devoted himself to her for the rest of the evening.

CHAPTER XXII

MR. AND MRS. DOUGLAS arrived at St. Mary's, bringing to Eliza satisfactory accounts of the Wentworth affair. Mrs. Douglas, to be sure, knew that there was no trust to be placed in any man on earth; they were all as hard as boards, and as fickle as the winds, and one more selfish than another. Therefore, if Mr. Wentworth jilted Sarah at last, it would not surprise her for a moment; but otherwise, she would have said, nobody could doubt his intentions.

"And, mamma," said Eliza, who had met her parents with unfeigned delight, "Sarah herself seems sure Mr. Wentworth likes her, and I am sure of it from what she says. So I dare say he is not so unfeeling as you think. I like him very much."

"Oh! my dear, I do not say there is any harm in him. In fact, I had rather have him for a son-in-law than such a Jerry as Sir William, such a goose as Lord Walden, or such a bashaw as Lord Teviot; but even if he is really attached to Sarah, that will not make me think better of men in general. And pray, Eliza, how does Lord Teviot behave to Helen, and at what time do they dine? It must be nearly dressing-time."

"You will hear the bell, mamma. It rings half an hour before dinner. Helen seems very happy, and Lord Beaufort and Colonel Beaufort and Miss Forrester are so fond of her, that she must be delighted while they are here."

There was an intonation in Eliza's voice, when the name of Colonel Beaufort occurred, that struck Mrs. Douglas's ear. No woman, be she ever so hardened or hackneyed in the ways of the world, can ever achieve an indifferent pronunciation, if the term may be allowed, of the name of the individual most interesting to her. There is no disguise she does not attempt; she drawls it out slowly, it will not be slighted. She runs it over quickly, it will not be slurred. She inserts it between two other commonplace names, it is still the guinea between the two halfpence. Still it is spoken in the tone of voice that belongs only to *him*.

" I have not seen Colonel Beaufort since he was quite a boy," said Mrs. Douglas. " I suppose he is like all the rest of the family, thoroughly grand and fine. I think you wrote word he was very conceited."

" No, mamma, affected. I thought him so at first; and perhaps he *is* a little affected. I do not think you will like him, mamma."

" I dare say not, my dear. I very seldom *do* like anybody; but probably he is not worse than Lord Teviot, nor so bad as Lord Beaufort. I have an idea that I shall prefer him to them."

Eliza was quite enchanted with such positive praise of her hero, but she defended Lord Beaufort valiantly; declared that he was the most good-natured man in the world, and not the least grand or fine.

" In short, the best of the two cousins? " asked Mrs. Douglas; " but now, my dear, we must dress, and when I have seen all your fine friends, I shall know better what to think of them. Ring for Hunt. How I hate these large rooms, where the bells are always a mile off! "

Mrs. Douglas found considerable food for observation in the party assembled at St. Mary's, and after the lapse of two or three days she had drawn from the events that were passing before her eyes the cheering conclusions,—that the Teviot *ménage* was not happy; that Lady Portmore, a beauty and a fine lady, was perfectly insupportable, and that it would be a virtuous action to be as disagreeable as possible to her; that Colonel Stuart was in his way quite as detestable; that there was no chance of Lord Beaufort's marrying Miss Forrester, and that Colonel Beaufort was a shade less languid when Eliza was talking to him than under any other circumstances.

The house was full of company, for the first week in September had arrived, and Lord Teviot's friends seemed to be unanimously possessed with an unusual eagerness to visit him. The breakfast table was covered every morning with letters from enterprising travellers who were naturally going to the other side of England; but who could make a *détour* to St. Mary's if they were wanted, and who added in a postscript that they should be there before an answer could arrive to stop them. Some, who did not know Lady Teviot, wrote to express their anxiety to make her acquaintance; and those who did were particularly desirous to renew it. Nobody said a word about partridges; but it was remarkable that from each carriage that arrived there was taken a long mahogany case, followed by a tin canister and a powder flask; and that each new-comer, in the course of the first evening, invariably asked if the harvest were well in, and if the birds were tolerably strong and numerous.

The crowd in which the Teviots lived was not favourable to the growth of their eventual happiness : at least, in nine cases out of ten, a young couple should be left very much to themselves during the first few months of their married lives. That complete dependence on each other, which insures habits of confidence and forbearance, is more easily acquired while the first dream of love lasts; and tastes and tempers amalgamate better in the end when there are no witnesses to observe that they do not quite fit at first.

Lord and Lady Teviot would, even if they had wished it, have found it impossible to be much together in their present train of life. He was out shooting all the morning with his friends; and in the afternoon she was riding or driving with hers: during dinner they were at opposite ends of a long table, and in the evening there were guests to be attended to, and the work of general amusement to carry on. Helen did not own it to herself, perhaps she did not know it, but it was a relief to her to be spared those *tête-à-têtes* with her husband, which she had found so alarming in the outset of her married life. Her youthful spirits were sufficient, and more than sufficient, to carry her through the many hours of amusement which each succeeding day presented. Joining great powers of enjoyment to a strong wish to please, and aided by adventitious circumstances, she moved amongst her guests the queen of a gay circle; and if she caught Lord Teviot's eyes fixed on her sometimes with sternness, sometimes with admiration, she merely thought, in the one case, that it was a pity he was so unlike everybody else, and in the other, that it was unfortunate she had not time to talk to him while he was in good humour; but in the meanwhile her impulse was to turn to her brother or her cousin for assistance in all her plans, and participation in all her gaieties.

So young and so lovely a mistress of a house was sure to attract; and Lady Portmore began to feel some frightful misgivings, not that Helen would eventually rival her in general admiration—no, she felt convinced that there never had been, and never could be such an universal favourite as herself, but she considered that she was at present in a false position, and had brought the real, genuine, well-established Portmore article into competition with a frivolous, tinselly, girlish plaything which derived a momentary value from peculiar circumstances. She began to think it time to assert herself, and to overthrow the usurper. She once tried to look bored, and apologized to the company for the dull evening which would necessarily ensue. But she found that it ended in her being left to nurse by herself the " touch of headache " she had announced, while the rest of the society were dancing in another room, and Mrs. Douglas took the opportunity of saying that she would come and sit quietly with her while the *young* people were amusing themselves.

So the next day she found it more expedient to declare that she was going to make the evening very amusing, and to arrange some charades.

" Come, Teviot, Ernest, all of you, you must each take a part."

" Who, I ? " said Colonel Beaufort, looking at her with an air of astonishment from the very depths of his arm-chair, where he was sitting very contentedly by the side of Eliza. " My dear lady, you may just as well ask me to go and break stones for Teviot's new road ; it would be quite as much in my line, and perhaps less trouble. I never shall forget what I went through last year at Kirwood Hall. I was asked there, and was foolishly good-natured enough to go. My mind misgave me the first evening that there was a screw loose,—that there was something sinister in the designs of the party. There were two or three abortive attempts at troublesome games, questions and answers, which entailed the bore of thinking ; and forfeits which gave an infinity of trouble, as a penalty for having thought wrong. Well, I put down these atrocities by a contemptuous smile or two, but the next evening I was overborne in my turn ; and I give you my honour, that I, who am by nature peaceable and inoffensive, and who had never done any harm to any human being in that house, was, during three hours, persecuted into being Lucius Junius Brutus, a village schoolmistress, the hind legs of a camelopard, and a wooden clock saying tick, tick, tick. The next morning I made an early transformation of myself into Colonel Beaufort in his travelling carriage ; but I doubt whether my constitution has ever quite recovered the trial of Kirwood Hall. No, no charades, for the love of mercy."

"Well," said Eliza, "I wish you did not object to them; I think they must be very amusing, and then you would act so well; I wish Lady Portmore would arrange one."

"How odd that you should always be ready to be amused! I am quite sorry I have destroyed your entertainment for the evening. What is to be done? Lady Portmore whisks about so fast, it would be vain for me to attempt to catch her. Shall I write her a note, and ask her to act for your diversion?"

"Oh, no! besides, nothing diverts me more than to hear you talk. Pray go on, and tell me more about Kirwood Hall, and the charades there." And it was by this naïve and genuine attention to his conversation, and this open delight in his society, that the unformed, candid Eliza attracted the languid, *blasé* Colonel Beaufort. The simple and melancholy fact was that she had fallen in love with him, which was an undignified measure, and if she had had only a year's knowledge of the world, she would carefully have concealed the preference she felt; but, as it was, she thought only that he was very pleasant, and that she was quite happy when he came and sat down by her; and she showed this without disguise. It was something so new, that Ernest was flattered by it. He did not care much about it at present; but if the chair that stood near her was as comfortable as any other in the room, he let himself drop into that by preference. He would, perhaps, even have put up with a cushion less.

Lady Portmore did not quite like his manner of passing his evenings, and when her particular plan of charades failed, she had nothing for it but to try to disturb the general comfort of the society. "Come, Miss Douglas," she said, moving her hands about as if she were playing on the pianoforte, "are we to have no harmony this evening? I am in the mood for a little music."

"I do not think Lady Teviot wishes for it," said Eliza,

who joined to a strong desire to contradict Lady Portmore a great disinclination to move.

" Oh, Lady Teviot has made over her powers to me this evening. I think, Teviot, your little wife has abdicated, and has become Helen Beaufort again. She and her brother have been reading letters and whispering to each other for the last half-hour. Are you shut out of their councils? "

" Lady Teviot has not had a very good account of her sister," he said, coldly, " and Beaufort was naturally anxious to see the letters."

" Dear, I am very sorry; I wish they had consulted me— I am a great homœopathist; I dare say Helen wishes us all away, that she might go to the Waldegraves; but really we have collected such a large party, that it will be difficult to disperse our forces. Pray who is that foreigner playing at whist? "

" Don't you know him? M. de la Grange; he comes over to England every year, and fancies himself a complete Englishman in language, pursuits, and habits, but without the slightest aptitude for either. He goes in the winter to any country-house of any description to which he can get himself invited, without much discrimination as to the society he meets there. ' It is all,' he says, ' the charming life of castle '; and between that and Melton, where he passes a miserable month of falls and fright, he makes out an existence which he thinks perfection. He is a good-natured animal, and I never grudge him a fortnight's shooting."

" You must introduce him to me; I dare say he has heard of me at Paris, and in London: all foreigners look to me as their patroness, as a matter of course. But come, Helen's colloquy is at an end. Beaufort, come here, I am so sorry your sister is ill, but I want you to sing. Miss Douglas is obdurate, but Mary will accompany you."

" Pardon me, Lady Portmore, but I must finish this bit of work to-night," said Miss Forrester.

" Oh, nonsense, only one song! Come, Beaufort "; but on looking round she discovered that Lord Beaufort had disappeared; and so that attempt fell to the ground, and Lady Portmore's gay evening was rather a greater failure than her dull one.

CHAPTER XXIII

" Mrs. Douglas," said Lady Portmore, " I am going to take quite the privilege of an old friend with you, but I feel as if I had known you all my life, and I am going to say something very impertinent."

Mrs. Douglas nodded. It was apparently a nod of acquiescence in the latter proposition.

" That dear little Eliza of yours, I am charmed with her; I am indeed. I would not say so if I were not; but if you will take my advice, you will not allow Colonel Beaufort to be so much with her."

" I think it would be difficult to prevent it," said Mrs. Douglas, with an affection of carelessness. " Colonel Beaufort seems to be, like most men, very much in the habit of taking his own way."

" Yes, but, my dear Mrs. Douglas, I am so afraid your gay, innocent Eliza, who is not aware how encouraging her frank manner is, should fancy that Ernest's attentions mean more than they do: I know him so thoroughly. He is a dear, kind-hearted creature, but rather a dangerous man. He means nothing by it, but he always seems as if he were making love to every woman he speaks to."

" That may be rather tiresome, and is very wrong," said Mrs. Douglas; " but it cannot be very dangerous. Those *seeming* lovers never take anybody in."

" Eliza is so young," continued Lady Portmore, who was longing to bring the conversation round to herself, " and very little attention turns those young heads; and what made me wish to put you on your guard, Mrs. Douglas, is that I know—this is of course entirely between ourselves, but I happen to know that Ernest is much attached to another person, quite a hopeless attachment, but so it is; he is very much in love with—a married woman."

" More shame for her. It is a pity she does not see him now," answered Mrs. Douglas, still preserving her coldness; " she would be thoroughly mortified, and it would do her a great deal of good. I have no patience with married women and their lovers."

" Oh! but you mistake me, dear Mrs. Douglas; I would not have you suppose for an instant, that because Ernest is in love with——, this person we are alluding to, she has ever thought of giving him the slightest encouragement."

" But it is what I do suppose, and always shall believe, Lady Portmore. I am not speaking of Colonel Beaufort individually. I never met him before, and shall not very much care if I never meet him again; but I shall always suppose that when a man makes love to a married woman it is entirely her fault, and it gives me the worst possible opinion of her."

" My dear Mrs. Douglas," said Lady Portmore, growing quite warm in the argument, " I do think you are a little too severe. I am sure I know some instances of married women, who are quite surrounded by admirers, who yet have conducted themselves in the most wonderful manner."

" I dare say they have," said Mrs. Douglas, significantly. " I know several instances myself, and very wonderful women they are. I cannot bear them."

" Ay! but I mean in the most exemplary manner. Now, Mrs. Douglas, only last year I knew a person, a married woman, very much admired," sinking her voice modestly, " who had reason to know that a man whom she met constantly in society was very much in love with her. He was in her opera box every evening, met her at every party

I

she went to, and passed half his mornings at her house.   She saw the folly of this, knew that she was in danger of being talked of, and without the least hesitation, without a thought of the inconvenience and trouble, she set off to Cornwall, and passed a whole week there with the most tiresome old aunt in the world.   This at once proved to the man that he had no chance, and he withdrew immediately, and affected a passion for somebody else.   Now, what do you think of that?"

"Why, that there never was anything half so absurd.   If your friend had given up her opera box, sent excuses to her balls, and said, 'Not at home,' for a week, the gentleman's passion would soon have come to an end; and if she had at first stayed at home with her husband and children, it never would have had a beginning.   That grand action of a sudden rush to Cornwall must have flattered him amazingly; it showed she was obliged to go to the Land's End for safety.   No, whenever I hear any of that cant about the difficult position of a married woman with her lovers, I know exactly what to think of her; I think her a good-for-nothing woman."

"Really, Mrs. Douglas, good-for-nothing is rather a strong term.   I must say I cannot go so far as that; good-for-nothing is an odd expression applied to a well-meaning woman."

"Why, what *is* she good for, Lady Portmore?   She is not a good wife, nor probably a good mother, and certainly not a good Christian; so I adhere to my expression, she is good for nothing."

"But if you lived in London, you would think differently, Mrs. Douglas; you would see how difficult it is for a woman of ordinary pretensions—— However, we will not argue, for, in fact, I am just like you, one of the strictest people possible, excessively strait-laced in all matters of principle; and, besides, we have wandered from our original topic.   I merely wished to put you on your guard about Ernest. He is just the sort of man to whose attentions I should object, for a daughter of my own."

" I forget whether you have any grown-up daughters? " asked Mrs. Douglas, with an innocent air of doubt.

" My dear Mrs. Douglas, I have not been married nine years—or ten at the very utmost."

" *In*-deed! " There was an emphasis on the first syllable, indicative of profound astonishment.

" And I was quite a child at the time; married literally from the school-room, before," with a half-sigh, " I knew what I was about."

" *In*-deed! " said Mrs. Douglas, still in a marked state of emphatic surprise. " Well, I am much obliged to you, Lady Portmore, for putting me on my guard about Colonel Beaufort, but these things must take their chance. Perhaps he would not show such a decided preference for Eliza's society if there were anything else to amuse him; but Miss Forrester does not seem inclined to take any notice of him; and Lady Teviot is so surrounded by all the other gentlemen, she has no time to attend to her cousin. So there are only you and I left, Lady Portmore, and apparently he has not the slightest taste for our society." And so saying, Mrs. Douglas, who had been rolling up her strips of canvas, and winding off her ends of worsted, quietly took her basket and walked away, leaving Lady Portmore thoroughly discomfited by the many offensive insinuations conveyed in her closing speech. She was regularly out of sorts, and in that soured state in which the wish to do a little mischief is a consoling idea. She was half inclined to leave St. Mary's, where her vanity felt half starved; but her faith in her power over Lord Teviot remained unshaken, and her wish to try it had become stronger. Besides, she could not go now, there was a great man coming.

CHAPTER XXIV

Mr. G. really was what is commonly called a great man. To the advantages of being a Secretary of State and Leader of the House of Commons, he joined those of being a brilliant orator and a very agreeable member of society. He had offered himself as a visitor at St. Mary's, which lay within reach of the large commercial town which he represented, and in which Lord Teviot possessed considerable property. There was to be a public meeting, and the opening of a new bridge, and a launch of a large ship, and much good eating, and still better speaking, at which Mr. G. and Lord Teviot were to assist.

Mr. G. had been a youthful friend of the late Lord Teviot's, and the kindness which he received from the father he now repaid to the son. He had a high opinion of Lord Teviot's talents, founded more on the intimate knowledge he had attained in private life of the acuteness and straightforwardness of his mind, than on the two or three successful speeches he had made in the House of Lords; and Mr. G. was anxious to remove, by the stir of official life, the shadow that Lord Teviot's shyness or sensitiveness threw over his higher qualities.

" Come, Teviot," said Lord Beaufort at breakfast, " I'll bet you what you like that you are in office before this day three months."

" What am I to be? a clerk in the Foreign Office? I do not see any other opening."

" Oh, they will make an opening fast enough, if you will go in at it. They can shove off old Lisle to India, or make out an embassy for Chaffont. You will be in, somehow, before Christmas."

" Not before Christmas, if at all. Nobody has time to be turned out during the holidays."

" How ver droll! " exclaimed La Grange; " but it is a truth of the most striking. We in England are so occupied with the chase and the sport, and with the life of the castle in the winter, that we forget entirely our politique. I am ver much delight to think I will meet Mr. G. in the ease of the country. He is one hero of mine. Does he voyage alone, my lord? "

" Ah! who comes with him, Teviot? "

" Only his private secretary, the faithful Fisherwick."

" Fisherwick! " repeated Colonel Stuart; " Heavens and earth! I trust not."

" Why, what harm do you know of him, Colonel Stuart? " said Lady Teviot.

" The gods forfend that I should know anything more or anything worse of him than his extraordinary cognomen; but imagine travelling with one of that curious species. Think of being shut up alone in a carriage with a live Fisherwick! It makes my blood run cold."

" Fisherveke! " repeated La Grange. " It is a difficult word, but I do know oder of that name—at least, I know a Mrs. Fisher very well, who live at Hampton Veke; so I suppose she is one relation. She is made to be painted, and most charming. Does your ladyship know Mrs. Fisher? " addressing Lady Portmore.

" Oh dear no; never heard of her," said Lady Portmore, tartly. She began to think La Grange not worth a civil answer. " But, Teviot, to return to this idea of your coming into office. It is what I have always wished for you; and I shall insist on G.'s making some arrangement that will bring you in. I can promise you Lord Portmore's support; he has a very high opinion of G."

" Poor G.!" whispered Ernest to his cousin. " I hope she won't let that be generally known; it might give him a shake in public estimation."

" And then, Helen," continued Lady Portmore, " when Teviot is in office, you and I must set about being popular, for the good of our friends. We must keep open house for the supporters of government. I will send you my list, and with a little of my help, you may make Teviot House of real importance to our party."

" I am sure," said Helen, laughing, " I should be puzzled to say what my party is, for at this moment I am very ignorant of all political matters; but if Lord Teviot comes into office, I suppose I shall grow as eager as most people are."

" Would you like me to take office, dear?" said Lord Teviot, who was pleased with this avowal.

" Yes, I think so! and yet——"

" Oh yes, to be sure you would," interrupted Lady Portmore; " everybody likes distinction; and you as well as the rest, Helen: and then you could be of use to all the Beauforts and Pelhams in creation, which would delight you."

" I need not begin to think of them yet. Lord Teviot is still unprovided for."

" No, Helen; and as you seem so well disposed for a political life, I am sorry to say that the whole thing is a vision of Lady Portmore's, and that G. has no more idea of giving me an office than I have of asking for one."

" I am thinking," said Lady Portmore, " if nothing else is available, which of the foreign embassies you could have?"

" Oh no! not an embassy," said Helen eagerly; " I could not bear to live abroad,—and to leave papa and mamma," she was about to add, but from some undefined feeling she stopped and said, " and to leave England and my own home."

" No, I think I might ask you in vain to do that," said Lord Teviot, coldly, for he rightly interpreted the meaning of the pause in her sentence. " I should not have a willing companion in my exile."

" Oh, you naughty girl ! " said Lady Portmore, affectedly, " to hesitate about following your husband wherever he goes—to say nothing of *such* a husband ! I am shocked at your hard-heartedness."

" I do not think Helen's hard-heartedness to be compared to yours, Lady Portmore," said Mary Forrester. " You have suddenly sent Lord and Lady Teviot out of the country, without the slightest warning. I have no doubt Lord Teviot would be just as sorry to leave his friends as Helen would be to leave hers. Of course I say nothing of *such* friends ! " she added, laughing, as she looked round the table. " In common politeness, neither he nor Helen can say that they could quite console each other for the loss of us."

" Very true," said Ernest, who saw Lady Portmore's game ; and " Very true," added Lord Beaufort, who was struck with Miss Forrester's energy and warmth ; but at the sound of his voice in approval, the colour that came into Mary's cheek, and the slight curl of her lip, reminded him that he was not privileged to offer his opinion to her. Since the unlucky conversation in the library, not a word had passed between them, not even a look ; she never seemed to see him. Once or twice it had nearly fallen to his lot to hand her in to dinner, but without any apparent premeditation, without a shadow of pique in her manner, she had contrived either to put Eliza forward, or by negligently continuing the conversation in which she might be engaged, to make it seem inevitable that Sir C. Smith, or Mr. Douglas, or Colonel Beaufort, should offer her an arm, and walk in before him. He did not quite like it ; he would have preferred an open war, an attempt at explanation, or a tart retort—but she did not deign to show her dislike in words.

CHAPTER XXV

Mr. G. arrived, of course too late for dinner; but as it was some years since he had seen either soup or fish in their best and hottest state of culinary excellence, he was quite satisfied—made the slightest possible apology for sitting down to dinner in his travelling dress, and looked like a gentleman and a well-dressed man.

Fisherwick looked horrid: he was, from his sedentary habits, averse to an open carriage, even in the dog-days; and the afternoon had been wet and foggy, so he was chilly to the last degree; and he always turned bright yellow tipped with blue when the fresh country air blew for any length of time on his worn-out Downing-street frame. His hair contrived to collect more dust than the usual laws of capillary attraction warranted. His black neckcloth turned browner and hung looser than common black cravats; his coat was a dingy brown—and, altogether, he had the air of an exhausted ink-bottle. If he had been allowed his luncheon on the road, and gallons of hot soap and water on his arrival, he would have been quite another Fisherwick; but, as it was, he looked like " a very unwashed artificer " indeed; and till he arrived at his third glass of champagne, he was as depressed and as uncomfortable as it was possible for a Cabinet Minister's private secretary, *né* Fisherwick, to be. But then he revived, and resumed his usual habits of official affability and courteous incommunicativeness, and his little dry pleasantries flowed forth, playfully cloaking his inflexible discretion.

" Any foreign news, Fisherwick? " said Sir Charles.
" I don't half like your last Spanish accounts."

" Ah, trust you country gentleman for croaking, and
for finding out what is not to be liked; you are never
satisfied."

" The last published details are anything but satisfactory.
Have you any later accounts? "

" I do not know the date of the last you saw."

" They were dated the 23rd; you must have heard
later news than that."

" We ought, certainly. For myself, I ask nothing more
from Spain than a glass of this excellent sherry."

" Are you asking about the Spanish news? " said Mr. G.
from the other end of the table. " Nothing can be worse;
our friends are in full retreat, and, in fact, the game is up."

" Now is not that so like him? " exclaimed Fisherwick
in an ecstasy. " I always say there is nothing like his
candour and courage. I never saw such a man."

" At what time did you start this morning? "

" At seven; he's always ready, you know."

" You must have found it coolish work, starting in the
rain and fog at that hour? "

" He never is cold," said the pinched and suffering
Fisherwick; " he said it was as fine a morning as we could
expect. He has the cheerfullest mind, and a power over
it that I never saw equalled.   What do you think he did the
last stage?—slept like a top, though I told him when we
changed horses that I was afraid we should be too late for
dinner.   ' We always are, my dear Fish,' he said, and went
to sleep again with the greatest composure. He has such
equable spirits."

" He looks well," said Lord Beaufort, " considering what
a bore of a session it has been."

" Does not he? " said Fisherwick, triumphantly. " I
am excessively glad your lordship has observed it; it is

quite remarkable. I never saw him look better"; and his dear dusty eyes filled with tears, for his devotion to his chief was as genuine as it was apparent, and he always took to himself the comments, whether complimentary or condemnatory, that were made on Mr. G. It made him *feel* well himself to be told that Mr. G. *looked* so.

Lady Portmore was not satisfied with her position at the dining-table. She was seated by Lord Teviot, and as the place next to Helen had been reserved for Mr. G., she was as far removed from the reigning great man as was possible; and to her surprise she saw Helen and Mr. G. talking and laughing with all the ease of old acquaintance. Once or twice she tried to enter into their conversation; but the distance was too great, and her sparkling remarks were lost in the steam of the entrées before they reached the head of the table.

"What a clever countenance my friend G. has," she said to Lord Teviot; "such a brow! If I met him without knowing who he was, I should say directly, That must be a clever man!"

"It is very unlucky," said Mrs. Douglas, who was seated on the other hand of Lord Teviot; "but I cannot agree with you at all. I never was more disappointed in my life with anybody's looks; he is so bald, and nearly gray—at least ten years older-looking than I had expected—and altogether very much like other people. But that is always the case. I never yet saw anybody who had been much cried up, who did not seem to me particularly commonplace."

"Wait till you hear him converse," said Lord Teviot; "perhaps you will then own that he is rather above the common herd."

"Yes," said Lady Portmore, "you will see how it will be this evening; he is perhaps more at his ease with me than with anybody, and I will lead him to talk on subjects that interest him, and you will be amazingly struck with his talent."

"At present I am more struck with his teeth. Pray, does he always laugh so much? amongst common characters that would be looked upon as a proof of folly."

"Perhaps G. will turn out to be a fool at last," said Lord Teviot.

"Oh, no!" interrupted Lady Portmore, who had not the first principles of a joke in her; "you may believe me, G. is no fool. I can answer for that; I have known him for ages, and can venture to say he is decidedly above par."

"Well, then, his laughter is only a proof that Lady Teviot amuses him; they certainly are very gay at that end of the table."

"Yes, absolutely noisy," said Lady Portmore, spitefully. "Now, my dear Teviot," she added, lowering her voice, "this shows you how right I was, when I told you that Helen required mixed society to put her in spirits. Only let your house be full, and she will be happy; and, perhaps, when she is a little older and wiser she will be content with a more domestic life." And with this food for meditation she left him, as she obeyed Helen's signal to retire.

CHAPTER XXVI

" DON'T you think Reginald Stuart very much out of spirits? " said Lady Portmore, when she was lingering over the breakfast-table, after the other ladies had withdrawn and Lord Teviot and Stuart had gone out shooting.

" Yes, I think he is," said Ernest, " rather out of spirits, and very much out of cash, I suspect; the old story of cause and effect."

" Poor fellow! " continued Lady Portmore; " it is a very deplorable case, for I don't believe that tiresome, poky brother of his, Lord Weybridge, will help him. In fact, between ourselves, I don't like Lord Weybridge; he is so hypocritical, he always pretends to be on good terms with our friend Reginald, and yet he lets him go on, distressed to the last degree for money."

" He did pay his debts once, you know, £16,000."

" Yes, but that was years ago; when Stuart was so young he hardly knew what he was spending. I have heard him say twenty times that he had no more idea how he spent all that money than the man in the moon. But now that he is older and wiser, I feel certain that if Lord Weybridge were to pay off what he owes, and give him something reasonable to live on, he would be very steady."

" Weybridge has six boys of his own, you must remember," said Lord Beaufort.

" Now, my dear Beaufort, do not you join to run down poor Stuart; you can have no idea of his position. There you are, an only son, with a large allowance, and Lord Eskdale ready to pay your debts at any moment."

" Is he? I am charmed to hear it, but I beg to observe that he has not had to pay £16,000 or even £1600 for me. And my run against Stuart consists simply in the observation that Lord Weybridge has six boys to provide for."

" What! those babies? Why the eldest is not eight years old; they can cost him nothing but a few yards of stuff for their frocks. Children can be clothed and fed for nothing now; and I only want him to put Stuart straight with the world, and then he may save for his own children, and welcome."

" I hope," said La Grange, " Colonel Stuart is not so much indebted. He have a horse which will run at Doncaster, and have taken one house at Melton."

" Yes, quite a cottage. I know he has given up the large house he had last year without a murmur; and as for his horse at Doncaster, he told me himself that he is sick of the turf, but he thinks it his absolute duty to try if he cannot recover a little money at Doncaster."

" Ah, then, he run that horse just for a matter of trade, as a lawyer makes a speech for fee."

" Exactly, that is his view of the case; and in all other respects I never saw a creature more unselfish. I know he came here with only a pair of horses; he has withdrawn his name from one club, if not more, and, except his riding-horses, he keeps nothing but a cabriolet."

" Ah! that cabriolet," said Mr. G.; " now that is one of the mysteries I wish you would solve for me, Lady Port-more. There are about sixty clerks in my office, most of them younger brothers of good family, with allowances of two or three hundred a year; and by writing eight hours daily they earn another hundred. And yet two-thirds of these youngsters keep a cab with a high-stepping horse and a diminutive groom. I do not know what it costs, as I never indulged in such a luxury myself; but I presume that above half of their income goes in this foolery."

" But what can they do? London is so large."

" Yes," said La Grange, " it is of such immense grandeur; and without a cab how can you bring yourself out of the affair? Suppose yourself with a visit to make in the high end of Portland Place, how would you get there from the Travellers'? "

" By Regent Street," said Mr. G., smiling.

" But how? I beg a thousand pardons."

" On foot."

" Oh, impossible," said Lady Portmore; " it would kill any of the young men of the present day to attempt such a walk; it must be four miles at least, or two, or some immense distance. No, I dare say a cab is rather an extravagance; but I own I think it an absolute necessity."

" Yes," said Lord Beaufort; " I do not see what a man is to do in London without a cab."

" No," said Ernest, " I quite agree with you; it is as indispensable as a coat."

" Exactly so," said La Grange.

" I am quite convinced of the fact by this unanimity of opinion," answered Mr. G. " I am only thankful I was born before this fatal cabriolet obligation was invented, and that I am able to walk every day from Grosvenor Square to Downing Street, and back again."

" But if it rains? "

" I put on my greatcoat, and put up my umbrella; and it is curious that I am generally accompanied by some man of my own standing, and that at every crossing we are either splashed or nearly run over by a tribe of young boys going nodding along in one of those puppet-shows on wheels. However, if it is necessary, I say no more; but I am not surprised to hear of so many young men deeply in debt "; and so saying he walked off to his red boxes and his Fisherwick.

" It is very sad, certainly, and G. may be partly right,"

said Lady Portmore; " but in Stuart's case his cabriolet is an actual measure of economy; he sold those magnificent carriage-horses when he set it up. I must repeat that I think he is in a very pitiable position. He is willing to submit to every sort of privation; but, as he says, what is the use of trying, if his family will not help him?"

" I thought his mother was very liberal to him."

" Yes, she makes him some sort of allowance; but she does not do all that he expected. And that is where I think his family so much to blame; they help him only to a certain extent. And that, as he says, puts him in a false position; he gets the reputation of having his debts paid over and over again, and yet he is never so entirely clear as to feel encouraged to live economically. No, it really makes my heart bleed to think of all those selfish Weybridges, and to see Stuart so unlike himself."

" Has not your friend Miss Forrester," said Lord Beaufort, " a great share of Stuart's low spirits to answer for?"

" If you mean that he cares about her," said Lady Portmore, " that is what he never did and never will, in my opinion; but at one time he had certainly a good right to expect that she would marry him, and it is a great pity she did not."

" She jilted him in the coolest manner when she inherited that fortune, did not she?" said Lord Beaufort.

" Had you not better look behind that screen, Beaufort, before you proceed?" whispered Ernest.

" Pho! nonsense," he said; but he started from his chair as he spoke, for, leaning against the door of the conservatory, where she and Eliza had gone to gather flowers, stood Mary Forrester, and any faint hopes which he might have entertained of not having been overheard were dissipated by the decided measure she took of walking straight up to the table and addressing him.

" This is the second time, Lord Beaufort, in which I have by chance overheard you accuse me of the most odious conduct to Colonel Stuart." She stopped, apparently choked by the violence of her emotion; her face was pale, but hot tears of shame and anger stood in her beaming eyes. After a moment's pause, which no one dared to interrupt except La Grange, who politely pushed a chair half an inch nearer to her, she passed her hands rapidly over her face, and said in a more collected tone, " But this is foolish, I am speaking as if I were angry and perhaps I was so, for a minute. At all events, it is evident that I am not calm enough ; not enough at my ease to make a good defence against your charges. But Lady Portmore has already borne witness that I never possessed the affections of Lord Beaufort's friend, and if Lord Beaufort will take the trouble to ask his sister how and when I became aware of that fact, she has my free leave to tell him all. I think she can exculpate me from the crime of jilting Colonel Stuart."

" I am sure," said Lord Beaufort—" I am certain—that is, I have no right to ask Helen."

" Perhaps not," she said, dejectedly; " but I ask it as a favour. You have only heard and repeated the statements of *your* friend. Hear what *my* friend, and Helen is my *real* and best friend, has to say for *me*. Perhaps you will still think me to blame; but I think your persecution of me," and she half smiled, " will not be so constant as it now seems to be." Again, there was a short pause; she leant with both hands on the table to steady herself, for she shook with timidity, as she added, " I am ashamed to say so much about myself, but the fortune that is supposed to have influenced me does not exist; I mean, that I am not the heiress Lord Beaufort thinks I am. The fortune is not mine now—I wish every one to know that. Now, Eliza, let us go "; and so swift was their retreat, that no one had time to speak before they were fairly housed in the next room, and Eliza had thrown her arms round her friend's neck, and given way to the burst of tears which had been gathering during the whole scene, while she said, " Never mind them, dear Miss Forrester, it is all ill-nature, and they had much the worst of it at last."

And so they had: there never was a more discomfited set of people, barring La Grange, who considered himself in high luck at having witnessed such a scene: it was an incident quite unmatched in his English recollections, and he was only longing to slip away, and write it down before he lost " the idiom " of Miss Forrester's expressions. Lord Beaufort was completely overpowered; even Lady Portmore was annoyed, for though she knew she could never be in the wrong, she thought she might have been more in the right if she had taken Mary's part more decidedly: but she was the first to speak. " Well, this is very unlucky."

" Very," said Ernest.

" Deuced unlucky," said La Grange, who was learned in vulgar English expletives.

" I hate the sort of thing," said Lady Portmore, " because, though I said nothing, Mary might think I did, and it will make such a *tracasserie*."

" Come, Beaufort, speak up," said Ernest, patting him on the shoulder.

" I cannot," said Lord Beaufort, rising and leaning his head against the chimney-piece. " It's a bad business."

" It certainly is," said Lady Portmore; " and those sort of scenes take away one's presence of mind so, or else I would have explained it all to Mary at once."

" It was very fine though: Mees Forster resembled very much Pasta, in *Medea*, at that grand moment when she says ' Io! ' " added La Grange.

" Can't you send him away?" whispered Lord Beaufort to Lady Portmore.

K

"M. La Grange, if you mean to go out shooting to-day, there are all the keepers now on the lawn."

"Ah! I see, Lady Portmore, you do think my chamber, I mean my room, better than my company, as we say in England; and I dare say I will disturb you if I stay. My lord, do not distress yourself; when Mees Forster think it over, she shall think it all fudge to be affronted just for so few words"; and with a hearty laugh at the excellence of his English vulgarity, which harmonized ill with the feelings of his hearers, La Grange walked off.

"I am glad he is gone," said Lady Portmore. "Do shut the door, Ernest, for fear he should hear me say how detestable he is; and now what are we all to do?"

"We have done enough for one morning," said Ernest.

"But what did Mary *mean* by the second time?" Lady Portmore asked.

"Beaufort gave her the benefit of his opinion once before, in the library, when she was in the gallery."

"No, did he? Really that is being imprudent, my dear Beaufort; and what distresses *me* particularly is, that Mary came in just when she did. If she had waited a moment, I was going to tell you that the engagement or attachment, or whatever it was, was at an end a fortnight before Mary ever heard of that fortune, and that she gave Stuart up on hearing of that unfortunate Mrs. Neville. In fact, I think Mrs. Neville sent her some of Stuart's letters, or wrote to her, or something of that kind."

"You might have told me that sooner, Lady Portmore, and then I should not have said what I did."

"How did I know you were not aware of it? I really think, Beaufort, the scrape is entirely your own, and you need not try to draw me into it. Besides, I am the last person in the world likely to say anything against Mary, who I am sure loves me better than anybody upon earth, though she did call Helen her best friend; but then she was angry. Why, I brought her here, you know, in my own carriage."

"It is rather a pity you did," said Ernest, "as things have turned out."

"Don't joke about it, Ernest," said Lord Beaufort, "for I am heartily vexed, and that is the truth. It does look like persecution, as she said."

"She came forward very gallantly," said Ernest. "I did not suspect she had so much spirit. We all looked remarkably small, I thought."

"As for that," said Lady Portmore, "I must beg to say that I did not look the least put out."

"My dear lady, I wish you could have seen yourself; such a look of guilt! I expected you to faint."

"Nonsense, Ernest, why should I? I was taking Mary's part; at least, I should have taken it, in another minute; but for fear of any mistake, I shall just go after her, and explain to her that I was quite innocent during the whole conversation."

"And I shall go to Helen," said Lord Beaufort.

"And I shall go and look for my own particular little Miss Douglas," said Ernest. "She looked aghast at the sudden breeze. The confidante's look of horror prevented me from giving my undivided attention to the principal performers. I shall like to hear what she thought of it."

"You really will persuade yourself that you care about that little Douglas girl if you carry on the joke much further," said Lady Portmore in a vexed tone. "Beaufort, I would advise you to wait a little, or you will find Mary with your sister."

"I don't very much care if I do. The meeting will be awkward, at any rate, and I had rather have it over when I am in the mood to say all that is humble"; and he walked off.

"It is rather unfair that he should see her first," said

Lady Portmore, " so I shall go to her room, and see if she is there."

" And when you have both exculpated yourselves for saying too much," said Ernest, " will you add in a note that I, according to my praiseworthy custom, was saying nothing."

CHAPTER XXVII

Lord Beaufort waited some time in his sister's room before she came to him. She had been with Mary, and had heard the history of the *contretemps* of the morning, and was prepared to pacify, and explain, and smooth, and conciliate, till all should be peace again. Such is the daily toil of the mistress of a large country-house. No laundress, ironing away at an obstinate row of plaits; no carpenter planing the roughest plank of wood; no gardener raking the stoniest soil, has half the trouble she has, to maintain a smooth surface in the aspect of her mixed society. Nothing more is asked. They may all hate, all envy, all rival each other; they may say everything that is ill-natured, and do everything that is mischievous, but the "general effect," as painters would call it, must be harmony; and this must be maintained by the tact of the hostess.

Such an outbreak as had occurred this morning was an unusual novelty; and Helen must quell that before the parties at variance met at dinner. She found Lord Beaufort most willing to do all in his power to deprecate Miss Forrester's resentment: her appeal to Helen had touched him, and as he hated to see a woman in tears, her struggle for composure had excited his admiration and gratitude. And when he heard her whole history he found further reason for regretting what he had said. Mary had received Colonel Stuart's attentions with pleasure during the time in which she believed him to be attached to her, and until she was surprised by a visit from a Mrs. Neville, who had good reason to suppose herself the object of Colonel Stuart's preference. Driven to desperation by the report of his marriage to Miss Forrester, she adopted the decisive expedient of making her rival her confidante. She told her story, and produced her vouchers, in the shape of some of Colonel Stuart's letters, and she cried over them, and her own guilt, and his treachery, and Mr. Neville's wrongs; and in the madness of her passion and her jealousy, threw away her own character, her pride, her delicacy, all, so that she could prove that the man she loved was a villain. She succeeded, so far as thwarting Colonel Stuart in his hope of marrying Mary could be called success. Whether disappointing him in his dearest hopes were a likely method to regain his affections she had not perhaps considered. Miss Forrester declined a continuance of Colonel Stuart's attentions, and when pressed by him to assign a reason for her change of manner, she frankly pleaded her knowledge of his want of principle, his seduction of Mrs. Neville, and his heartlessness in deserting her. He flew into a violent rage with Mrs. Neville, and ended by being scarcely less furious with Miss Forrester. A fortnight later when she became a rich heiress, his anger turned upon himself for having quarrelled so completely with her, and to save his own character he changed the date of their disagreement, and allowed his friends to suppose that *her* money had been the root of *his* evil fortune. All this Helen repeated to Lord Beaufort, and his knowledge of all parties gave him instant conviction of the truth of the story.

" But why does she say that the fortune is not hers now? "

" That is a point she would be unwilling to explain, but that she is anxious it should be understood now that she is not an heiress; and she imagines that it is ignorance on this subject which induced Colonel Stuart to follow her here. It was always supposed that the fortune which old Mrs. Forrester left to her would have been divided between her and two brothers: one is in the West Indies with his wife, and the other at sea. From some scruples about the will, not worth explaining, Mary is convinced that her brothers' claims are as good as her own; at least, so she chooses to say; and as she came of age two months ago, she has written to them, giving each of them a third of the property. I do not know the exact sum, but I believe she will have nearly £30,000 herself, which she says is quite enough for her."

" And does she really mean to give away £60,000? Well! she is a noble creature; I am in the humour just now to give her credit for every virtue under heaven; but I would rather not see her again. Can't you, dearest Nell, make the humblest apologies for me, and crown the whole by saying that as I am sure she must hate the sight of me, I have taken myself off to London? "

" Oh, no! dear Beaufort, you do not really mean you are going? that would be too absurd."

" But the best thing I can do. I shall look so foolish when I see her; and there is that blockhead, La Grange, to make his ungrammatical remarks on us; and, as I said before, she must hate the sight of me."

" No, indeed, she does not! perhaps she does not like you much at this moment, but it will all soon be forgotten. She is now waiting for me in my garden, to which she went that she might escape poor dear Lady Portmore."

" Ah! it is more than half Lady Portmore's fault. She *will* sit gossiping for an hour over the breakfast-table; and somehow people are always ill-natured at that early time of the day—bilious, I suppose; but those empty egg-cups and dirty plates always hear a great deal of scandal, and then Lady Portmore likes to *dénigrer* her dear friends."

" Well, never mind now; come with me to the garden, and make your speech of regret, etc."

" Oh, no, not with you, Nell! I could not say a word if you were standing by."

" Well then, go without me."

" That is a thousand times worse. No, the whole thing is a mess, and past cure, and the only resource is for me to take myself off."

" Oh! but that is so hard upon me," said Helen, with tears in her eyes. " You must stay, darling "; and she stooped down and kissed his forehead.

At this moment Lord Teviot entered, but, seeing how eagerly they were conversing, drew back. " Oh, come in, Teviot, pray come in! "

" I will come back presently, if you are engaged."

" No, I am not engaged, but Beaufort will insist on going away to-day; and I cannot possibly let him. Beaufort, may I tell Lord Teviot the whole story? "

" Certainly, my dear, if you like to repeat such a foolish business."

" If it is a family secret my curiosity is not ungovernable ; I had no idea you were closeted together for a mysterious story, or I would not have interrupted you."

" But it is no secret," said Helen; and she told him all that had passed, which threw him into such fits of laughter that Beaufort began to think the matter was not so serious as he had supposed.

" Then you advise him to stay? " said Helen.

" In his place I should go, but——"

" There, Helen, you hear what Teviot says."

" You did not let me finish my sentence," said Lord Teviot. " I was going to add that you cannot possibly go to-day, because you promised to dine with the Mayor of N—— to-morrow, and your going away would be an affront to him and to G. and to me, etc., etc."

" Yes, that is clear," said Helen. " Long live the Mayor of N——! and now, Beaufort, I will tell you how it shall all be. Mary and I will go out riding with Ernest only, and you shall join us accidentally, and make your peace while Ernest and I are cantering on first; and then follow us directly. You and Mary will, of course, hate each other for the rest of your lives, but that does not signify. So now it is all settled. You are going to drive Lady Portmore, of course, Teviot?"

"Of course," he replied, though provoked that Helen took it so coolly for granted.

"And the Douglases are going to pay a visit in the neighbourhood. Mr. G. may ride with us if he likes; he will never discover any little treaty of peace that is made under his eyes, and without a red box. The rest are out shooting, I believe. But there is poor Mr. Fisherwick, something really ought to be done for him."

"He is quite happy; there are despatches both from Lisbon and Madrid; quite enough to keep him in perfect content till dinner."

"Then we are all provided for," she said, and ran off to Mary. Everything came to pass as planned. The riding party set off. Lord Beaufort surprised them by a clever ambuscade from the stable wall; he told Mary he had been quite mistaken and wrong in what he had asserted, and was sorry that she had overheard it. Mary agreed with him in both these propositions, and said she should think no more of it, which was a bold assertion. He begged her to forgive him, for Helen's sake, and hoped she would shake hands to show they were friends. She suggested that their shaking hands might have an alarming effect on the nerves of the grooms who were riding behind them, but she forgave him with all her heart; and then she contrived to give Selim a slight touch with her whip, which brought him cleverly up to the rest of the party; and so the affair ended, with a little additional dislike on the lady's side, and some irksome recollections on the part of the gentleman.

Lady Portmore had already seen Mary, and proved to her that she had not such a friend as herself; that when she had said Mary was cold-hearted, she meant quite the reverse, and so on.   La Grange gave one or two mal-à-propos laughs when they met at dinner, which were put down by acclamation, and the only person who derived unmixed delight from the occurrence was Mrs. Douglas.   Eliza told the story to her, and she was charmed, because it enabled her to give a little hit at all parties.   She hoped it would cure Lady Portmore of that excessively improper practice of sitting gossiping half the morning with the gentlemen. She knew it was the right thing to say that Mary had not jilted Colonel Stuart, but somehow she, Mrs. Douglas, should never get rid of the impression that she had ; and she had never been more surprised than she was to hear that Mary was only just of age.   She looked six-and-twenty at least, and if Colonel Stuart were her only lover, much could not be said for her success in life.   She only wondered that Lord Beaufort did not get into more scrapes from his unguarded way of talking ; and she supposed that if Lady Teviot ever could believe him to have a fault, she could not be much pleased at finding he spent his mornings in taking away the reputation of her friends.   Colonel Stuart and Fisherwick were the only people not in the secret ; the first, because Lady Portmore had not had an opportunity of talking to him, and Fisherwick, because he had been writing from ten in the morning till the dressing-bell rang, when he took a run in the dark, round the shrubbery, and came down to dinner looking yellower and more narrow-chested than ever ; but declaring that nothing agreed so well with " us official men " as plenty of fresh air and exercise.

" I am afraid you had not time for a ride to-day, Mr. Fisherwick," said Lord Teviot, civilly.

" No, my lord, though it was rather an idle day with me ; but I indulged in a charming walk, only the sun was rather low " (it had been gone down about an hour) ;

"but he had a ride, I was happy to hear. Exercise is so good for him that I was delighted to find our despatches were not of a nature to keep him at home all day."

"Exemplary creature," murmured Ernest; "why have we not each a Fisherwick?"

Vain wish, unless each were a Cabinet Minister. There are hours in which the devoted lover grudges the attendance on his mistress which keeps him from Tattersall's; the devoted husband expects his wife to attend solely to him, and even the devoted parent has moments in which the impulse to give the idolized child a good shake is almost irresistible. All have their provocations and their fits of doubt and impatience. But the private secretary has none. He believes his chief to be faultless, and his official plans unequalled. He identifies himself with the man and the system. The minister and the red boxes, the treaties and the bills, the blue ribbon and the red tape, the members and the messengers, are all part and parcel of what he calls public life; they all stand on the same line; he looks upon them as the attributes of the individual who has made him a private secretary; and he worships and writes.

"Remember you are all up early for breakfast to-morrow," said Lord Teviot as the ladies withdrew at night: "we must be off in good time; there is the new bridge to open, and the collation to eat, and G.'s speech to hear, and we are six miles from the scene of action. Above all things, I recommend an elaborate *toilette*, for the sake of my friend the mayor, who hoped I should bring a 'smart party.'"

"An awful prospect! Will you tell my servant to call me the day after to-morrow?" said Ernest, turning to the groom of the chambers as he walked off to bed.

Mr. Phillips was too well educated to smile; but he thought it an excellent joke, and cut it over again on his own account to the steward's-room boy, which made all the ladies' maids nearly die of laughing.

CHAPTER XXVIII

THE important morning came, and with it the four carriages-and-four, and Lady Portmore, resplendent in feathers and silks, and much to be admired, till Helen came in, looking like a genuine angel, so soft and white and bright. It is difficult for the unlearned to explain the component parts of a becoming dress, but some of the party observed that the embroidery on her silk pelisse must have been done at Lyons, to which Mrs. Douglas subjoined the oracular remark, " that it was a pity that it was white upon white." There was also a quantity of shining lace, ordinarily, I believe, termed blonde, floating about, and forming an admirable cloud for the angel to float on.

" Well, Helen, you have gone and done it," said Ernest.

" Am not I *bien mise?* " she said, blushing; " I have really taken a great deal of pains about my dress, that the people at N—— may approve of Lord Teviot's taste. You know it is my first appearance there."

" And mine," said Lady Portmore.

" And mine," added Mrs. Douglas, in a tone that made everybody laugh except Lady Portmore, and she went on, never minding.

" But, my dear Helen, we must not expect to attract much notice to-day. There stands the real lion."

" My importance as a lion will not come into play till I begin roaring," said Mr. G.; " and my constituents will be glad to have something to look upon, even if they deign to listen to me. Really, my dear Teviot," he whispered as Helen moved on, " I never saw such perfection. I cannot take my eyes from her."

Such a speech from any other man would have given Lord Teviot a jet-black fit of jealousy, but it delighted him from Mr. G., who had established a right to make a little solemn political love to all the distinguished beauties of the day, and it was by no means a mere measure of custom and courtesy. He was as busy about his little flirtations, and as absorbed in his little sentiments, as if he had been a Lord Somebody Something just gone into the Guards, and doing his first London season, and nobody thought it odd. Half the women in London unblushingly paid court to him, and nobody said it was scandalous. If he got away from the House of Commons and came to a party, there was a sort of rustling sensation in the room, and two or three of his reigning loves immediately got up and made a circle round him, and drew their chairs close to his, and hated each other, and were as eager in their rivalries as if he had been thirty years younger, and were not absorbed in politics eleven hours out of every twelve.

Lady Teviot had taken his fancy prodigiously, and his unrivalled powers of pleasing were exerted for this young creature as if he were her own contemporary. Again, Lady Portmore was puzzled—in another point she was baffled. She wished to be in the same carriage as the hero of the day, but a Lord and Lady Middlesex had arrived the night before, solely for the sake of attending the ceremony. They were a remarkably dull couple—he, a quiet, magistraty sort of man, who never went into society except on a great county occasion—she, a little crooked woman, with an unpretending manner and a mistaken bonnet; but with all these drawbacks his peerage was a century older than Lord Portmore's, and upon a state occasion like this precedence must have its rights: so Lady Middlesex went with Lady Teviot in her carriage,

which also contained Mr. G. and Lord Teviot—the lion
and his keeper. Lady Portmore found herself actually
doomed to the second carriage, with Mrs. Douglas at her
side and Lord Middlesex opposite to her, and La Grange
going to make a spring at the fourth place. But despair
gave her energy, and she called to Ernest to take his
seat.

" Thank you," he said, " but I hate sitting backwards;
and Miss Douglas, who does not mind it, has promised to
change places with me if I go in her carriage."

" Indeed I never did, Colonel Beaufort."

" Well, but you will, I know; if not, I shall look so
frightfully pale that it will spoil the show and distress the
Mayor. Now, let us get in."

" Come then, Stuart," said Lady Portmore, " I will
have you here."

Lord Beaufort and Colonel Stuart, who had each their
reasons for wishing to avoid the carriage which contained
Miss Forrester, both hastened forward, and at last Lady
Portmore was gratified by Mrs. Douglas's declaration that
she should like to go in the fourth carriage, which had the
honour of conveying her husband; so Lady Portmore had
the pride of being escorted by three gentlemen, and the
pleasure of talking to them all the way.

The delay occasioned by these arrangements gave the
Teviot carriage some little advance, and the cheers with
which it was received reached Lady Portmore's ears
when she was in the midst of one of her confidential
harangues.

" What a noise! " she said. " All on G.'s account, of
course; . he is so extremely popular. I often tell him his
head will be turned. How they are cheering! it must be
for him. What is it all about? "

" We shall be in the thick of it soon," said Lord Beaufort;
" they are trying to take the horses off, and there is Teviot

imploring and gesticulating like a madman, and Helen standing up and curtseying; and now for such a hurrah."

A fresh mob rushed by. "Which is my lord's carriage —where is the young lady?"

"There, my good fellows, Lady Teviot is the lady in white."

"Why, you don't suppose," said Colonel Stuart, "they will go and take that estimable little hobgoblin, Lady Middlesex, for a bride?"

Another cheer, and, as the carriages moved slowly on, the murmur of comments on my lady's beauty and my lord's luck reached Lady Portmore's ears, and were encouraged by Lord Beaufort, who leaned out of the carriage and talked and laughed with the crowd, much to their mutual satisfaction. Lady Portmore waxed cross—wished she had known it would be such a mob, she would not have come; thought they had better wait a little, that the dust might subside; but no, on they went, the cheers becoming louder and the dust more opaque, and no vanquished king of the Huns, chained to the car of a Roman dictator, could feel his degradation more sensibly than Lady Portmore, following unnoticed in Helen's wake.

At last they arrived at the entrance of the bridge, and there stood the mayor and the magnates of the borough, with white staves in their hands and white ribbons in their button-holes, and white scarves over their shoulders; and Mrs. Mayoress, gorgeously arrayed, holding a bouquet to present to Lady Teviot; and the young mayors and mayoresses giggling at "the figure papa cut with a white shawl on," holding bouquets for the rest of the company.

The bridge was decked with flags, arches of laurel were thrown over it, and a barricade had been thrown across it to prevent any unhallowed foot from profaning the pavement till the proper moment. There was a dinner ready to be eaten at one end, and a balloon half ready to go up at the other.   The carriages had all arrived, and the company were all assembled.   Lord Teviot led up the mayor and mayoress and their goodly company, and introduced them to his bride; and Mr. G. accosted them all with the easy cordiality a well-practised member knows how to assume—perhaps really feels, though that is doubtful.   He had the knack of remembering their private histories and family connections, and was strong in his recollection of Christian names.

" Ah, Dowbiggin, glad to see you; I expected you would have been off after the grouse.   Charles Lloyd, you have been beat about the stone-coping of the bridge, I am glad to see.   Taylor, is your father here?   What! is that Nathaniel Curry?   you have been living on the fat of the land since last I saw you.   William, here's the sovereign I owe you—our bet about the steamer.   Mrs. Dowbiggin, this is my godson, I am certain.   I am expressly proud of George Dowbiggin, Lady Teviot; I must beg you to admire these curls.   And now for our bridge; it is a very handsome structure, upon my word.   Lady Teviot, you are to be the first to put your foot on our bridge.   Now for it."

The procession was put in motion, the mayor gave a signal with his wand, the flags were hoisted, the guns went off, and the band at the other end began playing that original and unhackneyed air, "See, the conquering hero comes."   But the barricade at the entrance had been made so particularly firm and good that none of the committee of management could move it, and it seemed probable that there would be a regular siege before the hero could either come, or with any propriety be called a conqueror.   The agitated mayor waved his wand wildly, and called for the clerk of the works; but he had gone to assist at the inflation of the balloon, and was in his turn storming at the gas-man for the inefficient supply of gas.

Still the band went on playing; still the barricade stood firm; and still the balloon remained flaccid. The mayor tore his white scarf in his attacks on the posts; the mayoress' face grew scarlet, but she periodically made little pokes at the powerful railing with the white ivory handle of her parasol, well meant but ineffective. La Grange proposed calling for boats, and attacking the bridge from the other side. "Impossible, quite impossible, my dear sir," said the mayor; "the boats are stationed here to convey the company to the launch; and the programme, sir, the programme specifies the south side of the bridge."

Happily, before the scene became perfectly ludicrous, the real carpenter arrived, the obstacles were removed, and the company advanced: it was really a pretty sight; the river was covered with boats—the quays and the adjoining buildings with people. The bridge was a very handsome structure, and no pains had been spared to make the temporary decorations accord with the occasion. As the procession turned to walk back again, the balloon rose just at the proper moment, carrying into the clouds, for the hundred and twenty-seventh time, the adventurous Mr. Brown, who assumed his most picturesque balloon attitude in bidding farewell to the old world and the new bridge. The supply of gas had been purposely stinted to save the credit of young Mr. Theodore Dowbiggin, who had announced his intention to become "an intrepid aeronaut," but had thought better of it as the time drew near. His intrepidity of course remained—that being a quality, like Dogberry's reading, that came by nature—but his aeronautcy was postponed. The well-paid Brown declared there was only gas enough for one, and the well-instructed engineer announced the impossibility of supplying another spoonful. Theodore loudly claimed to go up alone. Brown stuck to his balloon, and at last, as the papers announced, the high-spirited young man was borne away

L

from the spot by actual force, and the balloon rose majestically, bearing north-north-west, and was lost in the clouds. Not really lost: there is no occasion for alarm; it was found again two hours afterwards, hopping about on Framlingham Downs; Brown going through all the usual manœuvres of throwing out ballast, cutting cords, dragging anchors, etc., and extricating himself from all sorts of perils, from which he was eventually rescued by the Rev. Mr. Wilcox, who was taking his quiet afternoon walk, and was greatly surprised to see a Brobdignag humming-top skipping about his path, forty yards at a skip. Those who have the pleasure of knowing Mr. Wilcox will not doubt the readiness of the humanity with which he helped Brown—first to get out of his balloon, and then to catch it—nor the hospitality with which he offered him luncheon. A chaise was immediately procured; and Brown and his balloon were carefully packed up in it and on it, and returned to N—— in time to claim the last shouts of this shouting day.

Much had been done in the interim—a ship had been launched, and christened *The Helen* by Lady Teviot; the docks had been surveyed, and the whole party were assembled at dinner. Lady Portmore had contrived to hook herself on Lord Teviot's arm for the walk, which gave her an opportunity of writing the next day to all her friends that she had been universally taken for the bride; and at the collation she very cleverly jockeyed Lady Middlesex, and took her place next to Mr. G. The dinner had been laid in an enormous tent; and as it was a morning fête, it had been arranged that the ladies should remain and hear the speeches.

The toasts proceeded in the usual routine without any attempts at eloquence, till the mayor pronounced a magnificent oration on domestic " 'appiness in the 'igher classes " and the nobility in general, and concluded with proposing Lady Teviot's health. Air—"Happy, happy, happy pair." This was received with immense applause, which was increased by the sight of Lady Teviot's tears. She did not know exactly what to do, and so of course began to cry, but in a gentle becoming manner, though her nervousness increased when Lord Teviot got up to return thanks. She had never heard any public speaking, and expected that he would be unable to get safely through two or three inaudible sentences; therefore his gentleman-like easy flow of thanks struck her as a wonderful display of talent, and she was sorry when his speech ended, though it was by proposing the health of his friend Mr. G. Air—"Glorious Apollo." Immense cheering; and when that had subsided Glorious Apollo got up, and with a slight hesitation of voice and manner, as if he had not an idea what he was going to say, nor how to say it, and with an air of extreme surprise and gratitude at having his health drank at all, he started off in a brilliant speech that lasted three-quarters of an hour. As it was intended less for the edification of his present hearers than for an answer to the attacks of the Opposition papers, and a declaration of an important change in the commercial relations of the country, every word had been well weighed. It had been composed and revised and learnt by heart, and Fisherwick had copied it over five times with variations; but Mr. G. delivered it in an unstudied, off-hand manner, that gave it the air of a sudden burst of confidence to the 700 particular friends by whom he was surrounded. And by an artful allusion to the balloon, and the impracticable barricade, and one or two trifling events of the morning, he convinced the worthy mayor and corporation, who were not up to interpolations, that it was the sudden inspiration of the moment. Innocent creatures! their hearts burned with indignation when, on the following week, bitter leading articles dissected and misinterpreted and condemned every word of this speech; and they said it was most unfair that Mr. G. should be tried by words that were evidently spoken on the spur of the moment, and quite in confidence to themselves.

But in the meantime it was a magnificent display of eloquence, and the ladies of the party who were unused to public oratory were very much excited by it. Even Mrs. Douglas owned she was glad to have heard him once: she had no doubt that she should soon get used to the sort of thing, and see the fallacy and absurdity of long speeches; but for this once she had really rather have heard it than not, even though she had had the most uncomfortable bench to sit on that she had ever met with in her life, and though she was half starved in consequence of the waiter having whisked away her soup before she had touched it. Lady Portmore took joy on the occasion, in consequence of her having always prophesied that G. would make a capital speaker; and she could also venture to assert that his notions about trade were safe, and to be depended on, and she approved highly of what he had said. Mr. G., who liked a joke, contrived, by an allusion to foreign politics, to bring up La Grange, who was longing to astonish the natives by the purity of his English, and made a speech which in some respects was satisfactory, though he told them that the opening of the bridge was the finest imposition he had ever seen, that he should always consider that day the handsomest day of his life; that he was not to be regarded upon as a stranger, though he had never seen them before, for that he was as perfectly their compatriot in heart as in language; that it was his pride to be taken in as an Englishman wherever he went; and that from the bottom of his heart he drank their excellent healths.

The day concluded as satisfactorily as it had begun; Fisherwick came home slightly elevated, and so elated with the dinner and the speech, that after asking each of the company individually whether they had ever heard anything so fine in their lives, he found himself strong enough to read half a paragraph of an Opposition journal which contained a violent attack on his idol, and to rub his hands friskily while he hummed, *Ça m'est égal.*

CHAPTER XXIX

THE day after this fête, Helen received a letter from her mother that alarmed her much. Lady Eskdale thought Sophia's recovery far from satisfactory; she was weak and low, with a tendency to a cough, and was anxious to be moved to Eskdale Castle, which she thought agreed with her better than any other place, and, above all things, she wished to see Helen. " I must go to her," thought Lady Teviot; " there can be no difficulty about it. Mr. G. goes to-morrow, and the Douglases the next day, and I am sure Lady Portmore has been here long enough, and if she goes, there will only be some gentlemen left; and Lord Teviot may do very well without me, at all events, for a few days. Beaufort could go over to Eskdale with me." She did not like to investigate how much or how little she wished that some of their party should insist on remaining at St. Mary's, so as to keep Lord Teviot at home; but she went the length of thinking that he would be bored in a house where there was illness, and that she would be more useful to Sophia if she went without him.

She was pursuing this train of thought when he entered the room so suddenly as to startle her. She threw her handkerchief over the letter she was writing to her mother, hardly knowing why, but she always had in Lord Teviot's presence the painful consciousness that her feelings towards her family would be misunderstood or condemned. Perhaps she was wrong in dwelling on this idea, perhaps he was wrong in the manner that gave rise to it; but so it

166

was, and this difference of feeling, with which their married life had commenced, was every day creating and increasing fresh misunderstandings. Lord Teviot was so distractedly in love with his wife that the greatest devotion on her part would hardly have satisfied him; he had never had brothers or sisters of his own, and had no clue in his own life or feelings that could lead him to judge of the strength of early family affection. Helen was all in all to him, and he expected to be the same to her. She was too young and guileless to affect what she did not feel, and too inexperienced to trace to their right source the variations of Lord Teviot's temper. She had, as we have already seen, begun to fear him before her marriage; and this fear had been increased rather than diminished by his subsequent conduct. She saw that he was courteous and attentive to other women; therefore, the taunts and reproaches which he occasionally vented on her she imputed to dislike, and his want of sympathy in her affection for her family she ascribed to a desire to make her unhappy. She was totally unable to imagine that he could be jealous of sentiments so natural and right in themselves; for Helen was still almost a child, and the obliquities and injustices of strong passions were incomprehensible to her. She would have been surprised if she had known the trifles, the absolute nothings, by which, in the course of every day, she roused or irritated his jealousy—how he brooded over a careless word or a negligent look—how he tortured a kindness to another into an insult to himself, and an enjoyment into which she entered without him into a misery purposely inflicted on him. And numerous as were the little reproachful scenes that passed between them, she would have blessed her good fortune if she had known how many more she had escaped—if she had guessed the long array of her crimes and his wrongs, that he drew up against her, and which were not poured out, because some gentle, careless word of hers changed the current of his thoughts, and turned his rage to love.

He had now come to her with a proposition which, whatever interest it might have in itself, was important to him principally as a trial of his wife's feelings: it was one of those measures by which statesmen say they will stand or fall.

"Helen, I have been all the morning with G., transacting business, as the newspapers would call it. Do you remember Beaufort's prophecy about me?"

"What, that Mr. G. would bring you into office? Is that really settled? I am so glad. And what are you to be?"

"Nothing can be absolutely settled till Parliament meets, when I am probably to succeed Lisle, who takes the Privy Seal; but in the meanwhile, G. has another employment for me—one that I was at first unwilling to undertake. I hardly know what you will say to it."

"I know so little on those subjects, that I am afraid you cannot consult a less good adviser. But tell me what it is."

"He wants to send me off on a special mission to Lisbon." He looked earnestly at her as he spoke, and his heart swelled as he waited for her answer. He was divided between his wish to hear the degree of concern she would express for his departure, and his latent hope that she would insist on accompanying him.

"To Lisbon! Oh, Teviot, what an odious plan! What can make him think of sending you to that hot, dusty place? I do not like it at all. But a special mission entails only a short stay, does it? It is merely going out with a message and coming back again?"

"Something like that; the business may be concluded in a fortnight, or I may be detained there a month, and then the passage to and fro will take perhaps a week each time."

"The passage! Yes, and that dreadful Bay of Biscay

to cross, too. Well, I think it much the worst arrangement that could have been made. And have you actually consented to it?"

"Very nearly. I said I would first consult you; but I do not see how I can well refuse."

"And when are you to go?"

"Immediately; I must be off in less than a week if I am to be of any use. That does not leave much time for preparation." He looked wistfully at her, for her words had been so vague, he was still in doubt as to her intentions.

"No time at all. In every respect it is a bad scheme, except, to be sure, in one point,"—and she brightened as she spoke. "If it is to take place so soon, our company must all leave us directly."

"Of course."

"Well, then, I should be very dull here without you; and I should naturally pass the six weeks of your absence with my own people. Mamma writes me word that Sophia is very unwell and wants to see me; and, indeed, when you came in, I was just on the point of sending for you to ask when we could go to her."

"Go now—this afternoon, if you like. Please yourself."

Helen looked at him, and saw that one of his blackest clouds had come over his countenance. She went on in a hurried voice:

"No, not now; if you are to go so soon, I should like to be with you till the last moment," and she took his hand as she spoke.

"I can go before the end of the week if it will be any convenience to you"; and he coldly withdrew his hand. "I have half a mind to go up to town with Lady Portmore and Miss Forrester the day after to-morrow."

"Mary is going with me to Eskdale—at least, mamma asks her to come."

" Well, then, I shall go with Lady Portmore; she will be the more glad of my company." He got up, and walked moodily up and down the room. " You must have had a wonderful foreknowledge of my prospects, for you seem to have arranged all your plans with the certainty that I should not be here to interfere with them."

" Indeed, I have arranged nothing. I have not even asked Mary if she will go with me; and I never could have guessed or believed that you would go off to Lisbon in this sudden way."

" I have surpassed your fondest expectations, evidently, and given you a most agreeable surprise; but another time you shall have a longer notice of my departure, that you may be able to get up a little show of feeling on the occasion. You know it is usual, it is considered to be really almost indispensable to affect—only to affect—nobody would be so unreasonable as to expect you to feel; but you should affect some slight regret that your husband is going to leave you."

" I need not affect it," she said in a low, broken voice. " I am very sorry you will go."

" How flattering! it is a pity you did not think of mentioning it sooner."

" I did say so," she whispered through her tears. " I told you from the first I disliked your going."

" I had not the good fortune to hear you; you hardly think it worth while to raise your voice upon such an immaterial point as my coming or going. And moreover, I might have thought that you did not approve of the expedition on your own account; not that I did think so for a moment. I am cured of that, but many husbands would have expected that their wives would insist on accompanying them."

" Do you wish me to go with you? " and Helen felt that she ought to have offered to do so. " If you do, I can be ready in time."

" No, no, it is too late. I do not wish you, Lady Teviot, to give yourself any trouble on my account. I am the last person in the world to be gratified by *a sacrifice*. I have known all along, that you did not care for me, that you never have cared for me: and if I had wanted any further proof of the fact, I have been amply furnished with it in this conversation. No protestations, I beg, but leave me the pleasant conviction that in going abroad without you I am for once doing what you like."

" You are unjust, Teviot, you know you are."

" I do *not* know it. I appeal to yourself. Are you not in your inmost soul delighted that I am going? How should it be otherwise? Is there one of the name of Beaufort whom you do not love a thousand times better than me? I might ask, have you ever loved me at all? Why, did I not see you, in this very room, almost go down on your knees to your brother, to persuade him to stay a few more days? and when I tell you I am going away for six weeks, your countenance absolutely brightens; you almost said you were glad of it."

" Not glad that you were going; indeed I am not; but glad that I might go to Sophia without inconvenience to you. Indeed, Teviot, my sister is very ill. If you will read mamma's letter, you will see that I had good reason to be absorbed in that when you came in."

" It is no business of mine, why should I read it? "

" That you may see how ill poor Sophia is."

" I do not want to know anything about it," said Lord Teviot, who had worked himself up into such a rage that he hardly knew what he said. " I scarcely know Lady Sophia; why should I care whether she is ill or well? "

Helen's tears stopped instantly, and she gave him a look of indignation which startled him. It was the first he had ever seen. " Why indeed? No, it was foolish of me to expect you would."

She tore up her mother's letter as she spoke, and then, bending down over her own, employed herself with apparent eagerness in the attempt to finish it; but her hand trembled, and though her face was concealed, her round graceful throat was burning red, and the beatings of her full heart might almost be heard as she leaned against the table. Lord Teviot had done more towards losing his wife's affection by these few words than by all the taunting speeches he had ever addressed to her. Her natural gentleness and sweetness of temper enabled her to bear, with grief indeed, but without resentment, his starts of violence towards herself; but causeless unkindness to her sick sister she could not endure.

The utmost she could do was to keep silence, but perhaps she wished he might repeat his question, "Have you ever loved me?" that she might answer, "If I ever did, I do not now." But he saw he had gone too far, and a long silence ensued; she finished her letter, folded and directed it; still he walked up and down the room. She wished he would go. She wished somebody would come in; she should not have objected to hear that the house was on fire; a slight earthquake would not have been unacceptable, so that this scene might come to an end. At last the bright thought occurred to her of ringing for a lighted taper, and desiring the servant to wait while she sealed her letters; and Lord Teviot, who was by this time as eager for a finale as she was, took that opportunity to withdraw, merely saying, "Well, I shall tell G. I accept, and shall name Tuesday as *my* day."

"As you please," she answered, without looking at him; and he departed. The servant followed with the letters, and Helen threw herself back on the sofa, and gave herself up to melancholy and a bad headache.

At dressing-time she was obliged to account for her wan appearance to Mrs. Tomkinson, who was afraid her ladyship was not well, she looked " so bad."

" I am very uneasy about Lady Sophia, who is ill."

" Dear me! I am so sorry: I hope her ladyship is not dangerous."

" Not dangerously ill, you mean. No, I trust not, but I am very anxious to see her, and I shall go and meet her at Eskdale on Tuesday, so you must have everything ready for that morning."

" Yes, my lady; does my lord go with us?" This was asked in a stiff, affronted tone. " Mr. Phillips was speaking at the tea of my lord's being going to London on Tuesday, but I suppose he meant Eskdale Castle."

" No, my lord has business in London. Give me my gloves and some Eau de Cologne, my head aches so much."

" I wish your ladyship would let me bring you some dinner up here, and keep quiet against the evening. Them lights and all that clatter will be so bad for your head: just lie down for an hour, my lady."

" Well, perhaps it will be the best thing I can do."

" There's my lord's room door just gone to. Shall I call his lordship, and you tell him, my lady, that you don't feel well?"

" No, no, don't call him. There is no use in making a fuss about a headache. My handkerchief, Tomkinson, I will go down "; and she went.

" Well, if my lord has not turned out a brute at last, I'm much mistaken, and that is what I never was yet. I wish we'd never seen him; and to think of him, indeed, lording it over my lady, who is too good by half for him. See if I don't tell them all at Eskdale what he is; and yet I won't neither, for Lady Walden's maid is always casting up to me how happy her lord and lady is. And as for letting her have a triumph, I am not so mean as that neither. As for Lady Sophia's illness, I don't think much of that. She was always a one for making much of a little, and I think my lady's headache is all my lord's monstrous crossness. However, I shall put up my lady's very best gowns, just to make them think we are very happy. My lord *is* rich, that nobody can deny "; and with this consolation Mrs. Tomkinson descended to the housekeeper's room.

CHAPTER XXX

WHEN the party were assembled for dinner, Lord Teviot's appointment and consequent departure for Lisbon seemed to be generally known; indeed, so generally, that even Fisherwick ventured to make some dark allusions to it. Mr. G. asked Lady Teviot to thank him for sending her lord on such an interesting little expedition, and by not finding out her headache, nor appearing to think she could be out of spirits, did more for her recovery than Lady Portmore with all her condolences. *She* was in her greatest glory, and unusually overpowering. She had been fully occupied during dinner by admiration of her own propriety in not allowing Teviot a place in her carriage for the journey to London, which was, she said, a very different thing from going out with him in the phaeton at St. Mary's; and also by giving him instructions for his conduct at Lisbon; and her opinion of the state of parties there. Her advice was excellent after she had been rescued from a general confusion of Spain and Portugal, and from a particular predilection for the anti-English party at Lisbon, which she said was a mistake she had been led into by having lately talked over the subject with an Opposition member; but otherwise, she added, she knew more of Lisbon than anybody, and she had really half a mind to make Portmore run over there in his yacht, that she might assist Lord Teviot in doing the honours.

"Yes, pray do," he said, in hopes that Helen might hear; "you cannot have a pleasanter trip, and it will give me a brilliant start in my diplomatic career."

175

" Well, then, let us make a party. Ernest, will you go to Lisbon while Teviot is there? Portmore and I are going over in our yacht, and we will take you if you like to go."

" Not I; what! go tossing about the Bay of Biscay in October in that cockle-shell! I think I see myself. No, thank you; besides, my noble soul scorns the thought of being merely one of Teviot's suite."

" Ver good," said La Grange, " but more bitter than sweet. There, I have make one pon. I say, Lady Portmore, the colonel is more bitter than sweet; that is two pons."

" I doubt, M. la Grange, whether you understand the colonel better than I understand puns. I think that man much too detestable," said Lady Portmore to Lord Teviot, " and I see clearly I am in a sad scrape with Ernest. The truth is, I have neglected him rather shamefully, considering that he came here purposely to meet me; but he will soon come into good humour again. Beaufort, will you join our party?"

" I object to that," said Helen, looking up with sudden animation. " Beaufort is going *home* with me."

That one word was enough to explain to the refined ears of most of her hearers how matters stood between the husband and wife. It was discord to Lord Teviot, grief to Lord Beaufort and Mary, but music to Colonel Stuart, who was seated by Helen, and at that moment thought " My time is come."

" I fear Lady Sophia's health must make it necessarily only a family party at Eskdale," he said in his softest tones, " or I would accept an invitation your father was so good as to give me. I have been almost afraid to ask what your account was this afternoon?"

" Not good, certainly; but perhaps I see things *en noir* to-day. At all events, the less we talk about it the better; but you would do wisely, Colonel Stuart, to put off your visit to Eskdale till it would be a less dull one."

"It never could be dull; but whether it ever would be a wise measure, is more than I can say." His looks were intended to explain his oracular words, but Helen was too innocent to understand them. She had yet to learn that the first moment in which a woman lets it appear that she and her husband are at variance is the last in which she is safe from the impertinent admiration of others; and Colonel Stuart's looks and words were alike thrown away. Her mind was full of her own unparalleled griefs and wrongs. She was not sure she had been right in saying what she knew would vex Lord Teviot; but she felt rather the better for it too, and she was enabled to get through the remaining time at dinner without bursting into tears.

The conversation, in defiance of Mr. G.'s attempts to give it another turn, would revert to Lisbon. Fisherwick shrugged and signalled and whispered to La Grange, "I wish they would be a little more prudent before the servants. I see he is quite distressed. The Opposition papers will get hold of Lord Teviot's appointment before we gazette him, and there will be the deuce to pay with them."

"Are the journals so much dear to pay?" said La Grange, who hoped he had opened a new vein of information. Do you pay them yourself?"

"Pay them!" repeated Fisherwick. "My dear sir, do you really suppose we should deign to buy off any of those vile, libellous publications? What do we care for them? The papers that have any circulation are not to be bought, and as for the Opposition trash, it is not worth buying."

"I admire your papers beyond all that I see in England. We think much in our country of your liberty of the Press; but it far pass my hopes. It is the greatest of benefits to a stranger: it let him at once into secrets of society. You can tell to me, Fisherwick, if it be true what they do say, that Mr. G. have made these changes in

M

your trade-laws because his brother, who do own many vessels, will find it for his good."

"Is it possible, my dear sir," gasped Fisherwick, "that you can read and believe such detestable lies as are published in that infamous paper? not that I ever look at it, but he told me of that paragraph. He is magnanimous on those points to a degree of which I can give you no idea; but if anybody can really believe such libels—I must have these fellows pulled up."

"Ah! ah! you are angry, my dear Fisherwick. What! Mr. G. do then have a brother with shipping?"

"I angry!" said Fisherwick, puffing like an irate grampus; "if we official men were put out by such palpable calumnies as these, a blessed time we should have of it."

"But he have a brother which trades," pursued La Grange, shouting with delight as he felt he was driving Fisherwick to earth.

"He has three brothers, men of very distinguished ability and large fortune." This was enunciated with much majesty.

"And one in trade; ha, I have found you out; my paper did tell the trute."

Fisherwick turned from him in disgust, and had in consequence to endure a slap on the shoulder, and another triumphant laugh, as La Grange continued to repeat, "Found out."

After the ladies went to the drawing-room, Helen had Lady Portmore's high spirits and oppressive pity to bear; but much to her surprise was defended and protected by Mrs. Douglas, who sympathized with her headache, promoted her quiet, and snubbed Lady Portmore with great success.

Eliza was unfeignedly low at her own prospects; she thought she had only one more day of perfect happiness to come, and then there would be an end of refinement and Colonel Beaufort, and the reign of the Birketts and Thompsons would recommence; and she owned to herself that her tastes were sadly altered, and that she should like to live always in such society as she had met during the last few weeks.

When the gentlemen came in, the gaiety of the evening did not increase. Lady Portmore tried to get up a reconciliation with Ernest, who strenuously denied the existence of any quarrel. She begged his pardon for what she had said at dinner, and he declared he did not recollect what it was; and she ended by assuring him he was a strange creature, but that she saw that he was piqued, and felt sure that one day or other he would do her greater justice. Mr. G. and Fisherwick, who were to start at break of day, took leave overnight—Fisherwick hoping it might not be very cold in the morning, and Mr. G. with some suspicion that he had disturbed the peace of the Teviot *ménage*; but still he felt in his ambitious soul, " They would at all events have been tired of each other in six months, and perhaps then I could not have given Teviot such a good appointment." La Grange made his farewell speech, and announced that he was desolated to go, but that their excellent neighbour, Mrs. Dowbiggin, that charming woman, had done him the honour to invite him for a few days to N——, where he meant to initiate himself into all the details of trade and commerce. Lord and Lady Middlesex and various minor members of the society departed; and under these afflicting circumstances, the melancholy of the hostess and the forced gaiety of the host did them the highest credit. It gave them the amiable appearance of being actually sorry to lose their friends; and several of the party went away declaring, in the innocence of their hearts, that they should never forget the genuine grief with which their departure had affected those amiable Teviots.

CHAPTER XXXI

But Mrs. Douglas could not be so deceived. She could not allow such a promising bud of unhappiness to wither without, as Othello says, " smelling it on the tree." She was willing to prevent Lady Portmore from persecuting Helen; but she could not consent to deprive herself of the pleasure of pointing out the shadows of the Teviot picture.

" Well, Mr. Douglas!" she said, as soon as they were alone, " well!"

" Well, my dear; what now?"

" Why, what do you think of it all?"

" All what, my dear?"

" You know very well what I mean, love, only you don't choose to speak."

" I am quite ready to speak, Anne; but what is it to be about?"

" About this evening, to be sure. What did you think of it?"

" Between ourselves, I thought it not quite so pleasant as most of the evenings we have passed here. It was rather dull, was it not?"

" Now, Mr. Douglas, don't be tiresome, you are only affecting ignorance; pray what do you think of the Teviots now?"

" Very much what I always did; that they are very charming people, and keep a very pleasant house, and I am sorry to leave them."

" And you think they are a happy couple?"

" Very—not to-day, by the by, for he is going away for

a few weeks, which annoys her. I do not know whether you heard him say at dinner that he was to be sent on a special mission to Lisbon; and it strikes me that Lady Teviot was perhaps a little low at his going without her, which would account for the evening being dull. I have not an idea how those Portuguese and Spanish affairs are to end."

" Now, my dear Mr. Douglas, don't go off on those tiresome foreign affairs. What can it signify which conquers which, or who dethrones who, at that distance? Let them fight it out quietly. Besides, you need not pretend to understand national feuds if you have not found out what is passing under your eyes; but I cannot believe it, you must see what an unhappy couple these poor Teviots are."

" Unhappy, Anne, the Teviots! "

" Yes, by far the most unhappy young couple I know. In fact, I have been trying to recollect, but I cannot recall any instance of two young people separating so early in their married life."

" But, my dear Anne, you surely cannot twist this into a separation—an official trip, which is to last six weeks at the outside."

" As if the merest child could be taken in by that! I said from the first, Mr. Douglas, that Lord Teviot had a horrid temper, and that Helen did not care a straw for him; but Lady Eskdale was, I suppose, determined to catch a great *parti*, and now see what it has come to! There is he going off with a married woman, one of the most unprincipled people I ever encountered, and excessively old-looking; and there is Helen going back to her friends, quite broken-hearted. I declare I think it is very shocking, and that Lady Eskdale has a great deal to answer for. Then there is Sophia dying, by all accounts. I fancy they have wretched constitutions, though they look well for a time; but I will answer for it that all those Beauforts, before they are thirty, will have outlived their looks completely, and Helen is just the sort of person to fret herself into a decline."

" My dear, how you do run on, conjuring up one chance of unhappiness after another! and I cannot believe there is any foundation for any of them."

" No, because you do not choose to believe, Mr. Douglas; but I thought that even you must have observed Lord Teviot's guilty look when Helen said she was going home. You must have remarked that; and then that wicked Lady Portmore proposing, actually proposing to follow him in her yacht. I was quite annoyed that Eliza should hear such improper conversation. However, my belief is that she and Lord Teviot will go no further than London, and the Lisbon journey will be given up, now that, under pretence of it, he has got rid of his wife."

" I cannot think all this can be so, Anne; it is too bad to be true."

" Nothing is too bad to be true, Mr Douglas, and nothing is true that is not bad. Those are two axioms I never can persuade you to remember; and I am certain that we do not give that fine set credit for half the vices they practise. We may good-naturedly try to gloss over this Teviot story " (Mr. Douglas looked up, and shook his head); " but just consider what you would have said if the same circumstances had occurred in a lower rank of life. Why, when James Wheeler went off to America, and Sally Wheeler came home to her mother, what a fuss you and the churchwardens and the vestry made! and James only forsook his own wife, he did not carry off another person's."

" Neither will Lord Teviot. I must say, Anne, you have no right to put together such histories; still less to spread such reports. It is most ungrateful," he added, in an accent of deep displeasure, " after the kindness the Teviots have shown us; and if there be any foundation for your suppositions, it would certainly be becoming, and I should hope natural, that you would act by that young creature as you would wish her mother to act by one of your daughters in similar circumstances. You might have helped her with advice, if the circumstances you state are true. Lady Eskdale would have acted a kinder part by you, Anne."

Mr. Douglas was so seldom roused to anger that a lecture from him had a startling effect on his wife; and her conscience, moreover, rather reproached her on Helen's account; so she assured Mr. Douglas that her observations had been confided solely to him, and should go no further, and that if she saw any chance of being of use to Helen the next day, she would do what she could; but as for not thinking ill of Lord Teviot and Lady Portmore and Colonel Stuart, and indeed of most people, she really could not oblige him by going so far as that. It was a concession he did not appear to expect, so they ended very amicably.

CHAPTER XXXII

Not a word passed during the Monday between the Teviots, except on the most ordinary subjects. Helen hoped they were not to part on such bad terms, and wondered whether they were to write to each other. She would have been glad to forgive and forget his unkindness about her sister if he had wished it, and altogether was decidedly in favour of gliding back to peace and amity without explanation. But he did not take by any means this commonplace view of the subject: sometimes he had a glimmering idea that he might have been the aggressor in their quarrels; but that was only a momentary delusion. In general he saw clearly that he was the most unfortunate being on earth; that his wife hated him; that her family were his bitterest enemies; that he was driven from home by the unparalleled unhappiness of his daily life; and that this was the more provoking, because he happened to be a model husband, and certainly had loved Helen, though her marked preference of every living creature, from her father to her lap-dog, made it justifiable, indeed incumbent on him to give up caring about her. So much for his domestic life. As for his future prospects, they were of the gloomiest description. He knew many people thought his position enviable, and, indeed, there might be an appearance of prosperity in his lot. And he happened to have naturally the most marked and decided dispositions for enjoyment : he claimed no merit on that score, they were born with him; but Helen had blasted all this. It was entirely her doing. If she had shown one spark of affection for him, he should have stayed at home, the happiest of men; as it was, he was absolutely driven into exile. It was all very well to call it a mission, he called it banishment. As for coming back in six weeks, it was much more likely that he should not come back at all: he should certainly go on to Greece or Egypt. Timbuctoo seemed to be an interesting place; he should rather like to go there, just to see if Helen would think it worth while to be surprised. As for their ever being reconciled, that was out of the question; in fact, there was no quarrel; they were merely two people who did not suit each other, and so would be happier apart; and this being settled, he did the most unwise thing he could do. He sought out Lady Portmore, and made her the confidante of his fancied griefs. This was an attention that charmed her. She pitied him, told him that she had always dreaded his discovering what she had seen from the first, and had been kindly hinting to him ever since, that Helen did not care for him, and was not suited to him.

" She is your wife, my dear Teviot, so I have no right to speak; but from my heart I pity you. You require a wife who can understand your great qualities. You know I never flatter you, but there is really hardly a man of your standing who can be compared to you in talent, agreeableness, in everything that promises distinction; and then to see Helen so blind to all this; it is provoking; and I am foolishly warm where my friends are concerned. My advice to you is to go; absence may do much. She will miss you, miss the importance of her present position, for she prizes that; and perhaps she will grow wiser as she grows older. And in the meanwhile, my dear Teviot, trust to me for entering thoroughly into your interests. I ought not to say it, above all to you, but I know what it is to be linked to a being utterly incapable of entering into one's feelings. To no one but you could I trust myself on this point; but you know what Lord Portmore is "; and thereupon Lady Portmore launched into a sea of all poor Lord Portmore's little stupidities, with which every one of her male friends were indulged in their turn, and which at this moment interested Teviot, as he wanted to find out that all the world were as unhappy as himself.

Lady Portmore succeeded in hardening his heart against Helen, and the day—their last day—drew to a close without a word of kindness, regret, or reconciliation. Late in the evening, Helen, driven into action by desperation, went up to her husband and Lady Portmore, who were seated in earnest conversation, and, sitting down by them, asked Lady Portmore if she meant to go early the next morning; and then, turning to Lord Teviot, asked him the same question. On his reply in the affirmative, she said kindly, " Then can I speak to you for five minutes now, as you may not have time in the morning to give me your last orders? "

" I shall leave written directions about my letters, and Griffiths knows all that is to be done here."

" There is nothing like written directions to prevent mistakes," said Lady Portmore; " I always leave a positive book with my porter. But to return to this courier I want you to take—" and they resumed their conversation.

Helen looked disappointed, but retained her seat. Mary Forrester had watched her from the work-table at which she was sitting, and saw she was in need of assistance. She glanced round, but had not the heart to disturb Ernest and Eliza, who were also taking their last talk. These finales to a large party are full of sentiment and deep pathos. Mary had only one resource, as she did not choose to take Colonel Stuart into her counsels on this or any other subject; so she walked boldly up to Lord Beaufort, who was writing letters at the end of the room, and said, " Cannot you show Lady Portmore *now* the print you mentioned? "

She directed his eyes to the group in the distance, and added, " She is very much in your sister's way."

Lord Beaufort wanted no further explanation. He was as anxious as Miss Forrester could be that Lord and Lady Teviot should come to some explanation before they parted, for their estrangement was palpable to all eyes; so he immediately went to Lady Portmore and, offering her his arm, said, " Come, I am going to carry you off forcibly; you must not leave St. Mary's without seeing this picture, which I think has a great look of you."   She could not resist this piece of flattery, and went with him.   Lord Teviot rose to follow them, but Helen laid her hand on his arm, and said, " No, you cannot refuse me a few minutes on this our last evening."

" I am at your orders," he said coldly.

" Teviot, we surely are not to part on these terms.   Do not go without a kind word or look—I cannot bear it."

" I beg your pardon, I do not think I quite understand your grievance.   There was no necessity for our parting at all; but you decided that we should, and I can imagine no two people less called upon to affect any grief on that score.   Can I do anything for you in London? "

She turned very pale, and said, " Let me go with you that far, even if you will not let me go to Lisbon."

" Thank you, no; I shall be very much hurried, and you, you know, are going *home*."

" I was wrong when I said that—I knew it at the time; but I was hurt by what you and Lady Portmore said, and I spoke in anger.   Teviot, my home is with you."

" I fear it has not been a happy one, but all that is over now; discussions can do no good.   I have no doubt you will be very happy when you are with those you love, and as for me, allow me to take care of myself.   Any life that I make out for myself will be better than that I have led lately. Have you anything more to say? "

There was no answer; she attempted to rise, but sank back, and faintly murmured—" Nothing."

He looked at her for the first time, and was shocked at her ghastly appearance and fixed look of suffering. " Are you ill, Helen? " he said.

" Do not speak to me, I cannot bear any more cruel words. I must go to my own room, I cannot stay here with all these people looking on. Let me go——" and again she tried to rise.

" But you must let me assist you: take my arm, Helen."

" No, no; I must be alone."

" You shall be alone, but you cannot go by yourself, Helen. I will leave you when I have seen you safe to your room."

She had not energy to dispute the point: all she felt was a strong desire to be alone, and a certainty that she could not reach her room without assistance. He led her to it, supporting her trembling steps in silence. She disengaged her arm, and, waving her hand to him to leave her, rushed towards the ottoman, and, flinging herself on it, burst into a flood of tears. She sobbed like a child, and with the young passionate resentment of a child whose attempt to " make it up and be friends " has been misrepresented and repulsed. And as no resentment in her own heart was sufficiently powerful to give her any insight into the latent motives of Lord Teviot's violence, terror and helplessness were the chief consequences produced by his inexplicable language, accompanied by a sense of suffering under extreme injustice.

The relief of tears she had never before in her short, sunny life experienced to this extreme degree. She absolutely revelled in them, ignorant that her husband was a witness to her grief, till the sight of her sorrow overpowered him; and as he flung himself down by her side she heard him beseeching her to be calm and to forgive him, and to forget what he had said. " Say you forgive me, my poor Helen; I cannot bear to see you cry, and to feel that I have made you so unhappy. I am a violent, unfeeling wretch, and I know that I say a thousand things that I do not mean when I am angry: " and then followed all those inarticulate soothings and caresses which are so efficacious and healing after a quarrel. Then he persuaded her to look at him, and to see how sorry he was; and he brought a glass of water, and supported her while she drank it. And though they both abstained from any allusion to the original cause of their disagreement,—perhaps neither of them knew exactly what it was,—there was much concession on his part, and she had the comfort of thinking that they would now part on friendly terms. He advised her not to return to the drawing-room that evening, and tried in every way to quiet her shaken nerves. He told her St. Mary's would always be kept in readiness for her, and that Teviot House should be prepared for her in case she wished to be in London; and that he hoped she would at all events meet him there on his return. He gave the most minute direc- tions with respect to her letters, and begged her to write constantly; " and you will be sure to give me a particular account of Sophia," he added in a tone of deep humility.

" Thank you," she said dejectedly, " you are very good." She thought he was speaking only with the view of quieting her, and not from his heart. The tears still strayed slowly down her cheeks, and she looked so pale that at last Lord Teviot bethought himself of ringing for Tomkinson, and of putting the case into her hands. It was a charming spectacle for her, and quite overthrew her system of " my lord's good-for-nothingness."

" You never saw such a flustration as my lord was in," she afterwards told Mrs. Nelson, " just because her ladyship took on so, and got a little nervous on account of his lordship being obliged to go on that Portugee business; and he called

to me quite sharp for the sal-volatile, and my keys were
mislaid somehow—that always is the way with keys when
they are wanted; and there was my lord holding my lady's
hands and kissing them, which was distressing for me; but
I did not look that way much.   Indeed, I was rummaging
for those keys, and when I brought the sal-volatile my lord
gave it to her hisself, and my lord and me agreed that the
best thing for me to do was to get her ladyship to bed; and
my lord said, ' You had better stay by her, Mrs. Tomkins.'
To be sure it is very strange he cannot learn my name; but
anyhow I am satisfied about him and my lady, and I
suppose he will find out I am called Tomkinson at last, and
then everything will be as it should," which was a cheerful
prospect to end with.

CHAPTER XXXIII

THERE was a succession of hurried breakfasts the next morning, and of partings more or less painful. Lady Portmore went off first, comforting the friends she left by assurances that her visit had been very pleasant, and delicately affirming to the Douglas family that they would not find her one of those odious fine ladies who would cut them if ever they came to town, which last touch of grandeur made Mrs. Douglas remarkably angry. Colonel Beaufort, after ordering horses to take him the first stage to his own house in Lincolnshire, suddenly decided it would be less trouble to go to town with Lord Teviot. Miss Forrester had hesitated about accepting Lady Eskdale's invitation, as she thought she should be in the way till the family were more at ease about Lady Sophia, and to her great surprise found herself pressed by Mrs. Douglas to come and stay at Thornbank till she should like to remove to the castle.

" I really was obliged to ask her," Mrs. Douglas said; " though what she will do with herself I have not a guess. It is all Eliza's doing. She has taken one of those *engouements* for Miss Forrester which my girls set up all of a sudden. I cannot think where they learnt it. Not from me : I never took a fancy to anybody in my life. If people have any striking qualities, they are generally bad ones. However, Miss Forrester is less disagreeable than most of her set ; and the instant I saw *that* Lady Portmore making difficulties about taking her home again, I determined to be as civil to her as possible. Besides, poor thing! I should pity her if she had to go through all the fuss that Lady Eskdale will make about Lady Sophia. We shall hear enough of it at Thornbank, though I shall keep out of the way; and Miss Forrester is welcome to take shelter there till the great storm blows over."

Mary hoped that Lord Beaufort's stay at home would not be long, as in her own mind she had decided on postponing her visit to Eskdale till his was concluded; and, in the meantime, she was glad to be in Helen's neighbourhood: so she and the Douglases took their departure together. Eliza was desperately low, and looked back at St. Mary's as at a lost heaven; and after the tall column on the top of the hill had disappeared, the remainder of the journey seemed to her to be through a dreary flat, and she could not understand what Miss Forrester meant by thinking the country pretty. However, she found some consolation in the idea of the endless talks she could have with Sarah, and in the unacknowledged expectation that Colonel Beaufort must come at last to see his relations. At all events, there were others of his name in the neighbourhood; she might hear them mention him: in short, black as were her prospects, there were still gleams of light, and, to end where she began, she should tell Sarah all about it.

Poor girl! little did she think that while she sat quietly in the carriage, pondering over Colonel Beaufort's tritest remarks, hoarding up as most important recollections that he liked reading the newspaper, and did not care about poetry; that he thought London the best place to live in; and that his watch cost ninety guineas: little did she know that the ungrateful creature had dismissed from his mind all the conversations that had ever passed between them, and was given up to discussions on foreign politics with Lord Teviot, and half disposed to go abroad himself for a few years; and that she was merely to him a good-humoured little Miss Something whom he had met at St. Mary's. Shocking discrepancy! but so it will be, when young, ignorant girls fall in love as, I grieve to say, they often do with *blasés* men of the world. However, give them time and opportunity, and there is no saying whether the warm heart will not soften and conquer the hard one at last.

Lord and Lady Teviot parted in the most edifying manner. He handed her into the carriage, arranged her cloak round her, and insisted, in the hearing of Mrs. Tomkinson and the servants, on her writing to him by the first post, and then walked round the britzska to see that the apron was properly buttoned, and that Helen had shawls enough. This was all for the public: their private farewells had been perfectly amicable, though his misgivings had revived as her hysterics had subsided; but Helen was satisfied. She had her brother by her side, and Eskdale in prospect; the knowledge that she and her husband were on good terms now, and that he would have no opportunity for being angry with her again. So she was happy, and it was fortunate he did not know it.

CHAPTER XXXIV

THE respectable Douglas coach drove to the door at Thornbank. Mr. Douglas threw a paternal look at his sheep, who were tinkling their tiresome little bells and eating their rich grass in front of the house, and began to think St. Mary's was not such a very fine place after all, and that Thornbank had its attractions. Mrs. Douglas watched Miss Forrester, to see whether she turned contemptuous at the sight of a commonplace, moderate-sized home; and Eliza was eager for the first sight of Sarah. She was at the door, looking eager and happy in an unusual degree; and the next minute the important fact of Mr. Wentworth's proposal was made known to all the family; and in half an hour Eliza and Sarah were established in their own little room, perched on two hard cane chairs, with their shawls on to atone for the want of a fire, both talking at once, both listening, and both happy; but Sarah was the happiest, for though Eliza's gaieties had been the most brilliant, they were evanescent and fruitless, whereas Sarah was convinced that she had secured for life a comfortable little allotment of perfect bliss.

" Tell me more, Sarah; tell me exactly what he said."

" No, I can't indeed, Eliza; it seems so foolish to repeat those sort of things."

" Oh! not to me, your own sister. You really must, for I never have heard a real, live proposal, and I am so curious to know what they say. Just begin where you left off in your last letter, after he went over to my aunt's.

I suppose you were very anxious to know if he would call again? "

" Of course I was. I thought of nothing else; and yet I was sure he would, because he had said it. I do think, Eliza, he is the best man I ever heard of. Well, and so we went to church in the morning, and Mr. Briggs preached about taking no thought for the morrow. I am sure it was lucky he said nothing against taking thought for the day, for I could not help wondering if Mr. Wentworth would call; and while we were at luncheon there was a ring at the bell, and I felt myself colouring up, and who should come in but that horrid Ape Brown."

" No, really, did he? By the by, Sarah, he is not the least like Colonel Beaufort."

" No; I know," said Sarah, laughing. " I thought that likeness would soon wear off. Well, I began to give it up, when there was another ring, and this time it was all right. I saw my aunt give my uncle a look, and my uncle was so civil to Mr. Wentworth; and after luncheon we went out walking, and that dreadful Ape Brown came and offered me his arm."

" His paw you mean."

" Well, his paw; but my aunt called him off, and Mr. Wentworth instantly came, and said, ' I thought Mr. Brown was going to usurp my place,' which was so nice of him; and then, as I tell you, he proposed to me, and it was all settled."

" Oh! but, Sarah, that is not what he said; you must tell me."

" No, no, not now; besides, it is so cold sitting here, is not it? "

" No, not very, though I always had a fire in my room at St. Mary's. When you are Mrs. Wentworth, Sarah, you will have a fire in your dressing-room; and I think two arm-chairs would be a great improvement, don't you, on these uncomfortable articles? "

" So they would. You must come and see me constantly, Eliza. Mr. Wentworth says Broom House is very ugly, but I dare say I shall think it pretty. I like a flat place."

" So do I. Colonel Beaufort says his place in Lincoln-shire is about as cheerful as the Millbank Penitentiary, only without the river, and not so well built; but I am sure I should not dislike any place that belonged to a person I liked."

" How droll it will be when I have a house of my own, and order dinner, and keep accounts, like mamma! Mr. Wentworth is very particular about his dinner; and I have found out another of his tastes, Eliza, one which will make you angry."

" What is it, Sarah?—that he does not like people in the army? "

" No, not so bad as that; but he dislikes pink; so I shall not have any pink gowns in my trousseau. He will be here to-morrow. Eliza, I rather wish that Miss Forrester had not come just now, don't you? "

" I am not sure; I think you will like her; and then she will walk with me when you and Mr. Wentworth go out together; and she can give you the best advice about your trousseau. Colonel Beaufort says nobody dresses so well as she does."

" Oh, Eliza! I wish you were as happy as I am; but you will be soon. I feel sure Colonel Beaufort will come to Eskdale, and ride over here to luncheon, just as Mr. Wentworth did; and now I must go to mamma. To be sure, it is very lucky Mr. Wentworth happens to be perfect, because if he had had any faults, mamma is so clever, I think she would have found them out."

Sarah, happily, did not perceive that Mr. Wentworth's security was in his position, not in his perfectibility. Mrs. Douglas was too much charmed with the simple fact of a son-in-law to think of being censorious; but had he rashly engaged himself to a young lady who was not her daughter, she would have pointed out with the nicest discrimination that he was a very commonplace Mr. Wentworth indeed— fond of his dinner, inclining to fat and sleep, and drab- coloured in look, coat, and ideas. There was what artists would call a good deal of neutral tint in his composition; but he was well-principled, good-natured, reasonably wealthy, and attached to Sarah, so, as times go, she had reason to be thankful. It is well to lay hold of the excep- tion, when the rule generally is, that the men who may marry our daughters are neither good, rich, nor attached to anything but themselves.

Miss Forrester was vexed that her first visit should have taken place at such an inopportune time; but the interest she expressed in Sarah's happiness, and the kindness with which she entered into all the little arrangements of the family, made her of importance to them all, and at the end of the second day she found herself quite at home, and consulted by Mr. Wentworth about jewellery, by Sarah about dress, and by Mrs. Douglas on the difficult dilemma of the young couple being allowed to walk about without a chaperon. She had seen so many weddings that her opinion about the breakfast, the bridesmaids, etc. was considered valuable; and altogether Mrs. Douglas was in reality pleased with her guest, though it would have made a sad break in her habits to acknowledge it.

Lady Sophia's illness had proved to be measles; and though she was nearly well again, it had not hitherto been considered prudent to call at the Castle; but at last Mrs. Douglas thought the visit must be paid.

"I suppose, Miss Forrester, you would like to drive over to Eskdale Castle to-day? Mrs. Birkett tells me all fear of infection is over, but that Lady Sophia looks very ill; so I should like to see her."

"Because she looks ill?" asked Mr. Douglas. His wife

did not deign to answer this, and went on as if she had not heard it. "She is always full of fancies about her health, so a real, tangible illness must have delighted her. But we ought to make our due inquiries, and I suppose I ought to announce Sarah's marriage in form; not that Lady Eskdale will care about it. However, it must be done; so we may as well get it over to-day."

"The Waldens are there too, I believe," said Miss Forrester.

"That is rather against us; the whole family in full force, and the organ of Eskdaleism is by no means strongly developed in me; but if there is one of them I should find it more impossible to like than another, it is Lady Sophia. Now, Mr. Douglas, you are always saying I am censorious, but I appeal to you if Lady Sophia is not the most disagreeable young woman you ever met with?"

"Not quite that, Anne; but she is not so charming as the other two: a little spoiled and fanciful, and she snubs Waldegrave; but then he likes it, and she will grow wiser as she grows older."

"It is some time since Lady Sophia has done growing," said Mrs. Douglas. "We will go at three, my dear, if you please."

"And will you try and find out if they are expecting any company at Eskdale?" whispered Eliza to Miss Forrester, as they set off.

They found some of the family at home—Lady Eskdale sitting with Lady Walden, who had added a baby to the family—thereby giving Mrs. Douglas a third generation on which to vent her spleen; but, like most hard women, she had a weakness for babies, and was softened by the sight of it, though she did not "see why it was necessary to make such a fuss about a long roll of cambric, like a white bottle, with a little red head for a stopper." But the intelligence of Sarah's marriage was received with all the good-natured interest that Lady Eskdale took in the happiness of others; besides, it was a piece of county news, and that is always welcome in the country; and Mrs. Douglas had the pride of hearing it retailed three several times—to Lord Eskdale, Lady Teviot, and the Waldegraves, who all dropped in in the course of her visit.

"I am so tired!" said Lady Sophia, throwing herself on the sofa; "it is most oppressive weather for the time of year, or else one of my bad attacks in the head is coming on."

"Do you suffer much from headache now, Lady Sophia?"

"More than ever; that is, not from absolute headache, but from very peculiar feelings in my head. The measles may have made me worse just now; but that I have a tendency to apoplexy I am quite convinced; and if you look at me, Miss Forrester, you will see I have no strength for remedies."

"You do not look thin, Lady Sophia."

"That is fullness, not fat."

"And you have plenty of colour."

"That is determination of blood to the head: I have felt it the last two days. Dear William, please to put that ivory knife down; you twist it about till you will certainly bring on one of my fits of giddiness."

"I beg your pardon, my love; I dare say it is a tiresome trick of mine. Had you not better come out into the open air a little, dearest?"

"No, I thank you," she said, in a resigned tone. "It is kind of you to suggest it, dear Willy; but unless it would give you any pleasure I had rather not catch a bad cold in addition to my other ailments. Do you find the air of this county agree with you, Miss Forrester?"

"Any air agrees with me," said Mary; "I am never ill."

" I wish you could persuade Sophia not to think herself ill," said Sir William; " indeed, nobody but herself does think so."

Lady Sophia gave a smile of resignation as if forgiving him for insulting her dying agonies, but added, in the most caressing tone, " Poor dear Willy, I wish I had better health for your sake. Do open the window, dear, I feel faint."

" Were not you rather surprised, Lady Eskdale," said Mrs. Douglas, " to find Lady Teviot returning to you so soon? it must seem as if she had never left you. It is really a consolation to know that we mothers are not to lose our children by their marrying: not that I expect my Sarah will ever come to Thornbank without Mr. Wentworth."

" No, I would advise you to keep him out of political life; it is a complete knock-up to all comfort. I had set my heart on having dear Teviot here for a comfortable long visit, as we had been hurried away from St. Mary's; but it was very nice of him to let Helen come."

" I saw in the papers that Lord Teviot was detained in town, and had been dining at Lord Portmore's."

" Yes, but we have had letters from him at Lisbon; and it was fortunate for Teviot in the meantime that the Portmores were detained in town, as theirs is almost the only house open just now."

" I own I should not think it good fortune to be thrown into Lady Portmore's society anywhere or anyhow," said Mrs. Douglas, sharply; " I dislike her extremely."

" Oh, poor thing! some people do not take to her; but she is rather a favourite with most of my family: my son and my nephew both like her."

" So she gave me to understand," said Mrs. Douglas, so drily that there was a pause.

" Are you counting your features, love? " said Lady

Sophia, as Sir William passed his hand over his face. " I hope they are all safe "; and to the astonishment of Mrs. Douglas, who had hoped to see a little domestic quarrel, he burst into a genuine laugh, and seemed flattered by his wife's flippancy, and assured her that he was happy to say they were all right.

Soon after this Mrs. Douglas concluded her visit, and no sooner was the door closed than Lady Sophia jumped up from her sofa with a laugh, and said, " There! I have done it handsomely. I hear Mrs. Douglas says I am full of fancies, and worry Willy's heart out; so I have done my little possible to save her from the sin of spreading false reports. Mind, Willy, I do not give up the fact of my bad health, but I do not worry your heart out, do I? "

" No, my dear; on the contrary, you amuse me to the greatest degree by your good spirits, which I look upon as a proof of your excellent health, and by all your little fancied ailments; and upon the whole I should be sorry if you gave up this delusion. It makes you very diverting; so come and take a walk."

" It is very bad for me to go out in the east wind," she said, but smiled and put on her bonnet, Sir William wrapping her shawl carefully around her.

CHAPTER XXXV

Yes, Helen had returned again to her home. Again she was with those dear ones who had never looked at her but with admiration, and never spoken to her but with tenderness—again with those who had encircled her youthful days with blessings and love, and whom she had yearned to see with the deep longing of young affection. But she was not so happy when restored to them—at least, not quite so happy—as she had expected to be: there was a doubt whether she had done what was right; there was a slight feeling of mortification when she compared her sisters with herself, and saw *their* husbands treated as sons of the house, while she had returned unaccompanied by hers. She felt discontented with her own loneliness as she saw their fullness of companionship. The harsh words that used to terrify her were softened down by time and absence; they faded away as all offences will fade when the heart is tender and the mind well regulated; and the glowing words of love, the deep tones of passionate adoration, came back—

> " Apparelled in more precious habit,
>   More moving delicate, and full of life,"

than when she heard them from the lips of her husband. Sometimes the recollection of them stirred her very soul, and she pondered over them till she wondered at her own coldness, till she hated herself for not having prized them more, and began to pine for that from which she had voluntarily fled.

> " For it so falls out,
> That what we have we prize not to the worth
> While we enjoy it, but, being lack'd and lost,
> Why, then we reach its value ; then we find
> The virtue that possession did not show us
> While it was ours. So did it fare with Claudio."

And so was it beginning to fare with Helen. Moreover, she had not the same timidity in writing to her husband that she had felt in speaking to him; and the natural playfulness of her disposition sometimes broke out in her letters with far less restraint than she had felt in his actual presence. He too wrote to her openly, and she seemed to herself to grow better acquainted with him by writing than she had by words. Then she became curious to know what her own family thought of her position; how much Beaufort had observed at St. Mary's, and how much of the result of his observations he might have imparted to his mother. But in this respect she was soon reassured. Lady Eskdale had been *dorlotée* through a prosperous life into a quiet belief that everything was for the best; and well might she think so, for she had had the best of everything; and she could not imagine for a moment that her daughters were not to be as happy as she had been in their married lives; or happier, inasmuch as she thought them more perfect than herself. Therefore she merely lamented over dear Teviot's absence as a misfortune rendered endurable because it must be short; and she admired Helen more than ever for submitting with apparent fortitude to such a heavy trial. Lord Eskdale had the real manly political feeling about it. He would have thought it the height of absurdity if Helen had undertaken a voyage at that season, and with the prospect of such a short stay; and his cares turned solely on the success of Lord Teviot's negotiation, and the effect it might have on parties at home and abroad. And as he was in the habit every session of speaking—his enemies called it prosing—on the subject of foreign politics, he was delighted with the prospect of the information he should obtain from his son-in-law, and the certainty of good facts to go upon; a point in which his speeches had hitherto been rather deficient.

Amelia was the only one whose scrutiny Helen had to dread, if dread were the feeling it inspired; for, in fact, she would have been glad to talk over her griefs with her sister had she not been restrained by the strong rules of discretion which Lady Eskdale had laid down for the guidance of her daughters. Still she hoped that, without infringing her duty, she might consult her sister on some of her troubles; but Amelia was absorbed in her baby, and had hardly recovered from her confinement; and at all times there would have been insuperable difficulties in making her comprehend that there could be differences between husband and wife; so for the present Helen was left to her own cogitations and Lord Teviot's letters, and to the sense of her own inferiority as a wife and a happy woman when compared with her sisters.

Three or four days passed away; the invalids were all well again; the usual habits of the house were resumed, various guests arrived, and Helen drove over to Thornbank to claim Mary Forrester's promised visit. Eliza listened eagerly to the names of the company at Eskdale, and her disappointment at not being one of them was much mitigated when she found that her hero was not there; and on mature deliberation she came to the conclusion that as only a certain number of the days of her life could be passed at Eskdale, it would be a bad speculation to waste any of them on such a very incomplete party. So she was prepared with arguments against Mrs. Douglas's view of the case, which differed materially from hers.

" Well, that visit is over. I rather thought I liked Miss Forrester while she was here; but somehow I am not sorry she is gone. I always think that having people to stay in one's house gives more trouble than pleasure."

" But Mary did not give much trouble, mamma."

" I do not know what you call trouble, my dear; but there was a fire in her room all day; and we always had game for second course, and she drinks cocoa at breakfast, which is quite ridiculous. That is one of the pretensions which young people set up in these days; they care about their diet; that was never allowed in my time. I should like to have seen my aunt's face if I had asked for cocoa for breakfast when I was a girl."

" She has pleasant, lively manners," said Mr. Douglas.

" And likes a joke," added Mr. Wentworth. " How she laughed at my story about Hammond! "

" I don't wonder," said Sarah; " there are no stories so amusing as yours."

" You have not heard the fiftieth part of them yet. Why, when I was at Christchurch, Thompson, Hammond, and I used sometimes to sit up till two in the morning, telling good stories; and I suppose you never heard anything more amusing. Lady Teviot laughed at my pun about rain, did not she, Sarah? "

" That she did; she was quite delighted with it."

" The Beauforts all laugh as if they thought they had good teeth," said Mrs. Douglas.

" And so they have, Anne."

" My dear, I·am not disputing the fact, I merely observe that they are convinced of it themselves. Eliza, did Lady Teviot say anything to you about going there? "

" No, mamma; she said Lady Eskdale sent her love."

" What wonderful munificence! and Lady Teviot brought it quite safe all the way from the Castle. How very kind! I suppose when Lady Eskdale is left alone again you will be sent for."

" I shall like it just as well, mamma, when there is only a family party as when the house is full."

" I hope you will be invited then, my child; but I would not advise you to trust in any of these fine people; the Eskdales above all."

" They ought not to give themselves airs," said Mr. Wentworth; " I consider them quite a new family. I do not believe they were heard of before Henry the Seventh's time. My family dates back to the Conquest; and they have as little right to look down on Douglases as on Wentworths, if I am not mistaken."

" No right upon earth," said Mrs. Douglas, " but that they choose to set up for great people. I am not sorry they have not asked Eliza; though I shall always say it is very odd they have not; but nobody can live much with them without being more or less spoiled. Miss Forrester was civil enough while she was here, but she will be just like all the rest of that set when she has been with them a week. I beg to observe that Lady Sophia has not called here at all; and it would not the least surprise me if Lady Walden were not to send over a card of thanks, though I sent to inquire after her at immense inconvenience to myself."

CHAPTER XXXVI

LORD TEVIOT had been absent nearly five weeks, which had passed smoothly and pleasantly away at Eskdale Castle, when a sudden change of affairs took place; not only there, but all over England, to say nothing of Scotland and Ireland. The hapless individual who filled the office of Prime Minister under the gracious King of the above-named countries, having borne the fatigues of the situation for five years, long enough to have become unpopular with the people, wearisome to the King, and odious to all his own private friends, took one decided step to regain all he had lost with others, and to obtain a little rest for himself—he took to his bed and died.

His Cabinet was broken up. It had been, after the usage of all Cabinets, divided into two factions, opposed on all important points to each other, but forming what is by courtesy called a united Cabinet, under the gentle sway of the worn-out nonentity at their head. He was gone. Six or seven newspapers, with broad black borders, announced the death of one of the greatest men of the age,—recommended Westminster Abbey,—a subscription for a monument,—and one of his colleagues for a successor. An equal number of papers, after professing, with becoming candour and humanity, that they warred not with the dead, raked up all the old scandal they could collect against the deceased, denied him any talent whatever, and explained away all his virtues; they prophesied the utter annihilation of the ministerial party, and announced that in twenty-four hours they should be able to give a correct list of the new Cabinet about to be formed by the powerful leader of the Opposition. All the idle men in London rushed to their clubs, and such high betting had not been known since the last Epsom races.

After three days of wonderment, the King decided the bets by sending for Mr. G. The clubs were more thronged and more agitated than ever. One-half of St. James's Street said that England was lost, that the real crisis had come at last (there is generally a false crisis every Easter, in which England is all but lost, but she is found again towards Whitsuntide), and that Church and State, King and kingdom, Lords and Commons, were all to be knocked on the head at once. The club on the opposition side of the street was in ecstasies; its members shook each other by the hand till their arms ached; they declared the King to be the wisest monarch that had ever reigned, and Mr. G. the greatest statesman that had ever governed; that the country was saved, and revolution arrested. They met but to rejoice over the public good, and parted but to make private offers of their services to Mr. G.

And Fisherwick! how felt he? Never was there so happy a man; the world was not large enough to contain him, nothing was but the great room in Downing Street, which to him was greater than the world itself. He wrote faster than ever, and his adoration of his chief was yet more fervent; and when the list of the new ministry was drawn up by his own hand for the favoured evening paper, and when he had added thereto a paragraph announcing that Samuel Obadiah Fisherwick, Esq., had been appointed private secretary to the new premier, he felt that life had nothing greater to give. He had reached the summit of his Mont Blanc.

Mr. G.'s first measure was a dissolution of parliament. The roads swarmed with carriages, and the papers with addresses, the dying hatreds of former contests were roused into fresh life, and country houses became merely election committee rooms. Lord Teviot's name had been one of the first on Mr. G.'s list of his Cabinet, and a messenger had been despatched to recall him from Portugal. This appointment of his son-in-law gave additional energy to Lord Eskdale's ministerial politics. His son had been member for the neighbouring town of Boroughford in the last parliament; and if by any degree of exertion or expense —a gentlemanlike term for bribery—he could return his nephew for the second seat, it would be in many respects a clever stroke of policy. He should bring another vote in aid of the great G. cause; he should have the honour and glory of possessing, to all appearance, a borough of his own; and he should inflict a mortal blow on the Duke of Broughton, the lord-lieutenant of the county, with whose family he had invariably been on terms of polite rivalry and civil hatred, and who at the last election had contrived to insinuate one of his own nephews, Captain Luttridge, into the borough.

The only great difficulty Lord Eskdale anticipated was with Colonel Beaufort himself, whose habits of indolence would be much opposed to the work of canvassing. But in this he was mistaken. There is no stage of inertness and don't-carishness from which an Englishman may not be roused by the stimulus of politics; and a contested election is perhaps one of the finest remedies that can be applied to a confirmed languor, either of mind or body. Ernest caught eagerly at his uncle's proposal, travelled all night from town, and started on his canvass with his cousin an hour after his arrival, passed eleven hours on visits to the electors, and ended the day by making a speech at the Eskdale Arms to two hundred and fifty dirty-looking men, all smoking bad tobacco, and drinking worse beer; and most of whom were sufficiently drunk to insist on shaking hands with him four or five times in the course of the even-

o

ing. And yet when he and Lord Beaufort returned home at night, thirsty, tired, and smoke-dried, they declared they had had a " glorious day," and never saw a finer set of fellows than the electors of Boroughford.

" We shall beat the duke out of the field," said Lord Beaufort to his father. " Luttridge was going sneaking about the town with only half the number of supporters he had last time; and I cannot hear of a second candidate on their side. Besides, we have gained a valuable friend; Tom Rogerson is heart and soul with us."

" That is indeed a great *coup*," said Lord Eskdale. " He has cut the pinks dead, and is on our committee."

" What a clever speech he made at the Magpie and Stump!" said Ernest. " Eh, Beaufort, did it not strike you as something out of the common way? "

" Yes, excellent; but in election matters Tom Rogerson has not his equal on earth."

" Who is he, my dear? " said Lady Eskdale. " Where does he live? "

" Don't you know him? " said Ernest. " Well, I am astonished. I should have thought you must have known Mr. Rogerson, a neighbour; a man of talent, and a voter."

" No, my dear, I never heard of him till this moment; but I will ask him to dinner forthwith."

" Oh! pray do, there's a dear; he will be delighted to come: perhaps your hours are later than he is used to; but for once he might put up with that."

" Or we might dine earlier. I should not mind dining at seven to oblige a friend of yours; but where is he to be found? "

" I can give him your card when I see him to-morrow; he is very little at home now, but his ordinary abode is the front attic of No. 4, Hopscotch Alley, near the old market. I am not quite sure of the number, though I know Hopscotch Alley is the place."

" Now, my dear Beaufort, what does he mean ? "

" Do not mind what he says, dear; he is only trying to mystify you; the real truth being, that Tom Rogerson is a valuable ally, solely from his intimacy with all the rogues and knaves in the borough. He once kept an ale-house, and is now a very idle cobbler; but he is one of those odd shrewd characters who in all times of popular excitement make the fortunes of the party to which they attach themselves. We expect Rogerson will bring us in at least forty votes."

" Oh ! here is his name in my polling-book," said Helen, who was turning over the leaves of a small pamphlet.

" My dear Helen," cried Ernest, " what is that you say ? your polling-book ? "

" Yes, we have each got a polling-book, a list of voters, or whatever you call it, and have been studying them all day to see if there are any of our tradespeople or old friends in the village whom we could persuade to vote for you."

" No, have you really ? what treasures you all are ! If I were not so tired and smoky I should be tempted to make a complete tour of the room, just to kiss all your little hands. And there are several cases in which you may be of use to us. We want you to order a bonnet, which you need not wear, at Mrs. Vere's. Vere pretends to have opinions about Church reform."

" Yes, and Giles the ironmonger would not give us any promise to-day."

" Impossible, my dear Beaufort," said Lady Eskdale; " he has just finished all the ornamental wire-work for my new garden; he ought to be devoted to us."

" He ought, but he is not; for the duke has been speaking to him about iron flues for his hothouses."

" That is actual bribery," said Lady Eskdale, rising into real election energy; " but, if it comes to that, your father is going to have iron hurdles all round the pleasure-ground, and I may as well speak to Giles about them to-morrow."

"Then could you not call on Mrs. Birkett, and say something a little civil to her to-morrow?"

"Why, you do not mean to say," said Lady Walden, laughing, " that Mr. Birkett presumes to have any political opinions of his own, after having attended me so lately, and with the hope of vaccinating baby still before his eyes?"

"I do not exactly make him out; he said he should not like to disoblige the family, but that he would rather not pledge himself; that the duchess had asked Mrs. Birkett to her last ball, and that this was a great political crisis, and so on. I do not know what plot is hatching, but I fully expect the duke's agent will start a second candidate, and that people are hanging back till they see who he is. Mr. Douglas was rather stiff, I thought, to-day."

"Impossible, Beaufort; the Douglases must be with us," said Lady Walden. " Mrs. Douglas hates the duchess."

"Yes; but that is no great distinction likely to tell in our favour. Mrs. Douglas hates so many people."

"And Mr. Douglas was on your committee last time, and he is such an excellent man."

"Very true, so far as his excellence goes; but he has declined being on our committee now."

"Yes, there is a screw loose with the clan of Douglas evidently," said Ernest, " and if I had but time I should like to ride over and pay a few delicate attentions to my little Miss Douglas."

"We will all drive over there to-morrow," said Lady Eskdale, " and take Mrs. Birkett in our way: indeed, I believe Mary Forrester was at Thornbank yesterday; were not you, my dear?"

"Yes, I was, but I think with Colonel Beaufort, though not exactly in his words, that there *is* a screw loose. Mrs.

Douglas was very cold about the election, and Eliza seemed out of spirits."

" We must try what we can do to-morrow and bring Eliza back with us; so now to bed."

" It is time to go to bed," said Lord Beaufort, lighting his candle, " for we must be in Boroughford by nine.   Are you equal to that exertion, Ernest? "

" By nine, my dear fellow! that is full late.   I should have said eight; but then I hate anything like indolence."

CHAPTER XXXVII

THE mysterious coldness of the Douglases was unpleasantly explained the next day. The Duke of Broughton found it necessary to propose a second candidate, and he thought it advisable to choose a gentleman connected with the borough, rather than one of his own adherents. A requisition was got up in a few hours, and a deputation appointed to convey it to Mr. Douglas, and he was also assured by the duke's agent that he should be returned free of all expense if he would consent to be put in nomination.

Mr. Douglas would rather have declined the honour; he was no politician, he did not fancy the trouble of canvassing, and, above all, he did not like the idea of opposing the Eskdales. But this last contingency naturally delighted Mrs. Douglas, and her weight was forthwith thrown into the Broughton scale. The *château qui parle et femme qui écoute* are not more certain to capitulate than is the English gentleman who ponders over the requisition of a body of electors. After walking at least five miles up and down his library, contradicting in a sort of snappish agony every suggestion made by his wife, by Mr. Wentworth, and by Scrimshaw, the duke's agent, and after having declared fourteen several times that nothing should induce him to undertake the task of an election, he was sufficiently composed to sit down and write, under the dictation of Scrimshaw, his address to the electors, soliciting their votes. And at the moment in which Lady Eskdale drove to the door to solicit his support, he was making his entry into the town, preceded by two pink banners, and followed by Scrimshaw and ten shabby-looking men on horseback, riders and steeds covered with pink ribbons. The pinks said it was a very fine procession; the blues pitied " poor old Douglas " from the bottom of their souls for being mixed up with a paltry set of scamps, and for looking so " like a guy " himself. And now war was declared in good earnest.

The duke's nominees, as the opposite party of course termed Mr. Douglas and Captain Luttridge, were backed by many of the richer tradespeople, but they were unpopular with the mob; and, therefore, whatever might be the real results of the strife, its pleasures, while it lasted, were for the Beauforts. Ever, while you live, choose the popular side in an election; that is, if you have no particular regard for the good of your country, and no particular political prejudices of your own; for there is no comparison between a reception of cheers, applause, and good-will, and one of cabbage-stalks, groans, and bad eggs. Besides, there is something exhilarating in the real, genuine affection (while it lasts) of a mob for their favourite of a day. Lady Eskdale and her daughters had the full enjoyment of this position: they drove into the town constantly, and seemed suddenly to have discovered that they were without any of the necessaries or luxuries of life, for the extent of their dealings with well-thinking tradespeople was prodigious, and it might have been supposed that they were covertly sullying the purity of election; but, as they justly alleged, shopping was what every woman was born for, and could not, under any circumstances, be considered illegal; and every day they were received with cheers and applause by all the little dirty boys of the place, screaming like so many animated hurdy-gurdies, " Beaufort for ever! the Colonel for ever! "

Sometimes they met Mr. Douglas emerging from a careful

canvass of Five Courts Lane, or Stitcher's Row, and at first they thought it magnanimous to stop and shake hands with him. This greeting soon dwindled into a bow and a forced smile, with the remark that after all he had not behaved well to Beaufort; and at last they turned away their heads when they saw the pinks coming, and Lady Sophia asked her mother if she did not rather hate the sight of old Douglas.

The day of election arrived. Lord Beaufort and his cousin rode into the town, accompanied by a long train of Lord Eskdale's tenantry; and shortly after, Lady Eskdale, with the Waldegraves and Amelia, followed in her carriage; while Lady Teviot drove Miss Forrester in her pony phaeton. They were all deposited in the second floor of the house of Mrs. Harris, the milliner, which looked on the hustings. An election was a new sight to them, and they were, in their various ways, worked up to a high pitch of excitement. Mrs. Harris was overflowing with politeness, proud to receive " the Countess," prouder that she should be consulted on the probable results of the election, and proudest that she had made Harris vote against his conscience and inclination for my lord and the colonel.

Mrs. Douglas and her daughters were at the Broughton Arms, at the opposite corner of the market-place, and well was it for Eliza that pink was the badge of her party; it was her only chance of a tinge of colour, for she was as pale as ashes at the shocking contest between her father and her lover, as in her inmost heart she designated Colonel Beaufort. She looked upon her position as one of unprecedented difficulty, only to be paralleled perhaps by that of the daughter of Horatius, who figures in that interesting old romance which we obligingly call the Roman history. She had not seen Colonel Beaufort since his arrival, and now she was to appear to him decked out in this inimical colour. Moreover, he and his cousin were never named now by Mrs. Douglas but as " those horrid Beauforts."

The polling began, and for three hours was nearly equal on both sides; but at two o'clock Captain Luttridge was at the head of the poll, and Mr. Douglas was five ahead of Lord Beaufort, and eight of his cousin. Mrs. Douglas was delighted, threw open the window, and looked out with many smiles and much affectation. Lady Eskdale was low, and sent off a groom with a bulletin to Lord Eskdale, and tried to eat half a sandwich and drink a quarter of a glass of gooseberry wine, assuring Mrs. Harris that her bread and butter were superior to any at the Castle, and that she should have taken the gooseberry wine for champagne if she had not been forewarned. Helen felt sure that the next hour would do wonders; and Lady Sophia complained of her headache, and begged Sir William to stay quietly in the room, and not go and get crushed in the crowd.

The pinks marched by the window with their band playing and their banners streaming, and the mob groaned. Mr. Mullins and Mr. Dickson, and Mr. Wyvill and Mr. Winthrop, of the Beaufort committee—all great men in that, their day—rushed up the stairs at intervals to beg Lady Eskdale would not be alarmed, everything was going on well—they were sure to win. Lord Beaufort himself put his head in and said " Don't be afraid, all's right "; and Ernest, who was strutting about the town with Tom Rogerson, who had a very red face, and a great hole in his coat-sleeve, looked up and nodded a nod of encouragement.

Three o'clock came. The state of the poll still worse; Lord Beaufort twelve in arrear, and Colonel Beaufort twenty-one. Mrs. Douglas could not control her delight, and added much to it by making signs of astonishment, and throwing looks of commiseration in the direction of Mrs. Harris's house. Lady Eskdale sent off another groom to Lord Eskdale, and tried to finish her sandwich, but thought the bread was dry and the butter strong, and again sipped her gooseberry wine, and avowed that she never quite liked home-made wines. Lady Sophia's head-ache was exchanged for a violent palpitation, and she could not recover her astonishment that Sir William could remain quietly in the room, and was not exerting himself in the town.

The band of the pinks played louder than ever, and the groans of the mob became fiercer. Again Mullins, Dickson, Wyvill, and Winthrop rushed from the various polling-booths to assert that all was going on well. There was of course the most shameful bribery and intimidation on the other side; but Mullins would stake his head, and Dickson would pledge his life, and all the rest of the com-mittee would hazard stakes of equal value, that all would end well. Lord Beaufort had not time to come and see them, but they had a distant view of Ernest shaking hands with two pink butchers, who were giving up their colours; Tom Rogerson standing by, his arms folded, Coriolanus fashion, and his torn sleeve nearly detached from his coat by the force of his previous gesticulations. At four the first day's poll closed, and the numbers were:—

Luttridge	317
Douglas	300
Lord Beaufort	287
Colonel Beaufort	278

Deep and silent consternation in Mr. Harris's parlour, and riotous congratulations at the Broughton Arms. The mob thickened round the hustings, ostensibly to hear the speeches of the candidates, but, in fact, to prevent a word that they said from being heard. The unpopular gentle-men had to speak first, but, except by the movements of their lips and arms, it was difficult to guess whether they made any attempt to address their friends. The groans and hootings of the crowd below never ceased, and were intermingled with those odd accusations generally made by a mob against the objects of their spleen. " Now for it, Luttridge; who flogs the niggers? " " What was your grandfather's name? "   " Who killed the young donkey? " " Take a little donkey broth; it is good for the poor ": and then came a shower of thick black mud. " Want a black slave? here's one "; and a wretched little black kitten was thrown in Captain Luttridge's face. But a joke is a joke to the candidates who are at the head of the poll; and they seemed as much amused as their assailants. When Lord Beaufort appeared, there was an attempt made at silence, with such success that several words and half of one sentence were distinctly heard; and Lady Eskdale had tears in her eyes when she thought that such eloquence would perhaps be lost to the House of Commons. Then Ernest appeared, and made an oration so violent in words, and so languid and dawdling in manner, that it tickled the fancy of his hearers, and made even Captain Luttridge laugh. And then the fun ceased for that day, so far as the election was concerned.

But a little additional excitement was provided by the energy of the mob. Lady Eskdale's barouche drove safely off, and was soon out of sight. Helen and Miss Forrester waited five minutes longer, talking over the events of the day, and then, as a few drops of rain began to fall, Lord Beaufort hurried them into their little open carriage, and advised Helen to make the best of her way home. Either she had in her haste given the ponies their head too soon, or they were unused to be cheered on their way, which was their fate this day, but so it was, that they began with a little kicking and snorting, and then fairly ran away, which, of course, made several little boys call out, " Beaufort for ever!" more ecstatically than before. Lord Beaufort and Ernest followed at full gallop, and about half-way to the Castle they found the phaeton with one wheel in a ditch, Helen still seated in it, Miss Forrester standing at the ponies' heads, and the rain falling in torrents.

"I am so glad you are come," said Mary, looking at Colonel Beaufort; "we are in a most melancholy plight."

"Are you hurt? tell me, Helen, for mercy's sake," said Lord Beaufort, springing off his horse, and rushing up to her.

"No, not the least, but very much frightened," said Lady Teviot, half laughing, half crying. "I thought at first we were overturned; there was a crash, such a horrid crash——"

"Yes, the pole is broken, Colonel Beaufort; if you will have the kindness to take my place, I can go to Helen, she is still frightened"; and then Mary went to her, and taking off her own cloak wrapped it round Lady Teviot, so as to defend her from the rain, and soothed her, and talked so naturally and calmly that Helen began to recover her nerves.

"But how did you escape being thrown out?" said Lord Beaufort, who was still pale with alarm. "What a shock you must have had!"

"She had, indeed," said Mary; "but it is all over now, is not it, Helen, dear? I sent the groom on to Eskdale Castle to fetch the carriage; and now, if you would try to walk on and meet it, it would be much better for you than sitting there in the rain. Are you able to walk, love?"

"Perfectly, I am wiser now," said Lady Teviot, springing out; "but what nerves you have, Mary! I wanted to jump out at one moment, but she would not let me, and she stretched her arms out before me, to prevent my being thrown out; and when the wheel went into the ditch, and I did nothing but scream, she jumped out, and ran to those dreadful ponies' heads, and talked to them, and quieted them, though they were kicking dreadfully; and when the groom came up she sent him off for a carriage, and warned him not to tell mamma what had happened. In short, she thought of everything, and I could not think of anything but how frightened I was."

" She did indeed behave gallantly," said Lord Beaufort; " and now let us walk on, for you are both getting wet. Luckily there is the carriage in sight."

So, leaving Colonel Beaufort's servant with the recusant ponies, they hurried on; the ladies were hurried into the carriage, and the gentlemen rode on with them. Lord Beaufort was much struck by Mary's presence of mind and cheerfulness in a situation that was trying, to say the least of it; and when the carriage stopped at the lodge gate, he rode up to the side on which she was seated, and said, in a tone of great interest, " May I ask how you feel? I fear you must be both cold and exhausted."

" Your sister is on the other side," she said. " Helen, Lord Beaufort has come to ask you how you are."

" She really believes," he thought with vexation, " that I have not the common feelings of humanity where she is concerned; that I cannot ask her a civil question. How provoking it is—and she looked so handsome too! " and by dint of assiduous thought on this subject, he arrived too late to hand her out, and saw her and his sister run quickly up-stairs to change their wet clothes, and to break their disaster to Lady Eskdale.

As no real harm had occurred, their adventures served as a relief to the gloomy cogitations of the evening over the state of the poll. Several gentlemen of the committee had been asked to dinner, and of course the conversation turned exclusively on the events of the morning; and at any other time the family would have been the first to laugh at their own volubility and prejudices. When the ladies returned to the drawing-room, Lady Eskdale threw herself on the sofa with a deep sigh, which was echoed by her daughters as they ranged themselves round her.

" I feel quite desponding about the election to-night," she said, " and it is so mortifying to lose it; and I never heard anything so atrocious as the accounts of the bribery and intimidation on the other side. Mr. Mullins has been telling me all about it; he says it is quite unprecedented."

" So Mr. Winthrop says," added Lady Sophia.

" And Mr. Dickson," said Lady Teviot.

" And Mr. Wyvill," said Lady Walden.

" I cannot think such horrible wickedness can succeed," continued Lady Eskdale; " there will be a judgment upon it; and I really believe the Duke of Broughton is capable of anything atrocious. However, there is still a chance left; and if our friends are to be believed—and I quite put my faith in that nice Mr. Mullins—Beaufort and Ernest ought to succeed. There are 230 voters still unpolled, and Mr. Mullins assures me that of those we are sure of 120 or 130, I forget which; and so you see, my loves, we must subtract 130 from 250, and 287 from 130, and then add—— No, that is not right, sums are so difficult; but that the result would give us a majority I know, because Mullins says so."

" Mr. Winthrop says he is sure of it," added Lady Sophia.

" Mr. Dickson says we stand much higher than he had expected the first day," said Lady Teviot.

" So Mr. Wyvill says," added Lady Walden.

" I think I feel sure we shall win all the time," said Lady Eskdale.

" And so do I," said Mary, after a pause; " and yet I cannot help thinking, though of course these gentlemen know best, that we should feel *more* sure if we were at the head of the poll instead of being in a minority of thirty."

"Well, I think so too, Mary," said Lady Teviot; and then they were all silent again.

"Mamma," said Lady Sophia, "did it not strike you to-day that Mr. Douglas has a remarkably bad countenance? It never occurred to me before."

"Well, I thought so too, Sophia," said Lady Teviot; "he used to have such an open, good-humoured look, but after studying his face to-day when he was speaking, I thought it had a false, forbidding sort of expression."

"Perhaps so, my dear," said Lady Eskdale, resignedly; "he never at the best of times had a distinguished look, and I dare say, poor man, he must have moments of painful remorse for his treachery to Beaufort, and that tells on his countenance. However, if we have lost one friend, we have gained several others. I never saw anything like the devotion of all those dear good creatures in the next room. Mr. Mullins tells me he is quite as anxious for our success as if he were standing himself; he says he has hardly been in bed more than five hours this week, and he is quite hoarse with speaking. I like Mr. Mullins."

"And I dote upon Mr. Winthrop: he is not a bit less eager than your Mullins, mamma," said Lady Sophia.

"And my Mr. Dickson has not had a wink more sleep," said Lady Teviot.

"And I am proud to say Mr. Wyvill has completely lost his voice," said Lady Walden.

"Well, you may laugh, my dear children, but they are very delightful people, and I mean to see a great deal of them in future, and to ask them here constantly. And now let us rest till the gentlemen come, for I am half dead with the election, and that horrid accident with your phaeton, dearest Nell. I feel quite ill, and I think we have all agreed not to go into the town to-morrow; so now let us keep quiet."

To this they all consented heartily, and then, after a silence that lasted at least two minutes, they all recommenced their surmises and remarks. The gentlemen joined them, and till one in the morning they continued discussing the chances of each remaining vote without ever wearying of the subject. They parted with the avowed determination to get up very late the next day. At eight the following morning every bell was ringing, and each lady had decided that though it was advisable that the others should stay at home, she herself should be anxious and miserable at a distance from the scene of action. So at nine they were all on their way once more to the faithful Mrs. Harris, and full of renovated hopes.

CHAPTER XXXVIII

THE town was more crowded and more disorderly than ever; the mob more eager and considerably more drunk. The horses could hardly make their way through the crowd, and innumerable were the hands that were thrust into the carriage; and dirty as they were, Lady Eskdale shook them all heartily, though she afterwards assured her son that it was the greatest stretch of maternal affection she had ever made for him. Contrary to the general expectation, the Beauforts gained ground from the first hour, and at twelve o'clock Lord Beaufort was within one of Mr. Douglas, and Ernest within five. The agitation that had prevailed in Mrs. Harris's parlour began to evince itself at the Broughton Arms; and Mrs. Douglas was frantic with anger and spite, and added ten years at once to the ages of all the opposite party. Eliza, who had all along asserted that her father and Colonel Beaufort would and must win, adhered to that opinion, which no announcement of numbers, no force of calculation could possibly shake.

Another hour passed away. Lord Beaufort was at the head of the poll, and Colonel Beaufort within four of Captain Luttridge. Mullins and Co. were in a state of unexampled activity and triumph. Lady Eskdale and her daughters were speechless, for now that one Beaufort seemed secure their eagerness for Ernest's success was redoubled. A shout was heard, and a chaise whirled up. "Oh!" said Lady Walden, "there is my dear Wyvill waving his hat to us. Such a treasure of a man! but why has he powdered his face like a clown at Astley's?"

P

This was explained by his handing out of the chaise two very white millers, whom he had torn from their innocent farinaceous privacy into the pink and blue crowd. They polled for the Beauforts; Wyvill gave his own vote at the same time, and immediately after, Tom Rogerson was seen hauling along a very small pale-faced cripple, an iron-monger by trade, whom he had by dint of threats and brandy forced to the hustings; and who with faltering voice, and eyes fixed on Tom, voted for Colonel Beaufort and Mr. Douglas. " I allow the little wretch one vote," said Tom, with an air of condescension, " because he is his Grace's private tinker, and it does us no harm; but in a general way, I don't like to see such little hatomeys go for to think for theirselves." The numbers now were for—

Lord Beaufort	360
Colonel Beaufort	351
Captain Luttridge	351
Mr. Douglas	330

There was a pause for ten minutes, not another vote apparently to be had for love or money. The mayor had wisely abstained from giving any opinion, and neither party dared press him to vote: the delay became more aggravating every moment; at last there was a stir amongst the crowd as if some interesting event were in preparation at the end of the street. The ladies stretched their heads out of the windows quite as far as was safe; but their hearts misgave them, for there were no hurrahs to herald the approach of another Beaufortite. But yet the mob looked joyful, though so quiet; and at last there appeared, in grand procession, eight men bearing a bed, on which was laid an unfortunate master chimney-sweeper, who had broken his leg the day before, and who now was borne along, stretched at full length, with his wife's red cloak over his shoulders, and her flannel petticoat turbaned round his head, his face partially streaked with white, thanks to his forced seclusion from soot, and a blue flag thrown over his bed to conceal the patchwork quilt. Tom Rogerson was walking beside him, with a bottle of spirits (to be used in case of faintness) in one hand, and with the other making most imperative signs to the people not to agitate the sick man with their applause. It was a most impressive scene, particularly when the black lips opened in answer to the interrogation of the polling-clerk, and announced a plumper for Colonel Beaufort. There was a low murmur of delight, followed by a stern " Hush " from Tom Rogerson, who was so much affected that he was obliged to have recourse to the spirits which he had brought for the sick man. The procession moved on, and no sooner was the gallant chimney-sweeper out of hearing, than the numbers were again announced; and the shouts of the crowd burst forth. The election was decided; the five or six voters who had hung back all came in to the winning side; and in half an hour Lord Beaufort and his cousin were declared duly elected. Mrs. Douglas was in hysterics, and Lady Sophia, Lady Walden, and Lady Teviot were dancing a reel at the back of Mrs. Harris's parlour, out of sight of the street, and merely as a necessary relief to their over-excited spirits. Mrs. Harris was urging Lady Eskdale to drink the health of the new members in her gooseberry wine, to which request Lady Eskdale acceded, thought it tasted to-day much better than champagne, and begged for the receipt. Altogether it was a glorious day for Eskdale Castle. Every being in the house, from its owner down to steward's-room boy, was in a state of triumph, and the evening was passed in such hilarity that it was much to the credit of the establishment that there were enough sober servants to carry to bed those who were drunk.

CHAPTER XXXIX

Poor Eliza, she was the chief victim to the great Borough-ford contest. Mrs. Douglas said " Not at home," when Lady Eskdale, who could not keep up a quarrel for a week, called on her; and professed her intention of not returning such a hypocritical visit. The Castle was filled with company, but Mrs. Douglas sternly refused an invitation to dine there. Worse than all, Colonel Beaufort did not call at Thornbank. He thought of it, but one day the sun was out, and he should have a glaring dusty ride. The next day the sun went in, but he had no idea of catching cold for a mere morning visit, and he really had not courage " to face the irate Douglas *père et mère*," though he should rather have liked to see his little friend. He could not recollect her Christian name, but the little fair girl who had such a righteous horror of Lady Port-more. And for this man Eliza was undergoing all the pains and processes of a disappointment. She ate no breakfast and very little dinner, alternated from fits of absence in solitude to fits of impatience in society. She thought all the neighbours tiresome, and Thornbank dull; and finally set up an Extract Book, that last infirmity of blighted hopes. It opened, of course, with " She never told her love," though there was not an action in Eliza's life that did not tell it plainly if anybody had thought it worth while to interpret them. " The worm in the bud " was making a nice little feast in a quiet way. This quotation was followed by harrowing lines to the Bleeding heart and the False heart, and the Breaking heart and the Cold heart, and hearts in every variety of distress and wrong; and by short pithy scraps conveying the most cutting censures on man's inconstancy, or describing the withering lives and touching deaths of "The Lone One," or "The Early Lost," or words to that effect. And there was Colonel Beaufort, "cold, perjured, but adored" (p. 49, Extract Book), actually oblivious of her Christian name, and thinking of Parliament and Newmarket and pheasant shooting, and of anything but falling in love and marrying.

"I say, Helen," he muttered one morning after Lord Eskdale had mentioned that there would be no battue that week, "is there any chance of Teviot coming home soon? It will be monstrous if we are cut out of the pheasants he promised us by some trivial question of peace or war between two Great Powers, as they are pleased to call themselves. Do you know when he is coming back?"

"He seemed," said Helen, "in his last letter to think that his business at Lisbon might now easily be finished by others on the spot, and that he should come back to take possession of his new office."

"This is pleasing news for all of us," said Colonel Stuart, who was staying at the Castle, "and especially for you, Lady Teviot. Lady Portmore seemed sure of his return, for she asked me to meet him at Portsdown on the 10th, but, with every respect for our dear busy friend, I found 'metal more attractive' here than in one of her fussy crowds."

"Lady Portmore must be in ecstasies," said Lady Walden, "at the triumph of what she calls her party."

"Well, I am not so sure," said Colonel Stuart. "Mr. G. has failed to find out Portmore's merits, and my lady is rather wrathful at not having the offer of even a household place; and I hear she is beginning to make out that Mr. Sheffield is a distant cousin of hers, and that he leads the Opposition with great talent."

" So like her," said Lady Walden. " I wish she would take up the Sheffield side, and give up appropriating Mr. G. and his friends to herself."

" I am sure, so do I," said Helen, in an absent tone.

" And yet," pursued Colonel Stuart, " she is of use too. She has great power over her friends; how or why it is difficult to say; but in some instances," he added in a hesitating voice, " it is marvellous."

Helen was silent, she hardly seemed to hear what was passing. Amelia took up the argument against Lady Portmore—her charms and her agreeableness; and Colonel Stuart, with a manifest affectation of keeping back the facts that would tell best for him, ended by saying that somehow or other her influence over some people had been exerted with great success. Amelia left the room, and Helen, rousing herself from her fit of abstraction, asked Colonel Stuart " whether there was to be a large party at Portsdown."

" Lady Portmore did not name her guests, but said, as you probably know, that Lord Teviot would land at Southampton on the 9th, and that she expected him on the 10th." He put on a look of distress, and added, " I own this surprises me; and what is more, it provokes me. I cannot endure for your sake," he added in a low earnest tone, " the infatuation which can keep Teviot for an hour from such a home as his."

Helen looked surprised, but said coldly, " We have only Lady Portmore's word for the invitation that has been given; I very much doubt whether it will be accepted. I am thinking of meeting Lord Teviot at Southampton."

" Are you, indeed ? " and then he paused, and drawing his chair nearer to her, and looking at her with an air of deep compassion, said, " Perhaps you are right. If anything should occur to distress Teviot, I mean to annoy him, he *must* feel the comfort of having you near him. I cannot imagine he should not, and yet—— But I cannot speak on this subject. Whatsoever befalls him, Teviot will always be to me an object of envy."

" What do you mean? " said Helen, quietly; " there can have been no letters later than mine from him. He said he should be glad to get away from Lisbon, that it did not agree with him; he did not feel well. Colonel Stuart, you have not heard that he is *really* ill? "

" No, nothing of the sort; it was not to himself I was alluding. I was thinking of you. I cannot be calm and prudent where your happiness is concerned; and yet it was only a vague report."

" Oh! then do not tell it to me," she said, relapsing into her previous coldness. " If you had known anything connected with his health, you would have done well to tell me—any other reports I would rather hear from himself." She rose as she spoke, and without even a look at him left the room.

She went straight to Lady Walden, who was, for a wonder, not in the nursery. " Amelia," she said, " I cannot bear that Colonel Stuart. I do not know what he means. I cannot understand his looks and his manner. He has been trying to frighten me with some report which he says concerns my happiness. What business is it of his whether I am happy or not? Amelia, what does he mean? "

Lady Walden had seen looks of Colonel Stuart's that had aroused her suspicions, and she was sufficiently aware of his character and habits to have a distinct perception of his meaning; but she had no intention of enlightening Helen's innocent mind, and said, with an air of indifference, " Oh, nothing at all probably. He delights in petty mysteries, and in interference in the affairs of other people; and he fancies himself a good adviser, though it generally appears to me that his advice is wrong."

" Wrong or right," said Helen, " I do not wish for it,

and I am very glad Mary did not marry him. But I wish, dearest, you would ascertain, without seeming to care about it, whether he does know anything about Teviot. I dare say it is only some nonsense about that silly Lady Portmore; but still he has made me feel uncomfortable."

"And that is just what he intended," said Amelia; "but I will have a talk with him this evening. Till then do not let us think of him, and in the meanwhile may I ask, Nelly, if you ever in your life saw anything half so pretty as baby's hand?"

She put aside the curtain of the little white cradle that was on her sofa, and the sisters solaced themselves for the disturbance occasioned by Colonel Stuart's dark hints by a regular course of baby twaddle, kissing its waxy little hands, trying to roll the short down on its head into curls— an attempt in which they signally failed; and poking little holes in the corners of its mouth and the dimple on its chin, fancying they made it laugh. To impartial observers, the face made by baby under this manipulation was one of unutterable disgust and annoyance.

In the course of the evening Amelia fulfilled her promise to Helen, by engaging Colonel Stuart in conversation, and his vanity was gratified by her alluding to the hints he had given to her sister, and the impression they had made on her.

"You may imagine, Lady Walden," he said, rather solemnly, " that the last thing I should wish would be to give your sister a moment of uneasiness. I could not do it, such a bright, buoyant being as she is. How she can be undervalued or misunderstood! But this is not what I have to say. It had better be said to you than to her; and you can then impart the tidings to her or not, as you think best."

"But what tidings?" said Amelia, impatiently. "What is it that requires all this preparation?"

"Merely a report. I trust it is nothing more; but a report that materially affects Lord Teviot's position, should it prove true. Have you ever seen or heard of a certain Henry Lorimer, who lives not in the best society, but occasionally hangs about it?"

"You mean a tall, dark Mr. Lorimer, who is a connection of Lord Teviot's after a fashion, a natural son of Lord Robert's, Teviot's great-uncle. I believe that old Lord Robert was a shocking old man. Luckily for Teviot, he was never married."

"Ah!" said Colonel Stuart; "but this leads, unfortunately, to my mysterious report." And then he went on to explain to Lady Walden that this Henry Lorimer, after having consented to pass for some years as an illegitimate scion of the Teviot house, had suddenly asserted a private marriage of his father's, which he was prepared to prove, and consequently to lay claim to the Teviot title and estates. "This intelligence came to me through an odd, inexplicable channel; it is not yet generally known, but it soon must be, and I leave it to you to judge whether your sister had better hear it now, or on Teviot's return. It may be kept a secret a few days longer."

Colonel Stuart's intelligence always did come to him in strange, mysterious ways: but yet it generally proved to be correct, and Amelia felt that he was only asserting what he actually knew. She questioned him as to the grounds on which Mr. Lorimer had raised his claim; but on that point Colonel Stuart could or would say nothing. He confined himself to sighs and shakings of the head, after the fashion of Lord Burleigh, and an occasional word of pity for Lady Teviot.

She had watched this colloquy with great interest, and eagerly followed her sister out of the room when Amelia professed fatigue as an excuse for retiring early.

"Well, Amelia, what is it? Tell me at once. Is it anything about Lady Portmore? or about Teviot's health?"

"Neither the one nor the other, darling, and the story

may turn out false; but it is certainly very annoying ";
and then she repeated to her sister the facts stated to her
by Colonel Stuart.

" Oh! is that all? " said Helen, with a sigh of relief.
" In the first place, I do not believe it. I do not know
why it is, but I feel as if I should distrust anything and
everything asserted by Colonel Stuart; and then, supposing
it to be true, worse misfortunes might have happened. I
doubt whether very great riches and grandeur really do give
all the happiness we suppose. But Teviot, poor Teviot! "
she added, in an unusual tone of tenderness, " I am afraid he
will feel all this deeply, even if it ends well. He will hate the
discussions and all the publicity given to his family history;
and if it ends ill! Oh, Amelia, does he know it yet? "

" No, Colonel Stuart says that except ' the scamp,' as
he calls Mr. Lorimer, and his advisers, it is known to no
one but himself."

" I am glad," said Helen in a tone of deep feeling;
" for then I shall be with Teviot when he hears it, and I
think I shall be a comfort to him." There was silence
between the sisters for a few minutes, and then Helen,
throwing her arms round Amelia's neck, said in a faltering
voice, " Dearest, I have been wrong, very wrong, in the
whole course of my married life; so unlike what you would
have been. I cannot talk even to you about it; but the
worst of all is that I did not go with my husband to
Lisbon. Amelia, I am very unhappy, but to-morrow I
shall hear from him, and I mean to be at Southampton
before he lands. So whatever bad news may come, we
may hear it together."

" You are right, darling," said Amelia, who was too
honest and true-hearted to say that Helen condemned
herself unjustly. " It is better not to discuss the past if
it fret my Helen, but she will be a happy good little wife
for the future, and so good-night."

CHAPTER XL

THE next morning at an early hour Lady Eskdale was roused from that most pleasing of all the phases of sleep—the slight extra doze that follows the opening of the shutters—by Helen, who was looking pale and agitated, and had a letter in her hand.

"Mamma dear, I am so vexed to disturb you, but I am going to set off for Southampton directly. Poor Teviot has been ill; he has had a bad fever; he cannot write himself, but I have heard from his secretary, who says they were going to move him from that dreadful Lisbon directly; and that the doctors hoped that the voyage would be of use. He is at sea now. I shall hardly arrive at Southampton before him. Oh, dearest mamma, is it not sad?" and Helen burst into tears.

"My darling child," said Lady Eskdale, who was so little accustomed to be awakened by any misfortune that she could not collect her scattered senses nor untie her nightcap, "you must not cry; of course you must go to dear Teviot directly, but you must have some breakfast first, Helen; a fever did you say, dear? Do untie this knot for me. I am quite awake now, so let me see the letter; you have got frightened, my pet; I dare say it is only a slight attack."

But when she had read the letter she saw that Helen's alarm was well-founded, and her tears fell on her child's head, which had sunk on her pillow. Lord Teviot had been suddenly seized with a bad fever which was then raging at Lisbon; and guarded as was the account sent by his secretary, it was evidently written under great alarm and anxiety. Eight days of illness had been sufficient to prostrate mind and body. Friends were judging and acting for him whose will had been so absolute and actions so decided; and the strong man whom no fatigue had seemed to weary was to be borne in a litter, unconscious and helpless, to the ship which was to bring him home, or to be his grave.

Lady Eskdale was completely overcome. Her first thought was to accompany her daughter, but that Helen declined with a peremptoriness that admitted of no resistance. She said that it would be great fatigue for her mother, that her own preparations were made, and that she should be off in half an hour; that Amelia had offered to go with her, but that she had rather go alone, and would write from Southampton the moment she arrived there.

"But my dear child," said poor Lady Eskdale, who was gradually relapsing into bewilderment under the suddenness of this trouble, "you cannot possibly go alone to a great noisy hotel at a seaport town; it is not proper, though to be sure you are married, I forgot that; but still you are so young; and then all that anxiety about your dear husband; and how are you to get on board the packet? and the beds won't be aired. I must get up directly and ask Lord Eskdale about it. How tiresome it is that Nelson never will put my dressing-slippers ready! Oh dear, how little we know what the day may bring forth! I wish now you had gone with dear Teviot, though perhaps you might have caught this dreadful fever yourself."

"You cannot wish it more than I do," said Helen, fervently. "I ought to have been with him; but I shall not be alone at the hotel, mamma. Mary Forrester was, you know, going back this week to her aunt, who lives in that neighbourhood, and she will stay with me till Teviot arrives."

"But you two will be very helpless in that sort of place; Beaufort must go with you if you will not let papa and me go."

"No," said Helen, "no, I had rather go alone."

"Dear Nelly," said Lady Eskdale, looking with fond pity at the young fragile creature who was resting on the bed by her, looking miserable and pale, "you are not able to get through all this alone. Why should not Beaufort go with you?"

"Because, mamma," she said, throwing her arms round her mother's neck, "I do not think Teviot would like it. I did not like to tell you when first I came here, but at St. Mary's I was not quite happy. It was all my fault, but somehow poor Teviot was convinced that I thought too much of my own family; that I cared more for them than I did for him; and so—I cannot explain it, but I think he would be better pleased if I came by myself to meet him; and oh! if he is still very ill, I should like to nurse him and to wait upon him, and to make him happier than I did before. It would please him to have all my care to himself."

"You are right, darling; whatever will please your husband best it is your duty to do; so go, my child. I trust you will not want us, but if you do, we can come at any moment. God bless you, my dearest, and may all this trial end happily!"

"Yes, yes," said Helen, "it must, it will. Amelia has another grievance to tell you that will vex poor Teviot; but that does not signify if he gets well; and now I must go. Everything is ready; good-bye, my own dear mother." And before the company at the Castle met at breakfast, Helen and Mary were gone. Lord and Lady Eskdale had heard from Amelia the intelligence she had gathered from Colonel Stuart, and he, with all the guests, were preparing for their departure, feeling that the family, under their present circumstances, would be glad to be left to themselves. Colonel Stuart was in a high state of annoyance at Lady Teviot's sudden disappearance, and his own ignorance of the impression which his news had made on her; and suddenly determined to go to Portsdown, and hear Lady Portmore's views on the subject.

CHAPTER XLI

Lord Eskdale thought perhaps less of Lord Teviot's illness, and more of the threatened attack on his name and property, than Lady Eskdale did. He settled, as most men do, that a bad illness is only a decided step to a speedy recovery; and that whoever is very ill one day is sure to be much better the next. But a lawsuit he viewed in its truest and blackest colours; and where so much was at stake, he was eager to take some measures of defence, even before Lord Teviot's return. But the affair was still a mystery: and he could do nothing but wish and wonder. One measure for Helen's comfort he insisted upon, notwithstanding Lady Eskdale's assurances that Helen did not wish for it. He sent Lord Beaufort to join his sister a few hours after her departure; and even Helen felt it to be a relief when she saw her brother's carriage dash up to the door of the noisy, crowded hotel, where she and Mary had, after much difficulty, found rooms. There is something pleasant and cheerful in a large country inn, with a choice of clean, airy rooms, a warm welcome from a fat landlady, and the undivided attentions of *the* waiter. But at an hotel at a busy seaport town, where large parties land, eager to make a quick transit to London, where whole families arrive, equally eager to obtain accommodation till they enter the floating prisons which are already producing nausea by the view, from the windows, of their constant undulations; where the hall and landing-places are filled with packing-cases, and the entrance is blocked up by trucks; where all the bells are constantly ringing, and it seems to be nobody's business to answer them: all this is very dispiriting. Helen sank down in despair on the horse-hair sofa, which seemed to be constantly slipping from under her, while Mary attempted short voyages of discovery on the stairs, which were cut short by fresh shoals of arrivals and departures; the footman made a failure of his inquiries about packets; and Tomkinson utterly repudiated the bedrooms which were vouchsafed to her as a favour, and declined as an insult. This is one of the situations in which women acquire a wholesome sense of their helplessness, and a conviction that dependence on firmer minds and stronger frames than their own is their natural position in a world of petty difficulties, and Helen hailed her brother's arrival with pleasure.

Lord Beaufort set to work with authority, awed a dingy-looking waiter into attention; majestically intimated that Lady Teviot's room was not fitted for her, and obtained one less noisy and better furnished; and finally went himself to the packet-office, sent in his card, and obtained without difficulty the information he wanted.

"Helen, dearest!" he said on his return, "there is a steamer to start from hence to-morrow; but it seemed so certain by Le Geyt's letter that Teviot would leave Lisbon by the first conveyance, that in my opinion you had better stay here another day or two. Indeed, I am sure of it. You must be tired, and so must Miss Forrester. I advise you to follow her example, and go to bed."

"I am tired; but Mary is not gone to bed; you know her aunt lives about two miles off: and finding you were here to take care of me, she sent for a fly, and went to Mrs. Forrester's. She will come back early to-morrow," she added, seeing a look of surprise and disappointment on her brother's face.

"Yes, she must come back," he said moodily; and he

rose and leant against the chimney-piece with an air of painful abstraction.

" Dear Beaufort," said Helen, half smiling, " you do not imagine that Mary is thinking of your old quarrels, and has gone home to avoid you ? I assure you that is not the case."

" Is not it ? " he said, trying to return her smile; but he relapsed into his absent fit, and then, suddenly kissing his sister, said, " Good-night; you look very tired, and so am I. I hope Miss Forrester will come to breakfast."

" I suppose so," said Helen sleepily. " Good-night, dear. You are going to bed too ? "

" Of course " ; but when she had left the room, he drew the arm-chair to the fire, and, resting his feet on the fender, sank into deep and melancholy thought. He had met one or two people whom he knew slightly, who had either arrived by the last steamer themselves, or had seen friends who had. They all spoke of Lord Teviot's as a hopeless case. The agent at the office had mentioned that a packet might come in on the following day; it was waiting at Lisbon for a young lord who was very ill; but it was generally understood that he would not live to go on board. Lord Beaufort shuddered as he thought what the next morning might bring to Helen; he felt unequal to cope with her probable grief by himself; and ended by writing a note to Miss Forrester, telling her what he had heard, and imploring her to return as early as possible. He left this note with his servant, to be sent the first thing in the morning, and went to bed anxious, unhappy, and almost desponding.

The next morning Helen came down, looking more cheerful, though she suggested to her brother that she did not think the hotel would do for an invalid; that she had had a very noisy family lodged in the next room to hers; " and Teviot will perhaps be so weak that we may have

Q

to stay at Southampton for two or three days." She looked anxiously at her brother, who had hardly spoken all the time breakfast lasted, and intercepted a look of his at Mary that made her heart beat. She dared not ask the question that was on her lips.

"Very true," said Mary, seeing that Lord Beaufort was unable to answer his sister's mute appeal. "You must expect, dearest, that Lord Teviot will indeed be weak and want quiet. I think we might find some lodging just as near as this is to the pier. Indeed, I saw a house to be let some way back from the street, and standing by itself. It was, to be sure, very small."

"Oh, that would not signify if it is quiet. What do you think, Beaufort?"

"That it would be very desirable to get you out of this horrid hole," he said, starting up. "Miss Forrester, perhaps you will show me where this house is, and I will go and see if we can have it. Make some excuse to come with me," he whispered as she leant out of the window to point out the direction she was to take. "I must see you alone."

"Helen," said Mary, "as I have got my bonnet on, perhaps I had better go with Lord Beaufort and see the house. I shall know directly if it will suit you; and in the meanwhile you might be preparing for our moving."

"Very well," said Helen, listlessly. "I will speak to Tomkinson; any house will do, so that there is not this constant racket."

She saw them leave the room with a dreamy feeling of wonder that they should go together, and tried to smile as they went out; but when the door was closed she hid her face in her hands in a state of utter depression. She felt, without owning it to herself, that they knew more of her husband than they had told her; there was almost an angry feeling in her heart against the secrecy which she fancied they observed, and yet a shrinking dread of its being broken. Above all, there was a miserable presentiment of coming evil—that expectation of ill which quickens the hearing, blinds the sight, and seems to clench the heart with a grasp that tightens at every strange sound, at every sudden silence. She was still seated in the same place and position when Mary returned to say that the house was quiet and clean; that Lord Beaufort had hired it, and thought his sister had better go into it without delay. He was gone to make other arrangements for her comfort in the way of servants, provisions, etc., and would not return for another hour.

"He is gone to the pier, Mary?"

"Very likely," she said; "you know the packet may be in to-day."

"Yes, and you and Beaufort know more than that," said Helen, raising her heavy eyes, and fixing them on Mary; "you have heard something you do not choose to tell me. I do not want to hear it," she added, almost fiercely; "it can only be a vague report. I should not believe it."

"Perhaps you are right," said Mary, trying to speak calmly, though her voice was low and shaking. "But, darling, Lord Beaufort thought it better I should tell you that the accounts of your dear husband, brought by some of the passengers by the last steamer, were very alarming."

"We knew that," said Helen, impatiently. "There is always exaggeration in reports of illness. They cannot *know* so much as we do. Mary, Mary, why do you try to frighten me?"

"Your brother thought that you ought to know all, and I know my own dear friend," she said, fondly caressing her, "will exert herself for the sake of all who love her; for the sake of the husband who may want all her care, all her strength of mind and energy."

"He must, he shall want them and have them," said Helen. "He will be with me to-day." Suddenly her forced coldness gave way, and, throwing her arms round her friend, she said, "Oh, Mary, if I am not to see him alive, what a life of remorse and misery is before me!" Her tears flowed convulsively for a time, and then she said, softly, "God's will be done, but I hope this suspense will not last long; and now let us have everything in readiness."

She rose as she spoke, and began, with shaking hands, to collect the few things that were scattered on the table. She sent Mary to give the necessary orders to the servants, and in a few minutes they had left the hotel, which, for years after, Helen could never think of without a shudder.

CHAPTER XLII

THE house they had taken was quiet, and sequestered from the noise of the streets, and had a small garden attached to it. It had evidently been newly furnished, and Helen set about arranging the largest room in it for Lord Teviot, with better hopes than she had felt at the hotel. She dwelt again and again to Mary on the necessity of moving this sofa or that arm-chair to particular places, because Teviot might like to lie down near the fire, or to sit up near the window. The cook, who had been sent in by Lord Beaufort, was ordered to prepare a dinner that would suit a man in the strongest health, and with the same breath she ordered gruel, and arrow-root, and barley-water, and all the wretched slops that count for food when all wish for it is over. Tomkinson was so glad to get away from the uncomfortable attic into which she had been put at the hotel that she was quite condescending to Laurel Cottage, and with the help of Lord Beaufort's servant and Lord Teviot's footman collected a quantity of things from various tradesmen that could not possibly be of any use, further than the pleasure they gave her of passing herself off to herself as an excellent housekeeper. And as she was really good-hearted, she had great ideas of saving my lady trouble, now she was in such grief, and she magnanimously forgave Lord Teviot for calling her Tomkins, and, indeed, would have answered to " Tom," under present circumstances, without a murmur. Mary had ascertained from her aunt the name of the best medical man in the town;

245

and now everything was prepared, and they sat down to another hour of painful thought and miserable expectation.

At last Lord Beaufort appeared. " Helen, the packet is in sight, and they have signalled for a litter."

" Then he is alive; I shall see him again. Oh! Beaufort, let us go; I am ready."

She shook from head to foot, but with a strong effort suddenly composed herself, and taking her brother's arm walked rapidly on. Neither of them spoke, and yet this miserable demand for a litter had given them hopes they had not felt before. It is a hard method of testing our degree of hope when we find that what should have brought terror now brings relief.

The packet was now lying close to the pier. Lord Beaufort persuaded his sister to remain with Mary for a few minutes while he went on board to ascertain more precisely the state in which Lord Teviot was. They saw him speaking to a grave-looking man, evidently the ship's surgeon, and he was soon joined by Mr. Le Geyt, the secretary, and the captain. Helen watched their looks in breathless suspense, and at last, seeing Dr. Grey shake his head as he eagerly addressed Lord Beaufort, she rushed from the pier and the next moment was standing at her brother's side.

" My sister, Lady Teviot," said Lord Beaufort, looking meaningly at Dr. Grey.

" I am glad her ladyship is here," said Dr. Grey, looking painfully embarrassed, but speaking in a calm monotonous voice. " As I was observing to your lordship, Lord Teviot has had a very severe attack of fever, very severe indeed, and of course we must expect—— You know we always expect after that sort of seizure——"

" He is better? " said Helen.

" Well, yes, of course, otherwise——"

" Is he better? " she again repeated. " Do not look at

my brother, but look at me, sir, and tell me the truth, the whole truth. I can bear it better than this suspense."

Dr. Grey did look at her, and saw that she was indeed wound up to know and to bear all, and at once he told her that the fever which had attacked Lord Teviot was one of a very violent kind, and which had proved fatal in many instances at Lisbon; that when first Lord Teviot came on board there was little hope, but that the fever itself had subsided, and that the danger that now existed was from the frightful state of weakness to which he was reduced. "But his age and naturally strong constitution gave us hopes; certainly we have hopes."

"Thank you; and now that I know all, let me go to him."

"I should recommend to your ladyship to defer seeing him; there is the difficulty of the removal still to be encountered, and——"

"I mean to be with him when he is moved," said Helen firmly.

"And," continued Dr. Grey, in the quietest tone, "I must apprise your ladyship that though it is most unlikely that Lord Teviot should recognize you, yet if he does, and your ladyship should show any great degree of emotion, I cannot answer for the consequences."

"I shall not show any emotion, and I must see him," said Helen, who felt as if Dr. Grey were a personal enemy, and hated him as a man totally without feeling. She was quite wrong; he was kind-hearted, and felt the greatest interest in Lord Teviot's case; but for thirty years he had been floating about the world, or cooped up in barracks with rough and hardy seamen; and he fought the battle between life and death daily waged by the men of his profession with none of the amenities which he would have acquired in more polished society.

"Had you not better wait, dearest," said Lord Beaufort,

" till Teviot has been moved home? I will stay and assist Dr. Grey."

" No, no," she said, with tears in her eyes. " Beaufort, I should naturally have been with him if I had done my duty, and had gone out to Lisbon. I feel I can be quite composed; and now, Dr. Grey, show me to his cabin."

They saw that further opposition was useless, and Dr. Grey led her immediately down the ladder that led to Lord Teviot's cabin.

It was nearly dark; light was oppressive to that weary brain and those sunken eyes; and at first Helen could only dimly discern a figure lying motionless in a cot watched by a servant, who withdrew on seeing Dr. Grey.

" We have been obliged to exclude the light very much," Dr. Grey said; " it produced too much excitement, but now it might be as well to accustom him to it gradually before we move him." He withdrew one of the shutters as he spoke, and then Helen saw her husband. But how fearfully changed! She could hardly bear to look on the livid face, the closed eyes, the thin dilated nostrils, and the painful expression of powerlessness that met her sight. One bitter fixed glance she gave, and then sinking on her knees she seized the emaciated hand that rested on the bed, and covered it with kisses. But quickly rising, she turned to Dr. Grey and whispered, " You see I can restrain myself, and now tell me what is next to be done, and how you can make me of use." He saw that she had power over herself, and said kindly, " I see you will make a good nurse. The first step is to get him moved into some very quiet room."

" That is all ready."

" I should like further advice. I have other duties to attend to, and this is a case that requires unceasing care."

" Dr. Morant is already warned, and will meet you at any moment."

" Then now let me ask you to return to your brother,

and the bearers who are in waiting will take up Lord Teviot in his cot, and you shall direct us to your house."

He opened the cabin-door as he spoke, and a flood of light streamed in and fell on Helen as she stood by her husband's bedside. The light seemed to pain him, for his brow contracted into rigid furrows, and then the dim, filmy eyes opened and turned upon her. For one moment there was a ray of intelligence in them, but as Helen stooped to kiss the pale lips which she fancied had almost smiled on her, the feeble gaze turned away, and with a slight moan Lord Teviot relapsed into unconsciousness.

" Now, my good lady," said Dr. Grey, " the less we have of this sort of thing the better. Come away." He led her to the foot of the stairs, where she turned and said in a beseeching voice, " He knew me, Dr. Grey; say that you think he did."

" Well, perhaps so," said the doctor, who was moved by her youth and loveliness; " but don't try experiments, we have not strength for them. Here she is, my lord," he added, addressing Lord Beaufort. " Take her on deck, and we shall get under weigh directly."

Lord Beaufort looked at his sister with painful astonishment. She was quite colourless. Years seemed to have passed over her head in those few minutes that had been passed in that cabin. The girl whose short life had been spent in gay and young frivolity had now looked one of the sternest and hardest realities of life in the face; and that one look had changed her to the anxious, doubting woman. " The golden exhalations of the dawn " had passed away, and by the light of open day she saw the battle of life lying before her, and she roused herself for the encounter.

Dr. Grey soon reappeared with his charge. A curtain was thrown over the cot, by the side of which Helen walked, heedless, indeed unaware, of the compassionate looks of the bystanders, and they reached their home; and Lord Teviot was conveyed to his bed, showing no sign of consciousness of the change made in his position.

And now began for Helen the life of a nurse. Oh! who is there fortunate enough not to know the routine of those painful days and nights of anxiety, which seem never to have had a beginning, and never to know an end—so long, if measured by the intensity of the feelings—so short, if reckoned by the progress that has been made? Fallacious hopes followed by groundless despair; the promise of recovery that had shown itself in the morning, succeeded by the sudden relapse in the evening; the medical visits bringing with them hope, and leaving behind them a sensation of blank disappointment; letters of inquiry which seem cold or importunate, and full of advice that only perplexes the anxious watcher, and requesting answers for which there is neither time nor inclination. These are the minor troubles of the day; but who can describe the faint sickening of the heart of the young wife who had hitherto seen but little illness, and who now saw it in its most fearful form? The removal from the ship brought on a return of fever, and the voice which Helen had feared she would hear no more now rang in her ears with all the harshness of delirium; but it was harshness of tone only. She heard her own name repeated again and again with words of the fondest endearment; and when the silence of weakness followed, she almost regretted the terrors of the active paroxysm.

During that night, and several that followed it, she never quitted his room: there were hired nurses in attendance, medical men always at hand, and her brother ready and anxious to take her place, but she steadfastly refused to leave her husband. She slept on a mattress placed on the floor at the side of his bed; sometimes the short sleep ended with a start, and with a vague feeling that something dreadful was taking place; sometimes with the sound sleep of youth, but there she was, able to rouse herself and be of use on the slightest notice.

Lord Beaufort watched her with the tenderest care. He could not bear the sights and sounds of the sick-room with the quiet fortitude which she evinced. Lord Teviot's wanderings, and the death-like weakness that followed, completely overcame him; and after one peculiarly bad night, when the nurse had called him up to assist his sister, he came down into the breakfast-room quite worn out, and laying his head on the table, burst into a passion of tears.

Mary, who was writing letters to the various members of the family, looked at him with the warmest pity. The few last days had given her a new view of his character. She had once thought him cold and worldly; but his tenderness to his sister, his thoughtfulness and consideration for all about him, the confidence he showed to herself, and the deep interest they both took in Lord Teviot's illness, had brought them to a new understanding, and had entirely done away with the reserve that had once subsisted between them.

"What is it, dear Lord Beaufort?" she said, going to him and taking his hand as if he had been her brother. "Is he worse?"

"Yes, I fear he is; it has been a dreadful night. I cannot bear to see that fine fellow so utterly prostrated. And Helen, my darling Helen! it kills me to look at that angel; she will wear herself out, and she looks so miserable, and yet is so calm and self-possessed. She soothes him when no one else can. Sometimes I fancy he knows her, and yet he talks of her always as absent. Miss Forrester, it is hard upon you to be brought into all our distress."

"It would be far harder if I were kept away from it," she said; and she, too, had tears in her eyes; "but I am more sanguine than you. The doctor seemed more hopeful yesterday evening, and they told us we might expect a return of fever. I think I had better say nothing about the night to dear Lady Eskdale; do not you? Perhaps in the afternoon I shall be able to write word he is better; and now I will make your breakfast."

He kissed the hand that had held his, and said, " I think you are right not to alarm my mother more than can be helped; but if he is not better to-morrow, my father and she will certainly come."

However, the next day there was certainly some improvement; and in the evening there was less fever, and a greater disposition to sleep. The doctors recommended that food should be given every two hours, and Helen rose from her mattress each time to administer it herself. Once he seemed to sink back as if he were fainting; and she was about to call the nurse, when she heard the longed-for whisper —" Helen, my darling." She saw that she was recognized, and, stooping down, fondly caressed him. " Where am I? " were the next faint words. " You are with me, dearest, at Southampton; you have been very ill, but you are spared to me. Now you must not speak another word." She kissed his forehead, and, sinking on her knees, she poured forth, in a low tone, those eloquent words which gratitude wrings from the full heart that had seemed dead and cold, when all that it had at stake was to be wrestled for. The prayers had been faint and doubting, but the praise was full and fervent. Lord Teviot was too weak even to understand the thanksgiving offered by his wife, but the sound seemed to soothe him; and once more looking at her, he murmured, " Thank you, my own," and again sank into a quiet sleep.

CHAPTER XLIII

WHEN Lord Beaufort and Mary saw Helen in the morning, the first look was sufficient to assure them of the favourable change that had taken place. Pale and wearied as she was, the whole expression of her countenance was altered. " What would we have given a week ago for the chance of such a morning as this? " she said. " Even our sententious Dr. Grey is satisfied, and said, without moving a muscle, ' We are all right now '; but I know he is very glad: just look at the marks my rings have made in my fingers, in consequence of the warmth of his congratulatory squeeze; and Dr. Morant considers the danger quite over. Beaufort, dear, don't you think you ought to go to Eskdale, and tell them all this? Mamma will be so interested in all the details you can give her."

" Well," he said, looking at Mary, " perhaps it would be a good plan; but if I write to-day, and then take a confirmed good account to-morrow, that would be still more satisfactory."

" But you would be with them to-night, and, as I know by experience, a night of anxiety is a long, weary intervention. "

" Oh! Nelly, I see how it is," he said, laughingly. " You want to have Teviot all to yourself, and so turn me off, now I can be of no further use."

" No, no; what should I have done without you, Beaufort? you are always of use to me; but as to Teviot, it is true that when he is quite himself again, I had rather—I mean that he had rather I should tell him that we are quite alone. He must be kept quite quiet, you know."

" Yes, I see plainly that you want to get rid of us. Perhaps it is better; and a week or ten days hence he might like to see me, and I could come back again."

" I am sure he would like it," she said, eagerly, " and so should I; and now I must go back to him, and I will bring you a note for dear mamma. It is the first time I have had the heart to write to her. Dear Beaufort and Mary," she added, in a faltering voice, " I never can thank you enough for all you have done."

They were left alone. Beaufort walked straight up to Miss Forrester, and taking her hand, said " Yes; you have been all and everything to us, Mary; let me call you Mary, if only for this once. I know that I must formerly have been hateful to you; I know that I was most unjust; but all that is long gone by. You must have seen that it was. Have you seen, too, that you are now dearer to me than any other human being; that the wish of my heart is to gain your affection? Mary, speak to me, and tell me if I have any chance of success."

" Oh, take time," she said, with much emotion; " recollect how ill you thought of me only ten days ago."

" No, no," he said; " these last ten days have only shown me how perfect you are—how unselfish—how full of kindness; but long before that, at the time of the election, my love for you began: but you were so cold to me, I dared not show it. Mary, I was misled by the foolish assertions of a very unworthy friend. Even at the time I hardly believed what he said, and now! Mary, cannot you forget that I once thought you might have a fault? "

" Willingly, if you will go on believing that I have a great many. One of them, as we are confessing, I too will confess. I resented very foolishly the opinion you expressed of me; and was quite as unjust to you afterwards as you had formerly been to me. But since we have been here, we have understood each other better, and I look upon you now, Lord Beaufort, as a very sincere friend."

" Oh! pray don't do that; that is the last thing I should wish. No, Mary, I again repeat, I love you devotedly; my only hope is that you will consent to be my wife. Why do you look so distressed? "

She coloured violently, and seemed to find a difficulty in speaking; and could not even raise her eyes to his. But with a strong effort the cloud seemed to pass away, and she said, firmly, " Such frankness as yours deserves a frank answer. I will tell you the whole truth, Lord Beaufort; you know that I have loved before, and I had not a moment's happiness while that love lasted, for I had no trust. I feel," she added, timidly, " that towards you this distrust could not exist; on my side there would be perfect confidence; but you, you would remember my first choice, and you would perhaps always doubt one who had chosen so unworthily."

" Never for an instant: it was your discernment with regard to Stuart that first made me admire you; and when I found that your conduct with regard to him had been so true, so unlike what he had led me to believe, my shame at my own conduct was all that prevented me from telling you, long ago, how strong my admiration was. Mary, let me go to my mother with more than one piece of happy news. Let me tell her of my own happiness as well as Helen's."

What more was there to be said? Mary gave the " Yes " so earnestly requested; and by the time Lord Beaufort's carriage came to the door, they had talked themselves into the belief that they had liked each other from the first; that Mary had never had any real affection for

Colonel Stuart, and that Lord Beaufort was the only man whom she had ever or could ever have loved.

How warmly he was received at home, or how welcome his intelligence was to Lord and Lady Eskdale, may easily be guessed.

CHAPTER XLIV

COLONEL STUART's arrival at Portsdown was a great boon to Lady Portmore, who was living in a sea of *tracasseries* and explanations; to all of which he graciously inclined his ear. He delighted in a promising bud of *tracasserie*, and nursed it into a full-blown flower with all the care that a horticulturist bestows on a cankered yellow rose. He advised sharp letters in one direction, friendly appeals in another, epigrams were suggested here, and bemoanings there; wrongs dressed out, and rights suppressed, till it seemed somehow as if everybody were to blame; and the original petty affront widened into a circle of heart-burnings and coolnesses. He and Lady Portmore were adepts at this game, except that she was all fire and talk, and he all suavity and reason; but between them they made a great deal of mischief. She was now in a state of political transition, which gave great promise of involvements. To Mr. G.'s original offence of neglecting Lord Portmore, he had now added the sin of refusing an appointment to a very disreputable nephew of Lady Portmore's, who had been turned out of both army and navy, and therefore, as she pointedly observed, " Mr. G. must see that as the young man was not fit for the Church, there was nothing for it but to give him a good colonial appointment; he could not starve." Mr. G. asked, " Why not? " and thought a slight course of starvation would perhaps be wholesome; but, at all events, he declined peremptorily giving a good office to a very *mauvais sujet*. Lady Portmore was affronted. Mr. G. did not care.

R

She wrote eight pages of upbraiding and serious entreaty, which he answered by four lines of jocose denial; and the result was a complete and entire change in Lady Portmore's opinion on free trade, parliamentary reform, foreign policy, etc.   She did not state the precise nature of her new views, but was simply sorry to say that she and Lord Portmore had quite lost all confidence in G., and thought him a most dangerous minister, and were very thankful that the country had a Mr. Sheffield to look to. When Colonel Stuart arrived, she had given warning to all her old Government friends, and was organizing a large meeting of former enemies, in which she wanted his assistance.

Lord Teviot was of course included in the general proscription of Mr. G.'s friends, and therefore this history of the claims of Mr. Lorimer was not altogether unpleasant to her. Some little time ago she would have waged war to the knife against anyone who could have spread or believed such a report; but now, as it had been told to her in confidence, she began by writing it to fifteen intimate friends; and then took to dissecting it with her accustomed consistency.

" I really am quite grieved to the heart about this sad story of poor Teviot. Supposing it should turn out to be true—I am sure I hope it will not; what is to become of him?   G.'s Government cannot last a month after Parliament meets, so office will be no resource, even if G. does not turn upon him at once, of which he is quite capable. Such a blow to the Eskdales! Do they know this story? "

" I thought it advisable to mention it to Lady Walden, and I believe she told her sister; but a bad account of Lord Teviot hurried Lady Teviot away.   I did not see her again."

" Ah, Lady Teviot! Many people think her very pretty; I am not sure I do, and, by the by, she will not be

Lady Teviot if Mr. Lorimer gains his suit. How strange! What will she be?"

"Lady Helen Lorimer, unless there is some female title: Teviot may claim through some grandmother or great-grandmother."

"Oh no, I am sure there is not: I know a great deal about that family. I fancy we are connected in some way. No, you may depend upon it, she will be only Helen Lorimer, and they will be absolute paupers. This is really very sad"; and Lady Portmore looked radiant with sorrow.

"I should be very sorry if that old title went to such an unmitigated scamp as Harry Lorimer," said Colonel Stuart, "to say nothing of the loss to our friends at St. Mary's; but nobody in these days cares about their friends."

"I do," said Lady Portmore severely; "nobody is so constant to their friends as I am; and poor Teviot was quite devoted to me; but at the same time, if Harry Lorimer has a right to the title, of course he ought to have it, and he must be allowed to take his proper position in society. I think I have asked him before to some of my parties. Have I, Stuart? Is not he a man all over black hair, with great whiskers?"

"Yes, a regular tiger; but he is a good actor, and was tolerated at the Westerbys for the sake of their private theatricals."

"Dear me! how convenient it would be to have him here! we are in such want of a good Paul Pry; but, with my regard for the Teviots, it would not do, I suppose, to ask him just now. Besides, I am quite wretched about Teviot's illness, and must write by this post to Lady Eskdale, to ask how he is, and then we shall just have time for a rehearsal. I am very much disappointed in William Montague; he is a regular stick on the stage. Harry

Lorimer would be a treasure to us just now; but, as I said, I suppose the Teviots might hear of it. What do you think, Stuart, could I ask him?"

"Certainly not," said Colonel Stuart, who was alarmed at such an instance of want of tact and feeling; "besides, he is a vulgar dog at best."

"Oh, well! then that settles the point; and besides, Teviot is such a friend of mine, only I wish we could detach him from the G. politics. Mr. G. is just the sort of man to give him a peerage, if he loses his own. Such a job! However, I will write and ask the Sheffields; his attack on G. at that agricultural meeting was wonderfully clever."

And thus ended Lady Portmore's interest in one of her hundred dear friends. Even Mrs. Douglas felt more in her grumbling, unrefined way. Illness, independent of its merits as a destroyer of good looks, had always a certain charm for her. She was an excellent nurse, and now that the Teviots were in adversity, she warmed heartily to them; sent every day to the Castle for the latest accounts from Southampton; and though she continued to pity Lady Eskdale for having married her daughters so ill, she was unfeignedly grieved for Helen, and would have gone to Southampton herself if she could have been allowed to assist in attending on Lord Teviot.

CHAPTER XLV

But Helen wanted no assistance. The tameless energy of eighteen bore her through all the fatigues of broken nights and watchful days; and every hour her husband became dearer to her as she became more necessary to him. His eyes followed her with the tenderest gaze as she moved noiselessly about his room; the hand that brought him refreshment or medicine was warmly pressed to his lips; the fondest words of endearment fell gently from his pallid lips. If she left the room, he could have addressed her in the touching words of one of the best of English poetesses:

> " Watch me, oh, watch me still,
>   Through the long night's dreary hours—
> Uphold, by thy firm will,
>   Worn nature's sinking powers.
> While yet I see thee there
>   (Thy loose locks round thee flying),
> So young, and fresh, and fair,
>   I feel not I am dying."

Helen had expected, from former recollections, that the period of convalescence might be one of impatience and irritation. " All men are impatient when they are ill," she thought; " but somehow I do not think I shall mind it now. I know I can make him follow all Dr. Grey's directions, and that is all that is of real importance; and if he is low and vexed at times, it is only natural, poor fellow! " But he never was vexed or cross, which was the word that Helen had sedulously refrained from using, even in her thoughts. Once he was almost peremptory in his orders that she should go to her own room and take one good night's rest, leaving him to the care of the nurse; but he was met by an equally peremptory refusal, and an assertion that a mattress on the floor was the most comfortable bed possible; and he was also told that he was on no account to interfere with the arrangements of the sick-room, but to do what he was told, and get well as fast as he could. He only smiled, as he saw that all fear of him had passed away, and in the perfect ease of Helen's manner, amounting to playfulness, when he was well enough to be amused, he felt that the love which he had once doubted, and almost driven away, was again his own; and a quiet rest came over the weary heart which had loved with all the irritation of believing it met with no return.

She told him of her hurried journey, of her troubles at the hotel, and insisted on his thinking Laurel Cottage— which could hold only themselves and four servants—the most charming residence in the world.

" My poor Helen, what a quantity of trouble I have given you! but surely you ought not to have been alone at that horrible hotel."

" I was not," she said, quite frankly, for she felt that the days of jealousy were over. " Mary Forrester lives in this neighbourhood, and she came with me; and Beaufort joined us, and was so useful during that first dreadful week— sitting up half the night, and writing accounts of you half the day, and making love to Mary at all odd moments; and those two people who had hated each other fell in love on the strength of their mutual interest in your illness. You have made that marriage, dearest, simply by the fright you gave us."

" Dear old Beaufort! " said Lord Teviot; " he is a thorough good fellow. I fancied I had a vision of him one night by my bedside. Helen, I should so like to see him. Am not I well enough? "

"Not quite, dear; to-morrow Dr. Grey thinks you may be moved into the next room, and your servant has ambitious views of shaving you, and dressing you up in a splendid dressing-gown. After that I may perhaps allow you to 'see company,' on a limited scale; and Beaufort will come down to us whenever you like, but at present he is in London." She did not add that he was there engaged with lawyers on the subject of Harry Lorimer's claims; she was most anxious to keep that worrying history from her husband as long as possible.

"And your mother?" he said. "I do not suppose there is such another nurse in the world as my dear little wife; but still, Lady Eskdale must have great qualifications for that office. I should like her to pet me in her soft way; and if she were here, you would be satisfied to leave me with her, and go out for a little air and exercise."

"No, I should not. I take plenty of exercise, running about the house in your service; and mamma is so gentle, she would let you commit all sorts of imprudences." She was silent for a few moments, and a deep flush spread itself over her drooping face, then, suddenly raising her eyes, she said, "My own darling, I do not wish that anyone, not even mamma, should come between you and me just now." She threw her arms round him, and, with a fond kiss, added, "Teviot, you once thought I did not love you as you loved me. You do not think so now, do you? You never will think so again? I was afraid of you, I believe—perhaps at last a little jealous; but you were no sooner gone than I found out that I was very unhappy without you. Then came the news of your illness; and when I saw you in that wretched cabin, dying as I thought, I cannot tell you "— and she shuddered as she spoke—" my utter misery—the remorse I felt at having ever consented to leave you. How wrong I was!"

"No, no!" he interrupted her, as he pressed her to his

heart. " I do not wonder you were glad to get away from me. I behaved like an idiot and a brute, and frightened my poor child out of her senses, and expected her to love me all the more for it."

" Well," she said, smiling through her tears, " you have frightened me into them again. The terrors of the last fortnight have been much worse than those of St. Mary's; but they have satisfied me on one point—that when I thought I did not love you more than any other human being, I was only deceiving myself and you. Oh, Teviot, in all your wanderings and sufferings you were so good, so kind! Sometimes I thought my heart would break, when you spoke so lovingly of me, not knowing that I was by you. However, all this is over now! I cannot be thankful enough that you have been spared, and now only promise——"

" I will promise at once, without being asked, never to distrust my own Helen again. How can I ever doubt your affection," he said, with much emotion, " when I know that I owe my life, under Heaven, to your devotion? Kiss me once more, my darling, and then I will rest."

And the rest which succeeded this spontaneous avowal of his wife's true affection was the calmest and the most refreshing the invalid had yet known. Helen's mind was not so peaceful. She knew that there was yet a trial in store for him, and one that he would feel deeply. A number of letters were waiting for him; and at last the moment came in which he asked for them. Her hand shook as she gave them, and she said, with a faltering voice, " I hope there will be no bad news in them."

" No," he said; " I cannot anticipate any to-day. I feel so much better, and it is such a comfort to be by an open window, and to breathe the fresh air again! It is so very mild for the time of year, that I really wish, Nell, you would go out for a short walk. You ought to have had your carriage sent down; but we shall be moving soon to Teviot House. Will you take your maid, and go out? You see I have plenty of amusement," pointing to the heaps of letters that were lying by him.

"Well, I think I will go for half an hour, as you do not want me," said Helen, who dreaded the effect that the first announcement of Mr. Lorimer's pretensions might have on Lord Teviot in his present weak state; and conjectured that he would dislike having any witness of his first emotions. "I shall not be long away."

When she returned, she found him still lying on his sofa, looking exhausted, and with two red, feverish spots on his cheeks. A quantity of opened letters were strewed on the carpet beside him; others, unopened, were still on the table. She knelt down, and, taking his thin hand in hers, said, "You have been overtiring yourself with those tiresome letters."

"Perhaps so," he said, dejectedly.

"Do not open any more; let me look over the others for you."

"No, no," he said hastily. "You should not see them; they are full of vexation."

"That is all the more reason why I should, dear Teviot. Do not keep any vexations to yourself; we should bear them better together."

"It was for your sake I did not want you to know what I have heard. My poor Helen, what will you feel, when you know that, in marrying me, you may have married an unconscious impostor? that name, and fortune, and all——"

"You mean," she said, looking up at him with a smile, and kissing the hand she held, "that Harry Lorimer is trying to take it all from us. He means to be Lord Teviot himself. Happily he cannot be *my* Teviot, whatever happens; and who knows if he will not fail in all the rest!"

"Helen!" said Lord Teviot, starting up, "is it possible

that you have heard this history before? How long have you known it?"

"Before I left Eskdale."

"And you have had all this anxiety on your mind while you have been working like a slave in your attendance on me, and seeming to have no care but for my health."

"Why, you foolish old darling, don't you see that the great care swallowed up the little one? I hardly know how to explain myself, because I can understand that as you have been attached all your life to St. Mary's and Teviot House, and your name and station, it would be a cruel trial to you to lose all this; so I did feel at times very unhappy when I thought you had to hear it all as soon as you were strong enough to bear it; but so far as *I* am concerned, dear Teviot (do not think me unfeeling), but this is not the sort of trial that affects me very deeply."

He looked at her, and saw that she was speaking from her heart, and not merely with the intention of comforting him; and the suspicions he had once entertained, that it was for his position, and not for himself, that she had married him, were remembered but to be repented of, and forgotten for ever. He bent his head on hers, and whispered, "My treasure above all other treasures, whatever happens, I am not to be pitied. I have what I have longed for all my life—a real, true love to depend on."

The subject of the lawsuit once begun, it was of course a constant theme of discussion; but Lord Teviot was too feeble to take any active part even on a point of such moment, and was quite satisfied to know that Lord Eskdale was acting for him, and that Lord Beaufort was staying in London solely that he might be in consultation with the lawyers. The case, as Mr. Lorimer's advisers stated it, was a very simple one. Henry, Marquess of Teviot, had two brothers, Robert, the father of this Henry Lorimer, who was born, as had always been supposed, before the marriage of his parents, and Alfred, father of the present Lord Teviot. Lord Robert and Lord Alfred both died young, and on the death of Henry, Lord Teviot, the title and estates passed to the heir presumptive, Lord Alfred's son. Henry Lorimer now asserted that he had only recently discovered that his parents were married some months before his birth, and in proof of this, he produced a certificate of the marriage of Lord Robert Lorimer to Emma Scot, in January 18—, and a registry of the birth of their son, Henry Lorimer, in the following August. He could not undertake to explain why he had not at once succeeded to the title on his uncle's death, but Lord Robert was on bad terms with his two brothers, owing to the disreputable connection he had made; and he had probably never informed them that it had ended in a marriage. Both parents had died nearly at the same time; he had been left, when only three years old, to some of his mother's relations; and he affirmed that it was only on the recent death of the old aunt who had taken charge of him that he had found the certificate of his mother's marriage.

All this sounded plausible enough; but Lord Beaufort wrote in good spirits, and said that the lawyers were sanguine, and that there had already been two or three faint offers of a compromise, which confirmed them in the idea that Mr. Lorimer had but a weak case, and that they were waiting impatiently for Lord Teviot's return to London, when he would probably be able to direct them in their search for family papers, and to point out old servants or friends of the family, whose evidence would be important.

So Helen sometimes took a very obstinate line of disbelief, at others she would try to make Lord Teviot laugh by the plans she proposed to execute, if they were reduced to poverty, which she of course represented as extreme, Lord Teviot digging and ploughing for his life, and she cooking and ironing for hers, in a picturesque brown stuff

gown with short sleeves and white cuffs, and a little pink
silk half-handkerchief tied either round her throat or under
her chin—she did not exactly know which, but all reduced
heroines wore pink silk handkerchiefs, it was *de rigueur*,
after any loss of fortune.   Lord Teviot would not of course
object to the accustomed suit of velveteen.

No, he had an old shooting jacket, which would do well
enough on ploughing days; but he did not think that at
the worst they should be reduced to those extreme straits.
Perhaps Helen could sketch out a life for them a few grades
above that.

"Oh yes, dear, with the greatest ease. You would not
like to keep a shop?"

"Not at all, thank you."

"Nor I.   Could we afford to rent this dear little Laurel
Cottage, Teviot?"   He nodded.   "Oh! then nothing
can be pleasanter than our prospects.   I shall take care of
you till you are strong, and walk with you, and we can
occasionally afford ourselves a drive in a gig.   Phillips does
already the work of butler, valet, and footman; and as for
Tomkinson, no maid-of-all-work could have worked harder
than she has during your illness. Seriously, Teviot, it
is very easy to find fault with servants, and to be always
abusing them, as most of us do, but when illness or anxiety
comes, how kind and thoughtful they are!   Those two have
been indefatigable in their care of you, keeping the house
quiet, running for doctors at all hours, inventing *extempore*
meals; in short, acting like friends."

"Yes," said Lord Teviot, "I have observed them;
Phillips has been my servant ever since I left school, and I
knew his merits; but your little fly-away maid, with her
curls and graces, has quite astonished me.   She is so staid
and thoughtful, and the little woman actually cried when
she attempted to make me a congratulatory speech the
day I came into this room.   Of course we must make them

some handsome present; and in the meanwhile, there is a parcel of fine lace somewhere amongst my boxes, which I collected for you. I dare say we could find something there that would please your Mrs. Tomkins——"

" Tomkinson, dear; she is extremely distressed that you do not know her name, and I believe thinks you might just as well call mamma Lady Esk."

The parcel was soon found, and when Lord Teviot sent for Mrs. Tomkinson, and, addressing her by her proper name, presented her with a beautiful lace shawl, adding his warm thanks for her excellent nursing, she was completely overcome. After rushing up to her room, and taking a long survey of herself, she burst into a flood of tears, and then went down to the kitchen and made a cup of arrowroot flavoured with a double allowance of brandy, which she sent up with her duty to his lordship, and then returned to her looking-glass, which she visited at every spare moment during the rest of the day, snatching one half-hour for a letter to Mrs. Nelson, in which my lord's convalescence and real guipure, and my lady's goodness and the becomingness of black lace, were much mixed up together. The threatened lawsuit had now got into the newspapers, and become general property; so Mrs. Tomkinson added a fierce postscript, expressing her belief that Mr. Lorimer was " a vile imposture," and her hopes that she should live to see him hanged for forgery, and she should certainly not wear her black shawl as mourning for *him* indeed.

CHAPTER XLVI

Owing either to the arrowroot made by the grateful Tomkinson, or the excitement of the lawsuit, or the excellence of Lord Teviot's constitution, his strength returned so rapidly that his removal to Teviot House admitted of no further difficulty. Helen quitted her dear Laurel Cottage with some unwillingness, but was obliged to own, when she reached home, that there were advantages in a large luxurious house which she should be unwilling to forgo. Lord Teviot sent his secretary, Mr. Le Geyt, down to St. Mary's, to examine the chests of family papers that had accumulated there, and in the meanwhile the foreign affairs in which he had been engaged gave him all the occupation to which he was equal. Mr. G. came to see him immediately; entered with sense and friendliness into the affair of the lawsuit, to which, however, he did not attach great importance. He said he had seen too much of life to believe in these sudden discoveries of marriage certificates. A certificate that was worth anything was never missing for five-and-twenty years; and the old aunt, if *she* were worth anything, would have produced it long before. He felt sorry for whatever might give that perfect angel, Lady Teviot, a moment's anxiety, but was convinced it would soon be ended; and in the meanwhile Lord Teviot must contrive to be well enough to take office before Parliament met. Other acquaintances called, some with the gloomiest faces and forebodings; some with an affectation of considering the point decided in favour of Mr. Lorimer, and taking a degree of modest credit to themselves for still adhering to their poor fallen friends; but many with a real, hearty interest in what they called the real Teviots; and these true friends never vexed Helen by retailing to her any of the ill-natured remarks made by the false ones.

Lady Portmore's strength of purpose had given way, on the defalcation of one of her *corps dramatique*, who had been summoned home suddenly, and Harry Lorimer was established as Paul Pry *in esse*, and Lord Teviot *in posse*, at Portsdown. She wished to make a great mystery of this, but Mr. Lorimer took care to have the playbills of the private theatricals forwarded to the newspapers; and Helen would have been more than mortal if she had not delighted in the scornful smile with which Lord Teviot read the name of H. Lorimer, Esq., in the list of the " brilliant circle " assembled at Portsdown.

This was the last act of that series of trials which had had the effect of bringing the husband and wife into the closest bonds of confidence and affection. The very next morning Lord Beaufort, who had continued to act for his brother-in-law, rushed into the room with a bundle of papers, the result of Mr. Le Geyt's researches, and docketed by the late Lord Teviot—" Letters from my brother Lord Robert respecting his marriage." The last letter, written on his death-bed, from an obscure village on the south coast, announced that his infant heir had followed its mother to the grave, where he himself must shortly join them; and he implored his brother to show some kindness to the unfortunate boy he left behind him. " I gave him the Christian name which has always been given to the males in our family, in conjunction with my own, and though he has no legal right to be so called, it is a Harry Lorimer whom I commend to your care. Harry Alfred Lorimer, my second son, and heir, has been taken from me, and perhaps I have no right to complain that my death will be a loss to none but the unhappy boy who will remain a living proof of my guilt and folly." Enclosed were certificates of his marriage, and of the birth and death of his infant legitimate son. Whether the late Lord Teviot, a selfish, careless man, ever read this letter was doubtful. Certainly he never acted on it; and Harry Lorimer grew up ignorant of most of the details of his father's history. Whether he really believed himself to be what he now asserted, or merely made use of the papers he had found on his aunt's death, as a good speculation, wherewith to extract a sum of money from Lord Teviot, is a mystery that charity may leave unravelled. When his lawyer informed him that the papers which had been found did not " leave him a leg to stand on," he observed that he was not surprised; that he had begun life on one leg only, and was only astonished that he had stood so well and so long on it. " At all events," he added, " I have had my fun for my money, and have met with more civility during the last month than during the thirty preceding years of my existence. It is a shabby world to live in, but I do not mean to let the worshippers of the rising sun who took me up drop me again easily. So I shall go down to Portsdown. I suppose Teviot is not the sort of fellow to come down handsomely with a few thousands because I withdraw my claims. Is he? "

The lawyer said he rather thought not; and there ended Harry Lorimer's dream of grandeur. It had been short and vague, but, as he said, " rather good fun while it lasted; and he thought it would enable him to act Sly the tinker with considerable *verve*, if Lady Portmore felt inclined to get up ' The Taming of the Shrew.' "

CHAPTER XLVII

" HELEN," said Lord Teviot, " now that this law business is settled, and that I have given G. all my Lisbon
information, I think it would be very desirable to get away
from this foggy London. I shall never get strong so long
as we remain here."

" I am sure you will not," she said; " your doctors are
very anxious you should try change of air, indeed, so much
so, that I made Phillips write some days ago to St. Mary's,
to have all your rooms thoroughly aired, and to say that we
should probably be there in a few days."

" Then, my dear child, you said what is entirely untrue.
Certainly you may go to St. Mary's if you have set your
heart on it, but I cannot possibly have the honour of
accompanying you."

" Oh, Teviot, what do you mean? Why not? "

" Because I have set *my* heart on going to Eskdale," he
said, smiling. " I must see your mother and Amelia and
all the rest of them again, and we shall have the diversion
of watching dear old Beaufort making love. I really
wonder, Helen, you are not more eager to go and see all
our own belongings. I believe you are ashamed of showing
your scarecrow of a husband; but I want to go while I am
still looking interesting. I am sure your mother will
enjoy petting me and making much of me."

" Who would not, you darling? " said Helen, in a trans-
port of delight. " Oh dear, what a happy invention life is,
particularly when it has been a little chequered! just think
what a happy Christmas it will be; and how little we could

have expected it six weeks ago! Teviot, I sometimes think I am not half grateful enough for all the blessings I have."

"Well, they seem to agree with you," he said, looking at her with the fondest admiration. "I shall not be ashamed of showing my wife. I flatter myself, Helen, they will think you even handsomer than you were when you left Eskdale on our wedding-day."

"I should think so, indeed," she said, laughing. "I hope they will find me improved in all ways," she added more gravely. "I was a foolish spoiled child then, and now I am a happy woman."

Two days after this conversation, a large family party were assembled at Eskdale: Waldegraves, Waldens, Teviots, Ernest, and the reigning hero and heroine, Beaufort and Mary. Lord Teviot's appearance had at first caused considerable alarm in the circle, he looked so thin and pale; but Helen assured them that he was robust now, compared to what he had been, and that they would see improvement every day. So they all set about expediting his recovery, Lady Eskdale purring over him, and, as he foretold, petting him from morning to night; his sisters-in-law ready to amuse him at all hours, and Helen looking on with undisguised satisfaction at the daily improvement in his health, and feeling in her heart the enjoyment he evidently felt in having become a favourite member of a large and affectionate family.

"Yes, this is all very well," said Ernest one morning when he was sitting with the Teviots and Waldens. "You all seem very happy and settled, and of course had a perfect right to marry if you chose it. But now here is Beaufort going to set up his little altar to domestic felicity (I thought he would have stuck by me); and here am I, the only one of the family left in solitary grandeur.

> The last rose of summer, left blooming and lone,
> All my lovely companions well married and gone!

I declare it is very affecting."

" But pleasant for you," said Lord Teviot, " to have so many homes to go to; you know we all like to have you, and you will circulate amongst us without the slightest trouble to yourself."

" Yes; but I think I am getting too old now to be the odd man of the family; the dining-out Beaufort. And then, when I come home from one of your well-lit houses, or from my club, it will be very depressing to take out my latch-key, and to find a deplorable little lamp in the hall, which makes the whole house smell greasy; and to have to go tumbling up the dark stairs, to a darker room. I really wish I were married too "; and so saying, he drew his arm-chair almost into the fire, and tried to give a deep sigh.

" But why don't you marry? " said Helen.

" My dear soul, how can I? you can't expect me to go rushing about after all those London girls, who care for nothing but balls, and expect to be danced with, and to be handed to carriages standing miles off; and above all, to have their cloaks found for them. How I loathe a cloak-room, with No. 210 to be looked for, and of course it is underneath all the other wraps, and there are 209 bundles to be moved before one gets at it. No, I mean to eschew balls now I have got into Parliament."

" But there are plenty of girls in the country."

" Vulgar, I fear; and besides, how am I to make acquaintance with them? You can't expect me to go riding about the country, calling at all the neighbours' houses, and asking if the young ladies are at home. No, I do not see how I am to find a wife; but you must all of you set about arranging it. *Les grands parents* always do, you know, in French novels."

" I very much doubt, Ernest," said Helen, hesitatingly, " whether you would make a good husband. You will excuse me for mentioning it, but you are rather too selfish— I mean self-indulgent."

"Yes; that's just it. I have indulged myself to that degree, that I am, as you mildly observe, Helen, infernally selfish. But then, you know, my wife would be a part of myself; and I should indulge her, and we could both be selfish together. So do find one for me; and now I must go and take my ride. Who will come?"

"I will," said Lord Teviot. "I must try and get back to my old habits. Don't you think I might try a ride, Helen?"

"Decidedly not. You know, dearest, Dr. Grey said you were on no account to go out in an east wind; so I always look at the weathercock the first thing in the morning. It is due east, and bitterly cold."

"But he said I was to take exercise," Lord Teviot suggested very humbly.

"Well, then, come and play at billiards with me; as for going out in this weather, I can't allow it, love; so don't say any more about it."

"There!" said Ernest, as Lord Teviot walked off to the billiard-room, with his arm round his wife's waist. "Now, that is just what I want—somebody who knows which way the wind blows, and who will tell me what I may or may not do; and will make me stay at home when I want to go out, and *vice versâ*. Just see how it has improved Teviot: he used to look as black as thunder on the slightest contradiction, and now he is the mildest of men, and looks radiant when Helen vouchsafes to snub him. It is strange."

"Not very," said Amelia; "he sees that her whole heart is given up to him; and till he married, he never was really cared for by anybody. He had neither mother nor sisters; and the rest of the world only flattered him. Dear little Nell loves him—that makes all the difference, as you will see when Mrs. Ernest appears."

"I suppose it does," said Ernest; and this time he really sighed, and went off to his solitary ride.

It almost seemed as if Lady Eskdale must have overheard the foregoing conversation, for when she returned from her drive, she brought Eliza Douglas with her. The great election feud had nearly died out. Mr. Douglas had never wished to prolong it, and was in his heart rather pleased with a defeat which left him free to live with his cows and sheep and turnips; and, moreover, he liked the society of the Eskdales, and had a general hatred of neighbourly quarrels. Lord Teviot's dangerous illness had, as was said before, roused Mrs. Douglas's latent tenderness for Helen, and softened her towards Lady Eskdale. She said, indeed, that it might eventually be a great advantage to Helen to get rid of such an ill-tempered man, who was not even what he had pretended to be, probably not Lord Teviot at all; and who, if he lived, would most likely be a pauper; but still, there was something melancholy in Helen's story; and she thought it would be only neighbourly to call. And the first step made, the others were not difficult. The visit was returned. Lady Eskdale looked ill and harassed, which put Mrs. Douglas into extreme good humour. The failure of Mr. Lorimer's pretensions to the title was rather a trial; but Lord Teviot was civil and subdued, and Helen was so radiant with happiness that she was affectionate even to Mrs. Douglas; and altogether that lady was in a better disposition towards the Eskdales than she had been before the election. She had missed them as objects of observation, and had wanted somebody to find fault with.

So when Lady Eskdale invited Eliza to return with her to the Castle for a few days, no objection was made, and Eliza set off in a most hopeful state of mind. Her Extract Book, carefully padlocked, accompanied her, and it seemed likely that its gloomy contents might be enlivened with a few sonnets to " Hope," and " Peace of mind."

" Did you tell my aunt to ask her? " whispered Ernest to Helen, as they sat down to dinner nearly opposite to Eliza.

" Certainly not," she said, laughing; " she is a nice little thing; and I shall decidedly interfere, if you begin that course of philandering you pursued at St. Mary's."

" My dear Helen, I do not know what is the feminine of the word philanderer—perhaps philanderess; and I assure you she philanderessed with me in the most innocent but decided manner. But I won't begin again till I feel sure of my own honourable intentions."

He, however, occasionally addressed an observation to the opposite side of the table, and during second course observed to Helen that Miss Douglas had a very pretty hand and arm; and by the time that dessert was on the table, said he had made the discovery that she had a good perception of a joke, and smiled intelligently. " I really think, Helen, I am falling in love! I do not mean in the usual mad, bustling way in which most people set about it; but falling in love very creditably for me. What do you think? "

" That you have not the remotest idea even how to set about it; you are much too worldly and too *blasé* to appreciate or to please such a good, simple-minded girl as that is; but as you are only in jest, it does not much signify."

Ernest laughed, but he was very much piqued with Helen's views of the subject; and in the evening he took some pains to make himself agreeable to Eliza. But he did not find her so disposed to be amused and interested as she had been at St. Mary's. Mrs. Douglas, with her usual acuteness, had observed all that had passed there, which she thought fully accounted for her daughter's changed spirits since—and before Eliza went to Eskdale, her mother had spoken to her seriously on the subject of Colonel Beaufort's attentions, and without exactly saying that Eliza had invited rather than encouraged them, had desired her upon no account to *seek* his society; and, above all, to recollect that he " was a regular London fine man, without any heart, and thinking of nothing but his own amusement." In this opinion Eliza did not, of course, concur; but she most conscientiously acted upon it, and was as reserved in her manner as if her mother had been sitting opposite to her making cutting remarks at, and on, Ernest.

He was rather surprised at first at this change in their relations; then he became amused at seeing his attentions rebuffed, for sometimes he really took the trouble of being attentive after his languid fashion; and finally the slight difficulties placed in his way gave a degree of zest to the pursuit, and Lady Eskdale and her daughters took great delight in watching the activity with which Ernest stepped forward to hand Eliza in to dinner; and the patience with which he listened to her singing, openly avowing that he thought music a mere noise, and a painful interruption to the quiet and comfort of the evening. Whereupon Eliza, with a strong sense of filial duty, sang and played with additional ardour, and would have considered herself a little martyr, and pitied herself to a great amount, had she not perceived, with the keenness common on such subjects, that Ernest was, in fact, far more really interested in her now than he had been at St. Mary's. Page 28 of the Extract Book, dedicated to the sorrows of " The Neglected One," was torn out; and " Young Hopes," a poem by " T."—rather trashy, but extremely joyous—copied into the next leaf at full length.

CHAPTER XLVIII

" I WANT a talk with you, my dearly beloved aunt," said Ernest one morning, presenting himself at the door of Lady Eskdale's boudoir; " I want your advice."

" What is the matter, my dear? come in. Are you bilious, Ernest? I hope you have not got a touch of poor Teviot's fever."

" Oh no, it is nothing of that sort, but I am on the point of taking a desperate resolution, and I think your dear good soft mind is just the thing for my strong one to lean upon. You see, I make a joke of it to Amelia and Helen, they are so young and energetic. I never was either, but I am seriously thinking of marrying, and of asking Eliza Douglas if she will have me."

" My dear boy," said Lady Eskdale, who could not picture to herself life without husband and children, and had never brought herself to believe in the existence of an unhappy marriage, " how delighted I am! I am excessively fond of that girl. She is what very few people are, perfectly artless, and so thoroughly affectionate."

Lady Eskdale might well make that assertion, for Eliza felt for her that ardent love which girls in early youth often lavish on a woman far above them in age, position, and experience, whose kindness to themselves seems to be a distinction which raises them in their own estimation, and often influences the whole tenor of their after-lives. Lady Eskdale's loving nature gave her this power over many of the young people by whom she was surrounded. They felt sure of her sympathy, that great tie in all the friendships of life, and more especially valued, when it is found in those who are beyond us and before us in the race of life. Her gentle and caressing manner had a peculiar charm for Eliza, who lived in rather a hard atmosphere at home. She was firmly convinced that Lady Eskdale's opinion was infallible; that she was more beautiful in her middle age than the rest of the world in their prime; that her gown was better made, and her cap more becoming, than other women's caps and gowns; and that the very happy individual whom Ernest might select as his wife ought to count the blessing of becoming Lady Eskdale's niece one of the brightest ingredients in her lot. Young people may be foolish, perhaps are so generally, but there is something very attractive in the warmth of their grateful little hearts.

" I am very glad you like her, dear," said Ernest (all Lady Eskdale's *entourage* called her " dear "); " she seems to me as good a little creature as ever breathed; pretty and lady-like, and so serviceable; never minds what trouble she takes for other people. I think she will suit me exactly; we shall be very happy together."

Lady Eskdale laughed: " My dear Ernest, you amuse me with your cool way of taking that for granted. Eliza is all and much more than you say, for she has great intelligence and tact."

" Oh yes, of course, I forgot to mention that."

" And strong principles, which would lead her to be a good wife even to a bad husband; but she would be a very unhappy wife with a husband who did not care for her. Ernest, I never expect to see you very much in love, though I believe you affect to be colder than you really are, but are you quite sure you really care enough for my dear little Liz? "

" Quite sure," he said, speaking with more energy and warmth than was his custom. " As you say, I am not the sort of fellow who takes a romantic view of things, but the freshness and truth of Miss Douglas's mind have a great charm for me. I see how easily she may be made happy, and I am certain that I could never have for any of the hackneyed conventional set, in which it has been my good fortune to dwell, the same attachment that I have for her. You will see, dear, that we shall be a couple after your own heart."

" You seem to have no doubt that she will accept you ! " said Lady Eskdale, smiling.

" None whatever. I suppose I ought to say I have; but you and I have souls above that shallow sort of pretence; and as for Liz (I mean to call her Liz, it is such a nice short name), she has not a pretence in her. Half the fun of my proposal will be to see her look of delight. She is so easily pleased; that is one of her great merits."

" Well, dear Ernest," said Lady Eskdale, who could not help laughing, " you know best what will make you happy, and your choice pleases me particularly; but there is one more circumstance to be considered, your future wife's family."

" Ah, true," he said; " that is a consideration; but old Douglas is a thorough gentleman, and I like him; and as for the mother, she won't require me to be extravagantly fond of her; and if she occasionally squeezes a few drops of lemon-juice into my stagnant cup, it will be rather an advantage. I shall effervesce. I do not dislike ill-natured women; they are amusing at all events. Besides, a disagreeable mother-in-law is a very common crook in every man's lot, and I generally contrive to make my crooks sit very light; so thank you, dear, for having listened to me so patiently. I will let you know the moment I am engaged."

He did not give himself any great trouble to force an opportunity for his proposal, but was really more fidgety and nervous in manner than was usual with him. Lady Eskdale, with apparent carelessness, asked Eliza to fetch her some flowers from the conservatory, and there Ernest followed her, and a very few words on his part joined the destinies of two people about as unlike to each other, in habits, dispositions, and sentiments, as they could well be; but not the less likely on that account to be very happy in their married state.

Ernest was sincerely charmed with the shy but almost grateful assent given to his declaration by the lady of his love; and he was in an animated state of spirits when he led Eliza back to Lady Eskdale, and said, " We have forgotten your flowers, dear, but I have brought you a new niece, and you must make much of her, and coax her, for she is rather nervous, poor little soul."

Any deficiency in the art of coaxing could not possibly be attributed to Lady Eskdale, and she soon soothed the agitated girl into composure; and when Eliza had whispered, " I am so happy, too happy, but I must go to papa and mamma, and you must go with me, my dear, kind friend," the bell was rung, and the carriage ordered, and in a short time the lovers and the chaperon were on their way to Thornbank.

That the consent of Mr. and Mrs. Douglas was heartily given need not be doubted; and perhaps the most remarkable facts of this remarkable day were, that Colonel Beaufort so little liked the idea of being separated from " Liz " that he requested his aunt to send his servant and his things over to Thornbank, and settled himself there, to be fêted and worshipped, without even ascertaining whether the cookery were good, or the spare rooms comfortably furnished: the second fact was, that Mrs. Douglas was in a state of such intense felicity that when Lady Eskdale drove off, she observed to Colonel Beaufort, " How wonderfully handsome your aunt is looking to-day! even Mr. Douglas, who thought her altered the last time he saw her, must own she looks very young for her age."

Colonel Beaufort's *insouciance* seemed to have a peculiar fascination for Mrs. Douglas. It was a novelty in her experience of life; he was so smooth that she ceased to be rough; and to Eliza's intense delight, she saw her mother, who had seemed for two or three days rather puzzled by his careless way of announcing his intentions, and the deliberate calmness with which he seemed to expect they would be carried out, gradually yield to his gentlemanlike selfishness. At first with a slight sneer at herself, or him; but by degrees she took interest in pleasing him, and felt a degree of pride in seeing a man of such fastidious habits and manners perfectly happy at Thornbank. There is nothing so catching as refinement, and Mrs. Douglas began to act up, as well as she could, to Colonel Beaufort's habit of keeping the surface smooth. His gentle way of ignoring the complaints she was given to make of her servants, neighbours, etc., had a much better effect in checking them than argument or contradiction; and, with all his indolence, he was so naturally courteous that she found herself treated with a degree of easy kindness which few people had ever ventured to show her. It tamed her, and she fell slightly— and with the most perfect propriety—slightly in love with her intended son-in-law, and assured Eliza that she was a very fortunate girl, and once or twice went the length of reproaching her for not attending sufficiently to Ernest's wishes and fancies. This delighted him.

" Poor little Liz, who does nothing but try to please me, from morning to night, to be reproached with hardheartedness! Never mind, dear; I do you perfect justice, and think there never was such a good little angel before on this earth."

In his walks with Mr. Douglas, a new idea struck him. He had long felt that he ought to live more on his estate; but had always alleged that he fell into a lethargy when he was there, from which he could only be roused by immediate change of scene. But Mr. Douglas's interest in his farm, and his crops, and his labourers, and his cattle, led him to think that a little active occupation, added to the society of his wife, might make a few months, even in Lincolnshire, endurable.

" Liz," he said one day, after a saunter through the home farm, " would you like to live in the country? "

" Why, Ernest, I have never lived anywhere else; of course I should."

" But, you know, we must be in London during the session."

" Well, I should enjoy that still more. I have been so little in London."

" What a child you are for enjoying everything. I declare it is quite refreshing. But what I mean is, that I think we ought, instead of going loitering about during the recess at other people's houses, try to live in that dreary old barracks in the Fens, which calls itself my estate, and rejoices in the cockney name of Belleville, a name evidently derived from ' blue devils,' a malady from which I have suffered considerably there. But I think there would be some amusement, if I followed your father's example, and took part of the farm into my own hands."

" And I can help you to keep your accounts. I keep all papa's farm books in order."

" No; do you really? " he said, looking at her with extreme admiration. " That takes away my only difficulty. I did not feel up to grappling with account-books; but if you will take those in hand, we shall do very well."

" And may I have a school in the village, Ernest? "

" Of course, my child, two or three if you like—one for boys, one for girls, and one for adults, as great overgrown men and women choose to call themselves when they want to learn to read. Only don't ask me to come, Liz, to hear them stammer and stumble over their chapters and their sums; besides, I shall be busy with the farm. I must have some pigsties like your father's. I never saw anything equal to the comfort of those Chinese pigs, all brushed and cleaned, with their eyes obliterated by fat, and lying on their clean beds of straw, quite unequal to the fatigues of standing. I quite envied them. I have tried various amusements without much success; but I am convinced now that my real vocation is for Parliament and pigs. Yes, we will go to our own country place, and get your father and mother to come to us. Mrs. Douglas will help you to set up your schools, and your father will superintend the erection of my pigsties, and we shall all be as happy as the day is long."

"I have no doubt of that," said Eliza; "and perhaps Lady Eskdale will come and see us. Only think of the pleasure of having her staying with us!"

"Of course she will come," he said; "and now we must give your mother a hint to hurry on that trousseau; and then we can all go to Eskdale, and our wedding will come off with Beaufort's."

And so it was arranged. Mrs. Douglas immediately set to work to execute Ernest's directions, that she would exert her own excellent taste, and make Liz the best-dressed woman in England, with the greatest possible expedition; and as Mr. Douglas made no objection towards furnishing the necessary means, she found no difficulty in her way.

There is little more now to be said of the family whose veracious history has been here given. The cousins were married on the same day, in the chapel at the Castle; and on the marriage of her own daughter Mrs. Douglas made no complaints of the coldness of the pavement, or the glare of the painted windows; and even preserved a total silence on the subject of Lord Eskdale's grey hair. As the two couples drove off on their respective wedding tours, Amelia turned to Helen and said, "Well, there is no use in trying to calculate the amount of happiness married people will enjoy from their conduct when they are lovers. There were Walden and I, who both fell in love at first sight, *we* are happy. Beaufort and Mary began by hating each other; *they* are happy. In Ernest's case, the love was all on the lady's side; and now, did anybody ever see a man in such a state of felicity as he is? and as to you and Teviot, dear Nell, the love was all on the gentleman's side, and yet——"

"We are decidedly the happiest couple of the four, only that poor Teviot is a little henpecked; are not you, darling?"

"Not a little," he said, smiling; "but I like it. All men do. But the truth is, Amelia, that all you Beauforts have been brought up in a domestic atmosphere. Lord and Lady Eskdale are a model couple, and you have all been so accustomed to happy homes that when you are taken from one, you immediately set about making another. And I must own you succeed."

THE END.

THE
SEMI-DETACHED HOUSE

BY THE
HON. EMILY EDEN

THE SEMI-DETACHED HOUSE

CHAPTER I

" THE only fault of the house is that it is semi-detached."

" Oh, Aunt Sarah ! you don't mean that you expect me to live in a semi-detached house ? "

" Why not, my dear, if it suits you in other respects ? "

" Why, because I should hate my semi-detachment, or whatever the occupants of the other half of the house may call themselves."

" They call themselves Hopkinson," continued Aunt Sarah coolly.

" I knew it," said Blanche triumphantly. " I felt certain their name would be either Tomkinson or Hopkinson—I was not sure which—but I thought the chances were in favour of Hop rather than Tom."

Aunt Sarah did not smile, but drew the mesh out of her netting and began a fresh row.

" Go on, Aunt Sarah," said Blanche demurely.

" I am going on, thank you, my dear, very nicely ; I expect to finish this net this week."

Blanche looked at her aunt to ascertain if she looked angry, or piqued, or affronted ; but Aunt Sarah's countenance was totally incapable of any expression but that of imperturbable stolid sense and good-humour.   She did not care for Blanche's little vivacities.

" Do you know the Hopkinsons, Aunt Sarah ? "

" No, my dear."

" Nor their history, nor their number, nor their habits ? Recollect, Aunt Sarah, they will be under the same roof with your own pet Blanche."

" I have several pets, my dear—Tray, and Poll, and your sister, and——"

" Well, but she will be there, too, for I suppose the Lees will let Aileen come to me, now that I am to be deserted by Arthur," and Blanche's voice quivered, but she determined to brave it through. " Did you see any of the Hopkinsons when you went to look at the house ? "

" Yes, they went in at their door just as I went in at yours. The mother, as I suppose, and two daughters, and a little boy."

" Oh dear me ! a little boy, who will always be throwing stones at the palings and making me jump ; daughters who will always be playing *Partant pour la Syrie ;* and the mother——"

" Well, what will she do to offend your Highness ? "

" She will be immensely fat, wear mittens—thick, heavy mittens—and contrive to know what I have for dinner every day."

There was a silence, another row of netting and a turn of the mesh, and then Aunt Sarah said in her most composed tone :

" I often think, my dear, that it is a great pity you are so imaginative, and a still greater pity that you are so fastidious. You would be happier if you were as dull and as matter-of-fact as I am."

" Dear Aunt Sarah, don't say you are dull. There is nobody I like so much to talk to. You bring out such original remarks, such convincing truths, and in a quiet way, so that they do not make the black bruises which *les vérités dures* generally produce. But *am* I fastidious and imaginative ? "

" Yes, my dear, very painfully so. Now, just consider, Blanche ; you began this week by throwing yourself into a fever because Arthur was to leave you, on a mission that may be of great future advantage to him. He is to be away only three months, and is as much grieved as you are at the separation it involves. You immediately assert that he is going for a year at least, that he is to forget you instantly, and fall in love with any and every other woman he sees."

" No, only with that woman with the unpronounceable name that he used to dance with ; a very dangerous woman, Aunt Sarah."

" That he is to be smashed in the railroad to Folkestone, drowned off Antwerp, and finally die of a fever at Berlin ; and that in the meanwhile you are to have a dead child immediately, twins soon after, a very bad confinement, besides dying of consumption, and various other maladies," pursued Aunt Sarah in her steadiest tone. " Now, if those things are not vain imaginings, Blanche, I do not know what are."

" They sound plausible, though ; and, I assure you, Aunt, I did not imagine them ; they suggested themselves, and they look very like the ordinary facts of life. However, I grant it is a bad habit to look forward to evils that may not occur ; but then, you know, I am ill. I never had these grey thoughts when I was strong, and Arthur's going away has turned them all black. And now as to my fastidiousness."

" You always were fastidious, my child, easily jarred by the slightest want of tact and refinement, and I am not much surprised," added Aunt Sarah, as she looked fondly at her niece. There was something startling in the mobility of Blanche's beautiful features ; every thought that passed through her mind might be read in her kindling eyes and expressive lips ; she looked too ethereal for contact with the vulgar ills of life.

" I will allow you have some right to be fastidious, darling ; and it is only because it interferes with your comfort that I object to it. But you say you cannot go and stay with Lord Chesterton, because he calls you ' Blanket,' and thinks it a good joke ; nor with your sister-in-law, Lady Elinor, because Sir William is fond of money, and you foresee he will say that you cost him at least seventeen shillings and fourpence a day ; nor with your Aunt Carey, because the doctor who would attend you wears creaking boots, and calls you my Lady ; and now you object to a house that all your friends and your doctor recommend, because it is possible that your next-door neighbour may play on the pianoforte and wear black mittens. Dear Blanche, this is what I call over-fastidiousness ; and now I have finished my ten rows, and said all the disagreeable things I could think of, so I will go, and leave you to think how officious and particular old Aunt Sarah is."

" You know I shall think no such thing," said Blanche, half crying and half laughing, " but you must own, Aunt Sarah, that when you string all my fancies together, they are rather amusing—wrong, if you please, but amusing. However, I will try to reform, and if Arthur likes Pleasance, which he is gone to see, and if Dr. Ayscough persists in driving me out of London, I will establish myself in my semi-

B

detached villa, and try to get into the Hopkinson set."

It may be inferred from the above conversation that Blanche was slightly spoiled, but she was charming, nevertheless—sweet-tempered and playful, and with high spirits, now subdued by the approaching separation from her husband, to whom she had been married only six months. They were as foolishly in love as all young couples are or ought to be, and Lord Chester would willingly have declined the offer to join a special mission to Berlin, which had been made to him. Blanche could not conceive it possible that he should leave her in her very interesting state of health. Dr. Ayscough treated the notion of her being able to accompany her husband with the politest and most magnificent contempt ; and it seemed likely that the great national interests of Great Britain and Prussia would actually lose all the light which Arthur might throw upon them in the capacity of Secretary to a special mission. But old fathers see these matters in a different point of view from young sons. Lord Chesterton came fussing up to town full of admiration for her Majesty's Government in general, and for the Foreign Office in particular ; he must own he thought Clarendon very judicious in his diplomatic appointments, he might say very discriminative. And he was so profuse in his felicitations to Arthur on his appointment, and in his compliments to dear little Blanche, on her wisdom of letting her husband go without her—that neither of them had courage to say that they meant to decline the offer. And so it came to pass that Arthur was to go to Berlin, and Blanche to Pleasance. Dr. Ayscough wished her to leave London, but still to be within reach of his surveillance ; and Blanche, who had been under his care from the day of her birth, and who was delicate at all times, never supposed for a moment that his advice was not to be followed implicitly.

He went down with Arthur to look at Pleasance, they both approved of it, and when, soon after Aunt Sarah's departure, Arthur bounded upstairs, and declared that he had actually taken the prettiest villa in the world for his little Blanche, she warmed up to the idea. She made one faint inquiry as to whether he had seen her next-door neighbours. At first he denied their existence, but finally owned that there was a small house at the back of hers. " But that does not signify ; yours is a good large house, and such drawing-rooms, and such a conservatory, and a splendid lawn down to the river ; and there is a wall and a laurel hedge, and all sorts of conundrums to shut out these neighbours who seem to alarm you."

" Their name is Hopkinson, Arthur."

" And a very good name, too. Hopkinson was the name of the Captain of the ' Alert,' who

took me out to the Cape, and an excellent fellow
he was ; perhaps you would have thought him
vulgar, but he helped me through a bad fever,
which made rare havoc on board ; and Florence
Nightingale herself could not have made a better
nurse. I like the name of Hopkinson."

"Oh, well !" said Blanche, "then it will all
do very well, and I must write to Aunt Sarah,
and tell her we have taken her Semi-Detached
House. It is quite within reach of her daily
drive."

CHAPTER II

"HERE is poor Willis coming to see us," said Mrs. Hopkinson, from her commanding position in the window, to her two girls who were drawing and reading at the secluded end of the room. The girls looked at each other with a slight expression of dismay. Willis was not a favourite; he had married their step-sister, and it was thought a great thing for the Hopkinsons, when Mr. Willis of Columbia House, which boasted of a lodge and an entrance drive, a shrubbery and a paddock, and a two-stalled stable, and every sort of suburban magnificence, married pretty Mary Smith, who lived merely at No. 2, without a shilling of her own, and dependent on her step-father for a home. So when she became Mrs. Willis of Columbia House, and of Fenchurch Street, where Mr. Willis duly transacted some mysterious business that appeared to produce a large return of profit, the Hopkinsons thought her a very fortunate young woman, and so she thought herself, till she found out that she had married a man who was by profession a grumbler. He had a passion for being a victim ; when he was single, he grumbled for a wife, and when he had found a wife, he grumbled for the comforts of a bachelor. He grumbled for an heir to Columbia Lodge, and when the heir was born he grumbled because the child was frail and sickly. In short, he fairly grumbled poor gentle Mrs. Willis out of the world, and then grumbled at her for dying. But still her death was a gain to him. He took up the high bereaved line, was at all hours and in all societies the disconsolate mourner, wore a permanent crape round his hat, a rusty black coat in the city, and a shining one when he dined out. He professed himself " serious," and proved it by snubbing his friends when they were prosperous, and steadily declining to take the slightest interest in their adversities.

" What were their trials compared to his ? A lonely man—ah ! poor Mary ! don't talk to him of losses indeed ! " Certainly, though he might be the very good man he said he was, he was not an agreeable companion. His sisters-in-law were strong in that opinion. Mrs. Hopkinson took him at his own valuation, always called him " poor Willis " from respect to Mary's memory, and relieved him of the care of his sick child, which enabled him to sigh over the sacrifice he had made of his lost angel's legacy to her bereaved mother.

" I wonder what poor Willis will say, girls, when he hears that Pleasance is let ? "

"Something very unpleasant, mamma," answered Janet.

"Oh, my dears, you are hard upon poor Willis ! I am sure when I think of my dear Mary (what a wife she was to be sure !) I quite respect her dear husband's melancholy face and heavy sighs."

"But, mamma, don't you remember just after Mary had accepted him, and he came to ask for your consent, you said that he looked so gloomy, and sighed so deeply, that it was more like consenting to a funeral than a wedding ? "

"Did I ? " said Mrs. Hopkinson, trying not to laugh. "Well, he never was much in the cheerful line ; but don't talk of it, for here he is. Well, Willis, Charlie is a little better to-day ; and only think, Pleasance is let ! "

"Of course it is," answered a sepulchral voice.

"Well, it *is* a sweet place ! one can't wonder at anybody taking it ; but it has stood empty a long time."

"That I don't care about, that is Randall's loss ; but as I liked to smoke my cigar there in peace, and to take my lonely stroll by the river side, and as it suited my child to play in the garden—in short, as it was a sort of consolation to *me*—of course somebody else went and took it, that's all ! "

Janet and Rose tried to catch their mother's eye, but she was looking compassionately at Willis, the exile of Pleasance.

" It is a Lord Something who has taken it.
Mercy me, what a head I have, I remember
nothing ! What was his name ? It was one of
our great towns, Lord Leeds, Lord York, Lord
Birmingham—could it be either of those ? "

" As there are no such people I should think
not. I do wish, Mrs. H., I could persuade you to
read the ' Peerage ' a little more, these blunders
annoy me."

" Law, Willis, you'll be a conjuror if you
persuade me to read it at all. You might as
well ask me to read a list of Red Morocco Chiefs,"
(Mrs. Hopkinson somehow fancied that the
Morocco population was bright scarlet). " I am
just as likely to see them as all those peers you
are always studying."

" My studies are of a far more serious class,"
he said tartly ; " the ' Peerage ' is not of much
use to a broken heart. But I see nothing to be
proud of in ignorance on any subject ! "

Mrs. Hopkinson was in a reverie. " Chester ! "
she said at last, with a start that immediately
threw Mr. Willis into an attitude indicative of
a nervous headache, " Lord Chester, that was
the name ! "

" Viscount Chester, son of the Earl of Chesterton, married last year to Blanche, daughter of
the Honourable W. Grenville. I met them this
spring at the Lord Mayor's dinner. More
frivolous specimens of fashion you could hardly

see, all jewels, and laughter, and levity. Oh vanity of vanities!"

" Oh fun of fun!" exclaimed Rose. "A nice gay young couple. How glad I am! I dare say they will give parties and breakfasts, and there will be carriages continually down the lane, perhaps a band sometimes on the lawn. It will put you quite in spirits, Charles," she added, with a demure look.

He leant his head on his hands with a look of acute suffering.

" Got the headache, Charles?"

" One ache more or less makes little difference to me. I ought to have the headache. Have none of you found out who owns that dreadful macaw? It has been screaming all day."

Now it is a remarkable fact in natural history that in all the suburbs of London, consisting of detached houses, called by auctioneers 'small and elegant,' or on Terraces described as first-rate dwellings, there always is an invisible macaw, whose screaming keeps the hamlet or terrace in a constant state of irritation. Nobody at Dulham owned to having one, and detection was impossible, for there, as at all the suburban villages, the inhabitants lived by, and for, and with London. The men went daily to their offices or counting-houses, and the women depended for society on long morning visits from London friends and relations; and they did not, as they

observed with much pride, "visit at Dulham."
So the Macaw screeched on, and as his noise
seemed to come from fifty houses at once, everybody suspected everybody of keeping this plumed
atrocity. No. 3 sent to No. 5 to beg that the
bird might be shut up for a few days, as No. 3's
baby did nothing but start, and would not
wean. No. 3's messenger met No. 5's maid-of-
all-work, coming with a bold request that the
macaw might be sent away, as " Missus's mother-
in-law was subject to bad headaches, and was
driv half mad." As neither of the parties owned
even a linnet, in the way of bird, the nuisance
was not abated by this negotiation.

At one time there seemed to be a hope that
the mystery was discovered. A singular-looking
old lady walked into church with a bunch of
parrot's feathers in her bonnet. There was a
general nudging of elbows through the church
and a low murmur of " macaw." The lady
was looked upon with such abhorrence that
nobody would offer her a seat, and as for a
hymn book or a hassock, money would not have
procured them for her. The poor old thing might
have fainted away in the aisle if the pew-opener
had not sacrificed to her her own three-legged
stool. It turned out afterwards that she was
quite a stranger in the place, and had mistaken
the very humdrum Mr. Bosville for the popular
preacher of that name, who officiated at a church

five miles off. As she was stone deaf, she went away charmed with the sermon. And the macaw screamed on anonymously.

He was a treasure to Mr. Willis ; it was a daily and hourly grievance, and he made the most of it. This morning, after several splendid sighs, he withdrew with a cursory look at his child and a hoarse ejaculation, " Poor little sufferer ! " but in the afternoon, when the girls were out walking, Mrs. Hopkinson was surprised to see him return, his black coat buttoned up to the very top button, not a streak of white visible. This always portended a stern visit and much good advice.

" Look, ma'am, look there ! " and he presented her with a weekly paper of a disreputable character.

" Law, my dear, the *Weekly Lyre !* Thank you, I never read any of those abominable papers. Do carry it away for fear the girls should see it."

" For the sake of the girls, ma'am, you must read the paragraph I have marked."

Mrs. Hopkinson was half inclined to put on her gloves before she touched what she looked upon as poison. She had a pair of hideous dark green gauntlets that seemed made to encounter the *Weekly Lyre*. A broad black border, the work of Willis, encircled the following paragraph :—

" FRACAS IN HIGH LIFE.—It is our melancholy duty to report the separation of a young and

noble couple, whose appearance at the altar of
Hymen we detailed some months ago. Whether
the levity of the lady or the temper of the gentleman has brought about this *dénouement* we are
unable to say. Rumours of all sorts are rife—a
foreign court and a villa not one hundred miles
from London are the scenes of several piquant
anecdotes. Whether the last is tenanted by his
Lordship's wife, or his *chère amie*, we forbear to
say."

"Well, ma'am, what do you say to that?"
asked Willis, folding his arms, and looking as
like John Kemble as was feasible.

"Well, my dear, it is not much worse than
paragraphs I have read in the most decent
papers—I have seen things like that in the
Illustrated. It is odd that the nobility will
have 'Fracaws, and chère amies, and picking
anecdotes,' but I suppose in our class of life we
have the same things, only with English names.
Not that John and I ever had a fracaw, thank
goodness; but I am much obliged to you,
Willis, for the loan of the paper, and perhaps
you had better put it in your pocket, for fear
the girls should come home."

"But don't you see, ma'am, what it means?
Was not Lord Chester's marriage announced in
this very paper six months ago? Isn't he going
to a foreign court? and hasn't he taken a villa
not one hundred miles from London—and is

not a lady whose name is unknown coming to live in it? A nice neighbour for you, Mrs. Hopkinson."

"Oh, gracious goodness, Willis, you don't mean to say that Lord Chester is going to establish his mistress next door, and our back staircase looking on the lawn—in Dulham too! Such a quiet, proper place! Let me have another look at that dreadful paper! It must be so. What shall I do?"

"Bear the misfortune, ma'am—cheerfully as I do. Luckily my house is half a mile off."

"And we are under the very roof of Pleasance. I'll have the shutters of that staircase window shut and barred at once; the house will be as dark as pitch, but that can't be helped. Good-bye, Willis, I must be off to take my precautions. This *is* a business!"

Willis carried off his paper with something that would have been a smile if he had not been Willis, and Mrs. Hopkinson set to work to throw up her fortifications against the vices of the nobility.

In justice to the *Weekly Lyre*, it may be added that the paragraph in question had no reference whatever to Lord and Lady Chester, nor to any other Lord and Lady in Her Majesty's dominions; it was a stock paragraph inserted occasionally, and with variations, when the editor was distressed for news.

CHAPTER III

ARTHUR was gone. He brought his wife to Pleasance, and passed one day there with her, in order that he might fancy her way of life while he was absent ; and then departed, having promised positively not to dance with Madame von Moerkerke.

" I will not as you make a point of it ; but I cannot think why you are jealous of that yea and nay woman, who has but the one merit of being well dressed."

" Oh, Arthur dear, remember that ball at L—— House, where you devoted yourself to her, and never spoke to me at all."

" Of course I did not, for remember the morning of that day, when you let that fellow Hilton ride by your side for two hours, and talked to him all through dinner. I made a vow never to speak to you again, and, by the help of the angelic Moerkerke, kept it for a whole evening. The next day, you know, I was obliged to break it, in order to tell you I could not live without you."

Blanche felt the glow these words gave her, even when Arthur had left her, but still he was gone. She cried herself to sleep, and cried when she woke, and cried when Aileen arrived ; and then Dr. Ayscough drove down, and gave her a regular scolding, and assured her she would destroy her health and her hopes if she behaved so foolishly, and that he could see nothing to cry about. Mrs. Ayscough had been in Wales with her mother all the summer, and he did not go about sobbing to all his patients ; and he told Aileen to have a sofa placed out on the lawn, and make her sister pass the afternoon in the open air. Then Arthur's fond letter came, and after that matters mended considerably. There was the house to show to Aileen, and the garden to investigate, and all sorts of red and gold barges came careering up the river, with well-dressed people, looking slightly idiotical as they danced furiously in the hot sun. Aunt Sarah and one or two intimate friends drove down, and envied Blanche her shady trees and cool river, and even insinuated that Arthur was very lucky to have obtained such a good appointment. But there Blanche drew her line, she steadily refused that comfort. She had several visitors the first week, and Dulham Lane was, as Janet and Rose had hoped, much enlivened thereby.

But Mrs. Hopkinson sat with her broad back to the window, pertinaciously declining to look at all the wickedness on wheels that was rolling by her door. She had found that the plan of shutting her shutters would probably end in a fall down her narrow staircase, so she had told her girls not to look out of the window, that poor Willis had reason to believe that the people next door were not at all creditable ; and as Janet and Rose were singularly innocent in the ways of the world, and were always desirous to thwart Willis, and as they were particularly anxious to know whether flounces or double skirts were the prevailing fashion, they resented this exclusion from their only point of observation. Charlie missed his airings in the garden, and altogether the advent of Lady Chester had thrown a gloom over the Hopkinson circle.

When Sunday arrived, a fresh grievance occurred. The Hopkinsons had been allowed to make use of the pew belonging to Pleasance, and that was now occupied by Lady Chester and her sister. The slight bustle occasioned by the attempt to find a seat for Mrs. Hopkinson, who was of large dimensions, caused Blanche to look up, and with natural good breeding she opened her pew door, and beckoned to that lady to come in. She did so, and what with the heat of the day, and the thought of what Willis would say when he saw her sitting next to a lady of doubtful character, who had made a " fracaw in high life," she could hardly breathe. She inclosed herself in a palisade of hymn books and prayer books, sat close to the pew door, ready to burst through it at the slightest appearance of levity on the part of her companions, and it was only by dint of much fanning that she was enabled to sit through the service. She disappeared at the close of it before the sisters had finished their devotions.

" That poor woman seemed to feel the heat of the weather dreadfully," said Aileen.

" Yes, and I felt the heat of the poor woman, did not you ? It was like having a stove put into the pew ; but I am glad we were able to give her a seat, she looked troubled in mind. What a good sermon it was ! I think we ought to make acquaintance with the clergyman, but I do not know how to set about it."

" I mean to go to the school," said Aileen, " and I suppose he takes charge of that," and so the sisters sauntered home. Mrs. Hopkinson had in the meantime hurried to rejoin her daughters and Willis, who had found places in the gallery. She could hardly wait till they were out of the church before she began. " Oh, dear me ! I wished I had toiled up to the gallery with you, girls. Willis, where *do* you think I got a seat ? "

" On one of the tombs, ma'am ? " he gloomily asked.

" No, my dear, in the Pleasance pew, actually in the same pew with one of those shocking women who made the fracaw. I never was so uncomfortable, and they are so pretty, and what is odd, they were so attentive to the service, never

c

took their eyes off their prayer books, and they look so young to be so wicked."

" I forgot to tell you that my paper must have made a mistake," said Mr. Willis in his slowest and most complacent tone. " I saw the real Lady Chester and her sister drive by last Thursday and turn into the gate; fine horses she drives."

" And you have known it was the wife ever since Thursday ? " said Mrs. Hopkinson, stopping short in her toilsome walk, and facing her son-in-law, " and never told me ; and there was I, actually in church, fancying all sorts of shocking things about those pretty young creatures, and all because of you and your *Weekly Lyre*. If you bring that vile paper into the house, I will put it into the fire, I will, depend upon it," and she looked as if it were just possible that she might wrap Willis up in the paper before the conflagration commenced. He was almost frightened, his mother-in-law so seldom turned upon him.

" I did not know you cared about it ; indeed it rather surprises *me*, who can no longer take any interest in life, to see you so excited, and all for a woman who has separated herself from her husband."

" But we do not know that she has, it is only your paper that says so ; and, indeed, if she has, it is probably Lord Chester's fault. I have always observed that when man and wife part, the husband is a brute. And to think how I behaved, puffing and blowing, and going off at last without even saying thank you, and all on account of the *Weekly Lyre*." The warm-hearted woman was really vexed, the more so, that she did not see how any *amende* was to be made. However, chance befriended her.

Lady Chester was quite knocked up by the morning's exertion, so Aileen went alone to the afternoon service, and found her fat friend of the morning coming out of the adjoining house, accompanied by her slim daughters. They arrived at the church door together, and then Aileen said, " If you are not provided with a seat, my sister is not coming to church, and there will be room in our pew for all your party." She was surprised to see the difference in Mrs. Hopkinson's appearance since the morning. Her good-humoured face had its usual benevolent look ; she was actually cool, though the thermometer was some degrees higher than it had been, and her thanks were so cordial that Aileen felt pleased to find her little civility so much valued.

" Who do you think that lady was who sat with us this morning ? " Aileen said, as she rejoined Blanche on the lawn.

" How can I possibly guess, dear ? Somebody evidently perturbed in mind, and very uncomfortable in body ; but I have not an idea who she is."

" Neighbour Hopkinson," said Aileen quietly.

" You don't say so ! now do write a line to
Aunt Sarah forthwith, and beg her to come and
see my Semi-detachment, and judge for herself
if I am imaginative. I said Mrs. Hopkinson
would be immensely fat, and so she is ; you did
not happen to see if she wore mittens, did you,
Aileen ? "

" I did not observe what she wore this evening ; but I have a faint idea of a mitten holding
a fan, in the morning."

" No, have you ? " said Blanche joyfully.
" Tell Aunt Sarah to come early, and for the
whole day at least ! there are two of my imaginings verified, and perhaps the girls will begin
practising *Partant pour la Syrie* to-morrow."

" They are nice-looking girls," said Aileen,
" and I do not think you would have thought
the mother so fat this afternoon ; and she looked
so placid, I cannot think why she was so fussy in
the morning ; however, it is no business of ours,
and now, Blanche, come in, the dew is falling."

Aunt Sarah arrived, and, admitting the facts
of size and mittens, suggested that they could in
no way affect Blanche's daily comfort. While
she was sitting by the river side with her nieces,
a boat drew to the landing place, and Edwin
Grenville's joyous voice hailed his sisters—" Can
you give us some luncheon, Blanche ? we are
starving and tired,"

"Then pray come and eat; but who are *we?*"

"Harcourt, and Grey, and Hilton."

"Hilton," whispered Blanche. "Oh, Aunt Sarah, I wish Edwin would not bring him here, Arthur will be so angry."

"I cannot see why," said Aileen, hastily, and colouring up to the eyes.

"You are both much too young to receive morning visits from Edwin's brother officers," said Aunt Sarah, "and so I shall tell him; and I can safely undertake to make myself so unpleasant to his friends that they will be glad to go away again."

But there Aunt Sarah was signally mistaken. All her pithy remarks and sensible snubs were received by the young men as excellent jokes, and when they finally went away, Harcourt observed to Grey that "My Aunt was a jolly old fellow," and that he hoped she would be there next time they went. However, Blanche took the opportunity, when Aileen was walking by the river side with three of the gentlemen, to tell her brother that though it had been a very pleasant party, and though she was always glad to see *him*, yet, perhaps, he had better not bring his friends again. Arthur might not like it, he had rather a prejudice against Colonel Hilton.

"Oh, nonsense, Blanche! you must cure Arthur of prejudice; and the best of it is that it was Hilton who proposed our landing here."

" Ah, that's just it," said Blanche.

" Just what? " said Edwin. " Why, Blanche, I thought the great good of your being married was that you became a staid, sober chaperone for Aileen."

" Well, I am very staid, and quite sober and steady, as you would say of your groom ; but you know I am only eighteen, Edwin, and Arthur is away, and all circumstances considered, you had better come alone."

" Well ! I never heard such nonsense ; did you, Aunt Sarah ? "

" No, my dear, I think it is excellent sense, quite refreshing. I could have said nothing better myself, and as the tide has turned, you may as well go. Good-bye, Edwin, you have been lucky in your tides to-day ; generally they seem to me to run the wrong way. Aileen, bid your friends good-bye, for we are going in, Blanche is tired."

And so they all dispersed, and Blanche said to her sister, " I am glad Aunt Sarah was here. I shall tell Arthur how it was, and that I had nothing to do with Colonel Hilton's coming here. The next thing will be that we shall hear of Arthur's waltzing with that horrid Madame von Moerkerke."

Aileen smiled, but made no answer, though she was in such excellent spirits the rest of the day that it was obvious that *she* had no fear of Arthur or a rival.

CHAPTER IV

It was on this same day that the mournful event took place of the annual dinner given by Mr. Willis to his mother and sisters-in-law. Janet and Rose sighed and groaned about it considerably before it took place, because, as they justly observed, as nothing gave Charles any pleasure, and as it gave them none to see his melancholy face twice in the day instead of once, it was hard to have the trouble of dressing and to lose their comfortable evening at home. " Poor Mary has been dead now for three years ; I really think he might ask one or two people to meet us ; it is so absurd we four sitting in that gloomy dining-room, with nothing to say to each other. I feel always as if I should lose the use of my limbs before the first course is over, and I get the cramp in my feet, and a very peculiar headache. ' Charles's own headache ' I believe it is called in the medical books."

" Yes," said Rose, " and then Mamma always says, ' I wish you would not look so glum when we dine at Columbia Lodge, a little cheerful society is so good for poor Charles.' Now what connection there is between Charles and cheerfulness, except that they both begin with Ch, I do not know."

"Well, we must do our best to-day. I have a great mind to tell him of all those young men landing at Pleasance, and that lovely lilac gown of Lady Chester's, and the old lady in grey, and the grand carriage with the Duke's coronet that came afterwards; but somehow when I have collected a few little topics of a light kind, Charles looks so like a mute at a funeral that I cannot bring them out. However, one comfort is that our old grey gowns will do, and we want to wear them out."

But when they arrived at Columbia, the grey gowns proved to have been below the requirements of the day. A very showy coach drove up to the door, from which issued an equally showy lady, in a very bright pink gown, and two important-looking gentlemen, father and son, all three with such very high noses, and such jet black hair, and so obviously of Jewish descent, that it seemed impossible that they should not be announced as Baron and Baroness Sampson and Baron Moses Sampson. Consequently they were; and to the surprise of the girls, and much to their satisfaction, Mr. Greydon, the curate, immediately followed.

"Too much for me," whispered Willis to Mrs. Hopkinson with an agonised look, "but the Sampsons invited themselves, and as you know my respect for the church, I asked Greydon ; for, in fact, I wanted an eighth to make up my party."

It was altogether quite a lively affair. Baroness Sampson was full of facetious little affectations, absolutely affable to the Hopkinsons, and she did the honours of Willis's gravity with much pleasantry, and infinite want of tact, once arriving at calling him " you funny man," which threw Rose into an irrepressible fit of giggles.

It was obvious that Willis and Baron Sampson were leagued in some important speculation, which had brought about a degree of intimacy that might have been friendship, if either of them had been susceptible of that sentiment, and they would have liked to talk shares, and capital, and investments, if they had met with any encouragement. But Baron Moses was by way of being a fast young man about town, and bent on astonishing the Hopkinsons by anecdotes of the clubs, and the opera, and Prince Albert ; and the *sémillante* Baroness shook her black ringlets, and also her ear-rings, and chains, and bracelets to that extent, that they formed quite a musical accompaniment to her assertion that business was not to be attended to. She came for fresh air and fresh conversation.

" Do tell me something about Dulham, Mrs. Hopkinson. I want the Baron to take a villa.

I adore flowers and green lawns ; London kills me. It is such a stuffy, sad place, and *so* wicked ! " This last moral observation was addressed to Mr. Greydon in compliment to his clerical functions.

" Should I like Dulham, Willis ? Is there anybody here one knows ? "

" I should think not. But I am a sad recluse, I know nobody ! "

" Ah, now, I won't have you talk in that way ! If I have a villa here, I shall insist on your knowing everybody. Is there any house that would suit us ? I must have it on the banks of the river. That dear river—I really worship your Thames ! "

" Pleasance might have suited you, but Lord Chester has just taken it," said Mrs. Hopkinson.

" Lord Chester ! Dear me ! The man with the pretty wife, you mean. They are both quite the rage in our set."

" Do you know them, Baroness ? "

" Well, no, not exactly ; but still, living in the same set, and seeing them so constantly with my friend, Baroness Rothschild, I somehow feel as if I did." The Sampsons had been asked once to a large party at Gunnersbury. " And so *they* live here ? "

" She does, poor young thing ! Ah, it's a sad story ! "

" She does not seem very sad," said Mr. Greydon, quietly.

" Why, do you know them, Mr. Greydon ? " asked Janet, with some surprise.

" I had a note from Lady Chester this morning, asking me to call upon her. Her sister wished to know if she could be of any use in the school or village, and Lady Chester is anxious to do all she can, in her invalid state, for our little charities."

" Does Lady Chester look very ill ? "

" Very delicate, I should say ; but she seems to have high spirits. I enjoyed my visit, the two sisters were so unaffected and amiable, and extremely pretty."

Janet coloured. All the young ladies of Dulham, and many of the old ones, were more or less in love with Mr. Greydon, Janet rather more than less. None of them had well-grounded hopes of any return to their attachment. Mr. Greydon was an excellent young curate, a thorough gentleman, and lived on very good terms with his parishioners ; but any idea of marrying on £300 a year (the amount of his income) had never crossed his mind, and it was impossible for any one of his victims to boast of a word or a look of preference. Still Janet, in moments of extreme confidence, used to impart to Rose that if anybody gave Mr. Greydon a good living, or say, a bishopric (he

would make such a bishop !), or if a large fortune
were suddenly left him, she somehow felt sure
that he would marry, and that it would appear
he had distinguished her all the time.

Though Rose was, of course, very much
attached to him herself, yet, as she could conceive
the possibility of being happy with somebody
else, and as Janet was the eldest, and ought to
have the first choice, Rose gave in to these
flattering hopes, and always read what the
papers said of the illness of a bishop, or the death
of a dean, with great interest on Janet's account.

Admiration of Lady Chester Janet could have
borne, but she did not quite approve of his
thinking both sisters so pretty.

" There was such a grand carriage down our
lane to-day, Willis ; Charlie clapped his hands
and was quite in glee, poor little man ! four
horses, and postilions, and outriders, quite a
pretty sight, and such a grand-looking lady
in it."

" The Duchess of St. Maur," said Mr. Greydon.
" She came in while I was there."

" Dear me, one of the Queen's Ladies. She
went out of waiting last week, didn't she, girls ? "

Mrs. Hopkinson always read the Court Circular
and the Police Reports. The rest of the paper
was beyond her powers.

" Ah, the Duchess of St. Maur. Quite one
of your tip-tops," said the Baroness ; " the sort

of fine lady I carefully avoid. I suppose you were glad to get away, Mr. Greydon." She rather grudged to a curate the chance of becoming acquainted with a Duchess.

"I was going away just as she arrived, but Lady Chester made me stay. The Duchess takes a great interest in our Convalescent Hospital ; and I was not sorry to have an opportunity of interesting one of the Ladies' Committee in our improvements."

"And did she talk of the Queen and the Princess Royal?" asked Mrs. Hopkinson, who lived in a state of enthusiastic and loyal curiosity about the Court.

"No," he said, with a smile ; "we did not soar beyond Susan Hopkins's asthma, and Keziah Brown's rheumatism. The Duchess seemed well acquainted with all the old ladies."

"Well, I suppose the aristocracy are not so bad as we are told," said Mrs. Hopkinson, beaming with benevolence. "They seem to do a kind thing now and then."

"Now and then you may well say," murmured Willis. "What can they know of suffering? Ah ! let them once feel what real grief is, and there would be an end of their balls and *réunions*, and their postilions and outriders," he added, after an emphatic pause.

"But, I suppose," suggested Mrs. Hopkinson, doubtingly, "they do lose their friends and children like other people, and perhaps care about them."

Willis shook his head, and Mrs. Hopkinson again reverted to her favourite topic. " And did you hear nothing at all about the Queen, Mr. Greydon ? "

" Nothing. Oh yes ! there was some arrangement made about a concert at the Palace. The Duchess was to take Miss Grenville, as Lady Chester was not going."

" Ah ! not asked ; so like our good Queen. She would not invite anybody in Lady Chester's position, and yet is kind to her sister. There never *was* such a sovereign. Are you going to this concert, Baroness ? "

" No ; it seems odd, but we are not asked this time," said the Baroness with an air of modest pride. " I suspect we are out of favour at Court, but a Drawing-Room is my aversion, and I have been sadly remiss this year ; absolutely neglected the birthday, which was very naughty of me, and so I am left out of this party."

As that had been invariably her fate with regard to all parties at the Palace, the resignation she evinced had probably become a matter of habit ; but she hinted an intention of bringing the Queen to her senses by staying away from the next Drawing-Room too. She, however, enlivened the evening to the Hopkinsons by accounts of various splendid festivities, at which she said she had assisted ; and when the party dispersed, leaving Willis leaning against the chimney-piece with his head in his hands, the Hopkinsons walked home declaring the Baroness was very entertaining, and that the dinner had been really pleasant.

"And I am rather glad we wore our grey gowns," said Rose. "Do you know that when Janet was sitting by the Baroness, I thought she looked much the nicest of the two, more like a lady, without all those flowers and trinkets."

"I wonder Mr. Greydon did not offer to see us safe home," said Janet. "I suppose *that* Miss Grenville *is* very pretty."

CHAPTER V

THERE was no doubt, as Mr. Greydon had said, that Blanche *was* very delicate, and she was one of those exciteable people whose health fades when their spirits are depressed, and who expand into strength when their minds are at ease. She caught a slight cold by lingering near the river on a damp evening, and when Aunt Sarah paid her weekly visit to Pleasance, she found Blanche stretched on the sofa, pale and shrunk, with red eyes and hot hands, a feeble attempt at a cap at the very back of her head, and much Mechlin lace, and soft muslin and pink ribbon, professing to be an invalid's dressing-gown.

" My dear child ! what is the matter "

" All sorts of things, Aunt Sarah. In the first place, I am very ill—Aileen has sent for Dr. Ayscough. Now, just hear my cough."

" A failure, I think," said Aunt Sarah, " an attempt at a cough, rather than the thing itself."

" Then my throat is so sore. Do you think it will turn to that sore throat with the difficult name ? It kills people so rapidly, Aunt Sarah, that there will be no use in telegraphing for Arthur ; he could not arrive in time."

"Very well, my dear, then I will not send for him ; besides, I am not absolutely convinced that you have diphtheria."

"Then, after all I said to Edwin, he brought Colonel Hilton here again yesterday ; he said he could not help it, that Colonel Hilton *would* join him in his ride, and I have written to tell Arthur, and I know he will think I am flirting, and then he will begin to flirt himself. I assure you, Aunt Sarah, he did once before, just because Colonel Hilton rode with me. He owned it ; so it is not one of my fancies."

"Just lend me your scissors, Blanche ; this netting-silk knots so, I must cut it. I think it most likely, my dear, that Arthur—there ! another knot—what was I saying ? Oh, that though Arthur might be jealous, as a lover, of every man you spoke to, it is not very likely that with his good sense and warm feelings, and with the dependence he must have in your affection, he will suspect you of encouraging any attentions of Colonel Hilton. However, I am glad you write and tell him every-thing."

"Of course I do, and as you say, dear Aunt, it is very different now we are married. Arthur must know that I could not care now for any-body's admiration but his," and Blanche sat up

D

on her sofa, and slipped off her little cap, and
began to revive.

"But then I have not told you my worst misfortunes. I have had no letter for three days,
and those dreadful Miss Hopkinsons began to
play on their pianoforte this morning, and
actually played the *Dead March* in *Saul*, and
it gave me all sorts of shocking presentiments.
I thought Arthur must be ill because he did not
write—and in short, Aunt Sarah, I have made
up my mind to go to Berlin, and have sent
for Dr. Ayscough to tell him I am going."

There was a pause. "Aileen goes with me,
Aunt Sarah, and if Edwin can get leave, he will
go part of the way with us." Another pause.
"Why don't you speak, Aunt Sarah?"

"My dear, I have nothing so say, your plan
seems so complete, I can suggest no improvement; but I think you had better not begin
to pack up till your doctor comes—and here
he is. Lady Chester seems nervous to-day, Dr.
Ayscough, and will be the better for a talk
with you," and Aunt Sarah withdrew.

"Well, what is it? You must tell me quickly,
as I have not five minutes to spare. Why ain't
you dressed and out in the garden? It would
be a fine day for a row on the river."

"I have got a bad cold and a sore throat,
but that is of no consequence," said Blanche,
trying to look dignified. "What I wanted to

tell you is that I am very uneasy about Lord Chester, and I am going to join him at Berlin."

" To join him at Berlin, eh ? " said Dr. Ayscough, feeling her pulse in an absent manner, as if he had not the remotest idea that Blanche had a wrist, or that he had got hold of it. " And Lord Chester is ill, is he ? "

" How *can* I know ?   I have not had a letter from him these three days—not a line! "

" Oh ! " said Dr. Ayscough, and it was a satisfied oh ; expressing that he was now completely master of the case, and that the red eyes and fluttering pulse were precisely the symptoms he should expect to find.

" You are like my patient, Mrs. Armistead— her husband went with yours, I think—hers is a case of inflamed eyes ; and when I told her not to use them, she said ' she was not the least called upon to do so, as luckily she had not heard from Mr. Armistead for some days, so she was not obliged to write to him '."

" What a horrid woman ! but still it is a comfort to know she has had no letters either. But I want to consult you about my journey."

" When do you start ? "

" This afternoon, if you think I am equal to it," said Blanche, who began to want, at least, a show of opposition

" You would not go, I presume, if you did not feel *quite* equal to it," said Dr. Ayscough coolly.

" But there is only one more train to Folkestone this afternoon—you must make haste. Do you go by Ostend ? "

" I suppose so ; but Edwin will settle all that—I expect him soon. To say the truth, I do not well know my way to Berlin. It is a long journey, isn't it, Dr. Ayscough ? "

" That depends upon who undertakes it. Miss Grenville goes with you ? "

" Yes."

" And that little flighty French maid, who always calls calomel *le calmant*, and has about as much idea of being useful as that Dresden figure. Well, I wish you well through it ; I have left a prescription for your cold in case you do not get off to-day. Of course you have your passports ready ? " He felt certain she had not.

" Passports ! " said Blanche eagerly, " no, that I haven't. I never thought about them. Must I have a passport ? "

" It is generally considered necessary for travellers on the continent."

" Well then, I can't go to-day."

" I never supposed you could," said Dr. Ayscough, laughing. " I will come and see how the cold goes on to-morrow, and perhaps this evening's post may bring a letter ; and then you will not start for Berlin till the afternoon. Good morning."

He was waylaid in the hall by Aunt Sarah, who had somehow taken a diphtheria alarm, and by Aileen, who was frightened out of her senses at this sudden journey and her responsibility for her sister's safety.

"What do you think of her throat?"

"Ah, by the bye, her throat. I have not thought about it—there is nothing the matter with it."

"And this dreadful journey," Aileen said, "of course you have stopped that?"

"No, I have rather encouraged it."

"Oh dear, have you? what shall I do if she is taken ill on the road? and nothing but that silly Justine to help us, and I felt so sure you would stop it."

"There is nothing to stop, my dear Miss Grenville. Your sister has got into one of her nervous moods because she has not heard from Lord Chester. She knows as well as I do that she cannot undertake the journey; if she had been opposed, she would have worked herself up to the attempt. Give her the composing draught I have ordered; she will probably hear from Lord Chester by this evening's post, and to-morrow we can have a good laugh at her"; and he hurried off.

Blanche was, in truth, rather disappointed that he had made so light of her ailments and her heroism, but continued reading her Bradshaw and coughing till post time; then there came two letters from Arthur : one that had taken its natural course, and another that had gone a round by some Dulham in Yorkshire.

" Now is not that so like the Post Office ? " she said. " Letters that are of no consequence are always delivered directly, but when Arthur writes to me, they send his letters all over England. Arthur is quite well, and thinks that he shall get away before the three months are over, and Madame von Moerkerke is grown quite plain. Poor woman, after all she was a good-natured little thing ; and Arthur says just what you said, Aunt Sarah, about Colonel Hilton. I declare my throat is better, and if you will ring for Justine, Aileen, I will dress. What a horrid smell of smoke there is."

There certainly was. Justine came up quite *éperdue*, and in a high state of affected suffocation ; leaving the doors open to let all the smoke in, and shutting the windows to prevent it from going out. She had always heard it was right to shut the windows when the house was on fire ; and her eyes watered so, she really could not see to fasten mylady's hooks and eyes, and mylady's gown was all awry at last.

" But *is* the house on fire ? " said Blanche, half laughing, " because, if it is, we may as well make our escape."

" No," said Aileen, who had just run up stairs, " it is not on fire, but something has gone radically wrong with the kitchen flue; the smoke keeps pouring into the house, instead of going up the chimney, like well-behaved smoke; even the drawing-rooms are quite untenable."

"And my room gets worse every moment. We must take refuge in the summer-house, Aileen."

"But it is raining, and your cold?"

"Oh, that is not much, and anything is better than this. Give me heaps of shawls, Justine, and then we will rush into the drawing-room, and save our beloved Aunt Sarah, and carry her off to our wretched little asylum in the garden. Where are my letters? we will take them with us; and now, Aileen, I am ready."

They found all the servants in a state of dismay, ill-temper, and soot, and it really became necessary to leave the house, much to Aunt Sarah's dismay, who thought it a dangerous experiment. However, they settled Blanche on a hard bench, about as comfortable as a gridiron, and in a summer-house, half-trellis, half-earwigs, and Aileen glided backwards and forwards under an umbrella, bringing cushions, and cloaks, and clogs, and finally Aunt Sarah's netting; and the important butler came to announce that he had sent into the village for a person who understood the chimney and its strange ways; he really could not undertake it, and the smoke, as he phrased it, gained upon him every minute,

So, as Blanche said, they seemed likely to pass their afternoon in a mitigated shower bath ; but just then a portly figure was seen coming up the gravel walk, and Mrs. Hopkinson, in very short petticoats, displaying a pair of feet that left large impressions on the soaked gravel, a shawl tied over her cap, and with a black mittened hand, holding a cotton umbrella, presented herself.

She began the set speech which she had been composing ever since she took her resolution of offering shelter to the Pleasance ladies. " I heard accidentally through my cook " (Blanche pinched Aunt Sarah) " that your kitchen was on fire, and I came to ask if your Ladyship would not take shelter in my parlour. But, good gracious me ! " she exclaimed, in her natural manner, as she furled her umbrella and entered the arbour, " what a place for you ladies to be in ! Why, it's all of a slop, and dripping so. There ! there's a great drop gone down my collar. Why, you'll catch your deaths. Do, for goodness' sake, come into my house. Now, ma'am, take my arm—of course you've got your clogs on, and do wrap your shawl well round you."

" You are very kind," said Blanche, " but——"

" Very kind, indeed," interposed Aunt Sarah. " Perhaps you will give Lady Chester your arm, and Miss Grenville and I will follow. I am sure we are extremely obliged to you. Aileen, just pick up my netting mesh ; it is in that puddle. Now, Blanche."

And before Blanche could make any objections, she found herself under the blue umbrella, her hand under Mrs. Hopkinson's fat arm, and both of them wading through the little rivulet that usually passed for the gravel walk. " There," said Mrs. Hopkinson, as they reached her door, " now my girls will take care of you ; and as I am wet through, and can't well get wetter, I'll just step back and tell your maid to send you some dry things, and as I know that kitchen of old, I daresay I can give your servants a useful hint about the smoke."

The Miss Hopkinsons were as hospitable as their mother. A fire was lighted in the best parlour, a sofa wheeled round for Blanche, who was looking pale and blue, slippers and dressing-gowns produced, hot wine and water administered, and when Justine arrived with dry cloaks they quietly withdrew, and left the ladies to their own devices.

CHAPTER VI

"WELL, Aunt," said Blanche, "if you will candidly own that Mrs. Hopkinson *is* fat, and *does* wear mittens, and *does* know what passes in my kitchen, I will handsomely concede that she is a most hospitable neighbour, and that her dry room is very comfortable after our wet arbour."

"And you may add, my dear, that a semi-detached house has its merits ; if one half catches fire, you can take refuge in the other. And now, Blanche, you had better keep quiet where you are, and Aileen and I will go to our friends below and thank them. Just bring my netting, Aileen."

"But I should like to thank them, too, for it was very kind of the old lady to come swimming out to the rescue, and as I see ' hot tea ' expressed in every line of her benevolent countenance, I feel confident she will propose to bring me some ; so, if she does, will you encourage the idea ? "

Blanche was right. The tea-urn was on the table, brown bread and butter prepared, and a curious foreign china tea-service laid out, which excited the envy of Aileen, and the admiration of Aunt Sarah, who was learned in porcelain.

"Well, I believe it is reckoned curious; my husband brought it me when he came back from his third trip to China—no, it was his fourth, and he set so much store by it, that, of course, I could not say *I* thought it ugly; but I like the old willow-pattern best, and we only use this on great occasions. And now I should like to take Lady Chester a nice cup of hot tea, but perhaps I should disturb her."

"Oh no," said Aileen; "my sister was wishing for some tea, and if you do not mind the trouble, I am sure she would be very glad to see you, and thank you for your very great kindness."

"Kindness!—bless you, Miss Grenville!—why, where's the kindness in taking you three ladies out of the smoke and rain, I should like to know? If you have not all caught cold it's next to a miracle"; and Mrs. Hopkinson walked off with her tea and bread and butter. She was inclined —thanks to the *Weekly Lyre*—to be rather more formal with Lady Chester than she had been with the aunt and sister—she wished to show her strong disapprobation of a young wife separating herself voluntarily from her husband. She almost grudged her the Japan tea-cup and saucer, and thought the willow-pattern would have done, but somehow she could not keep up her sternness. Blanche received her so court-eously, was so earnest in her gratitude for the hospitality she had met with, and looked so fragile and pretty, that Mrs. Hopkinson subsided with a sigh into her usual motherly manner, and her conviction that it was all Lord Chester's fault.

"Well, you do not look much fit for any troubles in this world, and I hope you will have none worse than to-day's."

"Oh! it has been a very happy day really," said Blanche, smiling. "I had been very uneasy about some letters that had been mis-sent, and they came just before we were driven out of the house, so I did not mind that at all. Indeed, I think it was very good fun, now it is over, and it has given me the pleasure of making your acquaintance."

"You are very good," said Mrs. Hopkinson, "and I hope your letters were satisfactory."

"Oh, that they always are when they come! Arthur writes such excellent letters! but the post office has been very ill-managed lately—in fact, ever since he went abroad—and I foolishly fancied he must be ill, and I was on the point of setting off for Berlin."

"Law! my dear lady, the idea of your going off to Berlin, and in your situation, too! Why, I believe it is thousands of miles off, and the sea to cross and all! And Arthur is?"—

"Lord Chester, of course," said Blanche, laughing. "I ought to have called him so, I suppose. You see, Mrs. Hopkinson, he was sent

off quite suddenly on that tiresome mission to
Berlin, and we had never been parted for an
hour, and I thought I should die while he was
away, or that he would die while I was away.
In short, my aunt says I am full of fancies;
but you don't know how dreadfully lonely I
feel without Arthur!"

"Don't I, my dear?" said Mrs. Hopkinson,
quite warming up to the subject, and forgetting
what she called her company manners, "why,
John has been away the best part of every year
since we married. I am sure I might have been
a widow twenty times over for all the good I
have of his company! I have got used to it
now; but the first time that he went, just after
I was confined of Janet, I thought he would be
lost at sea every time the wind blew, and the
wind did nothing but blow that year, though
when John came back he said it was all my
fancy, and that he had made a remarkably
smooth passage."

"And John is?" asked Blanche.

"My husband, Captain Hopkinson."

"Captain Hopkinson!" exclaimed Blanche,
jumping up from the sofa, "and did he ever
command the *Alert?*"

"To be sure he did, and a regular tub she
was!"

"Well, this is curious!" and Blanche seized
Mrs. Hopkinson's fat hands, and pressed them

warmly, mittens and all. " Captain Hopkinson saved Arthur's life, by his care and kindness when Arthur caught that bad fever on his passage to the Cape."

" Not Lord Chester surely ! I always make John tell me the history of all his passengers. I don't half like those ladies from India, who are always coming home to their children, or going back to their husbands ; all I can say is, they don't fret on the voyage. I can trust John, but I always like to know who is on board, and I am sure I should have remembered Lord Chester's name ! "

" But his elder brother was alive then—he was only Captain Templeton."

" Captain Templeton ! " exclaimed Mrs. Hopkinson, jumping up in her turn. " You don't mean to say, Lady Chester, that your husband is that Captain Templeton who was the life and soul of the *Alert* till he caught that bad fever which carried off so many of John's best hands ? Goodness me ! why, John talked of nothing else when he came home from that voyage ! I thought I should have dropped off my chair sometimes with laughing at some of Captain Templeton's jokes ; and he came to see John when we were at Southsea—found him out though John was at home only for three weeks—and was so friendly, and shook hands with me, and said John was a capital fellow, which to be sure he is. And to think that he should be Lord Chester—and that you should be Lady Chester, and sitting in that wet arbour ! *That* is a curious coincidence ! "

Mrs. Hopkinson's ideas on the subject of coincidences were rather vague and ungrammatical, but Blanche was not disposed to be critical ; and when Aileen came up to say that Baxter had announced that the kitchen chimney had come to its senses, and that my Lady might come home—she found the two ladies both talking at once about the voyage of the *Alert*, and Blanche half sorry to go till she had heard more particulars of Arthur's cabin and his illness.

CHAPTER VII

"WELL, those are three as nice ladies as ever I
wish to see," said Mrs. Hopkinson, when her
guests had departed; "and as for that Lady
Chester, I'm quite in love with her. She thinks
so much of your father, and spoke in such a
way of him. I wish John had heard her!"

"Miss Grenville was very nice, too, mamma,
and took great notice of dear little Charlie, and
played at cat's cradle with him," said Rose.

"I did not think quite so much of her as of
the old lady," said Janet. "Did you make out
what her name was, mamma?"

"Lady Sarah Mortimer, my dear. She is
aunt to the two sisters, who are twins, and she
seems to have had charge of Lady Chester.
Miss Grenville lived with the other guardian."

"I cannot think how she comes to know so
much about schools," said Janet, who had
hitherto considered herself quite unequalled in
that line. "She seems to go to our school every
day, and says Mr. Greydon thinks this, and Mr.
Greydon wishes me to do that; and it appears
he called at Pleasance again to-day. Very odd,
he hardly ever speaks when I am at the school,

and as for calling, he has only called twice since he came to Dulham. However," she added humbly, " it is not very surprising he should like to go to Pleasance. He is so very superior himself that he naturally likes other superior people ; and, to be sure, Lady Chester and her sister are very different from any of us. Rose, don't you wish that mamma, and you, and I, were regular fine ladies ? "

" Oh, my dear," interrupted Mrs. Hopkinson, " don't talk so. You and Rose may try to be like those two pretty creatures if you please, and a nice job you will make of it ; but as for turning me into a fine lady, thank you for nothing. I should like to see John's face if I met him dressed in a grey moire antique and a lace mantle, and twiddling a little bit of netting silk over an ivory stick. No, my dears, you must let me be as I am, I'm too old to improve."

" You don't want a bit of improvement, dear old mother," said both her girls, giving her a good hug. " I was only joking," added Janet.

" And only a very leetle bit jealous of Miss Grenville," whispered Rose.

Blanche and Aileen went the next day to call on Mrs. Hopkinson, to repeat their thanks for her hospitalities, and to see the silver inkstand which Arthur had presented to the Captain.

" Such a sweet inscription," Mrs. Hopkinson said. " ' To Captain John Hopkinson, from his

E

obliged and faithful friend, Arthur Templeton.'
I don't suppose John would take one thousand
pounds for that inkstand. Would your Ladyship allow me to show you a picture of
John ? "

"I should like to see it of all things," said
Blanche.

" The only fault of it is that it is not the least
like him. John had it done at Macao, by a
Chinaman, Chiang Foo, who was supposed to
be a good artist ; and it was very kind of John
to think of it.   But considering that he is a stout,
florid man with blue eyes and a round face, I
don't think Chiang Foo has hit him off quite
cleverly " ; and Mrs. Hopkinson proceeded to
justify this assertion by producing the picture
of a sallow figure with half-shut black eyes and
high cheek bones, standing apparently on nothing,
and neither receiving nor casting the slightest
shadow.   Blanche could not help laughing ; but
Mrs. Hopkinson looked at it rather sentimentally,
and said, " At all events, it was done from John,
and the buttons on his coat are all right, and
look very natural."

" But I am sure it does not do him justice."

" No, indeed " ; and altogether Mrs. Hopkinson
felt gratified and interested in her new acquaintances.   Willis had called in the morning, and had
heard the history of the preceding day, on which
he made the obvious comment, that he did not

think much of a little smoke and rain. If it had been in Columbia Lodge, he had no doubt that the house would have been burnt down, but he was used to trials, and should quietly have submitted to that.

" I came to tell you, Mrs. Hopkinson, that you will probably have a visit from the Baroness to-day. She wrote me word she was coming to make a search for this villa she wants, and she wished me to accompany her; but if there is a thing in the world that depresses my spirits, it is rambling over a set of empty houses, smelling of damp and desolation. So I have left a note to say you would go with her, and I shall take myself off to town. The girls can just step to Randall's and get a list of the houses he has on hand. Where's Charlie? "

" He's asleep just now."

" Oh! when he wakes, you can give him this toy. I brought it for him; I saw it in the Strand, and it took my fancy."

It was a nice little model of a tomb, and when a spring was touched at the side, a skeleton jumped out, made a bow, and jumped in again. Willis looked at it with a grim satisfaction, which was not at all diminished by the positive refusal of his mother- and sisters-in-law to allow Charlie even to hear of it, much less to see it. Willis really was fond of his child, and did not press his pet skeleton on their acceptance when he found they thought it might frighten Charlie. In fact, he was rather glad to take it home again, for his own diversion.

Lady Chester and Aileen had hardly sat down in Mrs. Hopkinson's parlour, when the showy carriage appeared, and the Baroness and her son were announced.

" Do not say anything about us," whispered Blanche ; " we shall amuse ourselves with Charlie " ; and Mrs. Hopkinson took the hint, and turned her attention to the Baroness, who was overflowing with affability and grandeur.

" That naughty Willis has run off to London, and has referred me to you, Mrs.—Mrs.——"

" Dear Mrs. Hopkinson," said Aileen promptly, in her soft voice, " are you sure this is not your chair I have appropriated ? "

" To you, Mrs. Hopkinson," continued the Baroness, ignoring the audacious Aileen ; " he says you and your girls—where are they, by the bye ?—will help me in this difficult matter of a villa. I am afraid I am very particular, I am so spoiled. Now you, with this dear, tidy little cottage, can't guess what my troubles are, what with housekeeper's room, and the Baron's billiards, and Moses' smoking, and my own suite of apartments—a cottage, though I am sure I envy you, would not suit us."

" Here is a list my girls have brought from the house agent's ; there are not many houses vacant just now ; Acacia Place is one of the best, Baroness."

" It sounds citizenish," said that lady, who had passed all her early life in the very heart of that city ; " but to be sure," she added, with an air of deep thought, " I can change the name."

" I always admire Ivy Cottage as I pass it," said Blanche, trying to be civil to Mrs. Hopkinson's overpowering friend, " and I see a board up there."

" A cottage is out of the question for me," said the Baroness loftily, wishing to repress these intrusive young people. " So, Mrs. Hopkinson, we will go on with our business ; Bellevue —that sounds as though it might do."

" The house is tolerable, but unfortunately it is at the back of High Street, and you can see neither the river nor the common. Marble Hall, next to Columbia, is the one I should recommend."

" And a precious cheerful neighbourhood we should be in," said Baron Moses, confidentially, to the two sisters, whose beauty had made a great impression on him. " As the *belle-mère*, the mother-in-law," he translated condescendingly, " is occupied with my blessed mamma, and can't hear, I think I may venture to say that Mr. Willis is about the slowest coach I ever attempted to drive."

" Mr. Willis is my papa, and does not keep a coach," said Charlie, who was sitting on Aileen's knee, " so it could not go slow."

" Capital !   capital ! " said Moses, with an affected laugh. " Very true, my little man, *enfant terrible !*   It was the Miss Hopkinsons that I met at dinner at Columbia, not you, ladies, I think ? "

" No," said Blanche, demurely, " we have never had the honour of dining with Mr. Willis."

" Honour you may well call it, not pleasure ; but my mother, who is *entichée du beau Willis,* quite taken with him, means to humanise him, and make him give constant dinners. I presume I am speaking to residents of Dulham, and I hope we may have the pleasure of meeting at the festive board of the *égayant* Willis."

" I rather doubt whether Mr. Willis will ever ask *us,*" said Aileen, trying to look pensive.

" Oh ! but he shall. I hate exclusiveness, it's bad enough in London ; but in the country, where amusements are scarce, it is insufferable!"

" I am sorry to interrupt you, Moses," said the Baroness, " but the Baron will be frantic if I keep the greys standing ; I wish your father would not give such enormous prices for my horses. I am sure, Mrs. Hopkinson, your friends will excuse you if I take you away, but I am a perfect child in household matters, and your advice will be invaluable. Gunnersbury is my *beau idéal* of a villa, but that, of course, I cannot expect to find here ; so we will just look at Marble Hall. I wish I could have had Pleasance."

Blanche and Aileen immediately rose to depart.

" Yes, Pleasance is a stylish-looking concern," said Baron Moses, " though I only know it from the river. A charming spot for picnics."

" Ah," said the Baroness, " what suits the Chesters, would, of course, have suited me ; but, I fear, there is no chance of their giving it up. My friend Madame Steinbaum writes from Berlin——"

" Aileen," said Blanche, colouring and looking annoyed, " we really *must* go, we are detaining Mrs. Hopkinson ; and I have not made my petition. My sister goes to town to-morrow for a concert. Will you let little Charlie come and pay me a visit ? "

" Me will come," said Charlie, " me like you very much—me not like that black man," he added in a whisper, and with a look at Baron Moses.

" Well, then, that is settled. Good-bye, Mrs. Hopkinson," she said cordially to that lady, who followed her to the door, her face the colour of the coquelicot ribbon in her cap, and herself distracted by the grandeur and impertinence of the Baroness, which imposed upon her and shocked her. With a slight haughty bow to the Sampsons, Blanche departed.

"Then we will be off," said the Baroness. "I hope I did not affront your friends, Mrs. Hopkinson, whoever they may be; but they seemed inclined to put themselves forward, and I feared it might lead to their claiming acquaintance if I settle here, which would embarrass me. I am afraid I was *tant soit peu farouche*," (Mrs. Hopkinson wondered what that was, but settled that it was French for disagreeable,) "but it is a point with me to keep young people in their proper places."

"Of course," said Mrs. Hopkinson, who was quite bewildered, "*im*proper places are shocking things."

"Brava! brava!" said the Baron, clapping his hands, and then seeing that his hostess was beginning to look discomposed, he added graciously, "An excellent joke, but upon my soul, Mrs. Hopkinson, your friends are *belles à croquer*, that is to say, monstrous pretty creatures. Did not you think so, *madre adorata?*"

"Prettyish-looking girls, I believe, but they want style. Who are these damsels whom the Baron chooses to patronise?"

"I thought you knew Lady Chester and her sister at least by sight," said Mrs. Hopkinson, as sharply as her intense good-humour would allow.

"Lady Chester and her sister!" screamed the Baroness, falling back into her chair, and turning as pale as was possible under the amount of rouge she wore. " Good heavens ! Mrs. Hopkinson, why did you not name them ? why did you not present them to me ? I should have been too happy to show them every attention for the sake of our mutual friends the Rothschilds; in fact, I really wished to make Lady Chester's acquaintance, and I was scarcely civil, I am afraid."

" That I can answer for," said Baron Moses, who was in ecstasies with his mother's discomfiture, " civility was not your forte just at the moment. *I*," he added consequentially, " who can afford to follow my very vivid perceptions of what pleases *mon goût*, happily paid them every attention. I saw at once that they were intensely *comme il faut*." He sunk the fact of having offered to procure them an invitation to Willis's festive board.

" It is most distressing," said the Baroness faintly. " They must think me—*me* of all people in the world—-entirely without *usage du monde*. Why upon earth did you not introduce us, Mrs. Hopkinson ? "

" Lady Chester requested I would not," quietly replied Mrs. Hopkinson.

The Baroness received a vague and unpleasant impression that the request signified a disinclination on the part of Lady Chester to make her acquaintance, and with her mania for fashion and fashionable people this annoyed her extremely. Quite subdued, she set forth on her travels in search of a house, almost disposed to put up with the want of a billiard-table, and inclined to believe that Ivy Cottage would suit her better than Marble Hall. But a bright red flock paper in the dining-room of the latter mansion, with several vulgar chandeliers and over-gilt console tables, were too much for her: she thought the room would "light up sweetly." And having made Mrs. Hopkinson fag herself all over the house, to examine the attics, and the kitchen, and the cupboards, and the pumps, and do all the heavy work of the business, she dismissed her with the blandest apologies for requesting her to find her way home on foot, but "the Baron was very particular about his grey horses."

"Well," said Mrs. Hopkinson to the girls, as she was enjoying her tea after the fatigues of the day, " I'm regularly tired. That Baroness does not suit me nor my ways, and the airs she gave herself are not to be told. And there were those nice young ladies, *real* ladies to my mind, looking so simple and so quiet, and playing so prettily with Charlie, while that great storm of a woman swept over them. Don't tell Willis, my dears, but I can't help thinking she is very vulgar : and I see why the Queen don't ask her to her concerts."

CHAPTER VIII

"What a woman!" was all the comment Blanche made on the Baroness, "but I should like to know what she has heard from Berlin— should not you, Aileen? It must have been something about Arthur, because she implied that our stay at Pleasance would be prolonged. What could it be?"

"I daresay," said Aileen, laughing, "my imagination will not go so far as yours has gone— she probably meant to intimate to us, simple rustics, that she was in all the political secrets of the Berlin negotiation. I should not wonder if the Baron were a stock-jobber, whatever that may be ; but those sort of people always know, or pretend to know, the politics of the continent half an hour before the rest of the world. A hitch in the treaty may be worth money to the Sampsons."

"That would be bad enough," said Blanche. "It would keep Arthur longer abroad. Of course she could not mean that Arthur had got into any entanglement."

"Of course not. Oh, Blanche! Blanche! we want Aunt Sarah to keep you in order. And so you are going to have Charlie for your play-fellow to-morrow whilst I am away ? "

" Yes, I have taken quite a fancy to that poor little child. He looks so frail and suffering, and he told me he used to come every day to this garden to see the boats, till we took the house. I wish, Aileen, when you go out, you would go to Merton's and buy me a large Noah's ark, some picture books, and any toys of a laugh-able description ; that child wants to be amused. I wonder Dr. Ayscough has not been here to-day ? "

But he did not appear. When he came the following day, he found Blanche and little Charlie seated on the bank with a long proces-sion of small elephants, and gigantic lady-birds, all tending to an ark that did not seem adequate to house them, still less to admit eight yellow and red extinguishers, which were intended to represent Noah and his family.

" What now ? " said the Doctor. " Why are you playing at Noah's arks ? I thought you were at least half way to Berlin."

" No, you did not," said Blanche, " you thought no such thing, you were only, as usual, humouring me and laughing at me—I saw that all the time. It is a great pity that I have known you all my life, I see through you so well."

" Not half so clearly as I see through you, and it is a great advantage to you to have a steady old friend like myself, who withstands all your impetuosities. You were an impetuous baby when you were an hour old, and you are not tamed yet."

"But I am improving rapidly: I might have fretted over an obscure hint about Berlin that I had to-day, and that I could easily have magnified into a *bête noire*. Instead of which I have been sedulously at play with Charlie this last hour."

"And who is Charlie?" said the kind-hearted physician, taking the child's little wasted hand in his, and looking at him attentively. He could not see a sick child without trying to help it.

"He is the grandchild of my next door neighbour," and Blanche detailed the adventures of the preceding day, ending with an animated description of the magnificent Baroness.

"I know her," he said ; "she is always sending for me, because she has nothing the matter with her, and I have not yet succeeded in curing her of her good health. And now, I have a valuable document for you, which I have persuaded Mrs. Armistead to give me." It was an extract from a letter of Mr. Armistead's, in which he said that their Prussian negotiation was nearly at an end, that he might come home any day, "but I think of taking a look at Dresden and Vienna, and may perhaps push on to Prague. I want Chester to go with me, but he is spooney about his wife, and in a fidget to get home,"

"Oh, thank you, thank you," said Blanche. "Now, is not it a blessing to have a spooney husband? What does spooney mean? However, I do not much care, it evidently means that Arthur is soon coming home. Poor Mrs. Armistead, I suppose she is very much distressed."

"Not a bit. She said she was very glad, that she wanted to go to the sea, and that Armistead was always so bored at the sea-side, he was a worry to her, and now she could go in comfort."

Blanche shrugged her shoulders, and shuddered slightly at this painful picture of married life, and declined to believe that the Armisteads were a happy couple after their own fashion; and while she sat in a happy state of spooney meditation, Dr. Ayscough took her place with the Noah's ark. He settled Charlie on his knee and bowwowed, and growled, and mewed, and made Shem knock down Japheth, and Mrs. Shem catch the grasshopper; and then, putting the child down, he took Blanche aside, and said, "What are they doing with your little friend? He won't live unless he has proper medical treatment. He's a nice little fellow; make them bring him to my house to-morrow, and I will see him here again in a few days. Good-bye, my little man."

"Don't go," said the child, "stay and bark a little more."

" No, no, I have no time for more barking
to-day ; but you come and see me to-morrow
and bring Noah's dog with you ; and do you,"
he said to Blanche, " go and frighten the grandmother. That is *your* duty for the day."

Blanche did as she was bid. She took little
Charlie home, and when he had displayed his
toys and was sent up stairs, she repeated to Mrs.
Hopkinson the substance of her conversation
with the physician.

The tears rolled down the old lady's cheeks
as she thanked Lady Chester. " But, you see,
we must consult his father, and poor Willis is
rather a down-hearted man, and never believes
that anything can do good to anybody, or
that anybody can do good to anything. But
he is coming up the walk, and, perhaps, if your
Ladyship told him all this in your cheerful
way it might convince him. Ah, poor Willis,
he has never recovered the loss of his wife ! "

That was a state of affairs to interest Blanche,
and she received Willis with a degree of commiseration that flattered him extremely, and
satisfied his highest expectations in the way of
pity.

" Of course, I should wish my unfortunate
child to have every alleviation of which his
unhappy state admits. It will do no good ; he
is doomed, doomed, as every one connected
with me must be."

" Oh, don't say so, Charles," cried Janet. " Think of your sisters-in-law."

" But," he continued, with an added share of gloom, " it may be a satisfaction hereafter to think that I had the advice of such an eminent physician, however useless it may be."

" You must not be so desponding," said Blanche, with tears in her eyes ; she was actually a believer in Willis. " It is not surprising that, tried as you have been, you should tremble at the idea of a fresh bereavement ; but I assure you Dr. Ayscough is very sanguine about dear little Charlie."

" Sanguine ! " said Willis, throwing up his eyes, " ah, he little knows ! But I will not obtrude my sorrows on your Ladyship." In fact, he was in such a state of self-complacency at being recognised as a victim that he was in imminent danger of being betrayed into cheerfulness. " I shall, of course, follow your advice. How is the poor little sufferer to go, ma'am ? " he added, turning to Mrs. Hopkinson.

" Oh, there is no difficulty about that," said Blanche. " I am going to send the carriage to-morrow morning for my sister, and if Mrs. Hopkinson and Charlie will go in it, they can all come back together." She rose to go as she spoke, Willis opened the door with a degree of civility he seldom practised, and Mrs. Hopkinson followed her into the passage, and ended by giving Lady Chester a warm kiss and sobbing out, " Well, I beg your pardon, but I could not have helped it if you had paid me for it. Nobody knows what that poor child has gone through, and he such a little dear, too ! Only three years old ! and I only hope he will live to thank you himself ; for if ever there was a kind-hearted young creature it's yourself ! and now just take care how you go down those steps, and God bless you ! "

As Blanche sat by herself in the evening, she felt pleased with the recollection of the pleasure she had given, and planned another neighbourly act. She would try and see more of that interesting Mr. Willis, " and if I can persuade him," she thought, " to be a little more hopeful and resigned, it will add much to the comfort of that good-natured family. Indeed, I am not quite sure he is right to be so very miserable, and as everybody has their mission, they say, my present mission is to try and make Mr. Willis more resigned. I wonder whether he ever laughed in his life ? If so, he might be brought to laugh again."

The expedition to London was successful, and Mrs. Hopkinson had a great deal of interesting intelligence to impart to her daughters on her return. The carriage was so smooth, and Lady Chester had had quite a little bed of cushions made up for Charlie, " and as for that Doctor,

F

my dears, I should almost like a short illness
if he would attend me. He has put Charlie
quite on a new plan, and he has written down
all that is to be done ; but I suppose he saw,
easily enough, that I was as stupid as an old
post, and he will come and see him the first
time he goes to Pleasance. What a number of
good people there are in this world ! Then
we went to call for Miss Grenville in Grosvenor
Square, and she was so interested in Charlie,
and said that if anybody could do him good,
Dr. Ayscough would ; and I am sure that is
true. She had been at the Queen's concert,
and seeing I was curious, she told me all about
it ; only, unluckily, she had not remarked the
Queen's dress ; but she said the Princess Royal
wore a double skirt of white tarlatan looped
up with roses, which is a good thing to know,
and she said the Princess looked very happy,
and thought that Charlie would have to go to
the sea in time."

"Why, mamma, what *can* the Princess know
of Charlie ? "

"My dear," said Mrs. Hopkinson, laughing,
" of course I meant Miss Grenville said that, but
I have so much to tell, I mix it all somehow.
Madame Grisi sang beautifully. There were
at least twenty people waiting in the outer
room—I mean at the Doctor's—but directly he
saw little Charlie he called us in, and pretended

to be so glad to see the wooden dog. I have quite enjoyed my drive, and Miss Grenville's talk, and the only disappointment is that the Prince of Prussia was not there—at the Palace, I mean."

When Aileen arrived at her own door, she asked if there were any one with her sister, and seemed disappointed when she heard that Lord Chesterton was in the garden with my Lady— " No one else ? "

" No, ma'am, Colonel Hilton has been here, but he went away directly my Lord came."

Aileen brightened a little, but instead of attempting to join her sister, she went musingly into the drawing-room, and threw herself into an armchair, apparently for the enjoyment of her own thoughts ; and her absent manner so excited the curiosity of Baxter that he thought himself obliged to follow, and to ask if she would like to take any refreshment after her drive. And as she did not seem clearly to comprehend what refreshment meant, and declined it with an absent " No, thank you," he went down stairs to inform the housekeeper's room that " there was a screw loose somewhere," which announcement produced a considerable degree of excitement in those regions.

Aileen was not left long to herself and her absorption. Lord Chesterton and Blanche came in from the garden, Blanche with two bright red spots on her cheeks, and looking flurried, and Lord Chesterton, most elaborately polite, and slightly irritable. He was generally a model father-in-law, and Blanche was sincerely attached to him, and anxious to please him ; but there is no concealing the melancholy fact that he was by nature what may be called prim, and primness under high pressure is a very alarming quality. On his arrival at Pleasance, he had found a good-looking moustached young gentle-man sitting alone with Blanche in the most earnest conversation ; they both looked confused on seeing him, and the young officer withdrew in such haste, and in such manifest emotion, that Lord Chesterton's propriety took instant alarm and produced a degree of formal civility that almost came up to the courteousness of the last century. Blanche was no longer Bianca, or little Blanket, no paternal arm was passed round her waist, and no sportive admiration of her charms expressed. She became Lady Chester on the spot. Lord Chesterton almost bowed as he inquired after her health, and the frigidity with which he asked if she *ever* heard of Lord Chester froze her recollection of Arthur's animated letters, and they seemed to fade into thin sheets of blank paper.

To own the truth, Colonel Hilton's visit had annoyed her quite as much as it had discom-posed Lord Chesterton. His manner was odd and excited, he expressed, with needless repetition, his delight at finding her for once alone ; and Blanche tried in vain to believe that he had not attempted to take hold of her hand, as he began some disjointed sentences about past anxieties and present happiness. And it was at this crisis that Lord Chesterton arrived. No wonder he looked astonished, and that she felt almost guilty ; and the sound of Aileen's carriage was a relief to them both ; there would have been a scene if their *tête-à-tête* had lasted much longer ; so Blanche hurried her father-in-law into the house, and, by the help of Aileen and her London topics, conversation was carried on for a few more minutes : and then Lord Chesterton departed, or rather seemed to Blanche to vanish in a black cloud which would dissolve eventually into a letter to Arthur, warning him of the folly of his wife.

" Oh, dear Aileen, what shall I do ? he is so angry ! "

" What *is* the matter, darling ? I saw Lord Chesterton was not pleased, but don't cry about it—there must be some mistake. What has happened ? "

" Why, it is all that dreadful Colonel Hilton. He came here this morning, actually came in at the garden gate, without asking if I were at home, and he began to talk in such a strange way. I am sure I never gave him the slightest encouragement to talk to me of his feelings, and his happiness—I do not care if he is happy, or miserable ; and then Lord Chesterton came, and he looked astonished, as well he might, and then, to make matters worse, that odious Colonel Hilton rushed off like a madman, leaving my *beau-père* to suppose that he had disturbed an interesting *tête-à-tête*, and I know he will write to Berlin. Oh, Aileen ! what shall I say to Arthur ? "

" I will tell you," said Aileen, clasping her sister fondly in her arms : " tell Arthur that Colonel Hilton is going to be your brother-in-law, and he came to ask you to write to my uncle for us. Blanche, he proposed to me last night at the concert, and I thought I should have been at home two hours ago, and should have told you my story before he came. Dearest, I am so happy."

" Oh, Aileen ! my own darling, and so am I. Well, if ever there was a surprise thoroughly and entirely delightful it is this ! And so all these visits were for you ? Now I see how it was, and what a ridiculous goose I have been " ; and Blanche laughed like a child, till Aileen caught the infection, and laughed too, till she suddenly asked her sister what they were laughing at.

" Why, at me, child ; was there ever anybody so absurd as I have been ? How Aunt Sarah will triumph over me ! but it was Arthur's fault, originally—he put it into my head that he was jealous of Colonel Hilton ; so every time the poor man came here, I thought it was for love of me, or at all events that Arthur would think so ; and to-day I really believed he was going to make a declaration in form, and was doubting whether it were not my duty as a wife at least to jump into the river to avoid hearing it. I really do think, as Aunt Sarah says, that my imaginativeness is increasing, and in the wrong direction. Why did not I imagine he was in love with you ? nothing could be more natural, so I suppose that was the reason why I did not see it. But why did you not tell me, Aileen ? "

" Because I was not sure of it myself. Last year I saw a great deal of him at the Duchess of St. Maur's, and she always implied that her brother liked me ; but then, you know, there was that Chancery suit going on about his fortune."

" No, I did not know it ; I never read Chancery suits : but I will for the future—I shall look upon them now as connections. But go on Aileen, this is too interesting."

" Well, Uncle Leigh reads Chancery suits, for, if you recollect, he hurried me out of town last year, soon after you came to Aunt Sarah's."

" I know he did, and I have hated him ever since ; go on."

" He spoke to me about Colonel Hilton, and said he would have no encouragement given to a man who might be a pauper any day ; that the suit would probably go against him ; and as I would not promise to avoid him, he carried me to Leigh Hall."

" So like him."

" Well, Alfred—" said Aileen, with a little hesitation.

" And so his name is Alfred—one of my favourite names ; but go on."

" Alfred tried, after I was gone, to make a friend of you ; but after he had seen you twice, your marriage was declared, so that plan of carrying on our story failed, and as I heard nothing of him, and saw in the papers that he had gone abroad, I began to think he never had cared about me, but somehow that did not cure me of caring about him, and I was so unhappy, Blanche."

" My darling, I don't wonder, and you never told me a word about all this ! "

" I thought I had been so silly ; and when the lawsuit was decided in Alfred's favour, and he came into that immense fortune, Uncle Leigh began to suspect that *he* had been silly too, for he asked me if he should invite Colonel Hilton to Leigh Hall. Think of the degradation ; of course, I said *no*, decidedly ; but I believe Uncle Leigh thought there might be a chance of my meeting him at your house, or he would not so readily have let me come when you wanted me."

" And when you did come, there was I scowling away the very individual you wished to see," said Blanche, again relapsing into one of her laughing fits. " But, however, all's well that ends well ; only I wish I knew what had become of the unfortunate Alfred ; between me and my *beau-père*, he must have a low opinion of the manners of the Chestertons. Do you suppose he went back to town ? "

" I feel sure somehow that we shall see him in the course of the day," said Aileen, with a placid satisfied smile. " But you must not call Alfred odious any more," she whispered.

" I never did—I said that the Colonel Hilton of my imagination was odious ; but I like Alfred, who is to make my Aileen the happiest wife in the world, except her sister ; and I shall soon begin to love him. But now I must write to Lord Chesterton."

" Oh ! it is to be a secret, Blanche, for a few days."

" Yes, I know, dear—all marriages are secrets, till everybody has been told of them ; but Lord Chesterton must be enlightened for the good of my character ; and like all men embarked in great affairs, he loves a small confidence." So Blanche sat down and wrote :

"My Dear Lord Chesterton,—Your visit to-day was so unsatisfactory both to you and myself that you must come and see me again to-morrow or the next day at latest, and wish me joy of my darling Aileen's marriage to that Colonel Hilton who was sitting with me when you arrived to-day. I had never heard a word of their attachment, which it appears has been of many months' standing, and was brought to a happy conclusion at the concert last night. He came to be received as a brother, and found that Aileen had not returned, and that I was utterly ignorant of what had occurred. His unexpected visit and his confused manner distressed me, and when I saw how much you were annoyed, I felt that 'appearances were against me,' and I could not explain to you what was inexplicable to myself. Aileen's first few words made everything clear, and now you must come and be again the kind father you have always been to your poor little Blanket, who was a very wet blanket this morning. I could not help crying after you left me so coldly, but I am very happy now, and you have been always so kind to my sister that I know you will sympathise with her happiness, and I have extorted from her the permission to tell you what is to be a secret to the rest of the world for a few days.

"Your affectionate daughter,

"B. C."

Now there was nothing in the world pleased Lord Chesterton so much as a small confidence. He liked to feel that he had in his possession an actual secret : something that was made clear in black and white to *him*, and remained a blank to the rest of the world. He carried these confidential letters about in his waistcoat pocket, occasionally alluding to them mysteriously, and perhaps allowing to a very intimate friend the sight of one corner of the envelope, or of half the postage stamp.

Moreover, being very precise and reserved himself, the ease and frankness of his daughter-in-law were, to him, a constant source of surprise and amazement. He always recommended a *very little* more prudence in her conversation, and perhaps a *shade* less of rashness in her opinions, but he would have been extremely sorry had she attended to his recommendations. He liked her, as she was frank and open, and a perfect contrast to himself. He was touched by her note, by her sensitiveness to his blame or praise, and by her perception of the dignified manner in which he had shown his disapprobation of the slightest levity, and he arrived at Pleasance the following morning in a high state of paternal affection and affability. He shook hands warmly with Colonel Hilton, embraced Aileen, though not without some misgivings as to the propriety of the act, and presented her with a magnificent bracelet ; whereupon she returned his embrace, and thereby relieved him of his scruples.

The rest of his visit was passed in petting and admiring his daughter, and, having placed in her hand a gorgeous-looking *porte-monnaie*, he ventured to say, " that though it was hardly decorous he should allude to certain circumstances, yet he was aware that his good little Blanche must be making preparations for an expected happy event, and that he had brought his contribution to what he believed was called a *layette*." But this last word was too much for his delicacy, and he departed covered with confusion. The benevolent old villain was conscious that he had written to Arthur a mistaken statement of Blanche's conduct, and though the counter statement had followed immediately on the receipt of her note, he looked upon his offering partly as an atonement.

" It is a shame that Lord Chesterton should have given me this magnificent bracelet, and only that ' trifle from Paris ' to you," said Aileen.

But when a cheque for five hundred pounds presented itself, the chorus of approbation was loud and unanimous, and Blanche's mind, wrapped in a christening robe, was lost in a sea of Valenciennes and embroidery.

CHAPTER IX

" MAMMA," said Janet, a few days after this,
" are you going to return Lady Chester's visit ? "

" No, my dear, certainly not. It was very proper
of her to call, as she thought herself obliged to
us for shelter from that rain, and as for her kindness to little Charlie, it passes all belief, except
that everybody loves that child, but she don't
want me as a visitor, and a nice figure I should be
in her drawing-room. Why there's been as many as
eight or ten carriages there the last two afternoons,
with such fine people in them. That Duchess's
carriage is always there. I should be more out
of place there than the Baroness was here."

" That awful Baroness ! " said Rose ; " Charles
says she is to arrive at Marble Hall to-morrow
for good—did not you, Charles ? "

" I said she was coming to stay—*good* I never
anticipate, and in this case I anticipate considerable evil. She is too prosperous to enter into
my feelings. Look ! what she sent me to-day."
And he brought from an envelope black bordered
to the extent of half an inch four tickets of the
brightest blue, ornamented with Cupids per-
forming most dangerous antics on diminutive
rosebuds. " Tickets for a picnic, the Lord

Mayor's barge, and a band, and probably dancing ; in fact everything most repugnant to my tastes and habits—the Baroness should have a little more tact " ; and he almost groaned as he detailed this pointed affront to his reputation for complete broken-heartedness.

" To be sure, my dear, it was rather thoughtless ; but you see, she meant well, for the tickets are marked at a guinea each.   It was a handsome idea ; though why she should spend four guineas to make you do what you don't like, I cannot see."

" Is it possible ? " slowly murmured Willis, " can any one be so blind to the sordid side of human nature and picnics ? Ma'am, I am to pay her for them—that is, if I had kept them, I should have paid. She is a patroness, and has so many tickets she *must* dispose of, and she wished to pass four of them off on me, that's all " ; and he replaced them in the black envelope which contained a note in still deeper mourning, which note conveyed to the Baroness a stern intimation that " Mr. Willis never (two dashes under never) joined any (one dash) party of Pleasure, and was quite (two more dashes) unequal to the gaieties of a picnic." He looked at his note with a satisfied air of finished despondency.

" Miss Janet," said Charlie's nurse, presenting herself, " Lady Chester's compliments and she'd be much obliged if you would step in for a few minutes, if not ill-convenient."

" Nothing the matter with Charlie, is there ? " said Janet jumping up. The two young aunts doted on that child.

" Bless your heart, no, Miss ! except that he's in a fair way to be utterly spoiled. Missus told me to keep him out of the way, as my Lady was so kind about the garden ; but Law ! first one and then another comes, and the tall gentleman with the moustache who is there for everlasting wanted to put him cot and all into a boat and give him a row ; but I thought he might be drownded like, and I knowed I should be sea sick, so I said, no ; and now, Miss, will you come ? "

" Must I go, Mamma ? That poor Mrs. Thomson is dismissed from the hospital to-day, and she has not a friend nor a relation in the world, and I promised to go and see her, and consult with the matron as to what could be done for her."

" Is she a widow ? " asked Willis.

" Yes, her husband was drowned, and she met with some dreadful accident, and has been in the hospital for three months."

" Well, in consequence of her bereavement, I will give you the price of one of these tickets," said Willis, who was in high good humour at the notice taken of his child, and with himself for the dignified rebuke he had given the Baroness. " Yet money is no consolation."

" Oh, is not it ? " interrupted Janet ; " you would not say so, if you saw some of those poor creatures crying when they leave the hospital because they have no home to go to. I am sure I am very much obliged to you, Charles, your guinea will be such an assistance to that poor woman. Mamma, if I have not returned from Pleasance in a quarter of an hour, will you take it to her?" and so saying she departed.

She was shown into Blanche's boudoir, who apologised for having sent for her, but "We," she said, pointing to a tall distinguished-looking woman, very simply dressed, who was sitting by her, "are much interested about two or three poor women in the hospital here, and Mr. Greydon says that you know them all, and can give us more information about them than he can."

Janet's heart beat with delight. Mr. Greydon's praises were as unexpected as they were delightful, and she keenly felt, too, the possibility of benefiting some of her favourite *protégées*. Mrs. Thomson's case was considered and relieved, an ayslum procured for a young crippled orphan, and "Clara," as the dignified friend was called by Lady Chester, said she had heard much from the poor patients of Miss Hopkinson's assiduity in visiting and reading to them, and how they enjoyed hearing her and her sister sing.

"Oh, *do* you sing?" exclaimed Blanche, "I have not heard a song for ages ; you must give me one.'

"You would not call mine singing, Lady Chester," said Janet, smiling, "my sister and I have had very little instruction, and have scarcely ever heard any real music ; but we have taught ourselves a few chants and hymns, and some old-fashioned ballads, which please our poor sick friends, but I doubt if they would please anybody else. We moved our pianoforte into the back room when you came here, for fear our noise should disturb you."

The *Dead March* in *Saul* struck its melancholy old chords on Blanche's conscience, but she remembered that it was played with great expression, and again she begged Janet to sing, and opened the pianoforte ; but Janet said that an accompaniment was not necessary for the little she could do, and that little was not worth asking for twice. So without the slightest shyness she began *Old Robin Grey*, in a rich sweet voice that astonished her hearers. She seemed to be reciting the story, rather than singing the song, with a degree of pathos that overpowered them ; and just as the heroine's heart was ' like to break,' a sob from Lady Chester put an end to her griefs, and to Robin's hopes, and Janet's ballad.

" What *is* the matter, Lady Chester ? " she exclaimed.

" Why, your singing, child ; it's worse than the ' mither that did not speak,' for breaking hearts. It is the most touching thing I ever heard. Now is it not, Clara ? "

But Clara was wiping her eyes and did not answer.

" Dear Miss Hopkinson, what a gift that voice of yours is ; it would be so kind if you would let us come sometimes and hear you and your sister practise. Is her singing equal to yours ? "

" Rose sings much better than I do," said Janet simply, " and if you really think it would amuse you, and are not saying these kind things merely to please me, I am sure we should both be delighted to come and sing to you whenever you like. We are expecting dear papa home next month," she added, her eyes sparkling with delight, " and he is so fond of all these old ballads that we are very musical just now. If you have nothing more to ask about the hospital, Lady Chester, I should like to go there now, to tell Mrs. Thomson and Ellen Smith what will make them so happy ; and I will just run first into the garden, and send little Charlie home : I cannot tell you how much mamma feels your kindness to our poor little darling."

" He *is* a darling," said Blanche.

" And a great pet of mine," added Clara. " My carriage is at the door, Miss Hopkinson, and I will put you down at the hospital ; while you send your little nephew home, I will put on my bonnet, and we will meet you in the hall."

" Oh, thank you," said Janet, " then I am sure of being in time for Mrs. Thomson," and she ran hastily down stairs.

" Now that is what I call a pleasing girl,"

said the Duchess, " not shy nor awkward, and yet not forward ; and she is evidently spending her quiet little life in doing all the good that comes within her means. Then her singing ! My dear, I am ashamed of myself. I began to fancy that the Duke was old Robin Grey, and that I must have jilted some Jamie for him. You and Aileen, Blanche, have escaped being *fast*——"

" Thanks to Aunt Sarah," said Blanche.

" And thanks to your own good sense and taste ; but if you could see some of the young girls who have hardly been out a year ! their forward manners, the way in which they talk upon subjects which even now I should be ashamed to allude to—their careless manners to their mothers, and their extraordinary self-sufficiency—you would be shocked. That unaffected quiet girl is quite refreshing. I think I shall cultivate the Hopkinsons, Blanche."

In the hall, the Duchess found Janet, who, at the sight of the carriage, became aware of her companion's rank, and rather regretted the bold measure she had taken, in accepting a drive with an unknown friend. She did not know precisely how to address her ; had visionary ideas of saying your Grace, which she rejected as plebeian ; and then wondered at herself for having sung to a person whose concerts were constantly mentioned as the finest in London.

" However," as she told Rose afterwards, " the
Duchess was not half so grand as Baroness
Sampson, and quite unlike her ; and when I
have said that, it shows why I found myself
talking to her about you, and mamma, and the
poor people ; just as I should to any of our own
friends ; and when we reached the hospital, I
could not help begging her to come in, that she
might tell those poor women herself what arrangements she had made for them. It was so nice
to hear her talk to them, and then she is able
to do so much for them. How pleasant it must
be to be very rich. And then Mr. Greydon
came in," added Janet, blushing, " and do you
know she told him of my singing, and he said
he had never had the good fortune of hearing
the Miss Hopkinsons sing, except at church, and
she said he had then a great pleasure to come.
She wanted to bring me home. Again I thought
of the Baroness and her rudeness to dear mamma ;
but of course I preferred walking. Mr. Greydon
walked part of the way with me." And then
there followed a pause : the fact was too important
to be mixed up with meaner subjects ; and Mr.
Greydon's remarks on the promising crops, and
the prevalence of whooping cough in the school,
and the slight improvement of little Charlie,
were put up for private rumination. They were
too sacred to be imparted even to Rose.

CHAPTER X

" I HAD a funny note this morning from your friend the Baroness, Willis," said Mrs. Hopkinson. " It appears she has got into some dispute with Randall, and she, rather coolly, asks me to come and look over the inventory with him, as she cannot trust her servants, and is not accustomed to that sort of drudgery herself. Now I am sure I like to be neighbourly, but I do not see why I am to drudge for Baroness Sampson, and I don't want to get into a quarrel with Randall."

" Of course not, ma'am. You are quite right. It is an object with *me* to keep well with the Sampsons, and I suppose she thought, naturally enough, that *my* family would be civil to her. She is disappointed. That is not of the slightest consequence. Poor woman ! She has only just discovered the macaw. She says she never would have taken Marble Hall if she had been aware of that nuisance, and she thinks Randall ought to have told her, and wants him to get rid of it ; but he not only says he does not know where it is, but that he thought it sounded very cheerful. Ah well ! it's all of a piece with the rest of life, as I tell her. Incivility your only help, and a macaw's scream your only harmony. Life ! life ! "

" Law ! my dear, don't talk in that way. I did not mean to be uncivil."

" So I told her, ma'am, when she said how much your note had surprised and distressed her. I assured her you did not *mean* any incivility, and that indeed I felt certain, from the melancholy tie which binds you and me, that you could not have *intended* to annoy any friend of mine, and Miss Monteneros agreed with me. I had meant to have dined at Marble Hall—it will be a convenience to me in that sort of way—but it is in such confusion that I must go back to my solitary home."

Mrs. Hopkinson looked consternated at the view presented to her of her conduct, and professed her willingness to go instantly to Marble Hall and make herself of use, a concession that Willis accepted simply with a sigh—the true Willis sigh, to be had only of the inventor. The girls, who did not at all approve of his selfish management of their mother, said that as she had already refused, she could not go now unless a new request were made for her services.

" It has been made through me. I told Miss Monteneros I should go and fetch her."

" And who, upon earth, is Miss Monteneros ? " said Rose.

" Baron Sampson's niece, a very rich heiress and a charming girl."

This was said severely, and intended to make his sisters-in-law feel that *they* were not to be ranked in that category.

" Well, then, she might assist her aunt."

Willis shook his head, murmured, " How little you understand her," and then asked Mrs. Hopkinson if she were ready. He led his victim away in mournful triumph, leaving the girls in a high state of indignation, and with a slight hope that Miss Monteneros might eventually turn out his consoler. " And I trust she has a domineering temper," said Janet.

" And very high spirits," added Rose.

The Baroness received poor Mrs. Hopkinson very coldly. If that excellent woman had persisted in her refusal, the Baroness would probably have called on her the following day, and would have treated her with politeness as an equal. Now she saw an opening for transforming her into a slave, and a tame slave would be a useful addition to her establishment. Marble Hall was certainly in a great state of confusion—the butler and housekeeper at open war with each other, but united in their abuse of Randall ; one charwoman in a vociferous state of inebriation, another suffering under a sleepy form of the same disease, a housemaid in hysterics, and two ladies' maids drinking tea, and calmly

surveying a long row of unopened imperials
and cap boxes. The Baroness was scolding
them all in terms of such vulgar energy that
a faint thought crossed Mrs. Hopkinson's mind
that she must, at an early period of her life,
have been personally acquainted with the habits
and languages of the offices. At all events, her
manner of treating her servants was not calcu-
lated to excite either their attachment or respect.
At the sight of Mrs. Hopkinson she immediately
relapsed into the helpless fine lady : " Oh ! you
are come—I am so much obliged to Willis."
Again Mrs. Hopkinson thought that a little
gratitude to herself would have been an agreeable
variety. " Just step into the drawing-room, and
I will tell you all my difficulties, and I know,
you good soul, that you will undertake them for
me. You see my butler (I took him from the
Marquis Guadagni) is a very fine gentleman,
and he says he cannot undertake *hired* glass.
He has been used to the best cut of his own,
and he will have nothing to do with the inventory,
and that put it into my housekeeper's head to
say the same of the china ; and my maid and
Miss Monteneros' will not unpack our things
because they are not satisfied with the ward-
robes ; and then Randall will not furnish Psyche
glasses, and the women that came to help are
both drunk. This is really too much for even
my spirits," said the Baroness, sinking into an

armchair. "How Countess Montalbano would laugh if she saw me called upon to arrange all this *embarras*—poor me! and so now do take it all in hand, you kind creature, and see if you can make some order out of this chaos."

"I don't see much that I can do," said Mrs. Hopkinson bluntly, "I can ask Randall to send in another looking-glass or two—perhaps he will oblige me as an old neighbour—and I can recommend one or two steady charwomen in place of those you have; but you must get rid of the others first."

"Ah, yes!" said the Baroness, sinking deeper into her languor, "those creatures must go. Would you kindly send them away? and then if you would just run over the inventory with Randall, it would help my butler and house-keeper out of the dilemma in which they have placed themselves."

This was too much even for the goodnature of Mrs. Hopkinson, who was as nearly being angry as ever she was in her life; and at all events, it swept away all concern for Willis's feelings towards the Sampsons.

"Well, they must remain where they have placed themselves, if it depends on me to help them out of it. I am happy to say I know nothing about fine servants and their ways. Mine do what I tell them, and there is an end of it; and I would advise you, Baroness, to tell yours that if everything is not arranged in the course of the afternoon you will send them all away in the evening. If they obey, there is an end of your troubles ; if not, there is an end of your servants, and a good thing too."

" And about the inventory ? " said the Baroness, making a last attempt to treat Mrs. Hopkinson as a dependent.

" I have no doubt it is all right. If not, that young lady perhaps could see to it."

" Me ! " said Miss Monteneros, opening her very large eyes, and dropping the glass with which she had been surveying her aunt and Mrs. Hopkinson.

" Rachel taking an inventory ! " said the Baroness, with a scornful laugh, " that is not very likely."

" No, indeed," said Willis, " I am sure she is not equal to these household cares."

Again Rachel surveyed them through her glass, and then, turning away, murmured

> " Ye household cares, vex not my mind
>   With your inglorious strife,
>   Nor seek in sordid chains to bind
>   My free æsthetic life."

" Oh dear, that poetry ! " said the Baroness, who was thoroughly out of sorts, " am I never to hear anything else ? "

" You never heard that before, Aunt. I composed those lines while you and your friend were transacting business. What would become of us," she said in a sort of caressing manner to Mrs. Hopkinson, "without that meaning word æsthetic? Does not it express all and everything?"

"It may, my dear," said Mrs. Hopkinson, who could not help laughing at Rachel's drawling manner; "but I never heard it before, and do not know what it means now. If you had said asthmatic, I should have understood you at once; and now I must wish you all good morning; my girls will be expecting me."

The Baroness coldly said good-bye: the young lady seemed dreamingly disposed, and Willis, who was half-ashamed of his friends, condescended to escort his mother-in-law, and withdrew rather statelily.

"Now there!" said the Baroness, "I do believe that woman is affronted. She really gives herself airs—not that I care, provided she does not influence the precious Willis, the morose son-in-law."

"A little more than kin and less than kind," interposed Rachel.

"Now do give up that nonsensical habit—it has lasted a week and I am sick of it, and what is more, it does not take with Willis, and I tell you once more that it is of immense importance to the Baron to . . . . to . . . . " she was puzzled with the Baron's schemes, and perhaps ashamed to put them into words. "In short, Rachel, Mr. Willis must be——"

"Taken in, Aunt Rebecca?" She looked fixedly at her Aunt, and saw her shrink, but the Baroness rallied, and said :

"He must be civilly treated and made to feel that we are his real friends, and I must insist on your making our house agreeable to him."

"I cannot possibly combine the two very distinct ideas of Mr. Willis and agreeableness ; and if you object to my poetical vein, I am lost. You told me he was sentimental, and I had collected a splendid set of quotations, adapted to that state of mind, and now ' my tongue must be a stringless instrument.' What next, Aunt ? "

"There is no use in attempting to make you hear reason," said the Baroness, who was in a towering passion, to the great delight of Rachel ; "your uncle will be extremely angry, and now, as that tiresome woman will not help me, I must go and settle the house somehow. The Baron wants to give a great *fête* next week, and then there is that water-party, and half the tickets are still on my hands, and none of the arrangements made ; and *you*—what are *you* as a help ? lying on a sofa reading poetry—more of an encumbrance than a help."

"Thank you, Aunt. At all events it is a blessing to be something, if it be only an encumbrance ; and as you are going up stairs, will you ask the maids, if they have not drunk all the tea, to bring me a cup ? "

There was a slight approximation to a bang in the manner in which the Baroness shut the door ; but when it was closed, Rachel's whole expression and manner altered, her half insolent, half sleepy looks vanished, and the repressed air of drollery which characterised her countenance changed to a look of anxiety, as, resting her head on her clasped hands, she seemed to give herself up to deep and painful thoughts. She was trying to realise her position : days of childhood came before her—a home, a mother, young affections, strong and cherished ; and then a blank—both her parents swept away, and she the ward of Baron Sampson. Not a burden, for she inherited the wealth, that to one so young was valueless ; but no longer the child of Home, not uncared for, but unloved. Her school days had not been unhappy ; she found warm friends in some of her companions, and an able guide in her instructress, and by her own desire she remained at school till she was nineteen. Then the Baroness claimed her with an unaccountable eagerness. She was courted, flattered, petted ; but the instincts of youth are even clearer than the experience of age. She *felt* the falseness of the atmosphere in which she lived : all was false, the Baron's courtesy, the Baroness's caresses, the attentions of Cousin Moses. " We are all actors and actresses," she used to say, " and none of us quite up to our parts, though we act all day long."

This went on for two years. A month ago she came of age, and on her birthday her uncle presented her with a splendid *parure* of opals and diamonds, ("false, of course," she thought to herself) and, at the same time, requested her to sign some dreary looking parchments, which he called "releases—mere forms; but they relieve me from all responsibility with regard to your fortune, and they make you a very independent young lady." From that day the tone of the family had visibly changed, she felt she was treated with neglect, more as the poor relation than the wealthy ward, and there was less disguise practised as to the Baron's speculations and money matters.

The manner in which she had been almost ordered to decoy Willis into the house had awakened suspicions which her Aunt's change of countenance, when jestingly taxed with deceiving him, had confirmed; and she was now bringing herself to the conviction that the Baron's wealth was another falsity, and that her fortune had been, by some artifice connected with those parchments, placed in his power. "And I have not a relation nor a friend at hand whose aid I can demand, I live in a prison disguised as a palace, and take my share in the foolery that is to deceive the bystanders. But I will not lure others into the ruin that may have overtaken me. If that man's eyes cannot be opened, his mother shall be warned. How that woman's honesty warmed me ! I could have hugged her. I think I like my Aunt better since she has become openly uncivil—there is truth in that, and I suppose I shall have enough of it to satisfy me."

But there she was mistaken. The Baron arrived from the city and was for some time closeted with his wife, and when they all met at a very uncomfortable dinner, the old caressing manners were resumed. Rachel was, " dear child," and " lady fair," and " sweet thing," at every moment, and when the ladies withdrew, the Baroness was in fits of laughter at herself. " Those horrid servants had so annoyed her, that she supposed she must almost have lost her temper, and certainly must have lost her senses when she spoke as she had done to her little Rachel ; such a dear, and so amusing with her funny little quotations—the Baroness delighted in them, and would not miss one for the world."

" ' The world is a huge thing, a large price for a small vice.' That is from *Othello*, Aunt."

" You clever creature, what talents you have ! The Baron always says you are the shrewdest woman he ever saw—it would be impossible to deceive you."

" Then some deceit is intended," was the shrewd woman's thought, and she made up her mind to watch.

CHAPTER XI

WILLIS and Mrs. Hopkinson walked for some time in silence, and then she suddenly said,

" I don't like those people, Charles. I do not mind their rudeness to me; I suppose I look like a respectable housekeeper, and she thinks I am one—that does not matter; but I do not quite make out what *they* are. What do you know of them, my dear ? "

" He is one of the wealthiest men in the city," said Willis apologetically, for he was rather nettled that *his* mother-in-law should have been treated cavalierly, " and she is a very fine lady."

" Very fine, my dear, but not a lady, take my word for it ; I don't mind her not being ladylike in manner, nor, indeed, in look, which to my thinking she is not, but I hate her pretences."

" Pretensions, ma'am, you mean."

" No, I don't, Charles, I know what pretensions are, we all have them ; I mean pretences. Her helplessness, her ignorance, her nerves are all pretence, and before you have any dealings with that family in money matters—speculations I think you call them—I would advise you to know a little more of their history."

Willis was rather appalled at this. He had a great opinion of Mrs. Hopkinson's sterling sense, and he had an instinctive idea that her advice was good ; but it came too late. He had already, to some extent, embroiled himself in the Baron's schemes, and was on the point of embarking in a larger joint speculation. That he might avoid, and he determined to take his mother-in law's counsel, though, of course, with a murmur at her for offering it.

On their arrival at home, they found that Janet and Rose were at Pleasance. Mrs. Hopkinson read a note from Lady Chester, which they had left on the table, and showing it to Willis said, " Now I call that the note of a lady. She wants to hear them sing together, and wishes Lady Sarah to have that pleasure, too ; but she hopes they will not think of coming if they have any engagement whatever, but name some other time, and she invites me to come too."

" What is all this about the girls' music ? *Do* they sing well ? " asked Willis, who could not have distinguished *God save the Queen* from an Irish jig if his life had depended on it.

" I am sure I don't know if they sing well or not ; they sing to amuse themselves, and to please me ; and it's an odd kind of pleasure, too, for sometimes I sit and cry like a baby, when I listen to words about the deep sea and the wild waves roaring ; but then, of course, I am thinking

H

of John, and perhaps it is that that moves me—and yet there is something very particular in their voices, too, poor dears."

" Are you going to them, ma'am ? "

" No, my dear, they are all young at Pleasance, and don't want me. I had rather hear all about it from the girls."

And when they returned, they had so much to tell that they interrupted each other every ten words, then talked both together, and then stopped and tried to start fair again with their news.

" Oh, mamma ! what do you think ? You have seen Colonel Hilton ride by ? " said Janet.

" The tall officer who has taught Charlie——" said Rose.

" To call him Moustache," interrupted Janet.

" Who is brother to the Duchess of St. Maur——"

" And the Duchess of St. Maur is his sister."

Then they both added together, " And he is going to be married to Miss Grenville."

" One at a time," said their mother laughing. " Well, a wedding is a nice cheerful incident to my mind—and did you see the lovers ? "

" Yes, Colonel Hilton is what Lady Chester calls *Fanatico per la musica*, quite mad for music, and he did so admire Janet's *Ruth*."

" And he said Rose had one of the best contralto voices he ever heard ; and the Duchess was there, and oh, mamma, this is the nicest thing of all, she has actually asked us," and then they both spoke together, " to a morning concert at St. Maur House, to hear Piccolomini and Giuglini and all the great singers we have read about in the paper."

" You don't say so, my loves? but you two can't go alone amongst all that crowd of great people."

" Oh ! but she asked you, too, here is the card, she brought it with her—Mrs. Hopkinson and the Miss Hopkinsons."

Poor Mrs. Hopkinson did not respond at all to the radiant looks of her daughters : she was grieved to disappoint them ; but the notion of going to a large London party was one she could not entertain for a moment, and so she sorrowfully told them.

" I was afraid you would not like it, dearest old mammy, and so we did refuse at first, but then Lady Chester (she *is* so nice and so pretty, and so everything that she ought to be) said that Lady Sarah was to chaperon Miss Grenville, and that we might go with them in her carriage ; so if you have no objection, we should like to go."

" No objection at all to that," said Mrs. Hopkinson, clearing up instantly. " Only think if your father were to come home that day, and to hear that you were at a concert at St. Maur

House—he *would* be surprised ! Why, the Queen goes there, and though of course she will not be asked to meet you—I mean you would not be asked to meet her—still you are going to a house where you might have met Her Majesty." And Mrs. Hopkinson's loyalty waxed warm at the possibility.

Dress was the next subject of discussion, but Janet and Rose thought Lady Chester was so good-natured, they might venture to ask her for directions on that point, so that consideration was deferred ; and Mrs. Hopkinson narrated her morning experiences, which filled her daughters with indignation, and they issued peremptory orders to their mother never to go to Marble Hall again.

" Poor Willis ! " added Mrs. Hopkinson, " I suppose he is an unlucky man, as he says. He is certainly not fortunate in these friends ; the niece was the best of the set, though I did not understand what she was talking about, and she is pretty too."

" Does Charles think so ? " asked Janet.

" Charles ? I never thought to ask him. Why bless me, girls ! " Mrs. Hopkinson added, after a pause, " you don't mean to say that poor Willis will ever look up again after his sad loss— that he will ever think of a second wife? To be sure, I have no right to speak ; I had been a widow only two years when I married your father ; but then I was young and gay, and between ourselves, children, my poor dear first was not a man to grieve for long. Eh, dear ! we all have our faults, and he certainly had a good many. And somehow I was not very happy with him, but it is all made up to me now, and perhaps he meant well."

If so, he had certainly failed singularly in acting up to his intentions, for he had treated his young wife brutally ; and as there is no reason to suppose that the fall from his tandem which terminated his dissipated life was a voluntary act, or in any way meant as a kind attention or an atonement—it was charitable of Mrs. Hopkinson to endow him with even a limited amount of well meaning.

CHAPTER XII

THERE was to be a school feast at Dulham. This
is a modern innovation, which may be productive
of a certain amount of happiness, and is, at all
events, well intended on the part of those who
furnish the tea and the buns, and the steamer
and the vans; but there is always something
suspicious, to my mind, in the little shrill hurrahs
which are kept up by the youthful tea drinkers
at intervals during the whole day, to say nothing
of their being rather unmusical. It may not
be so, but sometimes it appears as if the five or
six charitable gentlemen in black coats and the
equally charitable ladies in black gowns who
conduct the festivity order the cheers as well
as the cheer; and that the hurrahs are *des
houras de commande*. However, this is being
hypercritical. The Dulham children were not
to be paraded to a tea execution in procession.
Mr. Greydon had asked for the use of the Pleasance lawn and garden, which was willingly
accorded by its inhabitants, who delighted in
the sights and sounds of childish merriment.
They had no anti-hurrah feelings. Aunt Sarah
came out strong on these occasions; she told

little stories to the children, which made them laugh ; she brought a provision of toys and sweetmeats, which were hidden in the most ingenius places, in thick shrubs, in wheelbarrows full of leaves, in Charlie's cot, and one great prize was discovered in Aunt Sarah's netting case. Mrs. Hopkinson, who felt she would not be out of place on this occasion, was invaluable ; she had known most of the children from the day of their birth, and had an individual knowledge of their ailments and their tempers, and their frocks and bonnets, and their little brothers and sisters, that made them familiar with her, and she could not walk across the lawn without half a dozen clinging to her skirts. Some of the young ladies of the parish came in the capacity of school-teachers, and Mr. Greydon, who brought several of his assistants, was absolutely frisky ; running races and flying kites, and cutting bread and butter in slices of astounding thickness—Janet thought that no loaf had ever before been so well divided.

Even Mlle. Justine was condescending ; she thought this *fête du village très-intéressante*, and withdrew her hands from her eternal apron pockets, to assist in tea making ; and Baxter deigned to carry one of the benches that had been sent up from the school half across the lawn. While the sports were at their height, they were suddenly suspended by the appearance of the Lord Mayor's barge coming majestically up

the River, flags flying, band playing, &c., &c.
Either from the attraction of the crowd of children
at Pleasance, or from the natural impulse to
stick in the mud which is the general character-
istic of boats, it came to, just opposite the house.
The children assembled on the bank, and greeted
it with spontaneous cheers, and Rose and Janet,
following to prevent them from falling into the
river in a mass, were met by the sight of Willis
moving majestically and sadly through the
mazes of a quadrille. They were speechless
with astonishment. If the monument had suddenly made them a low bow, or if the great
bell at St. Paul's had made a flippant remark
in good English, it would not have seemed more
unnatural than Willis dancing with a handsome
looking girl dressed in the smallest of bonnets
and the yellowest of gowns.

" Grey gloves too, and no crape on his hat,"
said Rose ; " he must be very near a proposal."

They fetched their mother to see this preter-
natural sight ; and when Willis came to a
triumphant termination of the *grand rond*, and
was making a stiff bow to Miss Monteneros, he
found himself confronted by his mother- and
sisters-in-law, and felt that the power of his
gloom, the charm of his misery, had passed
away for ever : he could not subside from that
last *chassé*, stiffly as it was performed, into the
bowed-down mourner.

Surprise had been felt on shore, but there was equal surprise on board. The Baroness who was doing the patroness, full of majesty, and also doing Cleopatra, minus the Nile, suddenly roused herself from a very effective attitude, and, beckoning to Willis, said, in an agitated voice, " Who is that leaning on Mrs. Hopkinson's arm ? "

" Lady Sarah Mortimer, ma'am."

" And the gentleman offering chairs to your sisters-in-law—two gentlemen indeed ? "

" One is Colonel Hilton, who is to marry Miss Grenville, and the other is, I think, her brother."

" Well, upon my word, they are free and easy young ladies, talking and laughing with those young men as though they had known them all their lives. This school feast has been a great introduction for them," said the Baroness spitefully. " I believe, in these days, a little attention to the poor is not a bad speculation." The Sampsons were always speculating.

" The Miss Hopkinsons are a great deal at Pleasance," Willis said stiffly ; " Lady Chester is constantly inviting them."

" Dear me ! I wish I had known that sooner," said the Baroness ; " I had no idea that they were at all in our set, or I would have phrased a little note I sent to them this morning differently."

She had actually written, in a fit of superb impertinence, to say that she had a *déjeuner dansant* on the 16th, and that if Mrs. and the Miss Hopkinsons liked to see it, they would have a good view of the company from some of the upper windows.

" Do, my dear Willis, explain to them that I had no idea that they would like to join in my little *fête*, but that I shall be happy to see them *as guests*. It will be very gratifying if Lady Chester and I, between us, bring these girls into society ; so mention that I will receive them *as guests ;* in fact, I will send them a regular card." She seemed to think that after that life had no further distinction to hope for.

" You can do as you like," said Willis stiffly ; the Sampsons were sinking hourly in his estimation ; " but I know they cannot come on the 16th. They are going to a morning concert at the Duchess of St. Maur's."

" At St. Maur House ? a subscription concert of course ; I am sorry now I fixed my *fête* for the 16th. I should have been happy to have taken tickets, and I shall feel quite distressed if my *réunion* should interfere with the Duchess's charitable intentions. It was very thoughtless of me to take her day. I am sure it is very kind of her to lend St. Maur House ; I can't think how it is that she and I have never visited, but we have not. I should have liked this opportunity of taking your sisters, Willis, if I had been going."

Willis was becoming frightfully clear-sighted to what Mrs. Hopkinson called the Sampson pretences, and received as much pleasure as it was in his nature to feel in baffling them.

" Lady Sarah Mortimer takes them ; and it is not a subscription concert, only one of the Duchess's morning *fêtes* ; begins at three, I think the card said."

A card ! a private party ! Lady Sarah for a chaperone ! the Baroness was absolutely silenced by astonishment and vexation at her mistaken treatment of the Hopkinsons. Rachel looked amused, and, viewing through her glass the groups on the lawn, observed that their picnic seemed to be going off successfully. This roused Baroness Sampson to a sense of her patroness duties. Various young men were despatched with peremptory messages to the red-coated bargemen, and finally the boat was induced to move slowly on, the band of course playing *Partant pour la Syrie*, a point of the globe the Lord Mayor's barge was most incompetent to reach.

" Now, Aunt," said Blanche, who had withdrawn with Lady Sarah to her own quiet room, " don't you think I am behaving very well, and that I am improving in habits of self-command ? You have not seen any signs of fretting, and yet I am very unhappy. Arthur did not write kindly, did he ? "

"He wrote under a misapprehension, caused by his father's letter ; and twenty-four hours later when he would have received the news of Aileen's engagement, he would certainly be much more unhappy than you are, my love, that he had been unjust to you. But I will own that you have borne this injustice wonderfully, and that my Blanche *has* improved in the art of self-control. And I have been thinking, my child, that you may soon see good come out of evil. Arthur will be so afraid of your fretting, and so ashamed of his pettishness, that I should not be at all surprised if he set off instantly to come home."

"Oh, Aunt Sarah ! do you really think so ? but then that wicked Mr. Armistead—who is clearly a very unprincipled man, and does not care about his wife—will never let Arthur off from that journey to Prague, now that he has made him promise to go. He will think it great fun to part Arthur and me, because he and his wife cannot agree."

"I have known the Armisteads for some years," said Aunt Sarah quietly. "Some people think him rather too evangelical, but that is no business of ours ; he does a great deal of good in a quiet way, and he makes his giddy little wife, who has no harm in her, very happy. She told me the other day, with tears in her eyes, that she never knew what goodness was till she married Mr. Armistead. You know what her own home was. And so as I was saying," pursued the old lady without raising her eyes from her netting, " I expect that in a very short time we shall have Arthur here—perhaps to-morrow."

" Oh, Aunt Sarah ! " said Blanche, throwing her arms round her Aunt's neck, " you know more than you tell me ; you have heard from Arthur, you are sure he is coming ; perhaps he is here," and she started up as if to go and meet him.

" My dear, dear child," said Lady Sarah, taking her by the arm, " will you be a little more reasonable, and above all, will you sit down quietly on the sofa ? I have *not* heard from Arthur ; but just before I came here, Mrs. Armistead came pirouetting into my room, and said she was furious with Lord Chester, who had made poor dear Armistead give up his Prague journey, and that they were probably coming home together directly. That little goose pretended to be in despair that her plan of going alone to Brighton was at an end ; but as she danced, and laughed, and sang scraps of French songs, and was overflowing with spirits, I imagine that she is not sorry to have her grave husband at home again. I did not mean to tell you this, thinking that you would rather learn it from Arthur's letter to-morrow, but now you know all that I know. Of course

Mrs. Armistead had forgotten to look at the date of her letter."

" Oh ! never mind dates. Now I am happy. They will be here soon—soon is a charming word, and as for Arthur's letter, I suppose I ought to be flattered by his jealousy, but I mean to be very dignified at first, Aunt."

" Very well, my dear ; we shall see."

" I really must, upon principle. It would never do to let Arthur get into a habit of mistrust—and to think of his saying he was going to Prague, when he never meant it ! "

" That journey may pair off with yours to Berlin, dear. But listen now to that song. How well those girls manage their voices."

The school children were all at tea, too much occupied with buns and muffins to make any noise, and Mr. Greydon, who seemed exhilarated by the day's work, suggested to Janet that it would be a good opportunity to give him the pleasure the Duchess had promised him of hearing her sing. If he had proposed to her to ride a steeple-chase, she would have attempted it, so she and Rose performed an echo song, the one sister concealing herself, and repeating from a distance, the clear notes of the other— the effect was perfect. Even Colonel Hilton and Aileen, who had retreated from the school-child world to a solitude in which they might uninterruptedly talk *to* each other *of* each other, abandoned their seclusion, and drew to the window in which Blanche's sofa was placed.

The long evening shadows were beginning to chequer the bright lawn, the still river, " one burnished sheet of living gold " reflected with unbroken clearness the picturesque barges that floated lazily by and the bright pleasure boats that stayed their rapid oars at the sound of the music from the garden. The summer air, rich with the perfume of the magnolias, breathed softly over all this beauty. It was a scene that might have made a philanthropist of Timon. Even the bargemen refrained, for the time, from the stream of oaths which seem to be their idea of common conversation, and if they swore at all, swore blandly and benevolently. Aunt Sarah actually suspended her netting, and as the last notes of the song died away, Blanche drew a long breath and said, " That is too beautiful—I only wish Arthur could hear it. '

" He has heard it," said a joyous voice at the door, and Blanche, turning hastily round, saw her wishes realised. There was a rush and a scream, and a soothing sound of endearments, with " darlings " and " dearests " intermixed ; and as Aunt Sarah precipitately fled, abandoning even her netting in the retreat, she was harassed by no fears that Arthur's sins would be visited with any undue amount of dignified coldness.

CHAPTER XIII

THE Sampson picnic did not end with any *coup de théâtre*, but upon the whole it might be called successful. No rain, no spoiled bonnets, the young ladies constantly dancing on deck, the old gentlemen constantly eating below, the Baroness treated as the great lady of the party— and to crown all, Willis and Miss Monteneros were much together ; and considering his usual taciturnity, and her habits of disdainful mockery, the Baroness was surprised to see them occasionally engaged in earnest eager conversation. She thought it augured well, and took occasion to observe to her niece the following morning that Willis improved very much on acquaintance, and was a thorough gentleman. To which Miss Monteneros made the obvious Shakespearian reply that " 'Twas never merry world since gentlemen came up," and that she thought the general merriment of the world would not be increased by this particular gentleman.

" At all events," said the Baroness, with a sweet smile which was slightly forced, " he shows good taste in one respect, I shan't say what. I should like to show some civility to his relations, Rachel ; but owing to one or two little *contretemps*, little mistakes that I made in my giddy way, I hardly know what to do."

" Or to undo," said Rachel, " for the interview with Mrs. Hopkinson and the note that followed are *des faits accomplis*. But, Aunt, as you don't want to have the Hopkinsons at your parties, and they don't want to come, why not let things remain as they are ? "

" For a thousand reasons," said the Baroness, pettishly. " It would be a great advantage to those girls to appear at my parties, and I like to do a good-natured thing." Rachel raised her glass and took a steady view of her Aunt ; it seemed as if she wished to study her in an entirely new character. " And if they really sing well, they might make themselves of great use to me." Rachel's glass dropped—there was nothing new in the Baroness as she was now revealing herself. " Then if the Duchess and Lady Chester have really taken up these Hopkinsons, there would be nothing derogatory in my doing the same."

" Nothing whatever," said Rachel emphatically, " even putting the Duchess and Lady Chester aside."

" Very true, Rachel. Of course, in my position, I can choose my own society. It would be a good thing for those girls to have the *entrée* of my house, and if through them I am drawn

I

into an acquaintance with their fine friends, their patronesses I ought to say, it really would make little difference to me to have to extend my visiting list. The Chesters I look upon as neighbours—I ought to ask them ; and I should not mind asking the Duchess if——"

" She would but come," said Rachel, " but to begin at the beginning, how are the Hopkinsons to be propitiated ?   What do you mean to do ? "

" Propitiated, indeed ! when I am offering them the greatest possible civility. Why, who are they ? the wife and daughters of an East Indian Captain, who have somehow crept into society quite out of their line. However, the Baron heard yesterday that Captain Hopkinson has made a large sum of money in the China trade, and if he comes safe home (I, for one, expect every ship to be wrecked) the Baron wants to make his acquaintance ! "

Rachel seemed to be in a fit of absence and murmured to herself, " ' If one should be a prey, how much better to fall before the lion than the wolf.' Well, as you say, Aunt, I believe Shakespeare gets too much into my head, I am always quoting him without rhyme or reason."

" That you certainly are," said the Baroness sharply. " However, I adore Shakespeare myself, and only wish I had time to read him. Indeed, I went once to see his *School for Scandal ;* but *revenons à nos moutons ;* I was thinking that

you, perhaps, could go and call on the Hopkinsons and ask them to our second *déjeuner* on
the 23rd, and tell them that my list is full for
the 16th ; that would put everything straight."

"No," said Rachel, "I do not know them ;
I do not want to bring them into this house,
and I had rather not call on them."

"Oh ! very well, take your own way ; and
perhaps, all things considered, I had better go
myself. Ring, and order the carriage " ; and
the Baroness departed, rather ashamed of herself
at heart, but still convinced she was doing the
Hopkinsons great honour.

Her arrival disturbed a very good-looking
young man, who was sitting talking to Mrs.
Hopkinson, and was making himself very agreeable, to judge from the sounds of laughter that
met the Baroness on the stairs. He jumped
up the instant she was announced, and said
that he was obliged to be on hard domestic
duty the first day of his return, so he could
not stay another minute. "But I could not
put off coming to thank you for all your
attention to my wife ; and I want to know
when my friend Hopkinson will be at home ?
Ah ! he abused the poor old *Alert*, but the
Alacrity seems to be the slowest tub of the
two."

"Oh ! you must not call the *Alacrity*
names ; John says it's the best voyage he has

ever made ; and that he is so rich now, he shall buy a place somewhere near Portsmouth, or Plymouth, and settle down into a country house ; but, bless your heart, till there's a dry deluge," (a new invention of Mrs. Hopkinson's, which she had to explain), " and the world is all land and no water, John will never be happy ashore."

" John will be happy any where, with the individuals whom he irreverently mentions ten times a-day at sea as his old woman and his kids ; and now I must bid the old woman good morning, and request the kids to attend to the summons they have received, or my little lady will suppose I have forgotten to give her note ; " and amidst a fresh burst of merriment Lord Chester departed.

Again the Baroness was surprised, and wondered who the distinguished looking young man was, who was on such easy terms with the family ; and she became more than ever anxious to put her acquaintance with the Hopkinsons on a better footing ; admired their room, looked at their work, and commented on the school feast. " It was quite an event in our expedition. And, by the bye, I wish you had been with us, we had a charming picnic, and I scolded that naughty Willis for not asking you. To be sure I ought to have done it myself, but somehow I took it into my head that you were *serious*," (there was no doubt of the fact in its literal sense at that moment : Janet and Rose were in a frozen state of dignity) " and that you would object to our frivolous amusements. But I am so glad to hear from Willis that you do go out. I have brought a card for my *déjeuner* on the 16th."

"Thank you," said Mrs. Hopkinson, " my girls are engaged."

" Oh ! you dissipated creatures " ; the Baroness glanced at the looking-glass ; there was no card paraded there, and she began to doubt the St. Maur concert. "But if it is a dinner engagement you can still come to me for the afternoon.'

The girls were determined not to gratify her curiosity, and merely said they were engaged for the day.

"Well, I hope I shall be more fortunate on the 23rd. I will leave a card to remind ; and as young ladies always have some young gentlemen to whom they like to show a little civility, I will leave another card or two. Ah ! I am very discreet, I shan't mention any names you may choose to add ; but when I see a charming young man sitting with two charming young ladies, I know what to think. Now I must run away ; my dear Rachel will miss me. I hope Captain Hopkinson will soon return. The Baron has heard a great deal about him, and will make a point of calling directly. Adieu, *au revoir*, on the 23rd."

"Thank you," again said Mrs. Hopkinson; but no acceptance of the invitation was given, and when the Baroness was again seated in her carriage, she had an unpleasant impression that "poor, dear, vulgar Mrs. Hop," as she habitually called her, had, in her simplicity and plainness, baffled all the flattery so adroitly offered; and if it were possible to admit such a monstrous thought, that she somehow looked down on herself, Baroness Sampson, of Lowndes Square and Marble Hall. She was rather glad Rachel had not been present. And then she had an unpleasant surprise with respect to her when she reached home; she found her sitting with a grey-haired, astucious looking man, who was tying up a bundle of parchments and taking his leave, assuring Miss Monteneros that she should soon hear from him.

"Who upon earth is that, Rachel?"

"Mr. Bolland, my solicitor," she said carelessly, "but have you secured the Hopkinsons, Aunt Rebecca?"

"Of course, but what is this new fancy about a solicitor?"

"Just what you call it, a new fancy. I found, on looking at my fortune, that it was unpleasantly large, and that it would give me a world of trouble if I undertook to manage it myself, so I have put it into Mr. Bolland's hands."

"I am sure your uncle would have been

glad to save you all trouble about it," said the Baroness in a faltering voice.

"I am sure of it, too," answered Rachel firmly. She looked at her Aunt, whose extreme paleness seemed to touch her, for she added more gently, "My uncle has so much business on his hands, I do not wish to trouble him with mine, and money matters are always better transacted with strangers. Besides," she added, trying to laugh, "there is something grand in the sound of a man of business—heiresses always talk of their man of business, as a part of the property; and as you are always telling me what a great heiress I am, I may as well have all the proper distinctions of the position. You look tired, Aunt—won't you have some tea?"

"No, I thank you, I have got a headache; I will go and lie down, for we have company at dinner, and I must rest." She almost tottered as she left the room. Rachel, too, could hardly stand. "Poor thing," she said to herself, "she knows it all—all what? Oh! these horrible suspicions! why were they ever put into my head? and why have they become almost certainties? Is money worth all the misery, the struggles it brings? Those Pauls, and Strahans, and Redpaths, have more to answer for than the pecuniary ruin they have wrought. They have ruined all confidence, all trust; they have made dishonesty the rule, and not the exception. Why did my Aunt ever marry that cold sactimonious man? His mere look always gave me a chill. Well, I must try to think I have done right; Mr. Bolland was my father's friend, and his warning was well meant; there are others, too, to be saved as well as me, else I think I would rather let my fortune go. It is not worth this wretchedness."

She heard the sound of the Baron's horses in the court-yard; and he came so seldom into her drawing-room that his immediate appearance there this afternoon took her by surprise. He looked harassed and heated, but greeted her with the fawning courtesy that always disgusted her.

"What, all alone, my fair niece? taking a little time, I have no doubt, for wise reflection. That is well; we men of business have too little time for thought, though I trust I neglect none of the opportunities that are given me. My happiest hours are those I spend in my library, where I can shut out all my earthly cares, and forget the world. Who is it calls it the workey day world? Sad! sad! that so it is to most men. I was not meant to live in all this money-making turmoil. It distracts me. By the bye, that reminds me that one of my distractions was forgetting to ask you to sign a paper that I ought to have given you with the others; quite a form, but a very necessary form. Perhaps

I have it about me ; ah, yes ; here it is," picking it out from a bundle of tracts, receipts of hospitals, &c. "It ought to be witnessed ; I will ring for two of the servants."

"Stay, let me look at it first, Uncle."

"That's right, always look at a paper before you sign it ; though whether my fashionable niece, Miss Monteneros, will be much the wiser for looking at a power of attorney I cannot say." He put it into her hand and again laid hold of the bell-rope.

"Do not ring, Uncle ; I cannot sign it to-day," and she put it into her pocket.

"Ah, not to-day ! Well, any day will do, but I should like to have the business settled."

"I have promised Mr. Bolland that I would not sign any paper till he had seen it," said Rachel, and she went to the window that she might not see the consternation with which she supposed the Baron would be overwhelmed ; but after a few moments' pause she heard him say in his usual bland voice :

"Ah ! Bolland the solicitor—a clever man— so you have consulted him ? "

"He was a great friend of my father's," said Rachel hurriedly, and still not looking round, "and you are always so busy, Uncle ; so I have put all my affairs into his hands."

"Indeed ! Well, you could not have done better," and still the voice sounded bland.

" Then you may as well give me back that paper; he can be one of your witnesses when he has seen it."

Rachel was half inclined to keep it, but she reflected that, unsigned, it could do *her* no harm, whatever it could do to her Uncle, so she returned it to him. He seemed in no flurry to take it, and kept turning over the other papers that had been in his pocket; but impassive as were his looks, she observed that his hands trembled.

" Here is the paper, Uncle."

" What paper, my dear? Oh! I beg your pardon, I had forgotten all about it. I was looking out a most interesting report on the Church Missions to Central Africa, to which you may like to subscribe. Ah, here it is; my name and subscription are made a little too prominent; I wished to have been put down merely as a ' friend,' but the Committee attached more weight to my name than it deserves. So here is one paper for another. Exchange is no robbery, Miss Rachel," and he sauntered carefully out of the room.

" Oh! what is truth? and where is it?" thought Rachel; " could he really be so calm if he were attempting to rob me? I will think no more," and she went up to dress for a large party.

CHAPTER XIV

ARTHUR'S return infused great animation into
the Pleasance life. There were all the Hilton
connections and relations to be invited and
feasted, and whole families of Grenvilles and
Chestertons were supposed to have become
suddenly possessed of the warmest feelings of
friendship for all the Hiltons and St. Maurs
that ever were born. Mr. Leigh, the uncle
and guardian, was invited to come and talk
settlements, and make difficulties which, as soon
as they had driven Colonel Hilton and Aileen
to despair, were detected as impostor difficulties,
and vanished. Mr. Leigh was so exacting in
the article of pin-money, so regularly aggravating, that Colonel Hilton, who would willingly
have permitted Aileen to spend half his fortune
or the whole of it, if she liked, was provoked
into saying that he did not see that she could
want any pin-money at all, she could ask him
for what money she required. But here Aunt
Sarah's good sense stepped in : she thought it
better that young married women should have
a fixed income, whatever it might be called,
pin-money or allowance. They knew then what

they ought to spend, and all their little charities, or any presents they wished to give, would be the fruits of their own self-denial, and she even hinted that the most devoted and liberal husbands would, after a certain term of married life, object to milliners' bills, and become possessed with an insane idea that their wives were extravagant and always asking for money. And although Colonel Hilton said it was impossible he could ever be such a brute as that, yet he thought Aunt Sarah's advice sensible, and named to her a much larger amount of pin-money than had been asked for by Mr. Leigh, "just to show the fellow what he could do, if he were not bullied;" and, moreover, he felt it due to the injured feelings of himself and Aileen to rush up to Hancock's and secure a diamond necklace that was on the point of being "submitted to the Empress Eugénie for approval," that being now the favourite term for buying and selling.

Lord Chesterton came to talk Prussian politics of the most mysterious and heavy description, and tried to throw an air of modest dignity over the love making that was going on in the house He at first attempted to follow the lovers in their rural walks, but found himself so obviously *de trop* that he resigned that occupation, with the observation that the manners of the present day had a certain freedom which surprised him. He had never been allowed to be *tête-à-tête* with Lady Chesterton before they married ; but, of course, if Lady Sarah did not object, he supposed there was not that impropriety in these rambles which struck his old-fashioned notions. Sir William and Lady Eleanor de Vescie came for a few days to see their brother, though, as Sir William observed, it was an expensive time to choose for their visit, as they would be expected to make wedding presents to Aileen ; and he accordingly bestowed upon her a carved wooden bread-plate, sold cheap, because it *would* spin round. As he had but thirty thousand a year, this was a handsome present for him.

There was boating on the river, and Edwin and his friends constantly rowing up to Pleasance. There were illustrious Prussians, new friends of Arthur, generally with a *faux air* of English corporals, to be entertained—and to many of these parties the Miss Hopkinsons were invited, not for their musical talents, but for their own amusement, and they were so unaffected and so merry that they became general favourites. There was one grand amateur musical evening, at the end of which Edwin imparted to his sisters that he thought Harcourt was smitten with Rose, and that, as he was a good sort of fellow, and had never had any particular father and mother, he could marry to please himself, and a good contralto voice might catch him any day. Mr. Greydon, who was an old college friend of Arthur's, was a constant guest, and Janet and he became better acquainted ; but it required a strong attachment and a very sanguine disposition on her side to derive that extreme gratification from these interviews which she found in them. However, she went on persuading herself that he liked her, and that he would show it more when he had a living, and in the meanwhile she was perfectly happy if he handed her into a boat or put on her shawl ; and there was one blissful day when he actually went back to the house to fetch her parasol which he observed she had forgotten. That parasol never saw the light of day again ; it was put into a favourite Chinese Cabinet and covered with lavender, and a new and inferior one bought for common use.

" The rival parties " on the 16th, as the Baroness always called them, went off well. An enemy, supposing it possible that the Baroness Sampson could *have* an enemy, might have said that the assemblage at Marble Hall looked like the recovery of one of the lost tribes of Israel ; but there were some fine sounding names among them : foreign Counts and Marquises, several members of Parliament, radical in politics, and unpolished in manner, and who had manfully voted for the removal of

Jewish disabilities. Whether they knew what the disabilities were, or what would be the effect of their removal, is doubtful ; but they somehow had an idea that they were voting against gentlemen and Bishops, and Church and State, and they felt proud of themselves. Then there were their wives and daughters, decidedly not ornamental. There were a few ladies of high sounding titles, who had either risen from the ranks, or fallen into them, but the chief part of the society was decidedly second-rate.

The breakfast was magnificent ; plate, wines, china, all of the finest description ; and it was evident that money was no object to the Baron, and, as he averred, gave him little enjoyment. The Baroness, he said, had a feminine taste for Sèvres China or it might be Dresden ; he did not know one from the other, but she pleased herself in those trifling concerns. He owned he thought that plate kept the dinner hotter, and when his friends were kind enough to come and see him he should be sorry if they found their dinner half cold and not fit to eat. He felt it a duty, with his means, to encourage the manufactures of the country (Sèvres and Dresden !), but for himself, a mutton chop on a common white plate was all he asked.

The Baroness was in the highest spirits, loudly regretting that the Duchess of St. Maur should

have carried off so many of her guests, but
that circumstance had apparently left her a
larger amount of condescension to divide amongst
the remainder. Miss Monteneros seemed to be
suffering either from a cold or the persevering
attentions of Baron Moses, and was more than
usually *distraite* and languid. Willis did not
appear till so late in the afternoon that the
Baron was quite uneasy about his friend, hoped
there had been no mistake about his card
(but there the Baroness reassured him), trusted
that dear little Rachel had not been cruel to
her admirer, to which he met with no answer
but a frown ; and finally asked if it could be
possible that he were gone to this grand London
party, which notion threw Baron Moses into
convulsions.

"Oh, my dear Sir, stop those ingenious
conjectures, or you will be the death of your
only son. The melancholy Jacques in the *salons
dorés* of St. Maur House. *Figurez-vous* that determined chief mourner *promenant ses ennuis* amongst
all that is of the gayest and the brightest."

"Would it be any trouble to you, Moses, to
speak either English *or* French ? " said Rachel.
" The two combined, neither of them very good
of their kind, obscure your meaning—to my
limited capacity, at least—and why Mr. Willis
should be more misplaced at a concert than a
breakfast, I do not see."

"Well, this is something *à faire dresser les cheveux*. The beautiful and accomplished Miss Monteneros avowing her interest in the obscure and freezing Willis ! Rachel, spare my feelings—*je suis jaloux comme un tigre*."

"And habited like a tiger," she said carelessly, as she turned away ; and taking the arm of one of her school friends, several of whom had been invited to the fête, " Let us go and set the dancers off. I am in that state of mind that I could dance in desperation, or sing, or laugh, or do anything extravagant."

"You are in one of your moods, my dear, as we used to call them at school," answered her friend, "when you used to begin to cry just as you were making us all laugh by your gaiety."

> " ' I have a smiling face,' she said,
> ' I have a jest for all I meet,
> I have a garland for my head,
>   And all its flowers are sweet,
> And so you call me gay,' she said,
>   'Grief's earnest, is life's play,' she said."

This was Rachel's answer.

And just as the music began the recreant Willis appeared. He hated now the very sound of the music. That one unfortunate quadrille into which he had been beguiled on board the barge had not only lowered him from his

K

high, disconsolate position in the world, but it had lowered him in his own eyes. He knew, in his inmost soul, that the fascinations of Rachel had lured him into that incongruous levity.

" Mary, the dear departed shade," was not only on the point of being superseded, but the figurative shade which she had thrown over him seemed to be departing too. This would not do. He had thought it all well over during the week ; Rachel was handsome, perhaps rich, though that had become a matter of doubt ; and to do him justice, he was not influenced by wealth. She had shown much sense and good feeling in the advice she had guardedly given him on the day of the water-party, when she had proposed their dancing together, as a cloak to her more serious purpose. The information she imparted had startled him. It gave him a fair promise of actual misfortune, over which he could pity himself for years to come. A thought of finding consolation in his informant crossed his mind at first ; but when she had once conscientiously and painfully warned him of the risks he ran in her Uncle's friendship, she relapsed into her usual supercilious manner, and that he did not like. He once thought of turning disappointed lover. There was a good deal that might be effective in that line : much sighing and moralising, great scope for sneering at women and life, and a good stroke of business to be done in the way of a bleeding heart. But still this was all common-place and hackneyed to the greatest degree. Everybody had been, or would be, disappointed in love ; hardly anybody but himself aspired to being hopelessly miserable, and invariably unlucky. So any little vague tenderness for Rachel was quelled, his coat was once more buttoned up to the chin, a fresh crape put to his hat, his grey gloves thrown into the fire, and, leaning, with his arms folded, under a cypress tree on the lawn of Marble Hall, Willis was himself again.

" You wicked man ! " said the Baroness, approaching him, " where have you been all day ? there is breakfast over without you. The Baron—he does so like to see his friends enjoy themselves at his house—was actually accusing me, poor me ! of making some mistake about your card. Now is that likely ? I'm a giddy thing, but not so bad as that. Why the Baron could not give a *fête* without you."

" I suppose not," said Willis, with one of his slight groans, which were so habitual that the Baroness did not mark its meaning character. " Captain Hopkinson arrived unexpectedly this morning, and that detained me."

" Oh ! that excellent Captain Hopkinson. I wish you had brought him with you. And so I suppose his daughters missed their concert," said the Baroness, her eyes brightening at the idea.

"No, they had been gone half an hour. It is always so, every pleasure comes exactly half an hour too late—Life! Life!"

"*They* will not think it too late—their fine friends are everything now," said the lady spitefully. "Baron!" she called to her husband, as he walked by in earnest conversation with a gentleman who looked like the Stock Exchange taking a little recreation. "Our friend's father-in-law is come; I was reproaching him for not bringing him here."

"I should have been delighted to see him. He is, I hear, an excellent man, has prayers for the sailors every morning, and keeps up a very strict tone of morals on board his ships. And virtue has its reward even in this life—I am told he has made a most successful voyage. Willis, you must introduce him to me. He can give us useful information," he added, turning to his friend, "relative to our Chinese railway business."

"Oh, no business here, if you please!" said the Baroness, who saw an additional shade of gloom coming over Willis's countenance; "you know I never allow that. Come, Willis, let me find you a partner."

"No—no dancing, the exertion I made in that way last week quite unhinged me. Go to

your gayer friends, Baroness, and leave me here
to look on and envy the light-hearted."

"No such thing; there is some charming
music going on in the saloon. That will divert
you, my dear friend," and so she carried off her
victim to listen to a comic song.

Now, if there is one thing more than another
conducive to low spirits, it is that depressing
invention—a comic song! The mere advertise-
ments—"I'm a merry laughing girl," or "I
too, am seventeen, Mamma!" if read early
in the morning, particularly before breakfast,
produce a degree of nausea that affects the health
for the whole day. And the treat offered by the
Baroness to Willis was to hear a young lady
with a prodigious colour, high cheek bones, and
a turned-up nose, sing with what was termed
"great archness," words to this effect :

"Yes, Sir ! I can waltz ! I can flirt !
    I'm out of the schoolroom at last !
  Pa' says I'm a romp, Ma' says I'm a pert,
    I say, I am fast ! I am fast !

"We girls love a lark ! It's the men who are stiff.
    Why that little Lord John's such a tease,
  If I ask him to dance, he turns off in a tiff,
    Law, Sir ! that is ease ! that is ease !

"I handle the ribbons ! I smoke my cigar !
    I polk till Aunt Jane looks aghast.
  I swim like a fish ! ride like young Lochinvar !
    In short, I am fast ! I am fas ! "

This last verse, illustrated by appropriate gestures of driving, riding, puffing smoke, &c., was received with thunders of applause, which were led by Baron Moses, and acknowledged by an imitation rustic courtesy, by the singer, Miss Corban, who, being eighteen, had quite outlived any youthful shyness. Some of the guests, who were what she would have called " *slow*," found themselves affected with alarming fits of dejection, accompanied by a distressing tingling in the ears and very burning cheeks.

Comic sings will occasionally produce these symptoms !

The music was suceeded by games on the lawn that would have been called romping twenty years ago—more dancing, and a grand display of fireworks, and terminated in a magnificent supper, and much champagne ; and the guests departed impressed with the idea that the Baron's immense wealth was spent with equal liberality.

CHAPTER XV

WHEN Janet and Rose returned from their concert, the door was opened for them by their father, and in the delight of this unexpected meeting, St. Maur House was for the time forgotten, almost in disgrace, for having taken them away just at the wrong moment. Captain Hopkinson was a particularly pleasant father, firmly and thoroughly convinced that his own children were superior to the children of all other fathers, that nobody ought to find fault with them, because, as he emphatically observed, they had no faults ! It was very odd, he had carried out to India hundreds of young women, well educated, amiable young women ; but some had bad tempers, some were nervous, some would flirt with the cadets, most of them were affected, and all of them sea-sick. " Now my girls are nice, natural, good-humoured girls, they would not give *that*" (whatever *that* is) " for the attentions of a whole regiment of those silly boys ; and the only time I gave them a trip in the *Alacrity* they were as steady on their pins as if they had been at sea all their lives." Janet was the shorter of the two, so at every return from his voyages he found out she had grown considerably, and as Rose was pale, he dwelt much on her blooming looks. Now that they burst upon him dressed, thanks to Mademoiselle Justine's supervision, in very becoming costumes, excited by the amusements of the day, and flushed with the delight of seeing him—he looked at them with the profoundest admiration, and when they left the room to take off their finery, he turned to his wife and said, " Well, old lady, those are not bad-looking girls, by any means. Why, the Miss Wallaces, who went out to Calcutta this last time, and were thought great beauties, and gave me no end of trouble because all the young fellows on board *would* propose to them—they were not to be named in a day with our girls."

" Law, my dear, you see them dressed out just for once in a way, and I don't think, John, you'll quite like the bill when you see it."

" Oh, hang the bills, I don't grudge them a little finery. Could not they always be dressed so, Jane? I should like to give them a walk in these gowns, one on each arm, just to see people stare."

" Stare! I should think they well might, if they saw our girls go flaunting about Dulham in those fly-away gowns. No, it's all very well for once in a way, as they had a fancy to hear this music ; and as the Duchess was so kind as to ask them, I thought it respectful to dress them out ; but we must go back to the old brown gowns, John. And to-morrow you must go and see that nice Captain Templeton, Lord Chester that was—no, is, I mean—and they are so kind to little Charlie. What have you brought for Charlie, John ? "

" For Charlie ? Well ! if I did not forget him altogether—I had no time for going about bazaars. Regent Street for my money if you want anything."

This was a little scene invariably enacted after every voyage. Captain Hopkinson always gave it to be understood that his family had been utterly forgotten by him from the hour he sailed ; and then, when the ship came up the river, immense stores of shawls, playthings and trinkets came pouring out for several days—rarities from every port at which he had touched.

The girls came back in their brown gowns, and hoped " Papa would not quite despise his Cinderella's," and still he thought them very superior to the Miss Wallaces, and hugged himself in the consciousness of two Indian shawls, now in his locker, on board the *Alacrity*. His arm-chair was brought from its banishment. Mrs. Hopkinson became so fidgety and so red in the face if anybody sat down in " John's chair," that the girls always removed it from the drawing-room when he was away; but this evening it was replaced at the head of the table, and when they all four sat down to their evening meal, and the Captain said grace, adding thanks for his return to his dear wife and children, they all began to cry as if the greatest misfortune had happened to them, till Mrs. Hopkinson, wiping her eyes, observed, " Well, if ever there were four fools in the world, here they sit. The idea of our crying because John's come home. It's just like Willis. How poor Willis would enjoy having a good cry with us—I wish he were here."

" Indeed, I don't mamma, it is the last thing I should like—spoiling papa's first day. I was just thinking of putting the chain over the door, and that we should all pretend to be out or asleep if he came. And, besides, we have so much to tell you. The concert was such fun, and St. Maur House is so magnificent."

" And then the music!" said Rose. " I think, mamma, they must be laughing at us when they admire our singing. If you could but have heard that duet of Piccolomini and Giuglini's, I wonder what you would have said. It quite took away my breath."

" Oh, I know the sort of thing," said Captain Hopkinson, " I used to go to the Opera at Lisbon, and such a quavering, and shaking, and screaming, with great loud crashes of the orchestra at the end, enough to deafen you. When I went on board again and heard John Leary, one of our best mizzen-top-men, sing *Home, sweet home*, the rest of the watch joining in the chorus, I thought *that was* music—the other was only noise."

"John Leary—he has sailed with you several times, my dear," said Mrs. Hopkinson, who was divided in mind between the *Alacrity* and St. Maur House, "he has a sweet voice; and his wife has had twins while he was away. But I dare say Pico—what's his name—is he a man or a woman?—sings very well too. One of the twins is called John. And, I suppose, the Duchess had not time to take any notice of you, girls?"

"But she did, indeed, mamma; you know we were with Lady Sarah, and the Duchess took such care of her, and took her and Miss Grenville to some of the best places in the room, and made us sit there with them, and when she was walking by with the Duchess of Cambridge and Princess Mary, she stopped to talk to us and asked how we liked the music."

"Did she indeed?" said Mrs. Hopkinson, looking extremely pleased; "and so you saw the Duchess of Cambridge and Princess Mary quite close. Only to think, John, of our girls being at a party with their Royal Highnesses. When you came in so suddenly and asked what had become of them, you little thought they were in such company, and all just because everybody is so very good-natured. Only think there was a Sir Somebody Something, who, it appears, asked your father to stay at his house at Garden Reach, all the time the *Alacrity* was at Calcutta ; and Lady Chester has given Charlie such a nice little dog. And, I dare say, if the Queen had come to St. Maur House, the Duchess would have been just the same to you. People are so kind. I suppose Her Majesty did not drop in ? " added Mrs. Hopkinson faintly.

" No, mamma."

" No, of course not ; what with all her children, and what with making war and making peace, and giving balls and proroguing Parliaments, and the Government always changing, she has not much time for visiting, poor thing ! I suppose you did not know any of the company ? "

" Oh yes, there were Lord Chester, and Colonel Hilton, and Mr. Grenville ; and Mr. Harcourt," said Janet, " got a seat next to Rose."

Captain Hopkinson thought Rose had really more colour now than her sister.

" And Mr. Greydon," said Rose, " took us to the refreshment room, and afterwards to the carriage."

Janet drew herself up, and her father said she was quite a tall woman now. Then the *Alacrity* became the topic for a time : there had been gales that sounded unpleasant to the hearers, but which were gales of great merit, as proving the wonderful sailing qualities of the ship ; then in a fog she had nearly run aground off the island of Tattyminibo, having mistaken it for the port of Tammyhominy, and no other ship could have behaved so unexceptionably under the circumstances as she did. Mrs. Hopkinson was convinced that it was the island which was to blame, and which had come and put itself in the way ; she knew of an island in the Mediterranean or Baffin's Bay that had played just the same trick ; and then, as she hated to hear of dangers at sea, she turned the conversation to her own doings during the day—how Lady Chester had sent for her to give her opinion upon some baby clothes that had been sent down to Pleasance ; and how she had recommended the cheapest, which were finer than any she had ever seen ; and how Lady Chester had always chosen the dearest ; and how they had had a nice chat about nurses and babies, and Charlie ; and how she had just got home and was thinking about the Valenciennes round the mantle, when John walked in.

And at this crisis in walked Willis, comfortably gloomy, after the Marble Hall festivities.

"All black again," whispered Rose to her sister, "even to his gloves; then there has been no proposal."

"Or a refusal," answered her sister; "he will be worse than ever."

But Willis was a different mannered man under the control of his sensible, straightforward father-in-law, from when he domineered over the good-natured Mrs. Hopkinson. Captain Hopkinson administered a large spoonful of good sense to every dose of querulousness— put aside the prospect of future grievances, as not worth consideration, and either disputed or laughed at the petty troubles of the day. Parade of real grief he looked upon as an impossibility. It was to be wrestled with alone, not forced on the attention of the public. And by persisting in the supposition that Willis *must* take some interest in the interests of others, and by steadily treating him as a member of his own very cheerful family, he always brought him into a more companionable shape. Willis did not quite like it, but he succumbed. In fact, it would have been difficult to resist the influence of that cheerful-looking room and that happy family. He finally deigned to ask if the girls had been amused, and hardly sighed when Mrs. Hopkinson asked if Princess Mary's gown was blue, though she ought to have known that the court was in mourning for the Prince of Saxe Badenheim. He even gave a succinct account of the breakfast at Marble Hall, comprised in the few words that there were a great many over-dressed people, that the tables were over-loaded, and the ball-room over-crowded.

"In short, it was nearly all 'over' with you, Charles," said Captain Hopkinson.

"With me?" said Willis, "oh, I see; a pun—I am not quick at puns. In fact, I am not in spirits to-night." (Janet and Rose looked at each other.) "The Baroness took me to hear the singing," and he shuddered naturally as he mentioned the comic song and the more comic songstress.

"But there is nothing dispiriting in that," said Janet; "you often hear us sing?"

"Yes, so often that it does not annoy me at all; I am quite used to it; I really hardly hear it. It does not even prevent me from attending to my book," and Willis thought that he was paying his sisters a most gratifying compliment, "but this Miss Corban screamed out her deplorable jokes, so that it was impossible to help hearing them. It was a pitiable spectacle!"

"Could not you just give us an idea, Charles, of the air, and some of the words?" said Rose.

"I! I sing a comic song! my dear Rose, do think a little before you speak. Have you ever seen anything in me that would lead you to suppose than I *can* sing?"

"No, but I never, till the other day, saw anything in you that led me to suppose you could dance. Singing may come next. Papa, you can't think how well Charles dances, such neat little *chassés* and *balancés*, and his *grand rond* was almost a round and a half. It was quite exhilarating to look at him."

Willis chafed up and down the room as Captain Hopkinson's peals of laughter hailed his saltatory triumphs, and took up his hat to go. But before he went, he announced that Baron Sampson was coming to make acquaintance with the Captain, and to gain some information that might be of importance to one of his schemes " ; and a twinge of conscience induced him to add, " He is rather a sanguine plausible man, and you had better take his statements, where any speculations are concerned, with a little abatement."

"He is not a bad fellow after all," said the Captain as the door closed on Willis.

"Who? poor dear Willis? Oh no! he is too tender-hearted, and cannot get over poor Mary's loss, otherwise, as I tell the girls, he would be as pleasant as everybody else." It need hardly be added that this comment was made by Mrs. Hopkinson.

CHAPTER XVI

LORD CHESTER was delighted to meet his old friend Hopkinson again, and carried him off to see Blanche, who seemed also to look on him as an old friend, and spoke so admiringly and kindly of his daughters, that, as Captain Hopkinson observed afterwards, it was very lucky that the girls were, perhaps, the nicest girls in the world, otherwise, all Lady Chester said might have sounded too complimentary; but, as it was, nothing could be more discriminating and satisfactory. Then Lord Chester took him to his stables, and offered him the use of any of his riding horses—a proposal that was peremptorily declined, probably to the saving of John's life, and much to the satisfaction of the groom, who observed that he never saw the use of putting a naval gentleman on the top of a horse—*he* never offered to go and navigate their ships, so why could not they let his horses alone? Finally, the gentlemen lit their cigars, and sauntered along the bank, where the sight of Mr. Harcourt in an out-rigger roused the Captain to give some strong opinions on the dangers of the river and the foolhardiness of young men.

To those who are not, like Wordsworth's prim-
rose, " dwellers on the river's brim," it may be
necessary to explain that an outrigger is an
apology for a boat, and, apparently, a feeble
imitation of a plank—that the individual who
hazards his own life in it is happily prevented,
by its absurd form, from making any other
person a sharer in his danger—that he is liable
to be overset by any passing steamer, or by the
slightest change of his own posture—that it is
difficult to conceive how he ever got into such
a thing, or how he is ever to get out of it again,
and that the effect he produces on an unpreju-
diced spectator is that of an aquatic mouse
caught in a boat-trap, from which he will never
emerge alive, notwithstanding the continual
struggle he appears to keep up.

"Well ; every man to his taste," said Captain
Hopkinson, " but so far as safety goes, commend
me to a gale off Cape Horn. There is less
chance of drowning, at all events. I must go
home. Pray does your Lordship know anything of a Baron Sampson who threatens me
with a neighbourly visit this morning ? "

"Nothing beyond his name, which figures
in every corner of the paper, wherever there is
a subscription or a company. He is supposed
to be worth millions, but latterly I have learnt
to mistrust that kind of reputation. I should
not mind detaching his grey horses from the

vulgar carriage containing his flashy-looking wife, and leading them into my own stables ; but I had rather have nothing else to say to him."

" Well, I hope he makes short visits, for I must be in town by three."

" So must I, so I will call for you in my dog-cart, and we will go together."

Captain Hopkinson shook his head, and said he looked upon a dog-cart as an outrigger on wheels, but still he accepted the offer, and, hearing the sound of the baronial coach, hurried home.

The Sampsons came in great force, for Miss Monteneros offered to accompany her uncle and aunt, much to their surprise, as she usually declined morning visiting ; and she established herself in the bow window where Janet and Rose were both busily at work embroidering a table cover, which ought to have been finished before their father's return, and at which they were now working with great zeal. Mrs. Hopkinson had of course warned John privately it was to be a surprise, so, though he ran against it and stumbled over it ten times a day, he was nominally unaware of its existence till the girls went up to bed, when he would light a candle and stand for a quarter of an hour admiring it to his heart's content.

" Do you like that sort of work ? " said Rachel, surveying both work and workers through her glass.

"Why, it is for papa," said Janet, with an air that showed she considered that answer to be a settler.

"But its being for papa does not make the actual needle-work less tedious."

"Does not it?" said Rose, looking at her with astonishment; "I should like to see the thing to be done for him—a dear as he is—that could possibly seem tedious. Besides Janet and I never think anything tiresome that we work at together."

Rachel sighed. She had come purposely to see a happy family, and even these few sentences had struck the dark chord of her life.

"Have you never had the pleasure, Miss Monteneros, of finishing off what you thought a successful piece of work to give to somebody you loved dearly?" said Janet.

"Never," said Rachel, in a low voice, "and for the best of reasons: I have nobody to love, I have never loved any one. My vocation is 'to roam along, the world's tired denizen, with none who bless me, none whom I can bless.'"

The girls looked at her with astonishment, and Janet, laying hold of her hand, said, "Do not talk so, it is not right—I beg your pardon, perhaps you are not speaking seriously. Nobody can exist unless they have somebody to love, and who loves them in return."

"True," said Rachel, "it is not existence, it is a myth.

> 'A dreary void,
> The leafless desert of the mind,
> The waste of feelings unemployed.'"

"But why not employ them?" said Rose, who was not learned in Byron; "you have a home."

"Such as it is."

"And relations."

"Such as they are. However, I did not come here to talk poetry and discontent—some people think them synonymous. But I have passed you in your walks, I have seen you at church, you have always looked happy and contented, and I thought I should like to talk to you and to know how you contrive to be so."

"There is no contrivance in it," said Janet, laughing; "Rose and I have good health and good spirits; we have plenty to do in the schools and the hospital; we have the dearest old father and mother in the world, and a comfortable home, and Charlie to play with. What more would you have, Miss Monteneros?"

"Nothing," she said sadly. "Affection, employment, and usefulness—you have, as you say, *all*. I envy you; you are happy, I am not."

The two sisters were excited by this style of conversation. It had never come into their minds to analyse life. They took it as it came, and to them it came happily ; and the idea that a young prosperous handsome woman should drop in for a morning visit and mention casually that her life was an entire failure, either for use or enjoyment, was so novel and startling that they hardly knew how to deal with it. They were induced to adopt their usual resource, and to call to mamma to come and rectify the disastrous state of Miss Monteneros' existence. She would know exactly what to do. But on looking towards her, they saw she had present woes of her own, and that she was nearly anni-hilated by the condescension of the Baroness, and the humility of the Baron—so Janet gallantly threw herself again into the fight.

" Miss Monteneros, you must not be angry," Rachel smiled ; " of course, you are much cleverer than we are, and know a great deal more about feelings, and poetry and that sort of thing ; but I do not like to hear you say you are not happy."

" I do not like it either," said Rachel languidly, " but it is a fact, though perhaps I need not have mentioned it to you."

" But I am glad you did, if you will let me say what I think. Have you no nearer rela-tions than an uncle and aunt ? "

"I have no other relations whatever; my father and mother died before I was two years old, and I never had either brother or sister."

"That is sad," said the sisters, looking at each other, "but still you have a home, and since you have no one else to look to, I suppose your uncle and aunt stand in the place of parents to you; could you not——" Janet stopped, she looked at the Baron and Baroness. It seemed really a waste of words to ask if anybody could love them.

"You are honest," said Rachel, with a hollow laugh, "I foresaw that that sentence could not come to a happy conclusion."

"But people say you are very rich," said Janet, "and just think what money can do for half the poor creatures in the world, and how soon you would attach yourself to any one whom you had relieved from real distress; I assure you Rose and I are often inclined to cry because we can do so little for sick people or starving children, and yet they are so grateful for that little. Miss Monteneros, don't you think that if you cared about others they would care about you?"

Rachel did not answer, but she leant over the work frame, and Janet felt a hot tear drop on her hand. But they said no more, for Captain Hopkinson came in in a great hurry apologising for his delay—making Charlie over to his aunts, stumbling over the eternal table-cover, and begging the girls to keep their embroidered gowns out of the way of his feet.

"You see papa has not an idea it is a table-cover for him," whispered the deluded Rose.

The Baron and the sailor were a fine contrast as they stood talking together; the one, sallow, with a broad wrinkled brow and a keen calculating eye, and having apparently speculated most of his hair off his head, his shoulders, bent, his chest contracted, his manner deferential, his voice unnaturally bland, he looked yellow, as if he had never breathed any air that was not tainted with the scent of gold. The other, tall, erect, fresh coloured, his crisp dark curls clustering over his manly looking head, and his keen blue eyes full of intelligence, giving his opinions or his information in a few words, and with a careless tone and manner that inspired confidence. He seemed to have no wish to *persuade*, and no anxiety as to the effect his assertion might make. "I suppose," thought Rachel, "my uncle might cajole me into believing what he has said; but I have faith beforehand in what Captain Hopkinson is going to say."

The conversation was gradually drawn by the Baron to foreign trade, to China, and finally to a projected Hongkong railroad. "I am delighted to obtain such valuable information from such excellent authority ; I have taken a few shares in this company—not, as you may imagine, with any idea of profit. With a certain twelve per cent. from our Banking Company, these railroad shares are, to me, a dead loss ; but my City friends did me the honour to wish for me as a director ; and then I feel that railroads, and harbours—in fact, facilities for trade are our best means for the conversion of our Eastern brethren. Don't you agree with me, Captain Hopkinson ? Though these railroads may carry opium, Christianity will have its ticket too."

" I hope it may, Baron ; but I am sorry to say that the Christian in the East carries little Christianity with him. However, we must hope for the best, and now I am afraid I must leave you to the care of my wife and daughters ; I am obliged to be in town at three, and have a friend waiting at the door for me."

" We must be going too," said the Baroness, rising ; " we have paid a most unconscionable visit. I hope Rachel has persuaded those young ladies to honour us on the 23rd, and to bring their music with them. We had a most delightful singer last Wednesday, Miss Corban, daughter of Corban, Isaacs & Co.— *elle chante à ravir,* such delightful comic songs. She does not sing generally at large parties, but she could not refuse *me*—nobody does, so remember that, young ladies."

At this juncture, the Baroness was interrupted by the rapid entrance of Lord Chester, who could not resist having a look at the owner of the grey horses ; though Blanche had charged him not to be drawn into an acquaintance with " that overpowering woman " on any account.

" Now, Hopkinson, are you ready ? " he said, with a sort of sweeping bow to the whole party. " I am sorry to hurry you, but we must be off ; and I had hardly time to run in, but my Lady charged me to say, Mrs. Hopkinson, that she cannot accept your excuse, and has thrown your note into the fire, and we expect you *all*—mind what I say—*all*, at half past seven, so no more nonsense about it."

" Well, my Lord, you *may* expect, but you will not get *me* to come to one of your grand late dinners ; they are quite out of my way, and I should be quite in your way ; John and the girls may go if they like."

" They have no option about it, and you had better not oblige me to come with two policemen and march you in to dinner too, I am quite capable of it. Now, John," and he hurried him off.

" Well, if ever there was a ridiculous, nonsensical dear boy, there he goes," said Mrs. Hopkinson in a pleased soliloquy.

" Lord Chester, I believe ? " said the Baroness, in a most subdued tone ; "not ill-looking by any means. Adieu, my dear Mrs. Hopkinson, *nous nous reverrons* on the 23rd."

" Good-bye," said Rachel, who lingered for a moment behind, " I see you do not mean to come, and you are right : but may I come again to see your daughters ? "

" Of course, my dear, whenever you like."

" And—and—can you tell Captain Hopkinson——"

" Rachel, your aunt is waiting," said the Baron, from the bottom of the stairs.

" Tell him," she added hurriedly, " not to begin mixing himself up with railroads and shares ; ask him to consult Mr. Willis first," and she ran down.

" Well now, what with the aunt's French and the niece's English, I am fairly puzzled ! " said Mrs. Hopkinson, throwing herself back with a sigh of relief. " I daresay they are very nice people, but I should not very much care if I were never to see any of them again."

" And what is your opinion of the Baron now ? " said Lord Chester as he drove off with Captain Hopkinson.

" A sharp fellow, and he seems to know what he is about, what is more than I do ; for I never could catch his eye, and I never feel sure of a man who will not look me in the face."

"Rachel," said the Baroness, who seemed slightly out of sorts, "I do wish you would not keep me waiting an hour while you are dawdling through your civilities to those people. Their heads will be quite turned. As for that coxcomb, Lord Chester, I can't think what he means—I suppose he was making a jest of the old lady."

"Perhaps," said the Baron, "he is in love with one of the young ones."

"Don't talk nonsense, my love," said the Baroness, sharply, "I never saw two more uninteresting girls—no manner, no *usage du monde*. What could you find to say to them, Rachel? I am sure you have seen nothing like them in my set."

"Nothing whatever that bears the slightest resemblance to them, Aunt."

"I thought so; and what did you make of the Captain, Baron?"

A shrug of the shoulders was the Baron's reply; but then, in his character of benevolent man, he added, "an honest, frank sailor, and it is not his fault if he does not spoil the view at Pleasance by setting the Thames on fire. I suspect he is well off, the fellow has such independent 'manners.'"

CHAPTER XVII

WHEN Captain Hopkinson returned late from town, he found an argument raging between his wife and daughters—she declining to go to the dinner at Pleasance, and they declaring they would not go without her.

"I am glad you are come, papa," said Janet; "here is mamma setting up a will of her own, and talking such nonsense that if it were Charlie she would be ashamed of him. Will you be so kind as to speak to her?"

"She is really getting beyond our management," added Rose, "and does not mind us even when we speak peremptorily to her."

"My dears," said Mrs. Hopkinson, her face radiant with delight, "you make me angry; you really are very disrespectful, and your papa will be quite displeased. It is all about this dinner at Pleasance, John. The girls want me to go, and I mean to stay at home, and so we are playing a game at cross purposes."

"Then the girls have won," said John, "for you are certainly going—I promised Arthur that I would bring you."

"Oh, John! how could you? I can't dine out, I'm so fat."

"Well, my dear, you can hardly expect to be as slim as you were at seventeen, but you are not half the size of your friend the Baroness; and this one dinner, unless you eat very voraciously, will not make you much fatter."

This idea threw Mrs. Hopkinson into one of her most comfortable fits of laughter. "You know that is not what I mean—but there is the butler, and all those footmen, they put me out; and they will snatch away my plate before I have finished; and there will be strangers who will be sure to wonder where Lord and Lady Chester picked up such a vulgar old woman; and then my face will become quite red. Why, goodness me! It is very silly; but I do believe I am shy like a young girl; so I had rather stay at home."

"But you will go to oblige me," said John, taking her hand kindly. "Lord and Lady Chester quite overrate the care I took of him in his illness; to be sure I never saw anyone recover from such an attack, but that was owing to his high spirits. However, they fancy I helped, and they seem to take pleasure in showing us attention, so don't let us thwart them. They have made the party on purpose—just a very few friends whom you know—Lady Sarah Mortimer."

"Well, I do not mind her—such a nice old lady—always netting and talking sense."

" Colonel Hilton."

" To be sure, I ought not to mind him, because he never takes his eyes off Miss Grenville."

" Sir William and Lady Eleanor de Vescie."

" Oh, my dear, I never saw them,—I really can't go ; and indeed, I don't think the blonde on my cap is quite fresh."

" They are only Lord Chester's brother and sister, mamma, so they cannot be called company ; and Rose and I have made your cap a perfect model of fashion," said Janet.

" Then you will like to meet Greydon ; and there is nobody else but young Grenville and one or two of his friends."

" Yes, young officers, full of jokes and quizzing. However, I don't mind being laughed at by them."

" Lord Chester did hint that perhaps his father might come," added John falteringly. " Lord Chesterton was so good as to say he wished to see me ; but you would not mind him, my dear."

" Lord Chesterton of all people—a Cabinet Minister—and I, who cannot read the *Times*, and should not know a Reform Bill from a Budget if you were to pay me for it ; and I don't even know if I have a new pair of gloves in the house. Oh, John, John, this all comes of your letting the *Alert* catch a fever on board. Girls, what is to be done about my gloves ? "

"There is a new pair all ready trimmed, mamma, and your grey brocade looks so imposing, so come and be dressed like a darling as you are."

"And will this be of any use?" said John, producing, according to custom, an attractive looking parcel, which proved to be a splendid lace mantilla. "There was a Mrs. Barlow on board who thought of nothing but finery. I believe if the ship had been going down she would have stepped into her cabin to put on a becoming drowning dress. When we put in at Funchal she was wild to have this thing, and as her husband would not let her, I secured it for you, and she went into hysterics."

"Poor woman!" said Mrs. Hopkinson, "there is nothing like a glass of cold water for hysterics; but to be sure, such lace as this is not often to be seen. I own I do love a bit of good lace."

"And these mantillas are all the fashion. It is just what we wanted for her, thank you, papa; this is the best venture you have ever made."

"Ah, they don't know yet about the Cashmere shawls; won't they be delighted?" thought Captain Hopkinson, as the girls carried their mother off to her toilette.

The result was most successful; the lace mantilla was, as Mrs. Hopkinson said, such a lady-like disguise that she made her entry at Pleasance without becoming unusually red in the face, and the quiet kindness with which she was greeted, and the unaffected gaiety of her hosts, put her quite at ease. Seated at dinner next to Lord Chester, who exerted himself to amuse her, Baxter and the footman lost their terrors, and her delight was great when Dr. Ayscough glided into the chair at her side. "I really think it is high time John should begin to be jealous of that man," she told her daughters afterwards. "Of course I did not mention Charlie—it would have been presuming; but he began talking of him directly, and when I said how wonderfully the child had improved, he said I should live to see him as fine a looking man as his grandfather; not that John is his grandfather, but he is a fine looking man all the same. And it seems there is such a grand murder in the paper—you must find it and read it to me, girls; a whole family poisoned by the father—just think of John poisoning us at breakfast, or, indeed, of his meddling with my tea-pot; and Lord Chester and Dr. Ayscough said such clever things about poisons; I thought I would remember them for fear of accidents; but I am not quite certain whether I have not forgotten part. However, I know it is not wholesome to take strychnine in any great quantity, so mind that, girls; arsenic, which is very apt to get into puddings and gruel, should be avoided, and you should take

M

something after it, if you do swallow any—
but I forget what. It was really very interesting,
and I like a good murder that can't be found
out; that is, of course, it is very shocking,
but I like to hear about it. Then I thought
I would take a hint about diet by watching
what the doctor ate. You know he told us
about Charlie that all young meat, and pork,
and raw vegetables, and sweet things, and
pastry were bad; and, my dear, he dined on
veal cutlets and roast pork, salad, and jam
tarts, and plum pudding. I suppose doctors
cure themselves when they get home after
they have dined out, and I am so partial to
him that he should have been welcome to my
veal cutlet, though it was deliciously tender,
and I also think we might manage that tomato
sauce at home—it sets off veal. They talked
a great deal too about Berlin, and the palace
our Princess is to have; altogether I was very
much pleased, though I had a sad fright about
my mantilla when a great gold tag that footman
had hanging from his shoulder—I wonder why?
—caught in it, but there was no harm done."

The dinner gave general satisfaction. Blanche,
who was seated between Lord Chesterton and
Captain Hopkinson, was gratified to see how
well they amalgamated; how Lord Chesterton
began by formal though genuine expressions
of gratitude for the kindness shown to his son,

and how this gradually expanded into curiosity as to the details of the late events in the East, and how he was evidently struck by the accuracy and observation which characterised Captain Hopkinson's remarks. Janet had contrived to sit next to her father, and as Mr. Greydon had taken her into dinner, he too joined in the conversation at that end of the table ; Janet's unaffected manner, her attention to her father, the intelligence with which she listened to what was passing, struck him, and for the first time it occurred to him that she was different from most of the young ladies he met at Dulham. He found himself watching for her opinions, entering into her jests with her father, trying to catch her eye when any amusing anecdote was related ; and when the ladies rose to retire, the look with which he returned to her her gloves and handkerchief, for which he had had of course to dive under the table, was a look of much meaning, one to be remembered for life. The great parasol day sank into insignificance.

Of course, before the first course was over, Blanche had composed a three volume novel of which Greydon was the hero and Janet the heroine. Pleasance was to be the scene at which interesting meetings were to take place ; she was to be the confidante of both parties, a living was to be found which should have every possible recommendation of situation, tithes, parsonage, &c., and finally a model clergyman was to be made happy with a model clergywoman. "Even Aunt Sarah herself must own that it requires no imagination to foresee all this," she thought, as she followed her guests out of the drawing-room ; and as she passed her hand through Janet's arm, the warm pressure with which it was met indicated a flow of happiness which could only expend itself in affection.

"Now, Mrs. Hopkinson, come and sit by me," said Blanche, when Aunt Sarah had settled her on the sofa. "I don't at all approve of the way in which you go on coquetting with Lord Chester ; it is not correct, and it affects my domestic happiness, and you are dressed for conquest. In my life I never saw such beautiful lace, what is it—Spanish ? "

"I'm sure I don't know," said Mrs. Hopkinson as soon as she could recover from the risible notion of her own coquetry. "It came from Funchal, though where that is I can't say ; John gave it to me just before I came out."

"There never was such a John ! and he is so agreeable too. I cannot think how you have the heart to go about flirting with other people's Arthurs when you have such a John of your own. Aunt Sarah, I have been so interested at dinner—it is really refreshing to hear conversation about facts, not about people. Captain Hopkinson told us such curious stories about China, and the nuns at Manilla, and their beautiful work ; and a great deal about opium and cotton that was too learned for me, but Lord Chesterton was so much interested in that, and in tariffs and custom duties, that I could not give the conversation a frivolous turn ; and besides, I always feel elevated when the conversation of my neighbours at dinner is above my comprehension. I always suppose they think me well-informed and I did pick up a great deal of information to-day. Now, tell me, Aunt Sarah, what you have heard."

" Not much, my dear ; Mr. Greydon's attention was taken up by the same conversation that you found so interesting."

" Not exactly," said Blanche, smiling.

" And Sir William, who was my other neighbour, was rather annoyed because he has received two letters to-day, one without any postage stamp, and the other with a stamp that did not cover the weight, so he had to pay fourpence for the carelessness of other people."

" Poor man," said Blanche, looking round to ascertain that Lady Eleanor was not within hearing ; " that is a serious loss, his limited means considered ; he will be obliged to cut down timber or mortgage the Hall if this sort of pillage goes on. Aunt Sarah, are you laughing ? "

"No, my dear, I am netting, the purse is for Sir William ; he asked me to net one for him, he is so careless about his money. He says he lost a shilling yesterday when he took some silver out of his waistcoat pocket to pay the omnibus fare, so I promised him a purse."

"And let us all subscribe and make up the shilling and fourpence he has lost, and you can present them to him in the purse ; will you, Aunt Sarah ? "

"If you continue to wish it, my dear, when my purse is finished."

"I am sure Sir William deserves it," said Mrs. Hopkinson ; "I see he has sent £1000 to that Refuge which was on the point of being closed for want of funds."

"There," cried Blanche, "now that is always happening to me ; I never take up a judgment against any one for a small fault, that he does not come out with some overpowering merit that I had never foreseen. Aunt Sarah, I withdraw my offer of the one and fourpence, and I allow that I was mistaken in thinking Sir William fond of money."

"You will make a great many mistakes yet, dear child, I hope ; for I do not want you to know the world well at eighteen. And I allow you to wonder, as I do, even at my age, why very wealthy men make many others happy by acts of great liberality, and make themselves uncomfortable by small meannesses ; but so it is, and we must make the best of it. This orange silk is not a good match, is it ? "

Blanche contrived to elicit some Sampson anecdotes from her friends, confirming her in her dislike of the supercilious Baroness, and the very different versions of Rachel given by Mrs. Hopkinson and her daughters interested her.

The girls were full of pity and admiration, and affirmed that when their mother understood Rachel a little better she would like her. " My dears, I had much better like her at once, if you wish it ; for if I wait till I understand her, I shall just be uncharitable for the rest of my days. I never know whether she is talking prose or poetry, or sense or nonsense ; but as you say she is very much to be pitied, I pity her with all my heart. But when she comes to call upon you, I think she had better be shown up to your own room at once."

There was music, of course, in the evening. A duet by Rose and Harcourt that was effective in more ways than one ; she accompanied him quite to his satisfaction, and on that point he was hard to please ; their voices went well together, and when he suggested what he termed a different interpretation of three or four bars, she was so compliant that though temper was with him quite a secondary consideration to voice, he thought that it would be very agreeable if Mrs. Harcourt, whoever she might eventually be, and Rose's good humour as well as her fine contralto voice.

" Is not that the young fellow we saw trying to drown himself the other day ? " said Captain Hopkinson to Lord Chester; " and yet in a room he does not look like a fool, and he sings well. That duet was not amiss, though I say it that should not. The girls have improved in their singing."

" I hope they will not improve any more," said Blanche ; "it is perfect as it is, in that simple touching style."

Captain Hopkinson tried to say something disparaging of his daughters' performances, but failed completely. He was rather absorbed in watching Mr. Harcourt's manner to Rose ; he did not like to own it to himself, but the young gentleman of the outrigger seemed more devoted to his daughter than was pleasant. Captain Hopkinson had no wish to have his family circle broken up just as he had come home to enjoy himself, and, moreover, he distrusted an individual who owned such an absurd boat. He did not observe another adversary : Mr. Greydon had come to that stage of admiration in which he fancied that everybody was watching him, that if he spoke to Janet all the bystanders would believe he was in love, which really would be too ridiculous. She was pretty, certainly, and an excellent girl, most useful in the village, and there could be no doubt that she sung better than her sister—but the idea of his falling in love ! Too absurd ! and so instead of walking boldly up to the singers with the other gentlemen, he coasted round the room, took a survey of the pictures on the wall and the books on the table, and so finally landed at the pianoforte, having, as he hoped, proved to himself and the bystanders that it was the last place in the apartment which presented any attraction to him.

Poor Greydon ! when he went home that evening to his small room over the grocer's shop, where the one-eyed awkward shop-girl had forgotten to place his candles, and had carefully closed his windows to insure a due amount of fustiness, where the furniture looked dusty, and where everything proclaimed " cheap lodgings for a single man without encumbrances," he sat down in a disconsolate state of mind. He longed for " encumbrances," he despised single men and cheap lodgings, he wished for a living ; and above all, he determined to go himself the following morning with a book that he had promised to lend Captain Hopkinson. He really rather liked that family, and he could imagine that girls brought up as they had been might make excellent wives to men who could afford to marry. He should not be surprised if Harcourt married one and Grenville the other.

The next morning he sallied forth with a very tiresome book on storms and currents in his pocket, and though Captain Hopkinson could not remember having expressed any wish to borrow it, he believed Mr. Greydon's assertion that he had—received him cordially, asked him to stay to luncheon, and after a visit that lasted two hours, the single man walked home to the cheap lodgings, not so certain as he had been that Janet should marry Grenville—Harcourt was quite welcome to Rose. He fairly owned to himself that he was in love, and, being of a hopeful turn of mind, began to think that some-body—he did not know who—might, some day—he did not know when—give him a living, he did not know where, and that Janet should habitually wear a blue muslin like that she had worn to-day. And just as this blissful vision was complete, the one-eyed maid knocked at the door with, " Please, Sir, missus sends the weekly bills." If he had had Rachel's turn for quotation, he could not have helped saying :

" He thought of her afar, his own fair bride,
    He turned and saw Gulnare the homicide."

He had always disliked this particular Gulnare, who passed in ordinary life by the appellation of Keziah Briggs ; but to-day she was unusually homicidal. And then those red books, with the odour of fat meat, stale fish and rancid butter that always steams up from them—he looked over them in despair. Janet, of course, would not eat much, but even an extra mutton chop, and French roll, and pat of butter would tell on the daily expenses ; and besides, she was used to every comfort at home. The luncheon at the cottage was a feast compared to his ordinary dinner. He put aside the red books and took up the *Times*, with a vague hope of finding a very unusual advertisement of wanted, A Vicar for a good living, &c., but found nothing more than a request from a poor curate with nine children for cast-off clothes and postage stamps. The notion of marrying Janet on a settlement of twelve stamps, and the reversion for himself of another man's coat and waistcoat ! and could it be expected that those whom Providence had blessed with the extreme of affluence should send Janet, in her utmost need, a blue light muslin with three flounces made in the last fashion ? No, it would be madness to think of her, and that being established as a fact, he thought of nothing else during the hours—they were but few—in which he was not occupied in the high duties of his calling.

CHAPTER XVIII

LADY CHESTER, too, had her thoughts on the subject. When the dinner party had dispersed, Lord Chesterton graciously signified his approval of her guests, which was a relief to her, as she had rather dreaded that the want of refinement or rather of vapidity, which was a safe quality in the society he ordinarily frequented, might have jarred him. But no ! he thought Captain Hopkinson a well-informed agreeable man, the daughters pretty, and the wife a worthy woman in her way ; and Mr. Greydon struck him as particularly gentleman-like. Was he a good clergyman ?

" One of the best I have ever met with," said Blanche, eagerly, " quite indefatigable in the schools and the hospital and the workhouse, and you should come here some Sunday to hear him preach—I really think that the advantage of hearing Mr. Greydon's sermons should have been considered in the rent of Pleasance."

" Is he the rector of Dulham ? "

" No, only the curate ; the rector has gone abroad for his health."

"Greydon always was a good fellow," said Arthur, "but just the sort of man who will be a poor curate all his life, and be satisfied. He will never push himself into a living."

"But I do not mean him to be always a poor curate," said Blanche. "Lord Chesterton, you always carry about in your pockets all sorts of interesting letters and useful information. Are you quite sure you have not got a good living in that left hand waistcoat pocket, or an advowson? whatever that may be. It sounds like something very advantageous and nice. You always give your little Blanche everything she asks for. Please give me an advowson if you have one about you."

Lord Chesterton thought it right to explain to her in the most technical language the difference between advowsons and presentations, and threw in a little good advice on the advantage it would be to Blanche if she studied greater correctness of expression, and if she always used precisely the right word, and the right number of words, and arranged those words grammatically. And Blanche thanked him so good-humouredly, and laughed at herself so heartily, that when she wound up her apologies by saying, "To speak tersely, I want a good living for Mr. Greydon; will you give me one?" he was induced to say, "Well, I will see what can be done for you." And, as Blanche afterwards observed to Arthur, she looked upon those few words as equal to an advowson and nearly as good as a presentation.

And so the evening ended happily ; but the night that followed was not so peaceful. At five in the morning the Hopkinsons were awakened by a loud peal from their door bell.

" Ah, there they are," said Mrs Hopkinson, jumping up in a fright. " Oh, John, what shall we do ? I knew they would come to us in our turn."

" Who would come, Jane ? " said Captain Hopkinson, who was half asleep.

" Why, the burglars, of course ! What will become of us ! Where's my purse ? I always keep a purse ready to give them, it makes them so good-humoured. Oh, dear, what a noise they make, and they will be quite savage if they are kept waiting," she said, as another violent ringing was heard. " John, John, you must not go down to them, they will knock you down. Let me go."

" I don't see," said John, laughing, " why I am to let you go and be knocked down instead of me ; but, my dear, there is no danger ; burglars do not come and ring the bell and ask to be let in like morning visitors. It must be the policeman."

" Ah, poor man ! I daresay, with his head

knocked to pieces with a life preserver, and
all over kicks and bites. But, perhaps, he is
only come to tell us that the house is on fire,"
said Mrs Hopkinson, with a sudden accession
of cheerfulness. " I should not mind that—
anything is better than robbers. Oh, John,
now don't put your head out so far, those ticket-
of-leave men fire in all directions. And do
keep calling out Thomas and James, and I
will answer with a gruff voice," said poor Mrs.
Hopkinson, who was so terrified her whisper
could scarcely be heard.

" My dear," said John, withdrawing his head,
" there is nothing to be alarmed at, it is Lord
Chester ; Lady Chester is taken ill, and he
wants you to go to her."

" And so that is all," said Mrs Hopkinson, instantly beginning to dress. " Ah, poor
soul ! of course I will. Well now, this *is* neighbourly of them, and I take it very kindly their
sending for me. Why, they are two babies
themselves, and they can't know what to do
with a third."

And so when Lord Chester met her with the
humblest apologies, he found her in a warm
fit of gratitude for having been called out of
her bed and frightened out of her senses, and
delighted to find that her experience as a mother
and a nurse was to be made available to her
neighbours at a most inconvenient hour.

Pleasance did not wear its usual cheerful aspect that morning; the drawing-room had that deplorable 'last night' look belonging to rooms that have not received the morning attentions of the housemaid. The chairs looked as if they had been dancing all night, and had rumpled their chintz covers, the books seemed to have fallen off the table in their sleep, and the music appeared to have quarrelled with the pianoforte in an attempt to place itself on the music stand. Only one shutter had been partially unclosed, and through the crack there came that struggling ray that ought to be light, but looks very much like dust.

Aileen came the moment she heard of Mrs. Hopkinson's arrival, looking pale and frightened, and she immediately hurried her neighbour upstairs, explaining that Blanche had been taken ill sooner than they expected, so that the nurse was not in the house. Arthur had sent for Dr. Ayscough, but in the mean time they had all become very nervous, and Blanche thought she should be happier if Mrs. Hopkinson was with her, and so they had taken the great liberty of asking her to come to them at that undue hour, &c., &c.

"My dear, don't say another word about it; what are we all sent into the world for, but to be of use to each other? and I am quite pleased that your dear little sister, bless her, fancies

having me with her ; and now, Miss Grenville,
don't you go to her with that frightened face,
there is nothing to be frightened about. There
is no want of babies coming safely into the
world, thank goodness, but go into her room
with your usual smiles, and tell her I'm come ;
and I'll just take off my bonnet, and then go
and stay with her till the doctor comes."

And very serviceable Mrs. Hopkinson was.
She found Aileen still with tears in her eyes,
Mademoiselle Justine occasionally proffering to
Blanche a little *tisane de fleur d'orange*, and watching an opportunity to slip out and dress herself
in a *petite robe de percale*, and a *bonnet à barbes*,
that she had prepared for the particular occasion ;
and which were not only becoming in themselves,
but so appropriate that even the Doctor and
the nurse must, she thought, be struck by her
wonderfully good taste in dress. Arthur was
fidgeting up and down the room, one minute
looking out of the window and wondering the
doctor did not come—the next assuring Blanche
that she was better, that she looked better,
felt better, and requesting her to agree with
him, a complete impossibility under the circumstances, so that poor Blanche became only
more nervous. Mrs. Hopkinson wisely hurried
them all out of the room, advised Justine
to see that the basket with the doll's caps, and
the absurd pin-cushion with its " Welcome,

N

little stranger," were all ready ; and told Arthur and Aileen to go and have some breakfast, and to send some to her ; and she gave an every day turn to the state of affairs that was soothing.

An hour after, Arthur came with a face of consternation : Dr. Ayscough had been telegraphed off to the other side of England, and the nurse could not possibly leave the place she was in till the afternoon.

" What are we to do, Mrs. Hopkinson ? it is really too bad ; what business had that woman in Yorkshire to telegraph for our doctor ? and then that other woman detaining Mrs. Smith—so selfish ! and my poor darling will have no doctor and no nurse—she will die."

" Oh no, she won't," said Mrs. Hopkinson, half laughing, " unless you go and put it into her head to do so. I hope I am as good a month nurse as any in the kingdom ; and you had better send for Mr. Duckett; of course he is not to be compared to Doctor Ayscough, but he is in good practice at Dulham, and we may as well have him in the house."

Mr. Duckett had always felt that Lady Chester ought to be his property ; he had occasionally attended at Pleasance, and during the last week his slumbers had been unusually light, and his attention to the sound of the night bell was unremitting. He came instantly ; Lady

Sarah arrived from London ; and finally, the important Mrs. Smith appeared in a hack cab that was almost concealed under a mass of trunks and cap boxes. The Duchess of St. Maur came to pay an early visit connected with Aileen's trousseau, and of course remained to hear the end of Blanche's troubles. Everybody was more or less in a fuss ; it was curious, considering that the birth of a baby is not a very unusual circumstance, to see the immense interest that the expectation of a young Chester created. Lady Sarah abandoned her netting ; and she, and the Duchess, and Aileen whispered and cried, and talked and laughed, and drank tea and coffee at odd hours, and put on *peignoirs*, and did what Shakespeare calls ' the gossips ' to perfection. Arthur walked up and down stairs unceasingly ; the tread-mill would have been repose to him that day, and he tried to cut little failures of jokes to Duckett on the useless fidgets of the ladies, who were models of quiescence as compared with himself. Duckett assumed a grand attitude of composure, repeated every half hour " we are going on admirably," and then tried to *égayer* Lord Chester by some horrible surgical anecdote, which in the best of times would have made him shudder, and now that he was nervous and frightened, made him feel that he was actually undergoing the actual operation described. He was certain that nobody had ever had such a wife as his, and that no woman had ever endured so much with so much fortitude. He went from Lady Sarah to the Duchess to be soothed, and when their matronly experience failed to console him, he turned to Aileen, and as for the brusque word or two which Mrs. Hopkinson occasionally found time to bestow on him, he accepted it as an oracle from heaven.

At last, there came the joyful whisper, "a fine boy"; perhaps the only moment of a fine boy's existence in which his presence is more agreeable than his absence, so let him make the most of it. But if in the whole course of woman's sensitive life there is one moment of happiness more keen, blissful, bright, than another, it is that in which the husband of her choice thanks her for his firstborn child. It was with heartfelt gratitude that Blanche whispered, " I thank God, love, that He has not taken me from you," for she felt, as Arthur pressed her to his heart, as with tears he thanked her for being so patient, so good—as he blessed her, not so much that she was the mother of his child, as that she was still his own, his wife, his Blanche ; yes, she felt that life was indeed to her most precious. " It would have been hard to die," she murmured, " I could not have left all these," and she kissed the hands of her aunt, her sister, and her friend ; and quiet tears of gratitude fell as she listened to the short prayer of thanksgiving which Aileen read as she knelt at her sister's bedside.

But there the pathos of the scene ended, then the bustling Mrs. Smith assumed her rights. " Come, come, we must have no more of this reading and talking, and all this crying. Now, my Lord, if you'll just go quite away I'll be particularly obliged to you ; and I must make bold to turn all you ladies out of the room, except this good lady," she added, turning to Mrs. Hopkinson, whose *savoir faire* had inspired her with confidence, " and, Miss Grenville, will you please to see that there is no noise made up those stairs, and I'll just shut the door after you, my Lord, if you will go."

" I must go to my father, who is down stairs," said Arthur ; " he is so delighted with his grandson, Blanche."

" Oh ! may I not see him for a moment before I settle for the night ? " asked Blanche.

" Oh, dear no, my Lady, not upon no account," said Mrs. Smith, colouring up as if the mere suggestion were a personal affront. " As sure as I'm alive, not another word shall be spoken here this blessed night. Tell Lady Blanche's papa, my Lord, that her Ladyship wishes him good night, and is very sorry she is not able to see him. No, no grandpapas indeed," she muttered, as she bustled about the room, and established that rustling disturbed sort of quiet which is the peculiar result of a regular nurse's exertions, and which is—strange to say—less irritating to the nerves of an invalid than the finished quiet of a lady-like attendant.

Lord Chesterton was extremely pleased with the birth of his grandson, for Arthur was the only heir to his old title and large estates—two possessions which he valued almost equally. He was informed of it at the House of Lords, and actually left that lively assembly in order to drive down to Pleasance, before the important debate on the Trawl and Seine herring fishing nets was brought to a close, a dereliction of public duty which weighed on his conscience ; but he tried to atone for it by filling his carriage with red boxes containing minutes about Hospodars, and statements of the wrongs of Dedarkhan Bux in the well known cause of the Jaghire of Munnydumdum. Public men keep up to this day the farce of saying that they read these papers. However, the absorbing interest they possessed did not prevent Lord Chesterton from entering heartily into the private rejoicings at Pleasance.

" I wish you had seen my father," Arthur afterwards said to Blanche ; " he thought it right to see the baby, because he looks upon that mite as a young earl and a sucking Secretary of State, but he was afraid of touching it, and contented himself with stroking it with the end of his gold pencil case and assuring Mrs. Smith that it was a remarkably fine child, and that he hoped she would take the greatest care of it, as its life was of immense importance. And to judge by the number and depth of Mrs. Smith's courtesies, he must have enforced this recommendation by lucrative arguments."

" Was baby good ? " asked Blanche with as much earnestness as if it had passed its six hours of life in deep study of the whole duty of man.

" Well, it gave a curious twitch of its chin not very becoming, but my father took it for a laugh. Blanche, he told me to tell you he thought he should have some good news for you by the time you were able to see him."

"Oh, Arthur, a living for Mr. Greydon ! and then suppose he does not propose to Janet after all? That would be distressing."

CHAPTER XIX

THERE seemed, however, no threatening of this danger for the present. Mr. Greydon had, till lately, so sedulously repressed any notion of falling in love, or of the possibility of marrying, that now he had once admitted the idea, he acted upon it with his usual energy. He said it was singular how often he met Captain Hopkinson and his daughters out walking—there must be a fatality about it—the fatality being that he looked out of his window, which commanded a partial view of their house, till they came out, and then, by walking very fast, he either overtook them or met them ; and in either case, by another strange fatality, he happened to have some parish work to do precisely in the direction in which they were going. Then he professed to feel so much interest in Lady Chester and her baby that it could only be satisfied by authentic accounts from Mrs. Hopkinson, who was constantly at Pleasance ; and if she happened to be there when he called, Captain Hopkinson received him and took him up to the drawing-room, and then there was a school talk, and perhaps a little music ; and altogether, if Mr. Greydon's income had increased at all in proportion to his passion, there would have been a Mrs. Greydon in a very few weeks. Captain Hopkinson saw how matters stood, and abstained from interference. He supposed if the young people liked each other they would make it out somehow : when Jane and he married they had not more than a hundred a year, and now they had more money than they could spend. Mr. Greydon might ask him for his daughter, and would, perhaps, be surprised to find that little Janet, would bring her fair share towards the expenses of a family, and in the meanwhile they were welcome to see as much of each other as they liked.

Willis, in former days, would not have observed whether anybody spoke to his sisters-in-law or not ; but some change had come over the spirit of his very melancholy dream. He looked more at what was passing around him, and less at his own petty grievances. It generally appeared that he had been dining with the Sampsons, or calling on them ; and he talked of the necessity of giving a great *fête* at Columbia Lodge to return the civilities that had been shown to him ; and, to the unutterable surprise of Janet and Rose, announced that he had had the pianoforte tuned, on which poor Mary had been used to play some little tunes that sounded like the wailings of a moulting linnet. "And if you will bring your music, girls, it will be a great treat for——" and then he added in one of his old querulous tones, "for the Baroness."

The girls were much flattered that Charles should think their singing a treat for anybody, and acute enough to guess what the pause in his sentence meant ; and when Miss Monteneros was announced soon after, the something almost amounting to animation in Willis's manner confirmed their suspicions. Rachel had called on them frequently lately ; sometimes with gifts for poor people, a list of whom she had obtained from Janet—sometimes in a moody humour, which she assured them could only be dispelled by talking it off to them—sometimes full of dry fun, and seeming to take life as a farce ; but whatever was the vein of the day, little Charlie was the "master of the situation."

The child had taken a fancy to her the first time he saw her, and Rachel had had so little experience of affection that his artless fondness touched her to the heart ; she loved him with a passionate love, she made herself his willing slave, told him odd amusing stories, and then again talked to him in sober earnest, as if he and she understood the world and each other better than any other two people on earth.

There is nothing so attractive to a child, particularly to a sick child, as being treated like a very old man. Charlie would sit on Rachel's knee, his eyes fixed admiringly on her, while she "fabled of green fields," or turned the white feathery clouds on the bright blue canopy above into troops of angels, to whose swift flight she gave fanciful destinations ; and Charlie would gravely say, "Yes, veddy true, pooty Rachel," and shake his head with an air of precocious wisdom that delighted her.

"Nay, never shake your gory locks at me, such dear little curling locks, too, as they are. And now, Charlie, your aunts have got some more visitors to entertain," she whispered, as Mr. Greydon was announced, "so you and I will go and sit in the shade in grandmamma's garden, and I will tell you such a funny story of a little kitten," and with a nod to the girls she carried him off. Willis looked fidgety, and did not lend himself to conversation with his usual asperity, and after a time he too disappeared in the direction of the garden. There he found Charlie in fits of laughter at the extraordinary sayings and doings of the supposititious kitten.

"You will spoil my poor little man, Miss Monteneros," looking at Charlie with an ominous shake of the head.

"Oh! nebber shake your golly locks at me," said the child.

"Now, was there ever such a darling?" said Rachel, "and I only said that once to him. He is too clever!"

"Ah, yes, poor little fellow," said Willis, with another shake of his "golly locks," meant to imply the probable fate of such early precocity.

"Charlie pet, go and pick me a quantity of daisies and I will make such a necklace for you. I sent him away, Mr. Willis, because I want to beg you not to speak so discouragingly of his health when he is present. He is old enough, or, at least, quick enough to understand, in some degree, your forebodings. I know," she added, in her most gracious manner, "that I am taking a very great liberty in saying this; but you are very fond of your little boy, and I am sure you will forgive me."

"More than that," said Mr. Willis, looking extremely complacent. "I feel very much obliged to you; I know I ought to conceal my habitual melancholy from the observation of that babe."

"Certainly," said Rachel, "and from everybody else. There is no great merit in bearing grief grievously, and there is certainly no great charm in habitual melancholy, be it real or artificial."

"I hope, Miss Monteneros, you do not suspect me of being artificial."

"Are not you? Well, I do not know, I am very artificial myself, a regular actress, but I

have always thought you outdid me in that
line. Why now, Mr. Willis, Hamlet, you know,
says that

> ' The inky cloak,
> That windy inspiration of forced breath,
> And the dejected 'haviour of the visage,'

are actions that a man may *seem*, they do not
' denote him *truly*.' Now, what good reason
have you for all this show of distress ? "

Willis was posed. He could hardly allege
to Rachel, with whom he was really in love,
that he was still inconsolable for the loss of a
wife for whom he had cared little while she
was alive, and when he came to think what
other griefs he had, he somehow could not
recollect them at that moment ; so he murmured something about a solitary home and
Charlie's health, a great bereavement and a
natural proneness to foresee the worst, &c.

" That is a misfortune, certainly," said Rachel ;
" many people would call it a fault. But dear
little Charlie's health is improving daily, so
there is one ray of happiness. With that kind
cheerful set of people we have just left, who
treat you like a son and brother, you can always
find a home that is *not* solitary. As for your
great bereavement, for which I heartily pity
you, time must have done something for you,
and as for the constant reference you constantly make to it, I long to say to you—but no,

I have no right to speak. Ah," she added, trying to relapse into her usual careless manner, " of all people in the world, I am about the last fitted to give good advice."

" No, you are not," said Willis, with more eagerness than he often evinced. " What is it you long to say ? "

" Why, just what the Quaker said to the Duchess of Buckingham, when he found her, two years after her husband's death, in a darkened room, hung with black, ' What, friend, hast thou not forgiven God Almighty yet ? ' And now I really must go to Charlie and his daisies," said Rachel, rising hastily and escaping, for she was half frightened at her own daring.

But thither Willis followed, staggered by her last stroke of wisdom, and slightly ashamed of her insight into his character, but flattered to the last degree by the interest she appeared to take in his happiness, and not at all aware that Charlie was at the bottom of all this plot against his querulousness. Rachel did not choose that Charlie should sit under the shadow of Willis's withered gourd, and she did not think that the gourd had any right to wither with such a Charlie to shine on it.

" Miss Monteneros," he began, " I hope you will allow me to thank you for the advice you have given me, and I beg to assure you——"

"Oh!" said Rachel, "if I have not affronted you, I am more than satisfied; and now for my daisy-chain. Papa must not interrupt us, must he, Charlie? we are decided on that point."

"Twite detided," said Charlie with great energy; "papa, please go."

"Are you not going to do what Charlie tells you?" said Rachel, smiling, finding after a time that Willis was still standing by them.

"I am not going," he said, rather moodily. "Miss Monteneros," he added after a pause, "you seem to take great interest in my little boy."

"The greatest possible; Charlie and I are intimate friends."

"Dat we are," said Charlie, "oh, veddy imitate."

"Cannot you extend that friendship to his father?"

"I am not much given to friendship," she said carelessly, and more occupied in tying her daisy bracelets round Charlie's wrists than in his father's remarks. "But if I had been your friend for the last twenty years, I could not have told you more crude, disagreeable truths than I did to-day. I can tell you as many again," she added, laughing, "if that proof of friendship will satisfy you."

"No, it will not," he said with some spirit; "I ask for more; the truths you have spoken

were not disagreeable, because they came from
you, and I hope you will see they have not
been spoken in vain. When you tell me to
be more cheerful, when you say my home might
be happy, Miss Monteneros, it is in your power
to verify your own prophecy."

Rachel looked up with an air of intense
astonishment.

"You are fond of that child—oh! Miss Monteneros, let him find in you the mother he has
lost. It is in your power to make both the
child and father happy."

"Oh, Mr. Willis, what are you saying?
Stay one moment——" Then there was a
pause and, to Willis's extreme surprise, she
burst into a hearty laugh.

"I beg your pardon," she said, "but to
think of all my exhortations to you to be happy
ending in your asking me to be your wife! Why,
of all the methods of being miserable which
you are so fond of trying, you could not have
invented one so certain to produce the desired
unhappy result as that. I suppose there are
not two people in England who would suit
each other so little as we should. We do not
care about each other, to begin with; and
there are you, still in the deepest mourning,
and avowedly inconsolable for the loss of your
first wife, asking a woman every way dissimilar
to her to be your second."

"But Mary did not suit me," faltered the unhappy Willis, "I could not love her; she was amiable certainly, but quite without the charm, the power that you have, Miss Monteneros. You would give an interest to my home that it has never had, and the gloom——"

"Say no more, Mr. Willis," said Rachel gravely; "you can hardly expect that I should have accepted your proposal under any circumstances, and we know each other so little that my refusal can give you but little pain. But think of the avowal you are now making; you have sought sympathy far and wide, and paraded sorrow in all directions, and yet you tell me that the Mary whose loss has been bewailed with such ostentation 'did not suit you,' you could not love her. Oh! where is Truth? am I never to find it? I can bear artifice in the frivolities and gauds of the world— it is all artificial in itself, all heartless—but sorrow should be as true as it is sacred. Falseness there appals and disgusts me."

She was trembling with excitement, but she took up Charlie as she spoke, and perhaps the sight of his wistful eyes and the touch of his tiny hand softened her, for she turned back and added: "Perhaps I have spoken too harshly, but the dead should never be named slightingly; she was Charlie's mother, too—do not say you never loved her."

o

And so she departed, leaving Willis more ashamed, more lowered in his own conceit than he could have supposed possible, and yet with a perception of the greatness and nobleness of truth that gave him an elevation of feeling he had hitherto never known.

Rachel deposited Charlie with his aunts, and walked home half annoyed, half amused with what had passed. " That comes of giving advice," she thought. " It never answers, but I did it for Charlie's sake ; and as the man has no real feeling, no great harm is done. I wish little Charlie had not been so funny and clever about the ' golly locks," it made me long to be his mother ; but to be sure it would not do to marry poor Mr. Willis on the strength of that one quotation."

CHAPTER XX

MRS. HOPKINSON was now released from her attendance on Blanche, to whom she had endeared herself by her unwearied kindness, and who looked up to her as a miracle of wisdom on the subject of babies in general, and this valuable baby in particular. As a proof that tact, which is only another name for consideration of the feelings of others, is compatible with unpolished manner, it may be mentioned that Mrs. Hopkinson and the nurse parted without having had one dissension ; and even with an admission on the part of Mrs. Smith " that that good lady knew very well what she was about, and that, considering how delicate Lady Chester was, and how little she knew about a nursery, it was quite a mercy she had Mrs. Hopkinson to look after her."

Lord Chesterton had informed Blanche that, by a happy coincidence, the living of Chesford, their own parish, had become vacant a very few days after she had intimated to him her wishes for Mr. Greydon ; and it was decided between them that on the important occasion of Albert Victor Chester's christening, Blanche should have the pleasure of announcing to Mr. Greydon his preferment.

She had now re-established herself on her sofa in the garden, and the old Pleasance habits were resumed. Janet and Rose were often asked to sit with her. Mr. Harcourt and his outrigger were again skimming on the surface and floating about Rose ; Mr. Greydon either had some excuse for calling on Arthur, or called without any excuse at all, except the old hackneyed one of " the fatality," and by his manner to Janet, Blanche was led to the comfortable conviction that, by giving Mr. Greydon this living, she should at once provide her village with an unexceptionable pastor, and pay off some of her debt of gratitude to the Hopkinson family.

The Sampsons continued to give their elaborate dinners, and their gorgeous *déjeuners*, and it almost appeared as if the Court Journal kept a special Sampson correspondent, so numerous were the paragraphs devoted to the sayings and doings, and givings and receivings of the Baroness. The Baron was more prosperous and more superbly humble than ever ; but it is to be hoped that the Baroness's guests derived more enjoyment from her hospitalities than she did, for she was constantly either irritable and dejected, or in a state of nervous high spirits, and she looked so ill that

Rachel suggested to her to have some medical advice.

" I cannot think what you mean," said her Aunt peevishly ; "I am sure with all my parties and *fêtes*, and all the luxuries that surround me, it would be strange if I wanted to complain to a doctor ; what do you suppose ails me, Rachel?"

" That is what I want to know, Aunt Rebecca ; you do not look well, and perhaps Dr. Ayscough——"

" Oh, don't talk to me of Dr. Ayscough, he really is too trying, never attaching the slightest importance to any of my symptoms, nor, in fact, to anything I say."

" Well, Mr. Duckett is reckoned clever, and is close at hand, and he has been attending Lady Chester."

" Oh, thank you, I am not going to trust my health to a country apothecary. It is all very well for the Chesters, who are, I suppose, as poor as` rats while Lord Chesterton lives. I think, with all our wealth, I might afford to see a physician."

" Can I write to any one for you? those nervous headaches——"

" I really must beg, Rachel, you will not take these strange fancies. What can make me nervous? me, who am notorious for high spirits !" whereupon the Baroness burst into tears, and became almost hysterical.

Rachel quietly administered all the usual remedies, and then in silence began arranging some flowers.

"Well," said the Baroness, "I must say you take things coolly. Having brought on this attack, you might as well send for assistance. I suppose you had better write and ask Dr. Ayscough to drive down here, for I must be quite myself on Wednesday. That will be the last and the best of our parties," she said with a ghastly smile.

And so the physician was summoned, and was received by the Baroness with all her accustomed graces, which generally were completely thrown away upon him; but to-day he seemed to study her looks with attention, and to bear her rambling statements with unusual patience.

"I really have nothing to tell you, my dear Sir, just a little headache—you know what a sensitive creature I am, and I think the wind is in the East. I always feel an East wind *jusqu'au bout des doigts*, and I have been overdoing my gaieties. I want rest, and change of air. The Baron is taking a splendid moor. Would the Highlands suit me?"

"Is the Baron thinking of going soon?"

"Oh, almost immediately," she said with some hesitation. "He talks of making a run down to Scotland to see the place before he buys it, and I am almost afraid he will not be here to receive his friends next Wednesday— the 12th of August is near at hand."

"And so you are making preparations for a start, eh? And Baron Sampson will give his friends the slip on Wednesday," and Dr. Ayscough felt the pulse in his hand give a sudden bound. "Well, I do not see that the journey would do you any harm, and change of air and scene would do you good. You are nervous."

"No, I am not; I cannot think what possesses everybody to suspect me of nerves. What reason upon earth can I have for being nervous?"

"That you must tell me," he said; "I can only assert the fact; and I am not bound to furnish reasons for the illnesses of you London fine ladies."

The Baroness was so charmed at finding herself classed by this fashionable physician with the fine ladies of the day that she rallied; and, while Dr. Ayscough was writing her prescription, tried a little light talk on the subject of the Chesters—pitied them for the privations that the poverty, with which she chose to endow them, imposed upon them—she believed Lady Chester sent for the village apothecary when she was taken ill, and depended for a nurse on the good offices of a Mrs. Hopkins, or some name of that kind, a neighbour. "To be sure,

young people are right not to run into debt ;
but I cannot fancy putting up with anything
second rate myself, indeed the Baron would
not hear it from me, he always says, ' Nothing
second rate for you, Baroness ; whatever money
can buy, you can have, only let it be the best.' "

" Well, if money can buy a Mrs. Hopkinson,"
said Dr. Ayscough, dryly, " it can do more
than I have ever supposed. Mrs. Hopkinson
has been a valuable friend to Lady Chester,
who required constant and great care for ten
days ; and now there are those pleasing young
girls to amuse her and sing to her during her
convalescence. They must be pleasant neighbours for you, Baroness."

" Oh dear ! I am much too insignificant
a person for the Miss Hopkinsons to notice.
Nothing but Duchesses and Viscountesses will
satisfy them ! I would have brought them
out at my *déjeuners*, out of mere good nature.
However, they are not worth talking of. Tell
me some news, Dr. Ayscough—you always hear
the last London reports."

" Unluckily, I have been out of town most
part of the day, so I cannot give you any gossip.
There are two more great failures in the city. I
wonder where these smashes will end."

" Two more ! " said the Baroness, faintly ;
" do you recollect their names ? not that I
should be much the wiser if you told me," she

added with a forced laugh. " The Baron happily
is quite independent of all these speculators."

" Corban's house was one, I know."

The Baroness turned pale. " The other
I forget, but I heard it was connected with
the Corbans."

" Ah, indeed ! Well, your time is so valuable,
I must not detain you—in fact it was absurd
to trouble you, I am so well." She sank back
in her chair, almost fainting.

Dr. Ayscough waited a few minutes, and
then said kindly, " You have something weigh-
ing on your mind." She shook her head, but
her colour was livid, and the hand she held
out to him trembled.

" Would it be a relief to you to tell me what
you apprehend ? You cannot suppose that
your confidence would be betrayed."

She looked fixedly at him, and the tears
stood in her eyes ; but suddenly she seemed by
a strong effort to calm herself, and, with a laugh
that was more distressing than her tears, she
said, " This is really too good ! what apprehen-
sions can I have ? except perhaps that we may
have rain on Wednesday, and that all my fireworks may fail. Good morning—I suppose it
is impossible to prevail on you to honour our
festivities with your presence ? "

" Quite impossible," he said. " Good morning."

" I always thought that Baron a very plausible rascal," was his reflection as he got into
the carriage, " and now I am sure of it. He
will be off before Wednesday, and she will
brazen it out to the last."

After the Doctor's departure, the Baroness
told Rachel that he had quite laughed at the
notion of her being nervous, and considered her
perfectly capable of a journey to the Highlands, and that he had recommended to her
to take her usual airing. So, as she should
probably be off to Scotland in a few days, she
thought of driving up to town, and depositing
her diamonds and trinkets at the banking house ;
and at the same time she could give directions
for packing up whatever she might want at
Lochingar. " I am afraid the house is small
for our establishment, and I almost doubt, my
dear Rachel, whether you will be lodged so
well as we could wish."

" Thank you, Aunt Rebecca, do not trouble
yourself about me ; I have always intended to
tell you that whenever you leave this villa, I
mean, as shopkeepers say, to set up for myself.
I am much obliged to you and to my uncle
for——". Rachel hesitated, she knew that the
very large allowance made for her during her
minority had more than saved her from any
pecuniary obligation, and she had met with
no affection. However, she added, " for the

home you have given me, and now I must
try what I can do for myself."

"And will such a very independent young
lady condescend to impart her plans for the
future? I should have thought I might have
been consulted, *si ce n'était que pour la forme*,"
said the Baroness, who, however willing and
anxious to get rid of a niece who was younger
and handsomer than herself, and addicted to
speaking plain truths, was yet piqued by the ease
with which their acquaintance was dissolved.

"I am thinking of going to the sea-side in
the first instance. My old governess will be
glad to pass the holidays with me, and that
little delicate boy of Mr. Willis's is advised to
try sea-bathing—so, if the Hopkinsons will let
me have him, he will go too."

"Upon my word, this is extremely flattering
to the melancholy Jacques, as you chose to
nickname my friend Mr. Willis. Well, nothing
in this world surprises me; but I must say
that after being accustomed to the society of
Moses, with his wit and vivacity and air of
fashion" (poor dear Moses, with his vulgar
jokes and flashy appearance), "I can hardly
understand this preference of that gloomy man.
Not that Moses is a marrying man. Don't go
and fancy that, and I am sure Willis is much
too devoted to the memory of his first wife to
think of a second, so you have no chance there."

" How distressing ! " said Rachel ; " but it will be interesting to sit on the rock and pine for either or both of them.

' Suppose I stand upon the sea-beach now,
　Mine arms thus, and mine hair blown with the
　　　wind,
Wild as the desert—and behind me—
　Make all a desolation—See ! See !

Aunt Rebecca,

　A miserable life of this poor picture.' "

Rachel knew that a good strong quotation always drove the Baroness out of the field, and her vivid delineation of Aspasia's misery had the desired effect. The Baroness was mystified into silence, and left the room merely saying, " Well, Moses is not likely to trouble you, at all events."

" No, I suppose not, after what I said to him last week," said Rachel, who knew from her cousin that his mother had urged him to weary her with constant proposals ; and so they parted.

" Oh dear ! how unamiable I am when I am with my uncle and aunt," thought Rachel, " thoroughly detestable I may say, and yet when I am with those girls, or little Charlie, I can be as good as gold, and so tame that that baby can lead me ; I do believe evil qualities are more catching than measles."

CHAPTER XXI

THE great event of the christening of Albert Victor took place the day before that fixed for Baroness Sampson's *fête* and a large party was assembled at Pleasance. It had been very trying to Blanche to keep the secret of the living at Chesford so long from Mr. Greydon; but then, as she observed to Aunt Sarah, the course of his true love seemed to run all the more rapidly because it was so far from being smooth. "I should like him to propose on his three hundred a-year, Aunt Sarah, it would be so romantic and touching."

"And so extraordinarily silly, my dear, that if he did, I should not think him fit to hold the living. Are you anxious he should have it, Blanche, because he is a good clergyman, or because you think he is attached to Janet?"

"A little of both, Aunt Sarah; but please do not say because I *think* he is attached. There can be no doubt of the fact. Don't you see yourself that he is desperately in love?"

"My love, it is more than half a century ago since I had any experience in love making, and all its little signs and follies are not so visible through my spectacles as they are to your young eyes ; but I daresay you are right, and I hope you are, for Janet is a pleasing good young woman, and will make an excellent wife for a clergyman."

" Oh yes, she will be so useful at Chesford, and such a nice neighbour for me ; and then if Rose marries Mr. Harcourt—— "

" What ! another love story ? My dear Blanche, I hope you are not going to turn into a match-maker ; of all the dangerous manufactories in the world, that is the worst, and the most unsatisfactory."

" Yes, if I sat down deliberately and said, there is the Reverend Horace Greydon, a friend of Arthur's, an excellent young man, and there is Janet Hopkinson who would exactly suit him, I will try and make up a match between them ; that would be wrong, and perhaps a year hence they would hate the sight of me for having thought of it. But when I see that they are mutually attached and longing to be married, then I step in like a beneficent fairy, and give them the means of meeting, and the means of living—and *my* manufactory, Aunt Sarah, only turns out the best finished articles of happiness. I *do* like to help young people in their love affairs," said Blanche in a reflective staid tone, implying that her long life of eighteen years and her twelve months of marriage had given her the experience and benevolence appropriate to a prosperous old age.

"But to return to Rose and Mr. Harcourt," said Aunt Sarah, smiling.

"I do not take quite such a lively interest in their affairs, there are no difficulties to overcome ; and though Mr. Harcourt is a good-natured gentleman-like young man, he is not to be compared to Mr. Greydon, and, moreover, he seems to me to sing out of tune. Rose will pass a life of accompaniments ; and she must be very much in love to change the time and the key of *Ah, si ben mio*, as she did last night, and yet to thank Mr. Harcourt for the signal failure he made of it at last."

"And what is to become of your friend Mrs. Hopkinson when you have married off both her daughters and her husband is again gone to sea ? "

"Ah, poor dear ! I have been fretting about her very much, and with all my imagination, Aunt Sarah, I have not yet imagined a fate that satisfies me for my darling old Hop. I should like her to be near baby, she understands him so thoroughly ; and if she would take care of him, I could take care of her. It is a pity that Chesterton is not semi-detached, that she had part of it. A semi-detached castle would be a novelty."

"Blanche, do you remember the fat mother with black mittens, and the daughters with the pianoforte, and the startling boy, and the horrors of a semi-detached house?"

"Perfectly, Aunt Sarah, and you see I was right as to the facts, except that Charlie does not throw stones, but wrong as to the conclusions I drew from them. However, I could not foresee that I should be housed with such excellent people. What a number of small kindnesses those Hopkinsons have shown me."

"My dear child!" said Lady Sarah, kissing her, "you are likely to meet with many kindnesses, small and great, in your journey through life, if you keep up that warm interest in the happiness of others which you feel now. Like will to like, and so my Blanche will find warm friends wherever she goes: and now go and dress for your christening—I hope you have no more matches to make."

"Not at this moment; but it strikes me, Aunt Sarah, that if the Duchess should have another little girl in a year or two, baby will certainly fall in love with her twenty years hence —that will be very interesting."

In the meantime, baby was christened, and immediately after their return home, Blanche drew Mr. Greydon aside, and said to him with tears in her eyes, "You have to-day been the instrument of conferring on my darling boy the greatest gift God has given to man; pray for him that he may be a Christian indeed—such a Christian as you, Mr. Greydon, are in heart and life. At this moment all earthly gifts seem to me but trifles, but I have one to offer to you."

"Oh, Lady Chester, do not speak of a gift to me. Do you suppose that the ceremony which has been performed to-day has not been most deeply interesting to me, that it was not a boon to myself to be allowed to bear my part in it? I assure you, I care much for the child of my earliest friend."

"I know you do, Mr. Greydon," said Blanche, holding out her hand to him, "and I was expressing myself foolishly. In fact, it is another boon I am going to ask you to bestow on us; I want you to come and look after us all at Chesford. That living is now vacant, and Lord Chesterton has commissioned me to offer it to you."

"To me!" said Mr. Greydon—"oh, Lady Chester, this is your doing. Chesford—where I shall be near you and Arthur—I cannot thank you, and at this moment too, you do not know——"

"Yes, I do," she said smiling, "at least I think I do, thanks to my own observation, not to any confidence that has been placed in me."

P

" What was there to confide ? " he said eagerly,
" but the utter hopelessness of an attachment
which strengthened every hour, in proportion
to that hopelessness. I had no prospect of
preferment, no possibility of offering to her a
home that was worthy of her ; but now—oh,
Lady Chester, I cannot tell you how happy
you have made me."

" And let us hope it will make her happy
too. You have not named her, but I always
guess right, and I assure you that the idea of
having her for my neighbour makes me doubly
happy ; and now go and say your say to Lord
Chesterton. He has been so kind."

Janet could not help observing Mr. Greydon's look of happiness during his short
colloquy with Lord Chesterton, nor the eagerness with which he afterwards advanced to
hand her in to luncheon. But she had
changed in due proportion to the change in
him. The time was gone by when she could
talk to Rose of her girlish fancy, of her
hopes that were more foolish than her fancy,
and her certainties that were more visionary
than her hopes. From the time that Mr.
Greydon really felt for her the preference
which she had imagined when it did not
exist, the distrust that always accompanies a
true love had seized her. She never mentioned his name to her sister, she shunned

rather than sought his attentions ; and the more marked they became, the less did she believe they could be intended for her ; and yet she had never been so happy. . Home was more prized by her than ever ; her father and mother had, she thought, never been so dear or so kind, and as for Rose, she could not pet her enough. She almost grew fond of Willis, and once suggested that the vulgarity and overbearingness of the Baroness were not quite so great as they had all supposed ; but this spark of that general benevolence, which arises from particular happiness, was instantly extinguished by the rest of the family, who still looked on life through its ordinary medium.

Janet sat down to luncheon in a doubtful state of happiness. She saw that something had occurred that excited Mr. Greydon, and gradually went on thinking the worst, till, from the frightful supposition that he thought her bonnet unbecoming, she arrived, by various gradations of misfortune, at thinking that he might have announced to Lady Chester his engagement to Miss Simpson, a remarkably plain, *not* young woman, who taught in the Sunday School, and was supposed to be an heiress. She was roused from this reverie by Lord Chesterton's rising and saying that he must propose one health in addition to that of the baby hero of the day, that of the new Rector of Chesford, the Rev. Horace Greydon,"—which announcement was hailed with the most marked approbation by the assembled company.

"Well, old fellow," said Arthur, "I give you joy with all my heart, and I give myself joy too; it will be rare fun having you for a neighbour. I daresay my father never told you that the Rectory is one of the prettiest houses in the neighbourhood."

"I am sure, Mr. Greydon," said Mrs. Hopkinson, "I never was so pleased in my life—what a thing it will be for Chesford to have such a clergyman. It makes me happy to think of it; but what upon earth is to become of us without you, I have not an idea; we shall all turn heathens"; and overcome by these adverse ideas, Mrs. Hopkinson fairly burst out crying.

"Pray accept my congratulations," said Sir William de Vescie, drawing Mr. Greydon aside. "It will give Lady Eleanor and myself great pleasure to continue the acquaintance so happily begun here. I believe the living is a remarkably good one; but I am afraid you will find coals rather dear—I know Lord Chesterton was giving 28s. the ton when we were giving only 26s., and butcher's meat was dearer the last time I was there than it was with us, but that might have been accidental. In all other respects it is a delightful residence."

Janet had said nothing; she gave a start when Lord Chesterton announced Mr. Greydon's preferment, and turned pale as she thought " he is going away." She did not know that *his* thought was, " will she go with me ? " But the next moment she found that her hand was taken and pressed between his, and though she pretended to believe that she had held it out to him in an attempt to wish him joy—a pleasing persuasion stole over her that her bonnet was not unbecoming, that Miss Simpson was at least five and thirty, and, heiress as she was, that Mr. Greydon did not care about her. " At all events," she thought, " he shows that he looks upon me as a friend, or he would not have shaken hands in that way." And she rose from luncheon in a flutter of happiness and shyness.

" And so you are really all going to-morrow to the Marble Hall *fête* ? " said Blanche, as her guests began to disperse. " That Baroness has conquered at last ; I can imagine it must be difficult to withstand that very imperious lady."

" Well," said Mrs. Hopkinson, " I am sure it is the last thing I wish, but John fancies it will be amusing ! and then that Miss

Monteneros, whom my girls *will* like so much, pressed them to come just to one of their *fêtes*, and she is so fond of little Charlie, that somehow I can't refuse her— though I did not quite know what she meant by saying it would be 'a tedious brief scene, and very tragical mirth, hot ice and wondrous strange snow.' But Rose says she was only quoting Shakespeare, and, of course, what Shakespeare says must be right, and besides, I should like to taste hot ice."

"Are you really going to these Simpsons or Sampsons?" said Harcourt to Rose. "I think it would be good fun to go too—suppose we all go! Arthur, will you come?"

"Oh, no, no," said Blanche, "it is quite impossible! besides, Arthur is not asked, happily."

"Oh, that is of no consequence," said Harcourt; "of course the Sampsons will take our going as a compliment. I don't suppose an invitation is necessary; they are just the sort of people to call us 'swells,' and to think it stylish of us to come uninvited."

"The Baroness gave me some cards for gentlemen," said Mrs. Hopkinson; "I believe she meant one of them for Lord Chester."

"Very likely," said Blanche, "but Mr. Harcourt can have it; Arthur is particularly engaged."

"I should like to go, Blanche."

"Oh no, dearest, you would not; you will be thinking next that you would like to take me. You should check these wild fancies, Arthur; I am never imaginative myself, am I, Aunt Sarah? Certainly not to the extent of supposing I should like to make acquaintance with Baroness Sampson; but seriously, if you go to her parties, we must ask her to ours—you would not like that?"

"No, decidedly not; I give it up, and Harcourt is 'swell' enough for two."

"Well then, Mrs. Hopkinson, recollect that I go to-morrow under your auspices. I shall have the pleasure of meeting you," Harcourt added in a low voice to Rose, "so it cannot be very tragical mirth to me."

CHAPTER XXII

THE *Times* of the following morning announced two more failures of large banking houses, and there were dark hints in the City article about a great capitalist, which were perfectly unintelligible to those who had not been brought up to talk Stock Exchange fluently, but explained by the more learned Willis to allude to Sampson's house. " I fully expect to hear that that fellow has gone off any day, and he will take some of your money with him, Charlie," he said to the little boy, who was sitting on his knee; "I am sorry on your account, but, never mind, we must make the best of it."

The idea of Willis making the best of anything was so startling, such a very astonishing novelty, that this announcement was received much as the intimation of a great misfortune would have been from anybody else. The Hopkinsons all looked at him with the greatest commiseration, and with some curiosity, just as people stare when a fresh beast arrives at the Zoological Gardens. A " Willis-making-the-best-of-it " was quite a new specimen, a rare and interesting animal; and when it further appeared that his black coat had disappeared, and that he was dressed like any other common-place gentleman, in an equally common-place dark coat, the pity of the family knew no bounds. If he had avowed that he had lost all his wealth and was going to hang himself, the girls would have laughed and said, " how like Charles "; but when he seemed to think that only part of his fortune was at stake, and that, except for Charlie's sake, he did not mean to be miserable about it, they were all in the greatest grief—Captain Hopkinson proffering assistance, Mrs. Hopkinson buried in her pocket handkerchief, and the girls, under pretence of coaxing Charlie, actually patting Willis on the shoulder, and stroking his hair, and going through all the usual sisterly methods of consolation.

" By the bye, young ladies, I have brought you some parasols suitable for the day," he said, producing two striking articles of guipure and white silk; " there is a terrible want of shade at Marble Hall, and you will be burnt alive."

" Really," said Rose afterwards to her sister, " I thought I should have fainted, if I had known how, when Charles gave us those parasols, and seemed to care whether we should be tanned or not. They are exactly like that parasol of Miss Monteneros' that we admired so much. Janet, he must be in love with Rachel, and all this change is her doing."

"I should not be surprised," said Janet, shaking her head sagely. "When people are in love they are so very benevolent—at least, so I have always heard ; of course, I know nothing about it. But I am sure there was something very interesting in that long talk he and Rachel had in the garden the other day : Charles has been a different man ever since. But now, Rose, it is time to dress."

When they arrived at Marble Hall, any misgivings as to the Sampson prosperity were quite set at rest. There were more servants in dazzling liveries, a thicker forest of green-house plants, more pineapples, and a greater variety of ices (not hot) than ever. The Baroness wore a gown of such very bright yellow that the sun was affronted and went in. She received her guests with the most painful affability—was so obliged to them for coming—so afraid that they would not be amused, as Mario and Bosio had failed her just at the last moment—and so much distressed that the Baron, who was busy about this tiresome Scotch property, had not

yet returned from town, that it seemed
difficult to respond to her civilities. She
wore a thick fall of lace over her face, on
pretence of a bad cold, but even through
that and a still thicker mask of rouge, a keen
observer could detect a livid face, blanched
lips, and red, restless eyes.

Rachel received her two friends with the
greatest warmth, and then devoted herself
to making Mrs. Hopkinson comfortable ; but
not before Willis, hovering in the background, had had the pleasure of seeing his
parasols examined and apparently admired,
and the unusual cordiality with which Rachel
afterwards met him convinced him that this
kindness to his sisters-in-law had given satisfaction to the lady of his love.

" I can't think what Lady Chester meant,"
said Harcourt, joining the two sisters, " by
talking of the Baroness as uncivil and important. I have had considerable difficulty
in escaping from her gratitude to me for
honouring her with my presence here to-day.
I felt like a Royal Duke, and half expected
to hear the band play *God save the Queen*
as I stepped with much dignity out on the
lawn. Now, Miss Rose, shall we go and
hear the music in the saloon, which the
Baroness assures me is not unworthy of my
notice ? "

Whether it were or not will never be known, for Harcourt and Rose passed the open windows of the saloon without appearing to perceive the volume of sound that issued from them, and strolled on to a bench in the flower garden, where they seemed to be engaged in earnest conversation. Indeed, Harcourt began their expedition by saying he had something very particular to say. Mr. Greydon asked Janet soon after if she would not like to follow her sister and, upon her assenting, he led her in an exactly opposite direction. Perhaps he too had something particular to say.

The sinister whispers respecting the absence of their host which were beginning to circulate among his City friends were stopped by his sudden appearance. He appeared to have escaped the influenza to which the Baroness attributed her changed appearance, and a veil that should conceal his intelligent eye, intellectual forehead, and general aspect of benevolence and morality would have been tantalising. As usual, he professed inattention to the amusements of the day, and was much occupied in talking over with his moneyed friends the deplorable state of the Corban family, and his intention to organise a subscription for them on a large scale.

" Corban may not have had a clear head for business, but I believe a more honest fellow does not exist, notwithstanding the cry some of his malicious creditors are raising against him. His family are, I am told, in a sad state. There was a talk of bringing out on the stage that charming Miss Corban, whom you have heard sing at my wife's parties. Now, on the score of morality, I must try to prevent this—her vocal talents, her beauty, her very archness, are all so many snares—I have put down my name for five hundred pounds, and hope to persuade many others to join in this good work. I believe there are sandwiches or some refreshments of that sort in the dining-room ; shall we adjourn there, and after dinner see what can be done for these poor Corbans ? "

And so they all went to the turtle, and venison, and pine-apple, that represented sandwiches, and invigorated themselves with a view of being charitable eventually.

Janet and Rose, looking very demure, had rejoined their father and mother ; and of course, by the merest accident, Mr. Greydon and Mr. Harcourt met them struggling through the crowd that was flocking into the dining-room, and offered their services. They found places not very far from the Baron, which was an advantageous position, inasmuch as they could hear an occasional axiom of morality, so well worded that it made an impression on the memory, and might be of use to them for life. His liberality, too, for he was still eager in the cause of the Corbans, was good as an example ; and Janet began to wonder whether a sovereign, the only one she had, might not be offered, more as a tribute to the influence of the Baron's example and exhortations than with any hope of its being of the smallest use. She doubted, indeed, whether he would know a mere single sovereign by sight, he seemed to deal with them so exclusively by hundreds and thousands.

However, at this moment it would have been impossible to address him ; a letter had been brought to him marked ' Immediate.' He read it with apparent unconcern, but his glasses fell from his hand as he removed them from his eyes. " Ah, my dear lady," he said, turning to the great lady of the party, who was seated at his right hand. "This is one of the petty torments of age, which you will one day have to endure ; I am always losing my spectacles or dropping my glasses. Do take care of your eyes ; mine are quite worn out."

As the friend he addressed was past sixty, and had for some years enjoyed, in the seclusion of home, the comfort of what she called clearers, she was particularly pleased

with this little address. The Baroness had
seen the letter arrive, and the trivial incident
of the falling glasses, perhaps, had a meaning
to her, which no one else could attach to
it. How often is the face of the husband,
when it seems utterly calm and unmoved to
the generality of society, full of strange
revelations and terror to the wife who knows
its slightest line, its most passing expression.
Baroness Sampson saw that, for one moment,
her husband's hand had been unnerved, and
to her this told all. She passed her handkerchief rapidly over her face, and then
suddenly rose from the table. Her pale
face and trembling movements confirming
the declaration she made of sudden faintness,
she left the room, murmuring that her influenza and the heat of the room had overcome her, and that Rachel must take her
place.

The Baron lingered a few minutes, explaining that his wife had been unwell for some
days, and then followed to inquire after her,
having first requested the company to adjourn
to the ball room and begin dancing. He
returned shortly, and said that the Baroness
was so completely knocked up, he feared she
would hardly be able to reappear ; and then,
taking the arm of his son, who had only
just arrived, he sauntered down the garden

walk which led to the river, and was seen no more.

The party dispersed soon after, with a vague feeling that "something was wrong," but merely expressing a wish not to disturb their hostess any longer ; the Hopkinson ladies had made their retreat as soon as dinner was over. Thanks to Rachel's attention, Mrs. Hopkinson had really been amused. A breakfast of this kind, with bands of music, singing, jugglers, &c., was quite a novelty to her ; and she came home in the highest spirits, making the most ample amends to the girls for ever having disliked their friend.

"She is a good, kind-hearted girl as ever lived, and very attentive to her elders, which I look upon as a very fine quality. I have come to the age when I enjoy a little attention from young people. To be sure she says a few odd things, but then I have been thinking that if everybody talked in the same way, if they were all as commonplace as I am, for example, it would be very dull, and Miss Monteneros is very amusing ; and, my dears, I am quite sure now, though I did not think so at first, that Charles admires her very much. He was always following us about, and that could not be for my sake, as he sees more than enough of me, and he was so civil and obliging. Well, she is fond of little Charlie, and she will make a good stepmother if he is to have one; and now here we are at home, and I have not heard a word from either of you. I am afraid you have not been so well amused as I have, and I can't get Willis out of my head. I really think we shall have a wedding soon in the family."

Janet burst out laughing, and Rose began to cry; and then they changed parts, Janet cried, and Rose laughed, while Mrs. Hopkinson, sinking back in her comfortable chair, and carefully taking off her best bonnet, stared at them with wonder. But the bonnet was twitched out of her hand and flung irreverently on the floor, and the daughters' arms were clasped round the mother's neck, before she could recover herself enough to speak, while Janet said:

"Mamma, dearest mamma, you talk of one wedding; what would you say to two more? Indeed, we liked the breakfast, and shall like the recollections of it all our lives; mamma, we are both so very happy, if it were not for the notion of leaving papa and you—Rose is engaged to Mr. Harcourt."

"And Janet to Mr. Greydon," added Rose.

"My dear, dear children," gasped Mrs. Hopkinson, "do stop a minute, I can't understand these sudden changes. Oh! where is

Q

John? He said it would be so, and I thought it was all nonsense; and so you are both engaged, and that dear Mr. Greydon will be our son; such a good man, and we have always looked up to him as something quite above us. And I shall like Mr. Harcourt, Janet—no, Rose, I mean—quite as much when I know him as well. And, my darlings, I will say that for you, that such good daughters will make excellent wives, and I hope you will both be as happy in your married lives as I have been. But I wish John would come home; and do, Janet, pick up my bonnet, I shall want it for the wedding, and then both of you sit down and tell me how all this came about, and you may both talk at once this time, though I do not like it in general."

They availed themselves of this permission, and Mrs. Hopkinson turned from one to the other, sometimes in a state of delight at their prospects, sometimes in a fit of desperation at her own, and finally she sank into a reverie, from which she awoke with a placid smile, saying, "My daughters, Mrs. Greydon and Mrs. Harcourt; well, if that is not droll; I had quite forgotten that you were not mere children still. Ah! there is John at last, how shall we tell him?"

But there was nothing to tell; he had

been detained by the lovers, not greatly to his surprise, as he had been more observant than his wife of the proceedings of the day, and he walked straight up to his daughters, and, with much emotion, congratulated them affectionately on their happy prospects.

" I assure you," he said to his wife, when the girls had withdrawn, " that those are two as fine young men as I ever wish to see ; I had rather a prejudice against Harcourt on account of that crinkum-crankum boat that he chooses to sport ; but he is really so well aware of Rosy's merits and so fond of her that, as there is no room for her in that absurd outrigger, I gave my consent very willingly. He is a liberal fellow. I said that I was afraid they would be disappointed in the portions I could give my daughters ; and Greydon said that with the excellent living Lord Chesterton had given him he wanted no more ; and then Harcourt took me aside, and said that he wished I would add to Janet's share whatever I meant to give to Rose. ' We shall have fortune enough of our own,' Harcourt said, ' and Mr. Greydon will do a great deal of good with the money. It would all go in opera tickets and concerts with me, which are of no earthly use, though very pleasant.' Altogether, Jane, I think we ought to be very thankful to see our two dear children so well settled."

"Yes, my dear, and I am most thankful, but I never was so miserable in all my life. It is all very well for you, John, who are used to be away from them a year at a time; but they are the daily happiness of my life, and I know you will be going to sea again, and then what is to become of me?"

"You must go with me, my love"; and there the matter ended for the present; poor Mrs. Hopkinson being as nearly selfish and fretful as ever she was in her life. She was somewhat consoled by a visit from Lady Chester, who came prepared to hear of great results from the *fête*, and was not disappointed. And she insisted on Mrs. Hopkinson's seeing the sunny side of this labyrinth, told her she was the luckiest mother in the world, and laid out a long avenue of grandchildren, leading anywhere but to the possibility of Mrs. Hopkinson's going off to India. In fact, Lady Chester assured her so solemnly that she had a presentiment that Captain Hopkinson would not go to sea again that Mrs. Hopkinson ended by believing her, and gave herself up to be considered singularly fortunate.

CHAPTER XXIII

JUST as the Hopkinsons had finished breakfast
the following morning, they were surprised by
an early visit from Willis, who seemed to be
in a state of unusual excitement ; and instead
of the congratulations they had expected, he
burst out with something like an oath, adding,
" And the rascal is actually gone—went off
while the dancing was going on ; the police
were waiting for him at the station, but I
suppose he had good intelligence, for he got into
a steamer, and has not been heard of since.
His precious wife must have feigned that illness,
for she is missing too ; and now, Mrs. Hopkinson,
I want you to do one of your good-natured
actions. Marble Hall is full of detectives, and
messengers from the Court of Bankruptcy, and
ruined tradesmen ; and that poor girl, Miss
Monteneros, is all alone, and I want you——"

" My dear, don't say another word, I'll go
and fetch her. Of course, she must come to us.
Dear me ! what a world it is ! nothing but
changes : the Sampsons gone off, and John
talking of a voyage, and both the girls going
to be married."

245

"Yes, I know," Willis said, "and I was coming to wish them joy," and he actually went and kissed his sisters-in-law, and said he was delighted. "And now, ma'am, are you ready?" While she went to put on her bonnet, Captain Hopkinson inquired into the probable amount of Willis's own loss. He said that if Baron Sampson's were a mere ordinary bankruptcy, he should lose but a few thousands; but there were rumours of forgeries to a great extent, and he could not yet know whether he might not be one of the victims. "Miss Monteneros does not know, either, whether her fortune is not gone too." However, thanks to the blindness of parents, the Sampsons had always believed that Moses was irresistible, and that Rachel would eventually marry him. Mr. Bolland's advice had averted the danger which she had run of putting the Baron legally in possession of her fortune, and his ruin had at last been so sudden and so complete that there had been no time to achieve the fraudulent embezzlement of her property.

Mrs. Hopkinson found the house in great confusion, and full of strange-looking men, some trying to seize valuable property which they looked upon as their own, as it had never been paid for—others guarding it for the general benefit of the creditors, and all heaping abuse, in no measured terms, on the head of the plausible swindler. Rachel was in her own room, preparing for departure, but sinking at times into gloomy reveries, which seemed to unfit her for any exertion. She was in one of these fits of exhaustion when Mrs. Hopkinson arrived, and the sight of an honest and friendly face broke up at once the icy gloom that had closed over her. She burst into a passion of tears, and, flinging her arms round Mrs. Hopkinson's neck, she sobbed out, "Ah! I shall be better now—I thought you would come to me."

"Of course, my dear, I am come *to* you and *for* you," said Mrs. Hopkinson cheerfully. "This is no place for you. John will be here directly to take care of your property, and you must come home with me. The girls are getting your room ready, and the sooner we go the better. When did the knowledge of all this come upon you?"

"Not till this morning; I was deceived to the last. After the party was over I went up stairs to see how my aunt was, and her maid met me and said her lady had such a bad headache she wished to keep quite quiet in her own room. At that moment she must have been on the railroad leaving England for ever. This morning I found this note on her table, and that is all I know."

"DEAR RACHEL,

"By a combination of untoward events, added to the easy credulity of your uncle, who is careless to a fault in money matters, our affairs have become so embroiled that we find it necessary to leave England for a short time. I have no doubt that justice will be done to your uncle, and that we shall soon be enabled to overcome the persecution, for I can call it nothing less, raised by his enemies, and a short tour abroad will not be disagreeable to me. Knowing the uncertainties of a commercial life, the dear good Baron, with his accustomed kindness and *prévoyance*, settled, some time ago, a handsome sum of money on me, payable to my own order, therefore, my dear Rachel, you need not be uneasy lest I should miss any of the luxuries to which I have been accustomed, and which, indeed, are to me absolutely indispensable. Should I find my own means insufficient, I shall apply to you without scruple, as, thanks to the Baron, you receive your *whole* fortune untouched; therefore I consider that we have some claims on you, though it is not likely we shall be driven to urge them. I will write from Paris.

"Your affectionate aunt,

"REBECCA, BARONESS SAMPSON."

"And so they are gone to Paris!"

"No," said Rachel with a deep sigh, "that is as false as all the rest. Two servants and some boxes went to Folkestone. My uncle and aunt went, I believe, to Hull, and sailed this morning for Norway. Mrs. Hopkinson, let me tell you all the truth at once ; as my relations, I feel deeply the disgrace that has fallen on them, the misery, the wide-spread ruin they have brought on others ; but as friends, I cannot affect to regret them. The Baroness is my mother's only sister ; I would have loved her, if she would have let me, in the very young days when my affections were warm—but it was impossible. There was nothing genial in her treatment of me, nothing true in her intercourse with others ; I cannot tell you how artificial, how mean, with all its splendour, our life was. She has made me what I am—cold, distrustful, unloved and unloving ; but at least I am not false."

" No, my dear, that you certainly are not ; I should say that, if anything, you were disposed to err the other way, to speak unpleasant truths, for fear you should not speak the truth at all."

" It may be so," said Rachel dejectedly ; " I certainly do not make myself generally liked. There is one truth more I must tell you before I enter your house—perhaps you will think it as unpleasant as all the others. One person in the world really does like me, at least, so he says, and that is your son-in-law ; and as my presence in your house might lead to constant meetings with him, or might interfere with your comfort, should he wisely stay away,

I feel you ought to know this before I accept your friendly offer. Now you know it, do you still choose to have me ? "

" Of course I do, my dear child, all the more for the confidence you have shown me. I am sure I wish with all my heart you would marry Charles, and take little Charlie under your care, for goodness knows what will become of him if I have to go to foreign parts with John ; and Willis has a great deal of good in him, if he had not got into such foolish habits of grumbling and groaning ; but we think he is very much improved lately, and what is more, we think it is your doing—so there you see, my dear, everybody can be useful somehow, and now come home. How pleased Charlie will be ! "

And Charlie became more than ever the charm and interest of Rachel's life. She entered warmly into the happiness of Janet and Rose, but she had little of their society. Mr. Greydon and Mr. Harcourt were always coming and going, and walking and talking, and Rachel looked on with amusement at the sight of four people foolishly and heartily in love. It was a new spectacle to her, and she thought it very entertaining, but rather incomprehensible.

However, she made herself extremely useful, especially in the matter of the trousseaux, not only by her advice and good taste, but by the magnificence of her contributions. In vain did Mrs. Hopkinson remonstrate; Rachel only laughed, and she said she knew best what Mrs. Greydon ought to wear when she dined at Chesterton Castle, and what Mrs. Harcourt would want when the regiment was quartered at Windsor, and she must request Mrs. Hopkinson not to interfere.

Willis was much occupied at this time by the settlement of his affairs with the assignees of the Sampson house; but he often passed his evenings with his relations, and Rachel could not but see that his interest in her increased rather than diminished. The only time in which he accidentally saw her alone he thanked her for her care of Charlie, and said he knew she would be glad to hear that his losses by the bankruptcy did not exceed the £10,000 which he had advanced to the Baron, and which, for some time, he had given up as a bad debt. Rachel looked distressed and ashamed; and became still more confused when he added that he did not mean to importune her with a repetition of his former declaration, however much his attachment might have strengthened—but he hoped she saw that her advice had not been thrown away, and that, at least, she no longer looked upon him as artificial and untrue.

" I hope we are both improved, and improving," she said kindly. " Who could do otherwise under the influence of these good-hearted people ? " and then she turned the conversation on the Hopkinsons, and the approaching marriages.

It had been her intention to settle herself at the sea-side after a fortnight's stay at Pleasance ; but Janet and Rose dwelt with such melancholy energy on the loneliness of their parents, and the comfort that she would be to their mother after they were gone, that she consented to stay till the return of the Harcourts from their wedding tour. Janet would not be able to leave Chesford, but Rose would then be within reach of Dulham ; perhaps in her heart Rachel dreaded to begin her lonely life, and clung to the kindness she met with at Pleasance.

Aileen's wedding was the first of the three that took place ; but as an accurate account of it may be read in any number of the *Court Journal* no description is required of it here. There is a frightful sameness in all those great weddings, but the day itself was propitious to the Hopkinsons. Their star was evidently on the ascendant this year. The Duke of St. Maur had engaged in one of those little light specula- tions with which people of colossal fortune are apt to amuse themselves, sometimes to the ruin, sometimes to the improvement of their overgrown incomes. He was muddling away 2 or £300,000 in making a pier and a harbour on the coast of a county half of which, at least, was his pro- perty. The agent in charge of these works had died suddenly ; and when the Duke mentioned, incidentally, the difficulty he had to find a trustworthy successor, it occurred to Arthur that Captain Hopkinson would be just the person for the situation. At Aileen's wedding Arthur had an opportunity of introducing his friend to the Duke, who was much pleased with his intelligence and frank gentlemanlike manner. The harbour works were such as Captain Hopkinson was peculiarly fitted to undertake, and after due inquiries and references, the offer was made and accepted, and Captain Hopkinson became the Duke's Agent for the Pier and Harbour of Seaview, with a good house and handsome salary.

"Well ! there never were such fortunate people as we are," said Mrs. Hopkinson. " There we shall be *at* the sea, which will make John happy, and not *on* it, which will make me the same—plenty to do, and of course, if any of you want change of air or sea-bathing, there you will be at once ! To be sure how things do come about, just from a little neighbourliness and kind feeling. For this is all the doing of that dear kind Lord and Lady Chester. If Lord Chester had not been so well cared for by John, he would have died, and there would have been no Lady Chester ; and if I had not stepped out in that blessed shower, with my great umbrella, she would never have known that I was John's wife, or anything but a vulgar old woman, which, to be sure, I am ; but I shall always think I saved that precious baby's life in that bad confinement of hers. And then if she had been grand and fine, she never would have brought my girls so forward ; but she made as much of them as if they were Duke's daughters, and that has ended in Harcourt's marrying Rose ; and she got that living for Greydon, without which he could not have married Janet ; and now by Lord Chester's introducing John to the Duke, he has got that good appointment. There never was anything like it. Well ! after to-morrow, when my poor darlings are married and gone, I shall have time to sit down and think it all over, and be thankful. At present, I think I should rather like a good cry."

The weddings of Janet and Rose took place in the quiet little church at Dulham ; there was no grand breakfast, no great gathering of mere acquaintances, no long speeches—but there were a few warm friends, much affection, hearts that responded warmly to the vows that were made solemnly, and a bright promise of happiness. Then came the hurried parting, and all was over, and they were gone.

"Oh ! Rachel, my dear," said the weeping mother, " you are almost another daughter to me. I wish you could make up your mind to marry Willis, and take my Mary's place, and then you would belong to us, and we should all be settled like the people at the end of a play. Could you not just fall in love with him ? "

" Quite impossible, my dear Mrs. Hopkinson, and no blame to Mr. Willis ; I do not believe it is in my power to fall in love with anybody."

" Then, my dear, you may just as well marry him as another. I think, with you, that you are not like my foolish children, capable of being desperately in love ; but then Willis is very much in love with you, and I almost think it is better that the love should be most on the husband's side ; and then he is afraid of you, and that is not amiss when the wife is cleverer than the husband. You are always telling me you want to make up to Charlie the loss that you think your uncle has inflicted on him. Depend upon it, Willis will not take a farthing of your money, unless he takes you with it, Rachel," added Mrs. Hopkinson in a quivering voice. " I see now why my poor Mary was not quite happy with him ; he married her because he thought it convenient to have a wife, who would do just what he liked, and have no will of her own, but he never cared for her and admired her as he does you. If he marries you, it is because he worships the ground you tread on, because he looks up to you as much as he looked down on her—because, in short, he has found out that there is something that he loves better than himself."

The effect of this exhortation cannot be known. The Chesters are departing to Chesterton Castle, the Hopkinsons hurrying off to Seaview. The scene is changed, the actors dispersed, but with a pleasing certainty that between Chesterton, Seaview, and Chesford they will constantly meet again ; but Pleasance is deserted, and once more there may be seen in the third column of the fourth page of the *Times* the old advertisement.

DULHAM.—To be let, a Semi-Detached House.

> The book is completed
>   And closed like the day,
> And the hand that has written it
>   Lays it away.

Postscript. Unfortunately the hand that has laid it away is obliged to take it up again. From the great importance of the events it contains, immediate publication was, of course, imperative, and the fate of one who played a great part in the history was left undecided ; but we have just received the following Telegram.

From Our Special Dulham Correspondent.

Dulham, 5.50 Saturday.

Willis has been accepted, and is in high spirits.

THE END.